COLLECTOR

LOST THINGS

COLLECTOR

LOST THINGS

{ A NOVEL }

JEREMY PAGE

PEGASUS BOOKS
NEW YORK LONDON

The Collector of Lost Things

Pegasus Books LLC
80 Broad Street, 5th Floor
New York, NY 10004

ISBN: 978-1-60598-485-8

10 9 8 7 8 6 5 4 3 2 1

Printed in the United States of America
Distributed by W. W. Norton & Company, Inc.

For Seth

1

Perhaps I would be too late to save them. The last dozen had been spotted on a remote island in the North Atlantic, on a bare ledge of rock, but it was already rumoured the final breeding pair had been killed – their skins sold to private collectors – and the single egg between them needlessly crushed. These were only rumours, I kept telling myself. But as I set out for the Liverpool docks, on that breezy April morning in 1845, I couldn't help hoping that I might be able to reach them in time, the last of the birds. I pictured myself surrounded by an inlet of seawater, listening to their strange and deep murmurs. An empty ocean in front of us, crisscrossed with the lines of migration that only they could sense, the fluxes in magnetism that has flowed through them for countless years. I would stand there, in awe, and I would be a barrier for them, beyond which there was only one thing: extinction. Yet I felt uneasy as I forced my way along the quayside, passing beneath the masses of wooden masts that towered above me, trying to untangle their rigging and spars and furled sails, trying, impossibly, to extract the shape of the *Amethyst* among them. It felt as though the ship was a tree among a forest of trees, further hidden by a thicket of thorns and climbers, rigging growing over her and the ships moored alongside, purposefully disguised, and this is a feeling that has remained with me, to this day. I couldn't see the ship and perhaps I never saw it for what it truly was.

I stepped over the hawsers, rounded the bollards, ducked under the ropes and avoided the piles of provisions, barrels, sacking and cable that littered the quay. Porters and lightermen called and whistled, *do that, move it, bring her down, steady now!* they shouted, a whole army of men dismantling what others seemed to be assembling. It was only my boarding papers, folded crisply and held firmly in my hand, that made any of it real. Men ignored me, but they read my papers and sent me on my way, directing me through this tangle. Eventually, crossing the decks of two larger ships, I was shown the gangway that led to the main deck of the *Amethyst*. A three-masted barque, lower than the previous ships, with worn planking that looked as though it had been rubbed down with salt. I had arrived upon it quite suddenly, without even realising it.

'Mr Saxby?'

'Yes,' I had answered, seeing a tall man striding towards me across the deck.

'The collector?'

'You could say that. Good morning.'

'Quinlan French, first mate,' he said, not offering his hand. He gave me a poorly disguised look of appraisal. 'The steward will show you to your cabin. I suppose I should say welcome ... to the ship, that is.'

With that, he promptly turned his back and marched across the deck, pointing at some aspect of the cargo that was being loaded, a rope that was trailing or a corner of sacking that needed to be tied. He leapt across the corner of the main hatch with such speed, and such sudden agility, that it seemed he was momentarily trying to play a game with his shadow, escape it perhaps, or fling it down into the hold. I, too, kept moving, feeling wary of a deck so full of work and dangers, towards a companionway I presumed led to the passenger cabins. As I crossed the ship my impression was of its size; the lofty structures of three masts rising high above me, cross-hatching the sky with a complicated pattern of wooden yards, held together with a web – yes, a web, I felt – of ropes and rigging. The bases of the masts were as wide as barrels where they pierced the deck. I thought, peculiarly, of candles pushed into a cake. And more than anything I tried to avoid the same wide-open cargo hatches, into which stores were busily being lowered by winches. Men with sleeves rolled up were col-lected around these wells, guiding the bundles and barrels down into a hold that loomed unnaturally dark and deep, as if the soul of this barque was cavernous and without measure and, above all, hungry.

Assailed by these images, I was relieved to descend the five steps of a companionway and find myself in a saloon that was calm and subdued and more like the drawing room of a coun-try house than I had expected. A stove, near the door, had already been lit, so I gladly stood next to it, holding my hands over the warming plate, listening to the soft tick of the coals burning inside. It was a very peaceful room, panelled in smooth honey-coloured oak, with cabin doors leading off it on both sides. A long darkly polished table reflected a skylight set above it. Beyond the table, I could see a wider space where settees and armchairs were arranged informally, with a tick-ing sheep's head clock on the far wall alongside a row of oil lamps. There was a smell of leather and polish and the scent of the burning coal, along with a hint of tobacco. It might have been in any country house, except that in the very centre of the saloon, the thick column of the mizzenmast speared through the room from ceiling to floor.

3

A panel slid open on my left and a small man in a buttoned white tunic appeared from what looked like a pantry. He carried a napkin hung over one forearm. Behind him, a dresser was neatly arranged, with cutlery lined up at precise right angles to the counter.

'Good morning, sir,' he said, in an accent that was not English. 'Are you Mr Saxby or Mr Bletchley?'

'Saxby.'

'Then your cabin is found right here, sir.' The steward opened a door cleverly concealed in the wood panelling, directly next to the pantry.

'Thank you,' I said, keen to establish a first glimpse of my room. Through the open door I could see a simple bunk with drawers underneath, and the corner of a canvas washstand.

'And the other cabins?' I asked.

'Next to you are the quarters of Mr French. He is first mate.'

'Yes, we met on deck.'

'A quick man. And tall?' He raised a hand, estimating Mr French's height. 'Good. Then at the end is the captain's cabin. It is larger than this, but then, he is captain.' He smiled softly.

'Quite so.'

He pointed to the doors on the opposite side of the saloon. 'Across there is the wash and the toilet. Then, that is chart room, first guest cabin, second guest cabin, and the cabin of Mr Talbot. He is second mate, but he is not very much in his cabin. He likes it on the deck. He is a big sea dog.'

I was amused by the description. 'And probably very useful,' I ventured.

'Yes. A useful man. Especially with ice.'

I stepped into my cabin and put my bag onto the bunk.

'I have this list on the desk where it is written down the general arrangement for the meals and the drinks,' he said, placing a finger on the list. 'It is there.'

'Are you Spanish?' I asked.

'Portuguese, sir. From São Miguel in the Azores. My name is Simao. That is a bell. You pull if you are in need of me. I shall bring you tea in some minutes.'

He gave me a small smile and looked quickly about the cabin, making sure all was in order, before going back to the pantry.

I closed the door behind him and sat on the end of the bunk. I tried not to feel anxious, but sitting there I felt overwhelmed, by the arduous cross-country journey I'd made from Norfolk and the night I'd spent at the lodging house near the dock. I had slept fitfully, haunted by troubling dreams and fleeting memories I could not place. Then an early breakfast in a sombre cold room, listening to the ticking of an overmantel clock, its pendulum swinging behind a small cut-out shape in the wood. The brisk walk along the wharf with the porters in tow, under the noisy and confusing masts and rigging aligned along the quayside, jumping the hawsers that were either tied to the bollards or threaded through iron rings each as wide as a man's neck, then the view of the open hatches of the cargo hold, a glimpse into a dungeon, and the first mate abruptly turning away from me – all this already seemed to have happened to another man, a braver man, a man without secrets.

The berth was small and practical, probably eight by six feet, clad entirely in shiplapped wood that had been lime washed. There was an almost imperceptible curve to the outer wall, along which the bunk was built. I lay down and wondered if I could already feel the motion of being afloat. The ship was still tied fast, but there was a strangeness about lying down, an unfamiliarity, a soft and unlikely gravity, that made me think I was already at sea. Peculiar sounds arose from deep below the cabin – the muffled hauling of barrels in a large dark space, the reverberation of wooden thwarts being struck and tapped. Above me, and to my side, footsteps paced on a deck that might be only inches away. I heard orders being given and answered, and calls from the tops of the masts that were as harsh and discordant as crows in the trees.

So this would be my home, a floating box that would carry me to the Arctic. I closed my eyes and tried whispering its name. *Arc-tic.* It sounded remote and tremendous. A word filled with sharp edges. I imagined ice growing across the sea, inching towards the ship, how the walls of my cabin would become cold to touch. It made me snap my eyes open in alarm. Momentarily, as I looked at the bare wooded ceiling, I felt a sense of drowning.

Not here, I whispered to myself, *please, not here.*

Simao brought me the tea, putting it on my desk and turning the handle of the cup in my direction. 'We will be casting off, sir,' he told me, thoughtfully. I wondered if it was his English that made him sound cautious, or whether there was something of concern. 'I close the door now, behind me?'

When I reached for the cup, my fingers went perfectly through the handle. I smiled at the precise nature of the steward, for whom I already felt a great liking. There was a biscuit of some kind next to the tea. It tasted buttery and had a crust of grated coconut. I had just eaten it when I heard a series of unusual noises outside my door – whispers and urgent scrapes of the furniture across the boards, which made me spring off the bunk and peer through the keyhole.

Across the saloon, I saw a beguiling sight: a person wrapped in a dark blue cloak being supported by two others. One of them I recognised as being Simao, trying to open the cabin door directly opposite mine while still supporting the figure in the cloak. The other person, who was giving the commands in hushed utterances, I could not see properly. Only his trousers, which were fashionably cut from a material which had a brightly checked design in yellows and teal. He was wearing riding boots, too, even though he was on a ship, made of gleaming brown leather. As for the person being supported, I thought that I wouldn't be able to see any part of them, for they were so thoroughly wrapped in the cloak, and the hood had been placed to cover the head. But at the entrance to the opposite cabin – as Simao shut the door behind them – I saw a merest glimpse of a pale cheek, an angle of the jaw and a corner of a tightly set mouth that caused me to feel instantly confused. I felt certain that I had seen this before, the cloaked person, the way they were being supported, the quiet manner in which they were being ushered into the room. This was real, but it had once been a dream, or I had seen it on another occasion.

Almost immediately I heard other footsteps scuttling down the companionway followed by a rap upon my door. My answer must have sounded startled, for it appeared that Mr French, the first mate, knew I had been spying when I opened the latch. I could see it in the man's expression. He gave me a curious glance, before purposefully checking his fob watch and informing me the ship was about to leave.

'Good,' I said, a little embarrassed. 'May I observe from on deck?'

'Naturally.' But rather than allowing me, he pushed me back with a single finger against my chest, and took a step into my cabin. 'A rabbit hutch, I'm afraid. Are you settled here, in your rabbit hutch?'

I nodded. We both looked at the cabin. He smelt strongly of eau de cologne.

'I have never met a collector before,' he said.

'Well, I wouldn't entirely call myself . . .'

'... Captain Sykes will lap you up. He thinks he is an expert on the natural world, but he is not. Not really. I know a lot more than he does. But he is the captain, so we won't tell him, will we?' He smiled, and I saw a row of thin teeth, slightly pointed, below the edge of his lips. 'You may put your books there, I suppose,' he said. 'Have you many books?'

'A few.'

'People like you have many books. I admire bookworms, burrowing their way. That's good. Working on a trading ship makes for a narrow mind and a mean outlook upon life. I shall be educated by you. I'm anxious to see what they are.'

'Oh yes, well, I have brought a range of volumes covering the key natural sciences, and some that detail Arctic obser-vations—'

'In good time,' he said, curtly. 'I am expected on deck.'

'Of course,' I replied, somewhat snubbed. 'Are there other passengers on board?'

Mr French regarded me, again rather curiously. He had ash-grey eyes, and an expression that showed a smile, not quite formed, or recently passed, that made him look vaguely mistrustful.

'A gentleman by the name of Bletchley, I believe. A good shot, he claims, although we will wait to see if he is also a good hunter, wouldn't you say? And one other passenger.' Here, the first mate did a strange thing. He mouthed a word, silently. He looked vexed when I failed to understand it. 'A *woman*,' he repeated.

I have often wondered whether, had I known what would happen, I would have left the *Amethyst* at that very moment. No. Truly, I think that even if I had known, I would do it all again, even though the voyage would change my life, alter the way I think about the world and the men who spoil it, and

8

probably there was nothing I might have done to alter the course of events. These things move towards us from the horizon, whether we set sail for them or not.

But on that morning all this was unknown to me. Standing on deck I let myself be thrilled by the spectacle of the ship's departure, watching as the hawsers were carried to the head of the quay by a team of men, all singing, bearing the ropes between them to encircle a pair of cast-iron capstans. Spars were slotted into the sockets and the men began to turn the axles, walking round them with a surprisingly smooth motion, while the ship, wound upon these giant's cotton reels, moved at a glide towards the wooden gates of the lock. As we approached, a vein of white light ran up the front of the gate, before it opened into a view of the sea beyond. The dock workers' caps rose in goodwill and farewell, the men shouted luck across to the ship and were answered back by those on board, as they clung to the ratlines or stood perilously on the ship's rail, one hand on a rope and the other pointing and waving. A tied bundle was thrown across the gap, an apple, too, gleaming like a cricket ball, tossed from the quayside to a man at the rail. It was bitten into at once, the sailor smiling wet-lipped with enormous satisfaction at his catch.

Still, as I remember how I had stood on deck as the ropes were thrown in the water and the caps were raised, sur-rounded by the web of rigging and the grind of machinery that turned and pulled in mysterious patterns, I see myself as an unenlightened man, poised leaning against the rail, watching the quay begin to slide away, a gap of smooth water opening alongside the length of our ship. I see myself, but I see through myself too. I was deluded.

2

I should have noticed more in the captain, that first glimpse I had of him, when we were moored a mile or two offshore. I had turned my collar against the sea breeze and was adjusting my hat when I saw him, already on deck and standing by the helm. He was small and rotund, dressed in a heavy tunic buttoned up the front, and older than I had expected, perhaps sixty years, with a quizzical – slightly monkeyish – expression, bald on the top of his head and blond wiry hair on either side of it. Without a hat, he had a vagrant appearance. It was only from his stance next to the wheel, with fleshy hands clasped behind his back, and the dutiful greeting Mr French gave him, that I realised this inconspicuous man must be Captain Kelvin Sykes. Together, they were discussing the breeze, looking aloft at the arrangements of the three masts and the movement of the flags. The captain licked a finger and turned it about his head and, at that moment, he caught my eye and gave me a barely perceptible wink.

'Is she coming about?' French asked the helmsman.

'Yes, sir. About slowly.'

French nodded at Sykes. The captain stroked his moustache and consulted his watch. 'Man the windlass, loose the sails and set the tops'l,' he ordered.

'Aye, sir,' French replied, then repeated the order to the men. 'And smart!' he added.

What began at that moment was unforgettable. The men climbed the ratlines and edged themselves along the yards working with their hands and arms in unison, loosening the canvas and letting it fall. A sail began to emerge, misshapen and bulky, an object that appeared casual and unconcerned by the breeze. It billowed and swayed while ropes were gathered and tightened, and I wondered how this plane of canvas – that so resembled a laundry sheet – might have any ability to move the ship. The air collected across the sail's face, a hesitant caress, then gently eased forward. Suddenly it filled in one smooth intake of breath and snapped taut, as if punched by a giant fist. At the same moment I heard the ropes stretch, and along their lines I saw a mist of droplets being wrung from them.

As the men climbed for the next sail, the mast began to lean, as the ship and its tall trees bent and pulled and began to move. What complete joy I felt. I rushed to the side and noticed the water beginning to stream alongside, the weed on the boards below the surface pulling in a current.

I missed, entirely, the arrival of the other passenger on the quarterdeck rail, until in the corner of my view I recognised the wild checked design of the trousers I had seen in the saloon, edging towards me.

'Splendid stuff!' he said.

My fellow passenger was a young man, possibly twenty-five, with bright sandy hair in long fashionable curls, and a wide uncomplicated grin on his face. He was wearing a cornflower blue pilot coat with large buttons and slanted pockets, had a golden cravat around his neck – as bright as a kestrel's throat – and a bamboo cane tucked under one arm.

'Edward Bletchley,' he said, offering his hand.

'Eliot Saxby.'

He shook my hand smartly, giving it a very strong squeeze, adjusted his coat and stared up at the sails in an appreciative manner.

'Mr French has told me we shall be setting twelve sails,' he said. 'He used all manner of names I cannot remember, but I shall learn them all, it can't be too hard.'

'I have just about figured out we are standing on a quarterdeck and that cabin before the mast with the two whaleboats on it is the fo'c'sle,' I replied.

'Very good!' Bletchley snorted. 'Now you must see this.' He angled a riding boot towards me: 'I have engraved a star into the toe of this one, to remind myself that this is my starboard side. How about that!'

'The wrong foot,' I said.

'No! Is it? Ah, I see you are joking. Very amusing.' He glanced towards the helm and whispered, 'Have you met the captain yet?'

'No.'

'Me neither. From the look of him he seems a quirky fellow.'

Bletchley wandered off, in the manner of a ship's officer, his hands behind his back and his cane stowed, while the sails continued to be set. Full of confidence, an easy charm and direct expression – a man I have always known I could never be. His clothes were flamboyant, his posture without apology. Yet even in that first glimpse of him, I believe I sensed something unusual. A glimmer in his eyes that was unsettled and furtive, at odds with the rest of his impeccable demeanour.

It was apparent, at supper that evening, that Bletchley's travelling companion had no intention of joining us. Her place at the table was glaringly empty. Mr French stood, formal and straight-backed, by the stove, warming his hands above the hotplate. He had the bearing of a naval officer, stiff collared and erect, smiling privately to himself. Perhaps he was amused by the impoliteness of the second mate, Mr Talbot, a most disagreeable fellow on first impressions, built as solidly as an ox, who refused to sit at the table or properly introduce himself. He merely stood at the far end, in a coat too thick for the warm room, regarding the companionway door, a frown on his face, occasionally sinking his fingers into his beard in the pursuit of an itch. When I went to introduce myself he looked back at me angrily, as if I had failed some requirement of proper approach. He refused to shake my outstretched hand so I quickly made my leave, choosing to stand near Bletchley instead, who was absorbed with studying a barometer fixed to the mast.

'It is gimballed,' he pointed out, 'to counteract the motion of the ship.'

'I see,' I answered. Bletchley was obviously wishing to be an expert in all things, and I worried that I might not be able to cope with his enthusiasms, in such confined quarters.

Talbot and French remained standing, Talbot like a tethered bull, uncomfortable in any room, and French as upright as an undertaker. Quite a couple, with little friendship between them. They remained awkward and formal, until the captain opened his cabin door and marched briskly to the table. As I'd noticed on deck, he was a short man, round in the belly, with a slightly florid face and a ram's horn look to the blond hair either side of his head. His bald pate gleamed surprisingly smooth in the candlelight. Immediately he began to speak in a brusque but not unfriendly manner:

'Good evening, Mr Bletchley, Mr Saxby, I am Captain Kelvin Sykes and I would like to formally welcome you to the

Amethyst. Please, your seats,' he instructed, taking his at the head of the table. 'She's a three-hundred-ton barque built in Bristol forty years ago. Not what we would call fast, but steady. She is made from a veritable forest – three hundred and twenty oak trees for her frame, and one hundred and forty long-grained Douglas fir for her decking, masts and yards. She is bound with no less than nine miles of rope. Nine miles, I say! And in her life she has sailed … well, how far, gentlemen? Would you like to guess?'

Bletchley was straight off the mark: 'Three times around the world.'

The captain rubbed his chin with a finger, contemplating. 'Mr Saxby?'

'I would say twice that.'

He laughed, satisfied. 'Wrong, sirs. She has sailed a distance equivalent to the moon and back.'

Sykes allowed us to feel dutifully impressed before he continued. 'She's a plump vessel, double walled with English oak between the wales to the six-foot waterline and a tripling of oak in the bows in addition to iron plating. Fortification timbers have been applied within the stem for resisting blows, and these consist – at considerable expense – of four large ice beams.' The captain made an estimate of their girth with his hands. 'From fine trees I personally chose in the yard. Thirteen inches square and twenty-six feet in length, each butted with its foremost end against strong fore-hooks. As you can appreciate, gentlemen, I am a keen engineer when it comes to the forces of man against nature.' He arranged his cutlery into rows, demonstrating his design. 'Each of these ice beams is connected in various places, here, and here, for example, by carlines, so that a blow to any part of the stem or bow will be communicated evenly across the shores of the timbers.' He scattered the cutlery with a strike of his palm.

'*Boom*, like that, gentlemen. It is quite marvellous.' The knives, fork and spoon looked a mess, a catastrophe, an approximation of a shipwreck. He drank thirstily from his wine. 'This year, I have also had fitted ice-knees beneath the bow. Your captain is a most cautious man, sirs, and you will be quite safe on board, in all circumstances.' He knocked the tabletop, for luck.

'To the business of our route, gentlemen, we will be sailing north-west directly into the Arctic Circle until we make a sighting of the sea ice, and will venture several excursions along the edge as required for hunting, Mr Bletchley. We will do that as soon as we are able, because I can see you are anxious to bag some skins, and it is the time of their cubbing, so we must not delay. At this time of year I shall expect us to be in the vicinity to the west and slightly to the north of Iceland before we encounter the floe. As is convenient, and winds and general weather permitting, we shall then leave the ice behind us and proceed to Mr Saxby's concerns.' He regarded me, his face lowered so he was effectively watching me through his eyebrows, seemingly in an act of permission to continue. I raised my glass to him.

'We have been asked to veer from our usual route in order that we might visit an island and various skerries to the south-east of Iceland,' he said, 'in accordance with Mr Saxby's duties as an agent for the collection of eggs and other natural artefacts for his influential acquaintances. We shall be looking for an extinct bird, I believe.' He paused. 'I see you are amused, Mr French, but we shall conduct this search for the bird because we have received payment to do so. Mr Saxby, you might settle an ornithological question that has long vexed me. The Scottish ptarmigan is black in summer and pure white in winter. So is it a black bird or a white bird?'

'It is both,' I replied.

15

'Exactly! You have passed my first test!

'So,' he continued, 'after our business with these extinct birds of yours, we shall be returning to our usual merchant route, passing Cape Farewell at the southern point of Greenland and delivering supplies to the whaling stations on the east coast of Davis Strait. At several points we shall offer trade with Esquimaux groups. Powder, rifles, flints and hooks and the like. Sheffield steel and plate is particularly admired there, as in the rest of the world. You will require your over-coats once more, as we travel north, again into the Arctic Circle. We shall navigate the western coast of Greenland, seeing many icebergs, gentlemen, but none so close that we shall touch them. I see you are excited at the prospect, Mr Bletchley! We will admire these bergs at distance, I say, and we shall pass the snouts of the finest glaciers in the Northern hemisphere, too, as they prod out to sea. It is a frozen and wondrous world up at the top. Our final destination, ice permitting – for it is very cluttered up there – will be Jakobshavn. It is 69 degrees north in latitude and you will be pinning your felt curtains over the portholes in your cabins, gentlemen, for it is light early. You might well observe the dipping-needle compass there, for it will be pointing largely down into the earth, rather than a flat north. That is where we shall embark upon our return journey.' Sykes took a healthy draught of his wine and dabbed his lips with the napkin.

'I have had many passengers on this vessel, and I look for-ward to becoming acquainted with you both. I would like to add that you are welcome to wander the ship at will, although the hold is not of interest and is of a dark and dan-gerous nature. Staves, hoops, manila sea rope, timber, scantling and coal tar is an excellent environment for break-ing an ankle. Any breakages of bones will be set by the ship's carpenter, which is not a pleasant prospect! Myself, Mr French the first mate or Mr Talbot the second mate will gladly explain all matters of the ship, when asked. They are both splendid seamen of great experience, particularly in the frigid waters of the North. You may talk to the crew but please be aware they are on board to work, and may not be convivial to idle conversation and in general do not match your education. At times when sails are to be furled or the windlass or capstans manned they are to perform these tasks quickly and should not be approached. I trust both of you will use your discretion with this. On a more delicate matter, most of the crew are Irish, and their land has once more been afflicted with the potato blight, which may have affected several of their number directly. I trust you will bear this in mind. But, enough of that! I believe the steward has provided you with a comprehensive list of times for drinks and meals and I suggest we start with the soup right away.'

Sykes sat back in his chair, greatly pleased, while the pantry door slid open and Simao wheeled in a tureen of soup.

'Mr Bletchley,' the captain asked, 'are you a good shot?'

'Unfailingly.'

'Game birds?'

'Mostly waterfowl. Duck, teal, widgeon and pintail. Grouse and pheasant in the season.'

'Nothing larger?'

'Deer.'

Captain Sykes stroked his moustache either side of his mouth, considering. 'The seal has no heart. It has to be shot in the head. You can kill it no other way. Mr Talbot will gladly show you how.'

'Thank you. Mr Talbot, I shall look forward to it.' The second mate looked up glumly from his plate and nodded at Bletchley.

17

The captain continued. 'Mr French informs me you have handmade rifles with you?'

'Absolutely. Mr Gallyon of Cambridge has personally manufactured them. I generally use a fowling-piece at the decoy, where the shoot is close and controlled by the dogs. With pheasants I prefer the trusty long-barrelled three-iron Damascus. But anticipating a relatively close shot I commissioned a shorter barrel and an easy breech. Mr Gallyon suggested a twenty-eight-inch barrel, rather than a thirty-six. And one even shorter than that, for when prey is close. He designs all my rifles, and I believe he has done a tremendous job on this occasion. I have had them personally engraved.'

Sykes looked as if he approved. 'I would like to try your guns in the morning, if I may?'

'I would be honoured.'

'In my time I could shoot the smirk from a duck's beak,' he said. 'Isn't that right, Mr French?'

'Yes, sir, and even on occasion you were known to make a kill.'

The captain grinned. 'Simao, what is this soup?' he asked.

'The bean and pork belly, sir.'

'Very good. We are lucky, gentleman, to have Simao on board. For the Portuguese are fine cooks, especially with salted cod. Cabinet pudding, too, if you're lucky!' Simao took the compliment with a neat bow and, at Sykes' instruction, began to clear away the empty place setting.

'Mr Bletchley, will we be seeing your wife?'

Bletchley, who at that moment had been drinking, nearly coughed on his wine. He looked at the captain, alarmed, before saying, 'Oh no, Captain Sykes, she is not my wife.'

Sykes was more interested than apologetic for his mistake. He let Bletchley continue.

'I'm afraid she is not well. Most faint, and troubled. I have given her a hop pillow to ease her mind. She doesn't want to leave her cabin.'

'Well,' the captain said, 'that is our loss, I am sure.'

'Why, yes,' Bletchley agreed. Momentarily, again, I saw something highly mistrustful in his expression.

Over the main course, which was beef that first evening, the captain turned his attention to me. He made it his duty to interview each of his passengers. I explained to the table that I would be collecting natural specimens for a group of individuals who had procured my services for the task and paid my passage.

'Who are these employers of yours?' the captain asked.

'Four gentlemen. I hardly know them.'

'But they wish to find this extinct bird?'

'It is somewhat more complicated than that,' I explained. 'I think they care little about the bird. But they do care whether it's extinct or not. They have made a bet on it.'

'A bet?'

'As gentlemen like to do.'

'Is this what you commonly undertake?' the captain asked. 'Settle pointless bets?'

'No,' I answered. 'It is unusual. But I have worked closely with museums and private enthusiasts, so the task of collecting natural wildlife and recording their habitats is something I relish. When these animals are presented in their display cases, it is important to be correct with all aspects of posture and environment.'

'Very interesting,' Sykes commented. 'You should consider stuffing Mr Talbot and placing him in a glass case, for he is one of the Arctic's most frequent visitors.'

Talbot, the second mate, looked back unamused, resolutely refusing to smile. Sykes laughed heartily at his own joke, undaunted. 'But what are these birds I have been told about?'

'The great auk,' I replied. 'It is a large flightless bird – you might regard it as a northern penguin. In recent years their numbers have suffered from hunting and loss of their colonies. It's believed that the final breeding couple were killed last year, on an uninhabited island off Iceland by three local fishermen. They killed the birds and smashed the egg. I, and the collectors I represent, would dearly love to find some remains.'

'Mr Saxby, steering my ship in the search for an extinct bird is one of the more peculiar charters I have accepted. But I dare say that if there are any remains, we shall find them. A beak or a foot at least for your display cabinets.'

'Let us hope so,' I said.

At that moment Mr Talbot decided to speak. 'I have eaten the auk,' he said.

The captain slapped the table with pleasure. 'Congratulations, Saxby! You have made our second mate speak,' he said with a flourish. 'So you have eaten this bird, Talbot?'

'Aye.'

'And what of it?'

'Oily.'

That was all he had to say on the matter. 'I will explain, gentlemen,' the captain continued. 'Mr Talbot is a man of few words. But before this cosy vessel he spent most of his life serving on whalers. He knows about all the Arctic creatures.'

'And how to kill them,' French added.

The captain laughed. 'Perhaps we should search for remnants of your bird among the hairs of his beard,' he joked.

For the first time Talbot showed some pleasure in the occasion. He looked up at me, deliberately I believe, and placed a large slice of beef into his mouth with his fork and continued to look at me while he chewed the meat. His beard was full and thick, but I could see the grease on his lips and the edges of his teeth. It was quite revolting, and I felt a warning of some form, aimed at me, although I had no idea what for. Still, I raised my glass and drank a toast to him, which he acknowledged, as he swallowed.

That first night, needing air and a space to myself, I went on deck and was thrilled to find it so deserted. It was almost completely without illumination, as if the ship was a solid featureless platform on which to walk above the sea. I was struck by how quiet a sailing ship was. Voices could easily be heard, and none of the sailors had cause to speak loudly. From the quarterdeck's rail – which was as wide as a church pew – I watched the waves running alongside, noticing how some would turn against the timbers and burst into white foam. Further out, the sea was dark and indistinguishable, with mysterious lines where the crest of a small wave was breaking. There was a clean sharp smell of salt and a soothing rush of water. The impression I'd had when I first stepped onto the *Amethyst*'s deck had been that I was entering a web of knots. I had almost expected to see giant spiders above me, each one as wide as a bale of hay, watching me as I stepped beneath them, and it was difficult to dispel that image. The bolsters in the rigging had resembled giant insects, wound in spider's silk.

I didn't venture far, for fear of snagging an ankle in some of the many ropes or blocks; instead I sat on a corner of the main hatch and listened to the sounds of the air and sails. I imagined how it must be, at the tops of these tall trees, with just the icy dome of the sky and stars above, riding the ship on the tip of a point a hundred feet in the air.

Sitting on the hatch, I was almost invisible, the only illumination on the main deck being the spill that emerged from the portholes of the fo'c'sle beyond the mainmast, and the open door of Simao's galley, which was a bright square shape cut into the darkness. Inside, I could see the corner of the cooking range, with a rail running around it to stop pots falling during rough weather, and several shelves and cupboards, all neatly ordered. A pendant was pinned to a shelf with the word Açores embroidered upon it. Simao was still busy. With two of the men he was arranging for meat to be hung from the rigging, where it would be kept cool and fresh. Double smoked sides of Wiltshire bacon had already been hauled up onto the mizzenmast, and two sides of an Aberdeenshire bullock had been roped to the mainmast, beneath the belaying pins where I sat.

On the quarterdeck it was just as dark, the only light being two partially masked dark-lanterns set above the twin binnacles at the helm, and the glimmer of brass along the skylights of the saloon. In a long sea cloak and cap, French was standing next to the wheel, his arms behind his back in a military fashion. He was as featureless as a churchyard shadow.

'Enjoy your meal?' he asked, on my approach.

'Yes, thank you.'

'We shall see if you keep it down,' he quipped, revealing a glint of teeth as he smiled. The compasses were gimballed, and in the glow from the lanterns their resolute needles shone like brilliant jewels set in their brass cylinders.

French continued: 'The captain bores me with his zeal for the ship and the journey. I have heard him say these things many times to passengers such as yourself – believe me, he is really not very sincere.'

I was surprised by his candour, and equally glad that in such darkness he wouldn't be able to scrutinise my expression. He seemed out to test me.

'But he knows his mind,' French added, suggesting that he'd gone too far. 'The Arctic needs a strength of mind. If you are weak, there are a thousand ways to die.'

'Or become crazed.'

'Yes, that too.'

'I have read many accounts of Arctic exploration,' I said.

'As have I. It is always wise, embarking upon a journey such as we are on, to consider the other members of the crew, in case forced by adversity we should have to eat one of them.' He chuckled, quickly, but without conviction.

I decided to rise to the challenge: 'Well, on first impressions, I believe Mr Talbot would make for a very unpleasant meal.'

He laughed. 'Yes, he is pure goat. Your boots would be preferable.'

Above me, the sides of bacon swayed eerily in the rigging, once, before settling again.

'I think I shall read for a while,' I informed French, wishing to take my leave. I had the feeling he was out to trick me into saying something I might regret.

'Yes. One of your splendid books,' he replied.

Back beneath the mast I wondered whether this was the absolute centre of the ship, the confluence of all the many balanced pressures of wind, sea and sail. Above me, the dark column of wood rose impressively into the sky. I could hear sounds, as one does under great trees, of the wooden limbs bending and turning. Ropes, too, stretching as the spars and yards tightened. Occasionally I heard the knock of iron upon iron, as bearings and fixings came together, and in waves I listened to the full enveloping sound of canvas filled with air. It arrived and sank with a whisper.

I smelt the salt of the sea and the caulked timber of the deck and the bloodied smell of the Aberdeen bullock where

Simao had tied it. I gazed once more at the sides of bacon that swung from the mizzenmast, wrapped in muslin, like the bodies of criminals hung in gibbets. As the ship swayed, they moved, in dreadful counterbalance.

By angling my book towards the portholes of the fo'c'sle, I was able to read the *Compendium of Arctic Fauna* I had brought with me, whose pages were already frayed from my countless hours of study. Each illustration was wholly familiar. The bull walrus, with tusks raised in fearless defence, dwarfing the Esquimaux who stands cautiously beyond reach, his spear held poised to strike. The razorbills and guillemots gathered on the ledges of some bleak northern skerry, huddled against a wind that couldn't be drawn but was no doubt there. Then the beasts of the sea, such as the elusive beluga, with its ghostlike countenance, its blind expression, or the narwhals, meeting in a lee of the ice floe, waving their unicorn tusks in strange unknowable greeting. The animals of the world became stranger, larger, more impenetrably skinned the higher north they were found.

On finishing his tasks, Simao approached and kindly hung a lantern above me, for the purposes of reading. I thanked him and he looked for a moment at the open book in my hands.

'May I see the bird you look for?' he asked, intrigued.

'Of course,' I replied, quickly turning to the page which was bookmarked with a jay's feather.

'This is the great auk, which man in his foolishness has made extinct.'

Under the pale flickering light of the lantern, I offered him the illustration. A single bird, the size of a goose, pictured on a ledge of dark rock, with squat legs and wide paddled feet, a stout neck and large spear-shaped bill.

Simao studied the picture for a long time. 'It is a great bird, sir,' he said, eventually.

'Yes, Simao,' I replied. 'It was.'

'Will we find it?'

'No, almost certainly not. We are too late.'

He nodded respectfully, and moved back to the galley.

I returned to the engraving, drawn to something I felt I might have previously missed. Something curious and intangible that I might have overlooked. The solitary bird faced me, inaccurately drawn and implausible, sketched from a collection of rare sightings and unreliable reconstructions, yet at that second, in that flickering lantern light, appearing to move in increments on the page. A trick of the light, yet for a brief moment it was as if the bird was alive.

I closed the book, pensively. The dead centre of the ship, I thought, surrounded by the dead, the animals tied to the mast and hanging from the rigging, and the illustration of the extinct, a last record of a bird that had now vanished. *We are too late.* It occurred to me, in a fleeting moment of total understanding, that I was on a journey of several mysteries, some surrounding me and within reach, but others as dark and impenetrable as the ocean beyond the ship. And with a glance towards the aft cabin I realised what had really been on my mind all that time: the absent presence of the female passenger, travelling with us, but so far completely hidden.

3

Of course, I didn't sleep, not that first night. The ship was full of strange sounds, coming from deep below me, articles of cargo shifting in the hold, or the scantling creaking, the planks of the hull making sudden eerie snaps. A knock, once or twice, from below the waterline, as if the ship were already nudging through the ice it was strengthened for. They bend, these ships. They stretch and bend and twist with the pressures of water and air. I have been told there is not a solid join among them, they are merely timbers bound with tallow and caulking tar.

I thought about my fellow passengers and wondered how each of them had come to be on this journey. Bletchley, with his gung-ho confidence, his popinjay clothes and that occasional glimpse of something dubious in his eyes. I have often made mistakes reading a man like him; such men carve out new identities for themselves each day. He had been revealing at supper, so enthusiastic about his guns, his steadiness of aim and ruthlessness of killing, then oddly childlike and uneasy when his companion was mentioned. And still we hadn't seen her, even though she was in a cabin a few feet away, in some state of illness or reclusion.

The first mate, French, had been interested in her, or

interested in gossiping about her. Yes, leaping Mr French, playing games with his shadow. That was another man I was reluctant to trust. He had a mocking air which might be his nature or might be practised. It amounted to the same. And his crude joke concerning cannibalism was not in keeping with the manner of a gentleman. I resolved to keep my distance from him, and also Talbot, of whom, frankly, I was afraid. The slightest provocation and he might throw a man overboard; he had that bear-like quality. He'd refused to shake my hand, that was clear, it wasn't that he hadn't seen it. And then that business of chewing his meat with an open mouth. Quite horrid. Of them all, only the captain – whom French had described as a bore – seemed to be a man I could rely upon.

I thought about these passengers, trying to sleep, while above me the early-hours watch paced the deck or gave out an order. I had heard French retire to his cabin, adjacent to mine, an hour or two beforehand. I had listened to him rinsing his face in the sink, and I had imagined how he might have looked at his reflection, studying those fleeting expressions of mockery and suspicion.

Around four or five in the morning, I became convinced that someone was watching me from the other side of the room. With fear, I stared at the canvas washstand at the end of my bed and, in the gloom, I was certain that a man's face was looking straight back at me. He remained quite still, intent, and poised. Gradually, I pulled the felt curtain away from my porthole. The little amount of light was enough to reveal that the face was nothing more than a towel, which I had left heaped on the side. I vowed always to hang it properly in the future. Yet even knowing that the face was imaginary did not settle me, and I have since wondered whether this might have been a vision. But that night I had, at least, an explanation.

Distracted with tiredness, I ventured into the saloon. The stove was shut tight. Inside I could see a well-nursed glow of coals ready to be stoked in the morning. Above it, a night lantern had been hung from a bracket. The long mahogany table was as still as a coffin, surrounded by neatly placed chairs whose emptiness now made me recollect glimpses of the meal we'd had. Talbot, chewing the beef while he looked at me, Bletchley, coughing on his drink when his female companion had been mentioned. Now, the empty chairs, and the settees beyond, cast shifting shadows on the floor as the ship swayed. It made the room feel dreamy, not fully real, mistrustful in its lines and dark spaces.

Dividing the two areas of eating and lounging was the bare wooden trunk of the mizzenmast. Its solid dense shape nailed through the room, much as a pin holds a display in a collector's cabinet. Crew and passengers, a scene impaled, it was a curious thought. I approached it, placed my palm against its smooth surface and felt a distinct tremble reverberating through the wood. Trapped deep within the mast, it must have been the current of vital energy transferring between the sky and ocean.

I was about to return to bed when I noticed a tray outside the cabin belonging to Bletchley's female companion. I crept towards it, mindful of creaking floorboards, and lifted the cloth laid over the plate and glass. A few crumbs, possibly the trace of a coconut biscuit similar to that which Simao had given me on arrival. Then a strange scent, coming from the glass. I bent to sniff it. A perfume, attar of roses possibly, but also something more medicinal, something unpleasant.

I missed breakfast, due to a late, thick sleep, so at mid morning I sat upon one of the settees at the far end of the saloon, hoping to read more of the *Compendium of Arctic Fauna*.

Simao poured me coffee, then offered to bring a little of the fried fish that was saved from breakfast. While I drank my coffee – which was excellent and dark and bitter – he must have gone to the galley in the fo'c'sle, for he came back with a bell-dish and set it before me. He laid three or four strips of fish on my plate, alongside cubes of fried potato.

'You have not the seasickness?' he asked.

'No.'

'Mr Bletchley was pale this morning. But he will become used to the motion.'

'I quite like it,' I replied.

He smiled with a hint of knowingness, before returning to the pantry. I tried some of the fish and discovered an unexpected spiciness.

'Simao, what are these that I'm eating?' I called.

'Codfish tongue.'

'*Tongues?*'

He peered from the pantry, touching the smooth stretch of skin below his chin. 'And sounds.'

'*Sounds* are the swim bladders of the cod,' the captain said, appearing rather abruptly from the chart room. For a man of his age and figure, he was surprisingly light on his feet. 'Simao devils them in mustard for me. It's the only way I can stomach them.'

I looked at my plate, no longer keen.

'Did you sleep?' he asked.

'Not really.'

'Only the innocent sleep, first night. The innocent and the drunk. Mr French does not drink.'

'He doesn't?'

'That, I would say, is a peculiar decision for a man to take. You enjoy a drink, I take it?'

'Yes.'

'Glad to hear it. Perhaps you would join me in my cabin, Mr Saxby, when you are done,' he said, in an instructive manner; it was not a request. 'And please, bring your nature book, too.' With that, he went to his cabin, tapping the face of the barometer on the mizzenmast as he passed.

I ate some bread and preserve, feeling uneasy, wondering what the captain wanted. I adjusted my necktie and waistcoat. It was at that moment I noticed the tray had vanished from its place on the boards outside the cabin door. Cleared away, no doubt, but its absence now made me question the moment in the night when, almost feverish with tiredness, I'd crouched to sniff the curious smell of the drinking glass.

Unlike the spartan furnishings of my cabin, the captain's berth had the sumptuous air of a rector's drawing room. Pictures and embroideries were hung on the walls, there was a garnet-red chaise longue in the centre, and a table with a fine oil lamp and cut-glass decanter of sherry placed upon it. His bed was partitioned from the room by a heavily patterned curtain.

'You have a refined cabin,' I told him, pleasantly surprised. 'It's quite a home.'

'It *is* my home, Mr Saxby. Mrs Sykes is under the assumption that she is the keeper of my home, but it is on land, and it has Mrs Sykes in it, so it is not a place I am comfortable in.'

'Maybe one day, when you retire, the ocean life might seem—'

'I would rather be lost at sea,' he interrupted, with startling emphasis. He pointed to a needlework picture hung in a frame on the wall. 'That, Mr Saxby, is where Mrs Sykes would like to see me housed. On dry land. Notice the roses planted by the front porch and the view of the church in the background.'

'It looks most acceptable in my eyes.'

'It disappoints me in almost every aspect. I shall tell you

something. My front door knocker is an anchor. Can you believe that!'

I laughed. 'Did your wife embroider the image?'

'No. I did that.' He looked at me, watchfully. A narrow band of dark pigment surrounded his cornea, the *arcus senilis* of old age. 'You seem surprised that a ship's captain makes pictures with needlework?'

'Well, a little.'

'It is my passion.' Sykes regarded me, before ringing a dainty bell on his desk. The door opened almost immediately, and Simao entered.

'We shall have coffee now,' Sykes instructed. He let Simao leave, then turned to me. 'And if you are willing, I would like to play a game of draughts with you.' He went to his desk and brought a board over and placed it on the table in front of us. The pieces were handmade and unusual. 'I like to beat all my passengers on each voyage. Mr Bletchley offered very little resistance, I can tell you that. A careless and impetuous player.'

'What are these made of?' I asked.

'The blacks are flattened bullets, and the whites are sections of seal bone – from here,' he pointed to his hand. 'Except, of course, they have flippers.'

I picked up a piece of bone and examined it.

'Do you wish to be bullet or bone?' he asked.

'I shall be bullet,' I answered.

'A fine choice. The bullet usually triumphs.' Sykes immediately made his first move. 'While we are away from the other men, you might tell me more about these extinct birds. I prefer to be fully informed and they sound most intriguing. I am fond of rare creatures.'

He appeared, at that moment, genuinely interested. I had with me the nature book, so I found the page relating to the great auk, and showed him the now familiar engraving of the

31

bird standing on the rocky ledge. The captain made a move and then turned to the book. He studied the illustration carefully, stroking his moustache while he examined the strange bird, its large hooked beak, its long sleek black back, its shortened legs and paddle-shaped feet. Eventually he spoke. 'This is a peculiar animal,' he said, thoughtfully. 'It has an extraordinary beak. How large do you think it is?'

'The size of a goose. Or perhaps a small child.'

'A small child, you say. Standing upon the rocks.'

'I have only ever seen a reconstructed one, in a display case, made from similar feathers from guillemots and razorbills.'

'Aha!' Sykes said, leapfrogging three chequers and removing them from the board. 'Talbot and I talked about these birds last night. Now, Mr Talbot is an extender of the truth, to suit his needs, but he nonetheless knew much about them. He told me that last century the tradition used to be that a whaler or Newfoundland trader would seek out their colonies. The locations were well known. All the ship had to do was moor alongside the nesting rocks and the men could wander at will, wringing necks or using hakapiks, whatever suited them best. These birds were docile and curious, and had no fear of man. Talbot said sometimes all that was required would be to fix a gang-board to the rocks and the birds would wander onto it, out of curiosity, I suppose. I believe most of them had never seen man nor ship before. Once on board, they could be encouraged towards the hatches and there could be clubbed, one after another, in a line.' The captain made a gesture with his hand, as if dispatching the birds in order. 'Thus, they would fall into the hold and be stacked or rendered as was fit. Doesn't it make you wonder? These birds following one another to their demise? It would make the sailors most amused, I believe, that in so many cases they didn't have to stand from their deckchairs, while their food and profit walked towards them.'

Simao returned, bringing a pot of coffee which he placed precisely on the table. Sykes was giving me a heavy thrashing on the draught-board. 'It is no wonder,' I said once Simao had left, 'that these birds are now extinct.'

'Yes, no wonder at all. Apparently they had stiff feathers that would pierce any material, but these ones, around the neck,' he tapped the back of his head, 'they were soft, and in addition more than a pound and a half of oil could be rendered from their flesh. Soft feathers, bodies fat with oil, and no fear of man! In Arctic waters that is an unlucky combination.'

'Unlucky is not really the right word.'

'Cursed, perhaps.'

The nature book was already several decades old, and time had moved fast for these birds. The accompanying text talked boldly of great auk colonies widespread across the waters of the North Atlantic and Arctic seas, from Norway to the outlying British Isles, Iceland and the Newfoundland coast.

'The last British great auk was killed in St Kilda five years ago,' I told him. 'A single bird was discovered on a beach and it was slaughtered because it was thought it might be a sea-witch.'

'A witch!' the captain exclaimed, looking at the engraving. 'You must refrain from telling that to the men, Mr Saxby. You understand they are a most superstitious lot. They are already spooked to have a woman on board.'

I continued, encouraged by the captain's apparent natural interest, although I wish I had stopped.

'For many years the birds had a small but flourishing colony on a rock called the Geirfuglasker off Iceland. It means "the rock of the great auks". It was a place that was impenetrable to man, due to the sheerness of the volcanic

33

cliffs that rose on all sides and dangerous currents offshore. It was the last colony of great auks in the world. But these rocks sank, and the birds had to flee.'

The captain chuckled. 'Rocks, Mr Saxby, do not sink,' he said.

'Of course, ordinarily that's correct. But in Iceland they have been known to, as a result of volcanic activity.'

'Their colony sank into the sea?'

'Yes.'

'It seems the Lord has it in for these birds of yours.'

'It appears so, yes. Ten years ago, the surviving birds – I believe their number was thirty or so – swam to the island of Eldey, a few miles away, where they joined an established colony of gannets and other sea fowl. When the great auk were discovered there in such perilous numbers, most of the museums of Europe and America rushed to procure a specimen.'

At this, the captain raised his eyebrows.

I explained: 'I suppose each museum and private collector felt it might be the last opportunity to own one of these birds, or one of their eggs.'

'A price on their heads, Mr Saxby?'

'Yes. They were hunted, one by one, and bought at a high price to be stuffed. For the sake of owning a specimen, the museums collectively made these birds extinct.'

With mournful finality, the captain closed my nature book and handed it back to me. He turned to the draught-board. 'I believe you have been roundly beaten,' he said.

'Yes.'

'Nature has triumphed over the bullet.' He cleared away the board and turned to me with a thoughtful look, as if assessing all that had been said. 'Thank you for educating me, Mr Saxby.'

*

For most of the day we sailed alongside the Irish coast which, as Mr French informed me, was about ten miles distant. I studied the remote harbours and the way the villages nestled into the cliffs, a smudged suggestion of peat smoke above them. I had never seen Ireland before. It was peculiar to watch it like this, at a distance, as if the view was a secret glimpse of lives I would never touch, but merely pass. This was how much of the world must seem, from the sea. The land must appear like a constantly arriving, constantly vanishing edge, often seen and just as often never reached.

Flocks of birds sped past, low and curious, waterfowl and ducks, heading along a migration route that we, also, were travelling. Their instinct was taking them north, braving the ocean until they could replenish in Iceland, and then on to the breeding grounds of Greenland, a route they had flown for thousands of years. High above the ship, similar lines of migration were being followed: formations of geese, slowly honking, their wings beating in unison, the leading bird changing position every now and then. I felt privileged to be beneath them, in step with their path, a slower participant in their ancient calling.

I saw little of Bletchley until late in the afternoon, when he brought his handmade guns on deck with great ceremony. There were three of them, each presented in a long case of walnut with the gunsmith's insignia embossed upon the lid. French, Talbot and the captain gathered round him, good humoured, while Bletchley laid the cases on the saloon roof. He lifted the guns, expertly preparing each one before handing them to the men, all of whom appraised the manufacture with a general feel of their weight and a practised aim along the barrels. I kept my distance, deciding to sit against the quarterdeck rail with one of my sketchbooks. Guns unnerve me, and in the hands of an enthusiast such as Bletchley – so childishly animated about his weapons – I thought it prudent to keep several yards distant, good shot or not. Instead, I occupied myself by sketching them, observing how each man raised and lowered his weapon. As a group they resembled territorial animals, raising metalled tusks at imaginary foes, similar to the illustration of the walrus in my *Compendium*. Off the stern, about a dozen gulls followed our progress. They had been there all day, looping and gliding and falling into the wake after any morsels they believed were being thrown overboard. Possibly the sea is churned by a ship as a plough churns the soil, and fish are brought to the surface. But now I looked at those same birds and knew they had become targets.

The first shots sounded and I watched the birds dividing and falling away from the gusts of hot lead. The gulls swooped low to the water, then swung back, buoyant, mindful of each other but still oblivious to the sights being levelled by the guns. Again, two more shots, and then a single report which tore the wing off one of the gulls. It plunged, immediately, while its wing – several yards behind – fell in a silent curved flight towards the sea. It was Bletchley's kill. He whooped with pleasure, and I saw deep boyish dimples on each of his cheeks as the other men congratulated him. More shots followed in quick succession, as rapidly as the men could load. A gull's brilliant white chest turned instantly red, as if a crimson flower had been pinned to it, and still the bird flew, three more beats, until it closed its wings and fell to the sea. Another gull had a leg blown off and as the leg and foot fell a second gull dived after it, curious.

I turned away, appalled at the carnage. I pretended to sketch in my book, and after I had stared at a few lines of pencil for ten minutes the shots abruptly ceased. When I went back to my cabin, I glanced astern. There were no more birds following the ship.

*

The afternoon's shooting was the major discussion over dinner that evening. I took little part and I suspected the men had already made a companionship that I had been excluded from. The captain was in a particularly jovial mood. He had claimed three birds, and was allowing Bletchley to tease him about whether or not a fourth bird had been his kill. Bletchley had the confidence of a man who had been the best shot, killing or fatally maiming at least eight birds. French, too, had killed. Only Talbot had repeatedly missed, and that was most amusing to the others.

Again, there was an empty place at the table. As with the night before, Simao cleared away the setting midway through the meal.

That night we passed the final black promontory of Ireland's Donegal coast. I had been told that most of the crew were Irish, and several of them had gathered to say their farewells. But it was only when I walked along the main deck towards their huddle that I realised they were in a vulgar mood. There was much laughter and the making of lewd comments about the Donegal girls. The men quietened as I approached, but I managed to hear salacious details of carnal desires acted upon in secret coves. I was quite shocked, but attended to my pipe as a distraction, already too close to back away.

'Good evening,' I announced. 'Saying a farewell to your homeland?'

One of the men stepped forward, still grinning. 'Aye, sir. Me and the lads was just speaking of its beauties.'

He was a tall man with wide shoulders, dark unkempt hair and quick eyes. Something unknown was being chewed in his mouth.

'And all them secret marshy places,' a voice behind him added. Again, I heard a sniggering.

'Thass right, all them *acushlas*!' someone said.

'Yes, gentlemen, I heard,' I said.

The tall man gave me a questioning look, before grinning. 'Apologies, if what you was hearing was a little crude,' he said, kindly.

'Are you two brothers?' I asked, seeing a chin and nose that bore a resemblance to the first man's.

'Aye, sir, we're the Herlihy brothers. Connor and Martin.'

'We own this ship,' his brother quipped.

'Aye, we do.'

'So, what is that over there?' I asked.

'Malin Head,' the taller one replied. 'Worst place God ever dragged up from the sea.'

Across the water, a dark blank featureless shape was cut out from the night's sky. A terrible void, an unmade part of the world, without definition or light. I shuddered to think it was solid rock that could tear a ship apart with a simple brush of its arm.

I took my leave of them, and walked back towards the quarterdeck. The captain was standing with a man at the wheel, and had clearly been observing me.

'Mixing with the men, Mr Saxby?'

'Yes,' I answered. 'They were saying their farewell to Donegal.'

'They do that. They'll be singing later. We won't be seeing land for a while now. Take your fill of it.'

'I will.'

'And I wouldn't spend too much time with the men, Mr Saxby. They're just Irish bastards after all.' He turned to the man at the helm. 'Aren't you – you're just one of my Irish bastards?'

The man stared forward, his mouth set inscrutably. 'That's right, sir,' he replied.

*

Later, wearing a sea coat, I walked uphill somewhat, to the very front of the ship. I leant against the capstan, listening to the swishing of the water parting below the bow. It was quite different in sound and aspect to any other part of the deck. Here, the curved bulk of the ship's sides were brought to a fine point, pinched, the timber planking woven to an unusual slenderness. It ended in a fine bowsprit that held a straight arm above the water, pointing towards an endlessness that was difficult to comprehend. In front of the ship was all the emptiness of the world, a world made of water, dark and without feature, without horizon or sky. The Atlantic void.

Three thousand miles away would be the coast of America. I thought of its seaports, its wooden clapboard houses on the edge of a country which, in turn, promised a new endlessness, of thousand-mile prairie, vast mountain ranges and impenetrable deserts and canyons. Beyond that, another ocean, even greater in size, with its own endlessly disappearing horizon. It was a dizzying thought. It felt, at the point of that ship, that the world was a series of frontiers, where man clung to the edges in huddled communities, a back turned on an endless nature.

The air was full of salt and a dampness that wasn't elsewhere on deck. I held the rail carefully and dared to look over the side, and could just see the very tip of the bow, far beneath, covered in iron plates, cutting smoothly through the sea, turning ink-black water into curling white foam.

A shanty had started inside the crew's quarters in the fo'c'sle. I jotted the words in my notebook.

He drank all the night till the night was no more
Found his bed on the Donegal shore
The tide rose for our Daragh, boy
The tide rose for our Daragh.

I went to the fo'c'sle and listened against the wood. The sound of the men's voices was great. I imagined it must be a confined space in there, full of hammocks swinging from hooks, and a stove in the corner surrounded by their boots.

Waves were the thing what woke him
From the dreams of the gal what broke him
Float for the grave is deep, boy
Float for the grave will keep, boy.

Won't drown me yet old Daragh goes,
Till you give me the stitch of twine in the nose
But the tide bore our Daragh out, boy.
The tide bore our Daragh out.

It sounded as if one of the men might have fallen over. The others stopped singing and began to laugh. A few words were said, although I couldn't distinguish them. Eventually they started singing again, first a single voice, then the others joining in.

Dead Donegal Daragh crossed the oceans vast
Saw coasts and reefs with his smile set fast
Till the stream brought our Daragh home, boy
The stream brought our Daragh home.

Finally, the one man finished the song:

I seen his ghost curse the rocks, boy,
The drink and the gal and the life, boy,
But never a word 'gainst the tide, boy,
Never a word 'gainst the tide.

The captain's Irish bastards sang well. But their small pocket-sized room of noise and light felt perilous and brief, like a candle being cupped in the hand as you walk across a large and draughty field. Your eyes watch the flame as it flickers against your skin, nursing its light constantly, but you are aware, also, of the impenetrable woods and hedgerows at the edge of your vision.

Fearing I might be caught listening, I returned to the main deck, passing beneath the two whaleboats that were hung from the davits on the fo'c'sle roof, and the open galley door where Simao was cleaning the cooking pots, towards the huge upright shape of the mainmast.

I stopped, as if a hand was pressed into my chest. Standing against the ship's rail, about thirty feet away, was the tall figure of the female passenger, wrapped in a shawl and holding her hair, to prevent it from blowing in the breeze. As if sensing my presence, she turned towards me. At that moment I saw her thin face and haunted expression, the paleness of her skin and the beseeching look of her eyes, and she was so incredibly familiar to me, so recognisable, it was as if I was seeing a ghost.

'Oh dear Christ,' I whispered, knowing her. 'Take me off this ship.'

4

How was it possible? How could she be on board? After all these years, never once seeing her since that fateful day. One moment was all it had taken, one misjudgement by me, leading to a decade of doubt and failure; failure to establish my career, and failure, too, in matters of the heart. In all that time I had never been remotely close to anyone, and it was all because of Celeste. For the second night I lay in my bunk and wondered whether sleep would come. Repeatedly I was confronted with images of the past, in that country house in Norfolk ten years earlier in the gloomy autumnal weather, while the wet leaves collected on the lawn and I sat in the conservatory, listening to the sounds of pheasants in the shadowy hedges beyond the grass and watching as the light faded. The light fades in Norfolk like nowhere else on earth. It recedes like a tide, leaving you stranded. I thought of the cool damp corridors of the house, its empty grand staircases, and of the times when I'd glimpse her, being led along the brick path outside, three circuits of the lawn, never once looking up, her hand limp in her mother's grasp.

By morning, I had finally collapsed into a deep and dreamless sleep. I dressed for breakfast as thoughtful as a condemned man, then studied my reflection in the mirror above the washstand while I shaved. Sleeplessness, below my eyes, gave me a solemnity I don't usually possess. I wondered how much I would be able to conceal, if asked a direct question. I have a tendency to freeze my expression when I am trying to avoid the truth. At that moment, my face was entirely readable – with every aspect of the previous years written on it. My eyes, ordinarily light and quick, stared back with a dull shine. *You thought you could escape, but you cannot.*

Beyond my cabin door I heard the sounds of people gathering for breakfast. Bletchley's piping tone, too loud and spirited for this hour, as he took his coffee, paced the room and asked questions with childlike persistence. I heard snatches of the topics he wished to discuss: the sciences of navigation, the azimuth compass, dead reckoning, the wisdoms of helmsmanship and the arrangement of sails. I sat on the edge of my bunk and whispered a prayer. *Please, Lord, allow me peace, let me face what is out there. Let me face the past with an unflinching eye.*

'Ah, Mr Saxby!' Bletchley exclaimed, as I entered the saloon, as if my appearance were a great surprise. 'At midday you and I shall be taking a sighting of the sun with the nautical sextant.'

'Good,' I managed, looking around anxiously for signs of her. 'I shall look forward to it.' But the only other person waiting for breakfast was Mr French, who was leaning against the sideboard, playing with the half-molten wax of a candle. He was in a world of his own, staring at the flame.

'We shall use Mr French's sextant,' Bletchley continued, like a dog with a bone, 'and the nearest recording to agree with his own reading shall receive a shilling.'

He grinned at me, open mouthed, expecting an answer. 'A whole shilling?' I asked.

'Penny, then.'

'Well, now you don't sound so confident, Mr Bletchley,' I said.

'Then it will be two shillings,' he replied, clapping his hands together in boyish delight.

As Simao brought the breakfast in from the pantry, I relaxed, with the certainty that Celeste would not be joining us. While Bletchley tucked lustily into his eggs, I took the opportunity to ask him where he was from.

'Ely,' he replied.

'Oh. I had the assumption that you were from Norfolk.'

'Why ever should you think that?'

'I am not sure.'

'My cousin used to live in Norfolk. Perhaps I mentioned that last night?' He carried on eating his eggs, as if it was his last meal on earth. He dabbed his mouth after every forkful, with annoying affectation. Choosing his moment, he leant forward and whispered: 'Her side of the family has all the *money*.' He sat back in his chair, satisfied.

'It seems peculiar for a lady to be travelling on a vessel bound for the Arctic.'

'Does it? Seems entirely natural to me. They're used to wearing fur – it's their second skin.' He appeared pleased with his observation. 'Do you know East Anglia?'

'Yes,' I said, wary of what I should reveal. East Anglia is a gossiper's paradise. 'I grew up in Suffolk, and have travelled widely in Norfolk.'

'A loathsome place,' Bletchley replied quickly. 'For the most part muddy, damp, and with an entirely bleak aspect. You can tell when you've shaken hands with a Norfolkman, because he has carrots growing under his fingernails. And he may try to plant potatoes in your pockets! As soon as I am back from this trip I shall be off to London.' Bletchley turned to French: 'What of you, sir – from which part of England did you crawl out?'

French glanced up at Bletchley. He waved his fork in an offhand gesture. 'Oh, it is not important.' He continued to regard the candle, ignoring us.

'I believe I saw your cousin on deck last night?' I said.

Bletchley frowned, curious. 'Really? I am surprised. Perhaps you are mistaken.'

'Well, perhaps so,' I said, knowing he was unlikely to offer more. 'It is easy to be mistaken.'

We never did perform the wager over the sighting of the sun. For at midday, a minor drama had overtaken the *Amethyst*. A greenfinch had been spotted, flitting between the ratlines of the mainmast and landing on the deck, where it looked startled and confused. Some of the men taunted it, knowing that the ship had taken it far out to sea beyond any possible chance of flying back to land. They tried to catch it by throwing sacking across the deck, but with each attempt, the finch flew up and landed in the rigging, or flew in a circle out to sea, before changing its course and returning to the ship, its only choice of a perch.

'The men are excited,' the captain said, watching the sport from the quarterdeck rail.

French was standing next to him. 'They think it's an omen,' he added. 'First they're skittish about having a woman on board, now this. They really are an ignorant lot.'

'An omen of what?' I asked. French looked at me and raised his eyebrows, inscrutably. 'Will they catch it?'

'The finch is already as good as dead,' he replied. 'They'll scare it off, then it will drown. It will fly away from the ship and lack the strength to catch up again.'

Sykes was listening to our exchange. 'Martin will get it,' he said, boasting. 'He courses hares.'

Some of the men climbed the first rungs of the ratlines,

preventing the bird from flying up, and I noticed the Herlihy brothers, acting in unison, cornering the finch towards the scuppers, where one of them managed to leap upon it, catching it below his cap.

'What did I tell you,' the captain remarked, satisfied. 'Should've had a bet with you, Quinlan – you should have faith in the men.' He called down to the deck: 'Well done, Martin!'

'A fast bird, sir,' Martin, replied, smiling broadly.

As the men gathered to examine the greenfinch, I asked French whether I could sketch it, so that I might make a painting.

'Good idea,' he replied. To the men he shouted: 'Bring that bird here.'

The men parted, still laughing, and Martin Herlihy brought the bird, captive in his hands, up the ladder of the quarterdeck.

'Mr Saxby will sketch the finch, while you hold it,' French explained.

'Aye, sir,' Martin replied. He stood in front of me, still sweating from the sport of catching it, immobile and obedient, opening a small gap between his hands in order for me to see the bird.

'Is it struggling?' I asked.

'Quite calm, sir,' Martin replied. Between his thumb and forefinger I peered in at the greenfinch, seeing its precise nostrils either side of a small polished beak. The eyes looked black and gleaming with fright, or exhaustion. 'Thank you,' I said. 'How did you manage to catch it?'

'Couldn't let me brother win,' he replied, grinning.

I began to sketch the bird, as quickly as I could, although it was far from ideal as most of it was concealed. Martin Herlihy angled his neck, watching my drawing, and obliging

46

me by trying to move his large fingers, one by one, to reveal different parts of the bird.

'You've got the look of it there, sir,' he said at one point.

'This is just a preliminary sketch,' I replied. 'I shall make a water-coloured painting of it later.'

'*Ahh*,' he said.

'Are you all right?'

'I think it may have shat itself,' Martin said, grimacing.

'Nearly finished?' French asked.

'Not quite,' I replied.

'It's shat for sure. It's shat on me finger.'

'Herlihy, you sound like a woman,' French said, watching as the man adjusted his hold on the bird. 'Keep it still now,' he ordered.

'I don't think I can, sir,' Herlihy grimaced. A dark wing with a vivid yellow flash slipped out between his fingers, accompanied by a hideous chirping that Herlihy tried to subdue.

'Ahh,' he said, again, spooked.

'Oh for God's sake!' French said, impatiently. 'Give it here, you fool.'

Quickly, he reached into Martin Herlihy's hands, held the frightened bird and, with a practised movement, wrung its neck. The finch jolted two or three times, its beak parting with surprise, before becoming limp. French laid it down on top of the saloon roof, as if it was a small cloth bag, and with a finger he moved the broken neck to arrange it properly.

'Thank you, Martin, you may resume your duties,' he said to the Irishman. 'You may sketch it at your leisure, now, Mr Saxby,' he told me, and even as he spoke he was turning away, quickly bored by the whole incident. I looked after him, shocked. As he approached the captain, I saw a devilish smile creep across Sykes' face, and I knew that French must have shared a very private look with him.

47

Martin Herlihy remained standing where he'd been, as though he'd been slapped. I could tell he felt responsible, and that the death of the bird would sit heavily on him. Strength of body and compassion of mind grow together. He shut his eyes for a second in prayer, before he moved off, wiping his hand on his trouser in a practical manner, but treading heavily, I thought.

I placed my sketchbook next to the dead greenfinch. My half-completed drawing confronted me: the sketch of a bird that was still living. Its similarity to the etching of the great auk in my Arctic book, an image created in all likelihood after the extinction of the species, felt eerie. They were the drawings of ghosts.

Catching the finch had been sport for the whole crew, but its death, and its body, belonged to me. I wondered whether I should drop it over the ship's rail, but feared this would be transgressing some superstitious custom; worse still, one of the gulls attending the ship would dive, immediately, and swallow it in front of all who watched.

But something had to be done with the body. I was just about to pick it up when surprisingly a hand took hold of my wrist. I heard a voice in my ear, calm and measured, a woman's voice:

'Why are the men always killing things?'

I glanced up and saw Celeste, bending to my level, with a woven shawl wrapped tightly round her. Her eyes seemed on the verge of tears, with dark rings below them and skin so shockingly pale it was almost translucent. Her mouth was set firm, as if in pain. She acted as if caught, clutching her arms in protection, holding herself, the only movement that of the curled ringlets of brown hair which hung either side of her face, stirred by the breeze.

'I don't know,' I said.

'You don't know what?' she replied, with a quick frown that was gone almost as it appeared.

My mouth felt dry. 'About the men. I don't know why they kill things.'

I waited for her to recognise me. It had been ten years since we had last seen each other, but I hadn't changed, not enough. She pressed a hand to her temple, as if suppressing a headache.

'You are staring at me,' she said, quietly.

I felt my skin prickling with heat. 'I'm sorry.'

She remained there, a little puzzled, looking sadly now at the bird laid next to us on the top of the saloon roof.

'Were you there at the moment it died?' she asked.

'Yes.'

'They have such tiny souls – perhaps the weight of a breath – that is all.' She smiled, consoling herself. 'But it is a soul, nonetheless, such as you and I possess, and who can say whether our souls are any more substantial. Was it in your hands?'

'When it died? No. That sailor held it.'

'Which one?'

I looked across the deck where the work of the ship had begun once more, spotting the Herlihy brothers talking to each other. 'By the galley door – the one with the neckerchief.'

She appraised him with a slight tilt of her head. 'A strong man, wouldn't you say? Strong hands, but I think he felt that soul depart. I see it in his face. He felt it as sure as an oak tree must feel the first leaf fall in autumn.' She performed a curious gesture with her hand, floating it downward as if emulating a leaf. Her hand came to rest on the wood of the roof, alongside the bird.

'Of course,' she said, more brightly, 'the answer is that men kill things because they enjoy it.'

49

'Not all men are like that,' I replied.

She smiled, conceding. 'Did it suffer?' she asked.

'It was scared when the men were trying to catch it. It became cornered over there, between the rail and hatches, and when it flew out over the sea I believe it was very agitated. It repeatedly changed course and was distressed to have no option – not knowing whether to be caught or drowned. But once it was captured it became quite calm. When Mr French killed it, he did it swiftly.'

'Dispatched in a proper manner,' she stated, unconvinced. I thought about how he had reached into Herlihy's grasp, impatiently, then how with a twist of his fingers the bird had died, quickly, without fuss and without choice.

'No. Actually he acted most improperly,' I said. 'I think he found pleasure in it.'

She looked back, startled. 'Yes,' she said, as a flush of colour rose in her cheeks.

'The bird was going to die,' I explained, 'either at sea or from exhaustion. But it had that right, I suppose – to have a natural death. It shouldn't have been killed.'

She touched the greenfinch with her finger, closing its beak and then stroking the intricate feathers of its crown. I watched, transfixed, as her fingertip pressed into the plumage of the neck, where the break had occurred, smoothing and flattening the feathers as if they were silk.

'Are you the collector?' she asked quietly.

'Yes.'

'May I ask your name?'

It's time, I thought; she will remember the name. 'Eliot,' I said. 'I'm Eliot Saxby.'

She regarded me, a little intrigued, but without any sign of recognition.

'My cousin has been telling me about you,' she said. 'He

is ... well, what should we say, he's very impressionable. He likes you.'

I felt confused. Surely she recalled my name? But her look revealed nothing. 'He is a very enthusiastic fellow,' I said.

'Sometimes too enthusiastic,' she replied, dryly. 'Like a puppy that keeps bouncing up at you – he needs the occasional rap upon the nose.'

'I shall bear that in mind.'

'Was it you I saw last night, listening to the men sing their shanty?' she asked.

'Yes.'

'You were hiding from them.'

'Was I?' I tried, attempting to deny it. I could see she wasn't going to be fooled. 'Yes. I suppose I was.'

Bletchley appeared, trotting up in a fine jacket and fashionable trousers. 'Shouldn't wander the deck at night, Eliot, you might fall in!' he said, looking as if he wished to be a part of the conversation as quickly as possible. He laughed loudly at his joke, underlining it with an impression of a drowning man.

'Quite,' I replied.

I was distinctly aware of two things: first Bletchley, nervously rocking on his heels, excitable and not trusting himself and inexplicably anxious, and secondly, a renewed stiffness in Celeste's posture. She put on her gloves and adjusted their fit. Bletchley waited for her, then held her wrist, rubbing the bare skin with a vigorous finger, a strange gesture which was unduly intimate. She bent towards him, compliant to his touch. Her expression clouded, as if a veil had been drawn across her face. When he addressed her, it was rather more for my benefit than hers. 'We must give you medicine,' he said.

She nodded, chastised. Urged to respond, I asked her

whether she had been unwell. She considered the question. 'I am always unwell.'

'But we shall get you better,' Bletchley bleated, anxious now to take charge and lead her away. I suspected complexities to their relationship that would be difficult to determine.

'Let us go,' she said. 'I feel tired.'

'Yes, dearest. You are. You are tired,' Bletchley continued, adopting her tone, both of them seeming to address me more than each other.

He clicked his heels in parting, and guided her towards the cabins. I noticed how she barely lifted her feet from the deck, and how pliant she was in his hold. I was struck by a deep sense of unease, of an atmosphere that felt charged and thorny, and effortlessly I remembered how she used to be led along the brick path across that autumnal lawn, her mother's grip a manacle around her hand.

Before she reached the companionway, she resisted Bletchley and turned back once more. 'Forgive me,' she said, smiling wanly, 'I failed to introduce myself, and it has been good to talk with you. My name is Clara.'

In my confusion, all I could think was that I must seek my cabin immediately. Close a door. There, sitting on the edge of my bunk, I wondered what had occurred. She had called herself *Clara*. It was unfathomable. Her name was Celeste! We had spoken for several minutes, without her giving the slightest hint that she knew me. Either she was pretending to be a stranger, or I had truly not been recognised. After all, much can happen in ten years, and the autumn months when I had known her had been far from ordinary.

The Norfolk manor house where she lived had been a shadowy and isolated environment. For the most part I had been left alone, in the chilly conservatory, restoring and cataloguing the collection, wearing fingerless gloves so I might handle the eggs safely. Each morning, I would see her through the panes of the conservatory windows, her outline rippled and made uncertain by the age of the glass, as she was led along the path by her mother. The mother was a thickened, severe figure next to Celeste's slender frame, but they had shared similarities – the length of their stride, the slope of their shoulders, the way they both looked up when the rooks called. In the tightness of her grip it had seemed, some mornings, as if the mother was holding onto a youthful version of herself, and was unable to let go. And Celeste, in turn, appeared held by the darkened presence of a future she wished to be no part of. I had had time to think these things. Celeste was young, no more than sixteen, and I had been twenty-two, I had been excited by the mystery of who she might be and the possibility that I might get to know her. Struck too by her beauty, her ghostly fragility, the dreamlike lift of her feet from the brick path, the thin soles of her shoes, the pearl whiteness of her gown against the deep wet softness of the lawn. She was graceful, almost transparent, it appeared, her figure almost floating. I had been mesmerised. Yet her presence in the house was never mentioned. In the three months I was there, my employer adamantly refused to acknowledge even the *existence* of his daughter. During the times when he was in the conservatory – while she was being led across the lawn – he would look anywhere but in her direction. Instead, he would pace the cold tiled floor, or drum his fingers on one of the shelves, daring me to glance at the girl beyond the glass. I had been certain I would be sacked if I asked about her, or even looked in her direction.

Clara joined us for supper that evening, for the first time since leaving Liverpool. She had prepared for dinner, and wore a dress of pale gold brocaded silk, trimmed with lacing and embroidered net mittens. But it was apparent from the way she sat, quietly and not wishing to look anyone in the eye, that she was far from comfortable. Bletchley was undaunted, mentioning several times that it was good to see her out of her cabin, getting better, getting stronger. Fit as a fiddle in no time. He kept patting her on the back of her hand, neither noticing the obvious flinch when he did so, nor the fact that she did not eat or drink.

Sykes was intrigued. 'It is a real pleasure to have a lady travelling with us,' he said, encouraging her to take part. 'As rare as one of Mr Saxby's birds, I believe. I do hope the rudimentary nature of life upon the sea is not a burden to you?'

'My cabin is perfectly comfortable,' she said, in a clipped and formal voice. Once again, she had been introduced to us as Clara.

'The men for'ard of the mast can be an uncouth and ill-bred rabble at times. You must excuse them if they tend to stare at the sight of a lady. They have their superstitions and the like, it is most annoying. I have noted it before.'

'Then I shall do my utmost not to be an object of fascination for your men, Captain Sykes.'

I tried not to look at her. But I wanted to study her face – the face that I had longed to see for so many years. The thin delicate nose, the fine bone of her forehead, the slender chin which was set, revealing nothing. She was so beautiful, so radiant. Celeste had grown into an elegant woman. If she had looked up at me and smiled I think I might have cried out.

'Of course,' Sykes continued, 'Mrs Sykes has been known to venture upon the *Amethyst* once in a while, but that is rather like having a heavy and shifting cargo in the hold. It makes me clumsy at the helm, irritable with the men and is no good on many accounts.'

'You seem very fond of her,' Bletchley exclaimed.

'Familiar, rather than fond, I would say. As one is familiar with a running nose in winter. Do you recollect that time, Mr French, when Mrs Sykes had us dig the ballast out?'

'I think of it often,' French replied. 'And also the occasion when she made the men brush their teeth.' Sitting at the opposite end of the table from the captain, he spoke with a modicum of effort. He had been quiet and distracted all evening.

'It is her duty to open my nostrils to the stinks it no longer registers,' Sykes said, enthusiastically. 'We must remind the men their yearly brushing is due once more, what do you think? But tell me,' he continued, not yet finished with Clara, 'why a lady such as yourself should be on a voyage to the Arctic, where it is nothing but cold and draughty and quite thoroughly miserable?'

Bletchley stepped in, keen to reply: 'I have dragged her along, sir, that is the short of it—'

'Thank you, Edward,' she interrupted. 'I am quite able to answer for myself.'

'Yes, yes,' he replied, hasty to backtrack, 'and your voice is so pretty, too, my pippin. You talk so very eloquently, also. I was merely saving you the effort.'

The look that she gave Bletchley was remarkable. It was piercing, as a heron's is piercing when it stares into the water ready to strike. Bletchley recoiled as if seared, his hands raised melodramatically in apology.

'I am on this ship,' she explained, 'for all the wrong reasons. Sometimes you can be at a place only because you can be at no other place. Will that suffice for an answer?'

Sykes seemed unsure how to reply.

'You might consider me as you did that finch this afternoon,' she continued, coming to the point. 'It landed upon this plank only because it could land nowhere else.'

She had momentarily silenced the room. Again Bletchley felt he needed to step in: 'It has also been generally agreed that clean cold air will greatly improve her health.'

'Strange. It's been the ruin of mine,' Sykes replied, glad of the opportunity to joke. 'Will you hunt?'

Clara regarded at him with a dark expression, wishing to be left alone. 'I abhor violence of any kind, Captain Sykes.'

'Very well said,' he replied, picking at his teeth with a fingernail. 'We will benefit from having a woman on board, it will civilise us, for men are very simple and brutish animals.'

Bletchley complimented at the captain, amused and excited, not knowing whether to take him seriously or not. 'I believe you are making a joke,' he said.

'Half,' Sykes replied, giving him a wink, but that too felt inconclusive. Clara sighed and Bletchley reached for her hand, but missed, patting the table instead.

She looked up, not at her cousin, but directly across the table at me. For a second she held my gaze – an expression in her eyes that was liquid and surprising, as if she was trying to figure out something I had said. In my confusion, which felt overwhelming, I heard her speak. *Save me from this place*, she said, and even as I heard her words, I knew that her lips had not moved and she had not spoken. I looked down at my plate, startled. *Not here*, I thought. *Be calm. Be focused.*

'Quinlan French!' the captain called out. 'For God's sake man, get your eyes off that candle!'

The first mate visibly jolted in his chair. I realised he had been intently gazing at one of the dining candles before him. 'I need your eyes to be good!' Sykes added.

French slid his plate away, before standing. 'I shall prepare for my watch now, sir. Gentlemen, Miss Gould, if you will forgive me.'

Sykes waved him off as he would a fly, waiting for him to

leave the room, then saying in a conspiratorial tone, 'The navy won't have the fellow, so he is left with us. It is our burden but we do our best.'

We listened to French's footsteps crossing the deck above us as he went to the helm. Almost immediately he must have turned, for we heard the same steps returning, rather more quickly. He came down the companionway and leant into the room.

'Captain, we are in sight of the Rock,' he said.

Sykes raised an eyebrow and consulted his watch. 'Very good, we shall come up on deck.'

The sight that awaited us was one of the most unforgettable of my life. Amid an almost totally tranquil sea, whose water was as smooth and reflective as polished steel, was the dark and foreboding profile of a single rock. It rose, as bold and as jagged as a dog's tooth, perhaps a hundred feet tall, but little more than the girth of a large house at its base.

'What is this thing?' I asked Mr French, as we stood at the rail to admire it.

'Rockall,' he replied. 'It is the furthest extremity of the British Isles. Beyond this point it is merely water.'

Sykes went to the wheel. 'Keep her to larboard, helmsman,' he said. 'Have you sighted the Hasselwood?'

'Yes, sir.'

'Very good. Keep your eye on the overfall.'

Such a blunt finger of solid crag in all this ocean was extraordinary. And even at this distance, of perhaps half a mile or so, the outline of the rock seemed to shimmer. I realised, by shielding my eyes against the setting sun, that its shifting profile was due to the many hundreds of birds that were flying from it, collecting almost in a haze above the isle as if their bodies had formed a smoke.

'Has man ever landed on this rock?' I asked Mr French.

'Certainly not,' he stressed. 'He would die in the attempt. The surge would destroy the tender and there is no purchase of any kind. A single ledge, I believe, that not even the birds use. It has no water and no other shelter. He would be mercilessly pecked at, blown off by the wind and swept away by waves.' He laughed. 'But the captain is fond of it. He always steers by the Rock. Is that not right, sir – you love this unholy spike of dry land?'

Sykes smiled broadly. 'She has a special place in my heart,' he said, patting his chest. 'I am attracted to the lost and the lonesome.'

Across the water, the eerie cries of the kittiwakes could be heard, alongside the rough barks of the fulmars and gannets. Several cormorants were lined along the top, their wings outstretched in cruciform shape.

I thought of the great auks that may have once sought out such a barren perch as this. A single rock several hundred miles from the mainland and surrounded by countless acres of empty ocean, yet even here they had been hunted down and destroyed. If they could not be safe in this most remote of places on the earth, then it was no wonder they were extinct.

Further along the ship's rail, I noticed Clara staring intently at the isle, her lips silently mouthing a prayer. A strange shine emanated from the pale gold of her dress, a flower grown where there could be no root. So, too, her skin, which was lit up by the evening sunlight.

'You seem enchanted by the sight,' I said, approaching her.

'Have you ever felt that you have seen a place before – but it's a place that you cannot possibly have been to?' She nodded towards the rock. 'Even though it is at the end of the world. Is it possible that I have seen this thing in my dreams?'

'I have felt such a thing, too.'

'You have? Yes, I can see you have.'

'You've seen this island before?' I asked.

'In dreams.'

'Then you're not just on the ship for all the wrong reasons.'

She smiled, quite wonderfully. 'I think you will be my only friend on this journey,' she said. 'Would you be my friend?'

'Yes, of course.'

She turned back to gaze at the rock. I studied her, closely. At that moment I really believe she saw something that no one else on board was able to perceive.

5

We turned due north, and for the next few days saw nothing but ocean. Occasionally, lines of birds would stream past us, so fast their wings were blurred. I made sketches as they raced by, noticing how their wingtips would touch the water at speed as the flocks repeatedly rearranged formation. The only other birds we saw were the deep ocean species that were able to live out here, rafting and diving, away from land. They were wild and spear shaped, barbarous skuas and petrels, passing the ship in sweeping glides, a cruel eye cast across the deck as if in their glance they weighed a man's soul.

I quickly learnt the sailors' names for the birds I knew. They called most gulls *mollies*, or *mallemokes*, and there were always five or six following us, at any one time, unless Bletchley was practising with his guns. Little auks were *dovekies*, Brünnich's guillemots were *looms*. Kittiwakes they had improved, with the name *tat-a-rats*, and ivory gulls were romanticised as *snowbirds*. Richardson's skuas were called *boatswains*, and glaucous gulls *burgomasters*. In all these names I sensed a relationship to nature that was practical, sometimes humorous, but not particularly affectionate.

I had learnt about birds during my childhood in Suffolk. Their times of flocking would announce the changes of season: mallard, widgeon, pintail, teal and geese in winter, greenshanks, redshanks, sandpipers, terns and stints in summer. I would study their migration and draw their eggs, and knew they were a connection to a world that existed beyond my horizons. Like the clouds, they came from distant lands. Arctic terns arrived from Africa and departed to the northern wastes of Greenland and Iceland. Swifts and swallows, arriving in summer, still had the dust of deserts falling from their wings. Swans, flying in formation from Russia and beyond; their secret calls and mutterings whispered great truths about a world I could only dream of.

The further north we sailed, the thicker the weather became. Fogs descended, as if the top of the world was hidden in clouds and vapours. Through the mist, curtains of stinging rain swept across the sea, drenching the decks in a matter of seconds. Cold steam rose from the wood. After these downpours, the rainwater poured away through the scuppers with a noisy gurgle of streams, returning to the ocean. Then all would be quiet again, the men would come out of the fo'c'sle and continue the jobs they had started, and the sails would drip and shine like faces of wet rock above them. The sea itself changed colour almost as rapidly, from a green-grey to an almost perfect black, and occasionally a vivid cloudy green as we drifted through fields of plankton.

It was in one of these lulls, between the rainstorms, that a ship was sighted, a few miles off, sliding between the veils of mist. I was on deck when it was seen, and was there to see it vanishing too, a dark low bulging shape removed, bit by bit, by the advance of the clouds. A mast remained, improbably, like the cross above a church steeple, before it too became grey, then faded, and was gone.

There was much excitement on the decks of the *Amethyst*. The men went forward, hoping to spot her again. In so many miles of ocean, in such strange weather, the view of the ship had been more ghostly than I could have imagined. A low brooding hulk that belonged to another century; but no one on deck seemed to share this superstitious feeling of mine. After a few minutes, through some motion of the fogs or direction of the vessels, the phantom emerged once more, angled to us but turning in our direction. I could see the churn of foam beneath its bow and, above deck, a solitary sail being furled among a peculiar arrangement of rigging.

'It's the *Jester*!' Sykes announced, balancing his telescope through a foothold in the rigging. 'Man, she has seen some weather! Helmsman, bring her abaft, she is slowing towards us.'

Not only was it heavier and built lower than the *Amethyst*, with four longboats tied to her side, but the tops of the masts had gone and part of the foremast had been tied off at a peculiar angle. Only the mainmast appeared to be functioning.

'Bray has nearly wrecked her!' Sykes continued, highly amused, to the men standing along the rail. 'Get the whale-boat ready. I shall be going across.'

The men went to the task, uncovering one of the whale-boats from the fo'c'sle roof and carrying it to the port-side davits, stowing the oars and making it ready to lower. It was a fine long craft, pointed at both ends, with a smooth carvel-built hull, partially covered in zinc to protect it from ice.

'Mr Saxby,' the captain called, searching for me on the deck. 'Ah, yes, there you are, always where I least expect you. Would you like to visit a whaling ship?'

Sykes, Talbot, Bletchley and myself were rowed over in the launch, shoulder to shoulder with each other on the simple benches. Bletchley, wearing bright mustard-coloured breeches, his blue pilot coat and his polished riding boots, looked dressed for a gallop in the country. Both ships towered darkly above us as the mist once more began to move in, drifting like bonfire smoke, obscuring the shapes of the rigging and masts. Surrounded by little more than the sound of dipping oars, we rowed through a mossy cloud of green plankton, and I imagined the depths of ocean that must be beneath us. The sensation of a small boat on a vast ocean made me uneasy. How could I have become used to the Atlantic, I wondered, when it was so terrifyingly deep as this?

Sykes noticed me gazing at the water. 'Good for whaling,' he said, pointing at the plankton. 'Makes the whales blinded, so the hunter has the advantage.'

We smelt the other ship before we reached it: a deep tarry smell of oil and smoke and butchery. The sides of the hull were as dark as bog oak, and streaked with long stains of what appeared to be blood. Gouges and lacerations covered the planks above the waterline, giving the cladding a splintered look that meant it couldn't have been watertight. Talbot grabbed the pilot ladder with a gaff hook, and Sykes hailed the other captain, repeating his joke that Bray had damned nearly wrecked his ship.

'Tried my best I did, Sykes,' came a call from above the black-strake, 'froze her and burnt her 'n' just about holed her through the stern but she just won't go down!'

We climbed the ladder, helped by some of the *Jester*'s crew, and were confronted by a scene of great disorder. In the centre of the deck, the fire-blackened blocks of a rendering house lay partly dismantled. The roof had gone, and two of the walls were blown, with bricks lying about in a ruined heap. Leading out from them, the deck planks were pitted and scarred with ruts of charred wood, the signs of a considerable blaze that must have stretched the entire width of the ship.

'Blast it, Bray, you're not fit for the sea!' Sykes stated, looking at the chaos with a mixture of disapproval and glee. 'What the devil has occurred here?'

'As I said,' came the reply. 'Just about all the gods have to throw, and some more than that, too.' Captain Timothy Bray was a short man, with a bald head and a straggly beard. Although small in stature, he was dressed in a long coat, more like a dressing gown, lined with animal fur. 'Careful of your dandy trousers, sir,' the captain said to Bletchley, 'you will pick up oil in no time.'

Bletchley nodded in agreement, keeping clear of snags. Bray raised his eyebrows at Sykes. 'Ferrying peacocks this time?' he said, for everyone to hear.

But it wasn't the condition of the ship that fascinated me. It was the state of the crew. To a man they were dirtied and ageless, with stained hands and faces and strong full beards the hue of tobacco. Their caps were the colour of grease, and their clothes were ragged and mended and appeared to have been woven from a material soaked in oil and smoke. Some of them wore hats of brown fur, the animal hide turned outwards, with rough stitching as if surgeon's scars were running across their heads.

'Mind the ropes,' Sykes advised, as he crossed the deck with his sprightly gait, heading for the other captain. 'So, the story?'

Bray was delighted to brag. 'The wind took her foremast tops off – whipped 'em like a dog pulling a stick. *Cer-rack!*' he cried. 'Then, of all curses, I must be a cursed man, the lightning nearly did for us with a fire.'

The deck felt greasy underfoot. It smelt horribly, of an animal flesh, partially decomposed, alongside the smells of fire and charred wood and a dark smell of mouldy ballast coming from the hatches. Flensing hooks hung from blocks the size of bull's heads, swinging freely above the deck and still coated with the remnants of meat or blubber that had dried onto the iron in strips. Ropes snaked carelessly across the decking, mixing with chains and gearing and more blocks and tackle, and at the opposite side, below the rail, several large grey bones each as long as a horse had been tied to the gunwale.

'Look,' I said to Bletchley, 'see the whale bones?'

Surprisingly, Bletchley had lost his usual enthusiasm. He glanced at the bones and then proceeded to put on a pair of calfskin gloves. 'Most unpleasant,' he said, with uncharacteristic disdain.

I noticed, in the fore-rigging, several other jawbones. They hung there dark and wet, and resembled the spars and yards that remained around them, but their presence made the ship seem half animal. I decided not to point them out to Bletchley. He was in a peculiar mood.

Sykes had had the foresight to bring our lunch over with us, suspecting the provisions on the *Jester* would be in a poor state. Bray was overjoyed, personally going through the hamper and finding the jugged rabbit, the Wiltshire ham, fresh eggs and suet pudding as if each parcel was a Christmas present. He ordered his own steward to lay the food out, and invited us to join him at his table. Below deck, the *Jester* had a similar layout to the *Amethyst*, but it was only when I saw the spartan nature of the walls, the lack of ornamentation or cushioning, the absence of settees, that I realised our own ship was rather more geared towards passengers than this one.

Sykes took a sip from his glass and theatrically spat it out onto the floor. 'Your water is foul, man!' he said, grimacing like a dying man.

Bray was greatly amused. 'Pond ice, sir. You've been harboured too long, Sykes.'

They continued in this vein, trading insults like school-children, neither of them making any concession to myself or Bletchley. Formal talk was thin and discarded easily out here. Bray talked enthusiastically, his eyes red-rimmed but sparkling with life, and he repeatedly glanced with a beady look at each of his guests, maintaining us as his audience. He had stories to tell, and had had no one new to listen for a long time.

He began by recounting how the *Jester* had overwintered in Cumberland Sound, a practice almost entirely unheard of, tied to an American whaler. 'A couple of the New Bedford lot tried it two years ago – no, I lie – three years back – and were almost destroyed with scurvy and madness and the blasted longing for their wives – not a thing I personally sub-scribe to. I believe you are the same Kelvin? Aha – a raised eyebrow I spotted there. Did you see it, gentlemen? Where was I – yes – we had such a poor season last year it wasn't worth our returning to port, so we sailed for Cumberland Sound before the weather changed. It's a good spot, well found by the Yankees,' he raised his hands dramatically: 'mountains this high, all sides, protect it from the wind, which means the bay ice forms with regularity and without much current. Oh, and yes, there is also a very friendly Esquimaux settlement there, which was most useful. We had one Esquimaux fellow, paddled out in his skin kayak – fif-teen feet long it was, adorned with knobs of ivory. His coat was lashed tight to repel the water, so there was no way of pulling him out from his craft – cork in a bottle, he was. So you know what we did? We lifted the whole boat on the flensing pulleys, with him in it, and set it down on the deck. He thought that was capital, you should have seen his smile. Great white teeth like piano keys.'

Captain Bray drained an entire glass of wine before

continuing. 'We anchored October, no, late September – it was the first week of October, it was, and spent many weeks trading and preparing for the winter and the like. I shot caribou, Sykes – you must try it, for they fall like oak trees – got the beast right in the ear – and the meat was hot-smoked and is excellent for avoiding the scurvy. We fetched this pond water and what provisions the locals could muster, although their diet is usually quite terrible. Most of their food remains in the gaps in their teeth. I arranged for the topmasts to be removed, and we tented the decks to protect against the ice.' Bray looked at me directly: 'You know that an icicle falling from the yards can kill a man? I heard of it happening, speared him right through from neck to heart. I think it was on Jan Mayen, but I might be wrong. We tied ourselves to the Yankee whaler, the *Mystic*, that had decided to overwinter with us. No, on Jan Mayen it was the frostbite, that's right. Where the man lost his nose. By late October there was no choice but to stick it out, you see. The bay ice had come in, uncommonly like porridge it was, with higher blocks coming in off the streams and fixing the sea rapidly. You could hear it growling and your instinct is to sail, sail, sail – you understand that, Sykes, don't you? We've all dreamt of ice.'

'I dream it before each voyage, without fail. In fact, if I didn't dream it, I might decide to stay on shore.'

'When the ice was as thick as this fist of mine, we weighed the anchors through these fine-cut holes we'd made. It was the ice that held us, nothing more. You would think it sets like a sheet of steel, gentlemen, but over the months we travelled several hundred yards across the bay. A snail's pace.'

Bletchley braved a question: 'So what did you do for all that time?'

Bray looked back at him, expansive. 'Oh, much fun, on

the whole. And plenty of hours for your fancy needlework, Sykes. Many evenings mallymarking with the Yankee boys and some with the Esquimaux. They cannot take their drink, no, not at all. Unlike the Americans, who can't take being sober. We had a Christmas dance and game of football on the ice.'

'Against the Americans?' Bletchley asked.

'Absolutely. The Esquimaux refuse to use their feet. They keep picking up the ball and running away with it.'

'What was the score?'

Bray slapped the table. 'A victory, gentlemen, of eight to five! With our goal only this much smaller than theirs!'

Bray was enjoying the sound of his own voice, and the taste of our food, often speaking through a mouth half filled with cold cut ham. He told us about the aurora lights that filled the night with eerie ribbons of colour, how the deck and ice and even the smoke from the men's pipes would be lit with these strange glows. 'Sometimes, you imagine a sound that accompanies the lights,' he said, oddly, then continued to tell us that he had found a new respect for the ice and the world it creates. 'When the sun returned it came first as a glow sitting on the horizon, as if a bonfire was set there, beneath the curve of the world. We stood on the ice to welcome it back – the entire crew. A curious thing, Sykes, I tell you, the sun broke through the horizon, yet our shadows all pointed towards it, for the moonlight was stronger.' He stopped, abruptly. 'Of course, here's me talking about this and yet with us is Mr Talbot, who knows more about surviving on the ice than the rest of us put together. When your ship was crushed, how long did you spend on the floe?'

I thought Talbot was not going to answer. He chewed his food for a good time, considering the question.

'Five weeks, sir.'

'Five weeks, you say? That is a length of time! What was your shelter – did you tent?'

'Carpenter built some shacks from the timber. We had the whaleboats, too, upturned. And six months of rum.'

'With reason to drink it,' Sykes added.

Talbot was surprisingly keen to say his part. 'What we done was have these two men on the edge of the floe, on the lookout for passing ships. The rest of us was just waiting, twenty mile off, roaring drunk for most of the time – I honestly remember little of it.'

'How cold did it become?' Bletchley asked. Talbot looked at him, as if being bothered by a mosquito.

'Like I says, I don't remember.' He sat still for a while. Neither captain spoke. Perhaps they knew that, given time, Talbot would continue.

Sure enough, he did. 'Only two things. The iron went brittle, it could shatter with just a tap here and there. And the rum began to freeze, even though it were wholesale strength. So we took turns keeping the barrels warm.'

'So you keep the liquor warm first, before the men!' Bray said.

'That's just about right, sir. It took 'em a month till those ones on the edge of the floe flagged a ship. But when they came back to our camp, bringing some of the other crew, that crew sat down on the ice and got drunk with us, too. Thing was, we couldn't carry all those barrels of rum, see, and not one of us wanted to leave it. So when we set out for the rescue ship, we was wandering in all disarray, and weren't prepared. We was nearly at the edge of the floe and that was when the blizzard came.'

'With no shelter?' Bray asked.

'Most of the men lay down and slept. Still drunk on the rum and that.'

69

'How long was the storm?'

'There were fifty-five men on that ship, plus twelve from the rescue ship, and six who made it off the ice.'

Talbot took a pause and Captain Bray leant over the table and filled his drink for him. Talbot thanked him, and held up his left hand in display. For the first time I noticed the ends of three of his fingers were missing. He let them be examined, turning his stumped fingers this way and that for all to see. They had the appearance of wax candles that might have been left on a windowsill, broken and half melted. I was quite amazed that I had never noticed them before. 'And I hant got no toes to count of,' he said, with a proud smile, directed at Bletchley and myself. Talbot had a shuffling walk, and he refused to shake hands with people. It made sudden sense.

'Yes, the Arctic is a cold mistress,' Bray answered in a similar vein. 'She will invite you into her bed and you are best not to sleep with her. The sea has options, but the ice, no. This spring, when the floe opened in March we sallied the ship and were quickly out.'

Bletchley interrupted: 'What does *sallied* mean?'

Sykes answered for the other captain by rocking his hand in the air. 'Most amusing to watch – the men run from side to side across the deck, forcing the ship to sway and break free of light ice.'

'Within a week we were in the hunting grounds,' Bray went on. 'We made many kills of Greenland whales, especially as the mothers were sluggish with their calving. Very fine hunting. But inexplicably the whale herd disappeared, we do not know where they went. There was nothing to be done. We killed a few dozen seals, but it was wasted effort. Then without warning we were in the most terrible storm. Those whales must have smelt it, you see. They knew and we didn't – we have only that brass barometer fixed there for us, whereas

70

they have their thick wise old heads. We had to bare-pole it, but even that was of no use. That's when we sprung the foremast and then lost it altogether, and we had just made good of that when we had the fire in the try-works on deck. One hell of a storm it was, too. It even rained fish, can you wonder at that. Bouncing on the deck as high as a man's waist! No, I am totally mistaken: first it was the fire, and then the storm. It doesn't matter – the wisdom of it is that we are returning to Hull, barrels still not made, and rather at a limp.'

The two captains had known each other for many years. They discussed at length the current conditions of ice and the advancement of the seasons, the patterning of bergs and the compaction of floes near glaciers, but I had the sense that neither one was really listening to the other. Rather, they were manufacturing the time necessary to drink several bottles of wine we had brought over. Fairly soon, I realised they were both quite drunk, and my own glass had been refilled so many times that I was viewing the room with a certainty of familiarity and uncertainty of focus, where both captains – being small, rotund and rounded in the back – appeared plausibly related or very possibly the same man. Bletchley, too, was being filled with wine. He repeatedly laughed with a shrill high-pitched giggle I had not heard before, and was not keen to hear again. Only Talbot appeared sober. Or his saturnine temperament gave him the impression of sobriety. Recounting the tale of being stuck on the ice had been the longest speech I had heard him construct, and it appeared to have exhausted him. For the rest of the meal he sat brooding under a contracted brow, as if he was carved of oak.

Bray leant forward and whispered carefully, 'I have something to show your passengers, Sykes. It will open their eyes.'

Sykes raised his eyebrows, drunkenly: 'By all means.'

'This way, gentlemen.' Bray pushed his seat back with a

loud scrape, letting it fall noisily behind him. He didn't bother to pick it up.

'Excuse the stink,' he said, amusing himself, as he led us onto a lower deck strewn with sacking and barrels, canvas, coils of rope, cooper's hoops, barrel staves, chains, hooks, tools and cases. I stood among the mess, feeling sick and disorientated. It looked as if the ship had rolled and the only things that had remained in place were the thirty or so hammocks that hung from bolts in the beams. In the dim light, I imagined that these hammocks – filled with blankets and one or two sleeping men – were the burial shrouds of some forgotten expedition.

'Careful where you tread, it is the flinch gut here, and still rather greasy,' Bray advised, perhaps viewing the disorder of his ship for the first time and attempting to tidy it up with a shove of his foot. 'There are men asleep. I think there are, anyhow.' I paled at the thought of an entire Arctic winter spent down here, with virtually no light, the air dense with smoke and the foul reek of unwashed men, while a howling wind tore down the slopes of barren mountains outside.

Bray was keen to explain: 'The gas from the blubber casks was so virulent, several of the men have been blinded. They are as sightless as worms down here. But I have seen it before, they'll be fine in a week or two. You might have noticed our brasswork has turned bluish-black? It is the effect of the gases.'

Approaching the end of the ship, the deck curved upwards at such an angle that even Bray had to bend his neck below the beams. There was a noticeable and inexplicable cooling of the air, and a scent of ice, as if part of this dirty, fire-blackened ship had remained frozen. I touched a beam and felt its cold damp surface, and quickly wiped my hand on my handkerchief.

It was now so dark on the lower deck Bray ordered a lamp to be brought. We passed it down the line, as miners might do in a pit. At the head of us, the captain was busy dismantling a rough wall which had been built of packing crates, talking to himself all the while, an image of derangement, as if he was intent on loosening the supports until the roof fell upon us.

At last, with a cry of satisfaction, he made an entrance of sorts among the packing crates. He turned to us, holding a gravedigger's lantern, and said: 'The most wondrous sight on earth.'

I followed Bletchley, who was for once totally quiet, into an enclosed space which was entirely floored with large blocks of cut ice. The captain hung his lantern on a beam nail and immediately we saw the spectacle he had led us to. Across the bed of ice, a giant white bear had been laid out. It was a vast animal, two or three feet high at the waist, and sloping in a thick hide of matted fur towards a head that was the size of several blacksmith's anvils.

'Christ!' Bletchley exclaimed.

'Your first bear?' the captain asked, his eyes glinting happily.

'Yes. Yes, absolutely.'

One after the other, Sykes and Talbot crawled into the space, and uttered amazement when they saw what was there.

'She came to the ships in January, during the night,' Bray said, proudly. 'I believe she was starving. She moaned on the ice below us and scratched at the hull. It was a quite terrible sound to listen to, and a dreadful sight. She was like a ghost down there – if you looked directly at her, then she vanished, she was as grey as bone, as was the ice. All you could see were her eyes, for they are as black as Whitby jet. On your departure, you might see the marks where her claws worked the wood. They're deep, gentlemen – make no mistake how soft

73

her claws would find the human body, if she were to bestow you one of her affections.'

'Who shot her?' I asked.

'I had the pleasure myself,' the captain replied, squinting an eye and pulling a trigger finger, once more, at his victim. 'But I was careful not to aim for the head, so it took a few bullets to finish her off. Her keel is full of lead ballast!'

'Why didn't you aim for the head?' Talbot asked.

'Because this, men, is a fortune you are looking at. I shall sell this white beast to a fat country squire who wants to scare his guests at Christmas by placing her in the entrance hall of his manor. When she's stuffed she will be worth several dozen barrels of finest spermaceti. With her I'll be able to fix much of the *Jester*.'

'Why haven't you skinned her?' Sykes asked.

'An Esquimaux boy was going to perform it for me, but an intact body is far more valuable. Without the bones and flesh the English taxidermist has very little accuracy in reconstructing its true size. They stuff 'em like settees, gentlemen, and then they're worthless.'

The neck lay stiff as a wooden bough, but the aspect of her expression was that of a sleeping animal. The weight of the jaw had created a slight dish to the ice below it, and the bear nestled into this hollow, as if at peace. Fortunately, I was positioned directly by the head, so I was able to crouch down to make an examination. She had a dark-lipped mouth, open enough for me to see the points of several teeth. With the stem of my tobacco pipe I parted the lips, gradually, though there was much resistance, until a fang the length of an index finger was revealed. Behind it, I saw a livid tongue vanishing into the deep shadow of her throat, and beyond that was the cruel wild interior of the animal. I wondered if this beast had killed a man. He would have had a similar view into this terrible aperture, just before his death. But now, on the bed of ice, the ferocity and malice of the bear had gone, especially as the tip of my pipe gave it an almost comical look, as if she was going to smoke with us.

'You must shake hands with her,' the captain suggested, pushing one of the paws towards us with his boot.

Bletchley tried first, lifting the great paw with both of his hands until it was just clear of the ice. He passed it to me. The weight of the bear's fist, and her arm, was considerable. The fur was so deep and dense my fingers disappeared far into it, yet still my hands were unable to reach either side of the paw. I felt the abrasive surfaces of the pads, as rough as tree bark, and the curve of several claws that had the smooth hard feel of carpenter's nails.

'It had a young with it,' Bray said, somewhat wistfully. 'It fled across the ice when we fired the guns,' he continued, his theatrical ringmaster tone returning. 'And you have shaken hands with its mother, now. That cub will smell her scent on you, gentlemen, beware.'

I realised his joke was not all humour. He looked back at me with a small-eyed stare, midway between amusement and something more diabolical, and I thought, it is you, Captain Bray, it is you who have the eyes as dark as Whitby jet.

6

Our two ships were separated by the same wind, one back to a British port, and the other towards an Arctic which was dangerous and unearthly. The evidence of fires and storms, the filth of butchery, the below-decks world of a charnel house where the bear was frozen, a corpse in a tomb, all these things had unsettled me. But it was the frost-blackened faces and dirty hands of the *Jester*'s crew – standing in threadbare clothes made good, mended, patched and neglected – that awoke in me an apprehension I could not control. They had had a look in their eyes that gauged – with a quick dark measured glance – the strength of your heart. And your chance of survival. The Arctic held a tragedy for any one of us. They measured these things effortlessly, with experience, and it had showed in the flicker of a smile at the corner of a mouth, or the suggestion of a raised eyebrow. Certainly, Bletchley, with his ridiculous mustard trousers and conker-polished riding boots, had been a figure of amusement: a fool, in a part of the world that had no time for fools. Me, they were probably less sure of. More than likely they had seen the clothes of a gentleman, and thought nothing more.

I think it was Captain Bray who, despite his showmanship

and theatrical manner, had sensed more in me than I have revealed for many years. He knew, while I was being led through the foul belly of his ship, that I was afraid. Afraid of the Arctic. Back in my cabin I was unable to forget the sight of the splintered hull of the *Jester*, where the ice had dragged its fangs along the timber, and the gouges where the polar bear had tried desperately to dig her way into a ship that smelt of food and human cargo. I lay on my bunk and imagined the bear's greyness in the polar night, how she must have looked as she stood on the ice by the ship, with hungry black eyes looking at the strange wooden vessel that was stuck fast in her world. Overhead, the spectral green streamers of the aurora borealis, twisting and lurking in the heavens with unknown intent. How could a man not lose his mind in such ice, such darkness, such absence as that?

On board the *Amethyst*, the routines continued as before. The bilge was pumped at eight bells, the log-line run almost every hour, and the sun sighted at noon. These things punctuated the day. But there was also much talk about Captain Bray's damaged ship, its failed cargo of whale oil and its frozen passenger on her bed of ice. Bletchley talked endlessly about a wish he'd had, since being a child, of being able to shoot one, how he could outwit it by circumnavigating the wind and using the sun to blind his approach on a flat white surface. He suggested a plan of hiding in a sealskin, laying ambush to a polar bear by shooting it at close range when it approached.

'Lay yourself out for his luncheon?' French had replied, with little-disguised derision. He was playing draughts against Bletchley. I noticed it was the captain's set, and French was playing 'bullet'.

'I would have two guns loaded, of course,' said Bletchley.

'And perhaps a napkin to tuck around his neck?'

Bletchley had laughed along with us at the joke, unaware that he was being mocked, continuing regardless: 'In all seriousness, I think it would be possible—'

'Of course, Mr Bletchley. Well, we must try it at the first opportunity.'

Seeing Talbot enter the saloon with his distinctive shuffle, Bletchley had turned excitedly towards him. 'We shall see bears, Mr Talbot?' he'd asked, hopefully.

Talbot glanced impatiently at Bletchley, before disappearing into his cabin with nothing to say on the matter and no wish to be drawn.

It was left to French to answer in his place. 'We will see seals, Mr Bletchley, and where we see seals, there are always bears.'

I had little time for this hunting talk. The reek of butchery that had clung to the *Jester* was difficult to overcome. In fragments, it had persisted – I had smelt it on the lapel of my jacket, on another occasion when I had combed my hair, and once even when I had turned the pages of a notebook. Death had been brought back to the *Amethyst*.

Only Clara seemed untouched. In fact, her health had begun to improve. Instead of the fragility of those first few days, when her sunken eyes and thin blue skin had suggested an entrenched illness, now she had a new vigour. During the day she and Bletchley took great pains to avoid each other, coming out on deck or retiring to their cabins like the figures on a weather-house clock, never out in the open at the same time. If, by chance, they passed each other, they would nod in cordial fashion; nothing more nor less. But the evening ushered in a quite different attitude. They would sit together on one of the settees, whispering or passing notes between them.

78

Once, while Clara appeared to be asleep at the end of the settee, I noticed Edward Bletchley looking about him, quite craftily, to see if he was being observed. Satisfied that he wasn't, he proceeded to stroke her upon the wrist and forearm. When she showed no response, he placed his hand upon her lap and let it rest there, motionless. I watched, transfixed. After a minute or two I realised he must have been forcing his hand down, for her dress had become depressed between her legs. I saw his fingers rapidly clench and deliver what must have been a strong pinch upon her thigh. Clara jolted with a start, her eyes springing open as she tried to suppress an astonished cry. But she didn't even look at her cousin, or acknowledge the errant hand that was still lying upon her lap. A minute or so passed, until I watched with horror as Bletchley's grip once more pinched her, slower this time, but with equal force and pain. Clara reacted, staring intently and drawing a breath through pursed lips until, with the sound of someone coming down the companionway, the offending hand was quickly removed.

Occasionally, if the cabin latches were not properly shut, the motion of the ship had the tendency to spring them open. This occurred one evening as I was retiring to bed. Both my door and – directly opposite – Clara's door swung open, as if mischievously pulled by an invisible thread. I leapt to close mine, and had a clear sight into Clara's cabin. Surprisingly, I saw Bletchley perched at the end of her bed. He was stooped intently over a board placed on the blankets. In front of him, Clara was leaning back against the wall, her eyes firmly shut as if in a deep trance. Seeing her door had opened, it was Bletchley who reacted – jumping from the bed as if he had been stung by a wasp. He nodded formally at me before closing the door with a firm click.

I was quite certain, in those days, that Clara hadn't

recognised me, and had no knowledge of the role I had once played in her life, on that fateful Sunday at the end of October in 1835. Her encounters with me on board were polite: wishing me good morning, or good evening, but never revealing anything else. Yet there were times when, facing her across the dinner table, I caught her glancing up at me in a most peculiar fashion. She would stare at my hands or smile inexplicably, and when I returned the smile it was as if she hadn't noticed me at all.

On May Day, the crew surprised us by blackening their faces with grease and soot. They came down to the passenger quarters in a procession, fantastically dressed in ribbons and tricorns, with epaulettes upon their shoulders. It was a startling and most unexpected sight. One of the Herlihy brothers, brandishing a wooden sword, approached Bletchley – who had been reading a book – ordering him to fetch 'them dandy trousers and the daft blue coat' in order that he could lead the men and women around the deck.

Bletchley had been startled by the wooden sword, but quickly sensed a game was in the offing. 'What women?' he asked.

'Them maidens,' the Herlihy brother said, pointing his sword. Two of the men stepped forward, with garishly painted faces and halved coconuts hung from their necks as grotesquely adorned breasts. The roughest, most hirsute of the crew had been chosen to be the girls.

'Oh,' Bletchley managed, quite taken aback. 'Of course. And delightfully pretty they are, too.'

Bletchley had been game that day, leading the ship's company around the deck, making gestures for the others to ape as they followed, while they banged kettles and frying pans and the like. It was an infernal noise. He grimaced and played up for about an hour, until he'd quite worn the crew out. At one point he stopped when he spotted me:

'That man there is not being enough of a monkey. Have him arrested!' The men approached en masse, but I swung my arms and chattered like a chimp and they thought fit to let me stay free.

'Quick thinking,' French whispered in my ear. 'It has been known for the leader to leap over the side, in which case we have to follow. Do you think Master B is quite as much a fool as that?' Bletchley, at that moment, was arranging for a pair of the coconut halves to be hung around his own neck.

'Perhaps. I have the sense that Edward has yet to reveal himself.'

'We have a lot of breasts this year, I've noticed,' French said, as a casual aside. 'It's because there's a woman on board. The sailors think we'll have bad weather – the naked breasts are meant to counteract that. We have no figurehead, you see, the sailors are all talking about it in their fetid quarters.' French tightened his cloak and pulled his cuffs straight. I couldn't gauge his mood. I smelt a whiff of eau de cologne on him. 'At least she's in her cabin now. May be for the best – the men are dead superstitious about having her up on deck.'

When, at long last, the festival wound to a close, Simao invited the passengers to join the officers in the saloon, where a platter of biscuits and pastries had been laid out. Coloured paper chains had been hung beneath the skylights and cotton doilies in the shape of snowflakes had been placed at our settings. Simao, with his customary precision, invited us to stand in a line alongside the table. We stood, like as many schoolchildren, while Simao went to the captain's cabin and knocked once upon the door. Sykes answered, entering the saloon wearing a velvet cloak and a crown of sorts, made from a cooper's hoop.

'I say, Captain Sykes, what's all this about?' Bletchley piped up, grinning so wide his dimples were like upholstery buttons.

Sykes eyed him, regally. 'I do not know this captain you speak of. As you all may see, my name is Neptune, and I have the great pleasure to inform you that not only is this the first day of May, but at noon we crossed into the Arctic Circle.'

Bletchley beamed with delight, skittish as a kitten, and promptly made us all shake hands.

'Wonderful news!' he said. 'Wonderful!'

'I have upon my hand a bishop's ring of rough amethyst crystal,' Sykes continued, holding up a hand to show us. '*Amethyst*, as you are aware, is also the name of this fine ship, and I wish you all to bless her with a kiss of the Episcopal ring, after which you may attack the cakes our steward has prepared, with as much excessive gluttony as you wish.'

Sykes moved along the line, inviting myself, Bletchley and Clara to kiss the ring, which we did. He shook our hands. 'Welcome to the Arctic,' he said to each of us, in turn.

I remember the feel of French's hand, which was surprisingly dry, and a handshake that was brief and quickly dispatched. Sykes' hand felt small and vigorous, like the hind thigh of a whippet, twitching with energy.

Remarkably, for the second time, Talbot refused to offer his hand as I approached. Instead he stared me down with anxious consternation. Clara noticed this exchange – or rather lack of exchange – and came to save me, guiding me away from the taciturn second mate and offering her cheek for me to kiss. Doing so, I heard her whisper *I think you will find what you are looking for*, by way of a wish, or blessing. I felt her squeeze my elbow, affectionately, but as I pulled away from her I was aware of a hot and unpleasant look that French gave me, as if I had behaved improperly.

That was the occasion when I saw Clara happily eating several of the coconut biscuits. Simao, excessively relieved, kept offering her more, in the manner of a grateful mother whose child has just regained its appetite. She laughed when Bletchley insisted he try on Neptune's crown. I was struck by the fact that I had never heard her laugh before. For the time being, I was happy too. I gazed at her, full of contentment. A happy woman is a righted world, I thought.

I had thought about Celeste since that autumn when I had worked at the manor house near Somerleyton in Norfolk, sitting in the conservatory, organising the egg collection. Each day I'd watched her being led across the lawn, bronze leaves blowing about her feet, a shawl tied closely around her shoulders. It hadn't taken me long to work out where she was for the rest of the time. She was shut away in her bedroom, kept behind a locked door, in an unheated part of the manor house, held distant from myself and any other visitors as if we might be a threat or bring contagion.

During those weeks I had been exposed to a mystery. In a largely silent house filled only with the distant ticking of several clocks, a girl was apparently a virtual prisoner of her parents. Every day she was guided in a kind of trance, the processional circuit of an invalid, led by her mother. At each turn of the walk, before her feet touched the brick edging, I would see a glimpse of her face, eyes turned down in meditation, her cheek pale and bloodless in the chill, her hair tied simply and without ornamentation. My work was tedious, assembling the fragments of rare eggshell into complete specimens, strengthening them with careful plaster moulding, and then arranging the collection by zoological group and species. It was easy for my mind to create its fantasies – what the fleeting appearances on the lawn meant, or the nature of her illness. I made small discoveries: her name was Celeste, she was the daughter of the house, an only child, and she had recently been withdrawn from all public interaction. It was not much to go on, and rather than appease my curiosity, it inflamed it.

Before long, in the hour after lunch, I began to explore the house, using the servants' staircases and passages, pacing the cold-carpeted corridors that were left unheated. It was a damp and chilled place. A large wood-burner roared in the entrance hall, but its heat was channelled elsewhere, into the library and drawing rooms. At the very top of the house I found her bedroom. It was locked from the outside.

It took me a couple of weeks before I began to pass her door on a daily basis, and longer still until I lingered there. I would press my ear to the wooden panels. Occasionally I was able to discern sounds of her moving, or pacing the rug with bare feet, or the clink of glass bottles being arranged on the marble surface of a dressing table. Once or twice, while I was looking at the light that crept below her door, a shadow would pass.

At those times, I felt a very real presence of the girl inside the room, and she must have also sensed me, for it wasn't long before my visits to the door were noticed. I would stop, lean my ear against the cold paint and listen to the sound of her approaching. With just an inch of wood between us, I could hear the faint sound of her breaths and could imagine the softness of her hair, virtually touching mine. I held the palm of my hand against the wood. A finger lightly drummed against the other side, and I replied, mimicking the rhythm.

I began to rely on visiting the corridor, never letting a day pass without going there, and I felt that Celeste looked forward to these moments too. Strangely, neither of us spoke, even though a whisper would have been heard. It was as if to speak might break the spell. Sometimes, during her walks on the lawn, I had noticed that she looked up to glance in my direction, her face still tilted down but her eyes searching for mine as I sat at my desk.

It was she who spoke first. With my head leaning against the wood one afternoon, her voice was soft.

'Is it you again?' she asked.

It was as if I woke from a dream. I started, unsure of how to react.

'Can you hear me?' she asked.

'Yes.'

'Good. That is very good. Why do you come here, every day?'

I felt like running. What was I doing? I'd been hired for a job, to be in the conservatory, curating the egg collection. What on earth was I thinking, leaning against this bedroom door in a part of the house I had no right to be in?

'I must go,' I said.

'Please ...' she urged. 'Stay.'

I had taken a step away from the door, but I returned and leant my head against it once more.

'My name is Celeste,' she whispered.

'Mine is Eliot.'

'Eliot,' she repeated, trying the name. 'Are you the man who is helping my father?'

'Yes.'

'Is your work nearly done?'

'A few more days.'

'I have seen you, working in a very careful manner.'

I waited, knowing that at any minute I might be discovered, knowing also that this would lead to my instant dismissal, but still I was unable to leave.

'My father has spent a great deal of time and money collecting those eggs,' she said. 'I wish you would smash them all.'

7

I will save you, I had promised. Each day, sitting at that bench alone in the draughty conservatory, mending the eggs, the same thought. Save her from that dreadful captivity, that torment. Each day I would creep up the staircase and listen outside her door. I will save you, I would whisper, so quiet she would not be able to hear me.

But you didn't, I said to myself, standing on the deck of the *Amethyst*. You didn't save her. Out to sea a dense pall of fog rolled towards the ship. It felt like the arrival of a dark and malevolent force. A brooding shadow that was accompanying the voyage, out there, getting closer, gaining on us. Others on deck had noticed it too, stopping their duties to stare at the purplish tinge in the clouds, the colour of Welsh slate. Soon the fog overran us, and a dense storm of snow sped past the ship's side and through the rigging, fast as smoke, clinging and settling on any exposed part of the deck. Within minutes the entire ship had been transformed under a covering of fine white powder, crisp to the touch on any exposed piece of wood or rope. I expected it to soften and melt, becoming slippery and wet, but instead it had a brittle and grainy texture that remained for an hour or two, setting my teeth on edge as I stepped through it, until some of the men used deck brushes to clear the working areas. Talbot, at the helm, merely turned his collar up against the weather, purposely ignoring it, even though his beard quickly developed a dusting. French, on the other hand, wanted no part of it. I saw him duck into the galley as soon as the snow was sighted, and he remained in there until long afterwards.

After watching the blizzard, startled by the sight of the mast tops spearing through the snow, I needed to go to the saloon for warmth. There, I pressed my ear against the base of the mizzenmast, wondering whether I'd be able to hear the vibrations of the storm: distant sounds carried through the wood, of ropes and cables, the whole living sinews of the ship bearing the forces of the weather. The rest of the room was unnaturally hushed, punctuated by the regular creak of oil lamps swinging above the table and the ticking of the sheep's head clock by the captain's cabin. It was only then that I realised Clara was sitting in the second part of the saloon, on one of the settees, studying me.

I quickly removed my ear from the mast. 'It's snowing outside,' I explained.

'It is?' She put her book on the cushion and came to the mast, placing a palm against the wood.

'It feels so incredibly strong, don't you think? This whole ship feels quite … unbreakable. Like the forest of oaks it once was.' She stood very close, so that I could see the complicated arrangement of her hair – drawn into a plaited knot at the back, with a similar plaited band across the top of her head and loose ringlets that hung either side. It must take concerted preparation, each day, I thought. I noticed a single grey hair, among the brown.

'Seeing as I have you all to myself,' she began, 'I have been wondering whether you might show me the drawings you have made? You seem quite inseparable from your sketch-book.'

'Yes, I suppose that's true. Of course, I shall fetch it.' The sketchbook was in my cabin. On the way back I stopped, took a breath and examined my reflection in the mirror above the washstand.

'*Careful*,' I whispered.

We sat on the settee behind the mast while she looked at the sketches. My approximation of the dock at Liverpool, with the tangled riggings of dozens of ships, the distant coast of Ireland, with its small fishing harbours, a view into Simao's galley in the fo'c'sle, his colourful pendant to remind him of his island home pinned to the shelf. A pot on the range and the pie hole behind it, where food was passed through to the men. More sketches, of the masts and their sails, of seascapes and clouds, and the isolated view of Rockall that she had been so affected by. Gannets, cormorants, the gulls that had followed the ship before Bletchley and the officers shot them, then the half-finished sketch of the poor greenfinch, held between the strong fingers of Martin Herlihy. Finally, an impression of the polar bear, lying on her slab of ice, in the darkly confined lower deck of the whaling ship. Clara examined this drawing for a long time, tracing her finger along the line of its head.

'Edward told me about this bear in great detail. I'm glad I stayed on the *Amethyst*. I don't think I could stand seeing something as sad as that. Did you touch it?'

'Yes. I held the paw.'

'Like this?' she asked, reaching across and holding my hand. Her skin felt smooth and cold.

'This way,' I said.

'What was it like?'

'It was heavy, and the claws had a cruel hard curve. They were not retracted.'

'I meant not how it felt, but how *you* felt?'

'I felt afraid. It made me think of a total whiteness, and only this white bear within it.'

'Yes,' she said, thoughtfully. She turned to a blank page in my sketchbook. 'So, now to a challenge for you. Do you think it possible to draw me?'

It must have been her intention all along. 'I would be honoured.'

'Good,' she said, 'although I can instantly feel myself blushing – it is a weakness of mine. Shall I sit here?'

'Yes, under the skylight.'

I fetched my drawing charcoals and immediately started drafting her outline, noticing as I did how she grew poised and stiff. Her hands held each other in her lap and her shoulders grew tense.

'You must relax,' I suggested.

'I am sorry. It feels strange for a man to be drawing me. Should I look at you?'

'If you feel comfortable.'

She considered it, then turned directly towards me, looking steadily into my eyes. I was struck by the flat brown quality of her irises, large and innocent, yet with a pooled darkness within them that was troubling. I began to draw the curve of the line below her eye. The placing of her ringlets either side of her face. The youthful jut of her chin and the sadness of her mouth, pursed and thin lipped.

'Do you think you will find the birds you are looking for?' she asked.

'No.'

'Why are you so certain?'

'The great auk is extinct. However, there's a part of me that

90

refuses to believe it. I suppose that's the part of me that is known as hope. There is always a chance that remains of them might at least be found, on the breeding ledges. Even those would be valuable, not just in monetary terms, but because man should have a reminder of what he has done.'

'Because of hunting?'

'Entirely. They used to be plentiful, swimming across the ocean – you are aware they were flightless? To think, they'd been doing that for thousands of years, and it has only taken a couple of hundred years, since ships like this began to plunder the Arctic, for them to face extinction.'

'I can tell you are a man of belief. So if they are to be found, it is you who will achieve it. If only there was a place where man had not reached.'

'Yes.'

'I used to have this notion, when I was a child, that God had created a special place beyond the edges of the world, where all the lost souls could go in order to live their lives in peace. I used to imagine it was an island – like the ones in the Norfolk Broads – that are tangled with trees. Only, you could never see this island, unless you too were a lost soul. God had made it, as an afterthought, knowing man would be cruel enough to drive all that was precious away from him.'

'I like that.'

'A piece of the world that was left over, when it was made. I still think of it. I think of it when I make pastry, curiously, with the pieces that are left behind after the cutting. I cherish them.'

'Then I shall, too, in future. Do you still believe in this place – for all that has been lost?'

She shook her head sweetly. 'Not since I found it.'

'You found it?' I asked. 'What do you mean you found it?'

She held a hand to her chest. 'It's in here. It's in you, too.'

I laid the charcoal on the paper. Her eyes shone with feeling. I was quite enthralled by it.

'I would like to know more about you,' she said. 'Edward told me you are an agent for private collectors. Are your employers very influential?'

'Well, they are rich.'

'But are they naturalists, such as yourself?'

I wondered how to answer. There were four men who, over drinks at White's club on St James's Street, had made a wager that, contrary to belief, they could procure the last great auk in the world and bring it to London. White's was famous for such wagers. One of the men was associated with the British Museum, but beyond that, no, they were not naturalists. They were men who liked to make wagers, whether it was gambling on which door might open first to their private lounge, or whether a species could be pulled back from the oblivion of extinction. They had read the reports in the newspapers, they had been drinking, it was a February afternoon, and they made wagers.

'No,' I replied. 'They are merely collectors. They want to own something that no other man has.'

'Is it really that simple?' she asked.

'Yes. Men are really that simple.'

She looked a little surprised. 'So why did you agree?'

'They paid my passage. More than that I am free to do as I wish.'

'But what if you return empty-handed?'

I shrugged. 'They will bet on something else. Their whims are not mine. If they wish to waste their money on idle wagers, so be it. For me, I have studied birds my whole life and the chance to find one of this species, to find the merest feather that once belonged to them, or even stand in the place where they have so recently vanished – it would be a privilege.'

'Yes, I understand.'

'I ... I would love to save something.' I suddenly felt my feelings were open and might easily become beyond my control. 'I'm sorry,' I said, 'I am forgetting to draw you.'

She gave me a reassuring smile. 'Are you happy with the likeness?'

'I think so.' I considered it. 'It's so very hard to capture what you see.'

'Do you think my face is a pleasant one?'

I halted. 'Yes. Very pleasant.'

'I'm not so sure. Edward says I'm attractive, but there again he says what you wish to hear. He's like my father in that respect. My father is excellent in knowing what people want to hear. Personally, I think my face is too thin, and my eyes are too dark.'

'You told me you live with an aunt?' I asked.

'In Aldeburgh, on the Suffolk coast. A very damp and creaky house, but it has a view of the North Sea. And mobbed by gulls every hour of the day. Have you been to the town?'

'Yes,' I answered, briskly. 'But several years ago.'

'It changes little.'

'I expect so.'

'It will be washed away one day, God willing. What was the nature of your visit?'

I decided to lie. 'A funeral,' I said. A funeral is rarely questioned. If I told her the truth, my identity would likely be revealed. Although I grew up in Suffolk, for the last ten years I had been afraid to set foot in Aldeburgh, knowing that her father often went there as a county magistrate, and would spend his evenings hunting for birds and coursing for hares

93

on Orford Ness. If I had run into her father again, I did not know how he might have reacted or what he would have done to me. He might have shot me.

'I may not ever see my father again,' she said, quite unexpectedly. I was alarmed, having just thought of the man, to hear him mentioned. 'I don't know why he sprang to mind just now,' she added. 'Thinking of Aldeburgh, I suppose. He wanted me to stay in sleepy Aldeburgh, and I'm here, with Edward. Can you believe it?'

'Does he know you are on this ship?'

'Oh yes, he knows,' she replied, implying a subject that was still raw. 'And I can feel his disapproval, even here in this room. He has not always been a kind man,' she said, as if it needed explaining. I looked at her, noticing a new liquid quality to her expression. The shape of the mouth I had drawn no longer resembled that of the woman before me.

'Why do you say that?'

She shook her head, sadly. 'We don't choose our parents. We don't choose ourselves either. If only we could. I would start with brighter eyes and a brighter outlook to go with them.'

'Clara, did Edward persuade you to come on this journey?'

She regarded me curiously. 'Edward needs to prove himself as a hunter.' The idea brought a very private smile to her face. 'He still believes every man needs a trophy wall. He is so young, he still has those boyish dimples, doesn't he? But he's already old enough to think he's a failed hunter.'

'But why should you agree to accompany him?' I persisted.

'He ... Always I am talking about Edward as if he owns me! It's ridiculous. He needs me, in a way that is quite unusual. It's absurd – I should never have come. But I did, and shall have to face the consequences when I return.' She sighed, exasperated. 'What am I saying – it was Edward's idea. He wanted to shoot seals and I needed to escape.'

'Escape your father?'

'Escape myself. The truth is, Edward likes to keep an eye on me. That is why I'm here. I receive medicine, Mr Saxby. Edward administers it to me in the morning and at night.'

I continued to draw, glad to be occupied by the charcoal, but feeling uneasy listening to a growing confession. The face that was emerging on the page already felt a betrayal of what was truly there, before me. Clara had changed in a matter of seconds, her skin had darkened below her eyes and her expression looked haunted and captive.

'I don't sleep, Eliot.'

I tried to remain composed, but felt quarried by a changing situation. She must have planned this, intending either to reveal something to me, or extract it. 'Is it the motion of the ship?' I asked.

She smiled, quickly. 'No, it is not that at all. I am afflicted with night terrors. If I sleep, I have *visions*.'

She looked at me with a directness that effortlessly pinned me to the spot. I felt paled by the force behind her eyes.

'What visions?'

'The cruelties of mankind,' she replied, quickly. 'When I dream, I see people – some are my family, but most are unknown. Blue devils. They are real and very present in my room. They sit and tell me what is in their hearts, and it feels as if they have no concealment. It is quite horrible.'

As she told me this, I closed the sketchbook, unable to continue. I conjured up the image of how she had been as a girl of just sixteen, her name not Clara Gould, but Celeste Cottesloe. How she used to whisper similar things to me, through the locked door to her bedroom. Her nightmares and daydreams, a world full of anguish and fear. I had heard this

95

same voice in that chilled corridor at the top of her parents' house. My poor Celeste! She had told me about visions she'd had of a poacher living in the woods. A frightening man wreathed in smoke, who would not cease to chase her.

My mouth felt dry. 'Do these visitations appear every night?'

'No. Sometimes my medicine is very strong. It renders me a dreamless sleep that I remember nothing of.'

'And it is only at night that you suffer in this way?'

She considered the question carefully. 'There are times, during the day, when my mind relaxes. I feel that my mind, it ...' she did a curious motion with her hand, a sliding motion, '... it slips. At those moments I feel as if I am among shadows. That I am not entirely alone.'

Celeste, I thought, *just reach out your hand and hold me. Remember I loved you, I wanted to save you, I still want to save you.*

'May I be honest with you, Mr Saxby?' she continued. 'I sometimes care little for my well-being. You may be shocked but I care little whether the ship is cut open by the ice and is quickly sunk.'

'Please, do not talk like this.'

'You asked why I am on this voyage? Well, I feel I can tell you. I sometimes think I would like to walk across the ice sheet into that total whiteness you spoke of, and—'

'And what?'

'*Vanish.*'

'Clara,' I insisted. 'You *must* stop talking like this.' Instinctively I leant forward and held her hand. It felt cool and thin in my own, and totally without resistance. I continued to hold her, and gradually I felt her fingers begin to curl into my own. She gave a shy smile.

At that moment, a cabin door was wrenched open, and like

a gust of wind Bletchley was standing in the saloon, in disarray, with wild hair and an expression of having just woken. Instantly he saw that I was holding hands with Clara and he gave me a most livid glance. Quickly, as soon as it had appeared, he managed to control it, collecting himself and turning to his cousin.

'Why, are you feeling all right, my pippin?'

Clara, immediately composed, met her cousin's question head on. 'A little faint, Edward. I wonder what concoction you have for me in your doctor's chest?'

Bletchley ran his hands through his hair, brushing it one way, then the next, confused and placed on the spot. 'Now, now, Clara,' he said. 'Don't be silly.'

I saw that I had released her hand. Bletchley walked up to her and took her by her wrist. He did it quite firmly.

'Let me take you for a lie down,' he said, giving her no choice in the matter. As he led her away to her cabin, she smiled gracefully at me.

'You have a poetic soul, Mr Saxby. I will listen to the mast, as you have taught me to do. Thank you.'

I found it difficult to sleep that night. I lay, troubled, worrying that Clara might be visited by known and unknown visions. The sea sounded restless beyond the ship's wall. Increasingly, I had found the ocean harder to contemplate at night. During the day, the horizon gave both a connection and continuity to a world I understood. There was always busy work and duties to be performed around me. But the night was different. The sea had a terrible black depth, fathomless and intense, which gave it a menacing aspect. It seemed to disappear, becoming a noiseless void that terrified me. Looking down the side of the *Amethyst* I would see a glimmer of black water, nothing else. Sometimes a passing flicker of phosphorescence. I would quickly retreat to my cabin, but the lamplight shining on the wooden surfaces only emphasised what was out there, beyond the ship. Nothing.

Perhaps it was for this reason that the crew drank heavily in the evenings. The alcohol mollified them, they became more relaxed, but I had also noticed they became more reflective. It was at these times they told me their true feelings about the Arctic. During the day the stories tended to be practical: the hardships of working with ropes that have iced over, or the effort of cleaning and storing sail. They bragged about a cold so intense that skin would freeze to metal, how it burnt inside the nostrils with a hot dryness, how a mug of boiling tea would turn to ice as it was thrown, and how the ship's woodwork, exposed to a frost-rime, became as serrated as a saw, as if it had grown multitudinous rows of shark's teeth. There were tales of frostbite, of applying spirits of lime to blackened fingers or rubbing them with snow. Some of these tales were tall, and were said to impress me, I knew. Or scare me. But at night, when rum had been drunk, different stories emerged. They described seawater growing thick and sluggish, as if it developed a new nature that was not entirely lifeless. How it spat and hissed as a wave rolled through it. Some had seen God in the water there, in the way the ice would encircle a ship. They'd told me of the air that arrives, gritty and stinging, although it looks no different. Or the beasts that surface from time to time through the limpid water. Dead fish, floating with monstrous size, their bodies inflated with gas, passing the side of the ship. Or pale bleached whales – the solitary beluga or the spectral narwhal – seen at midnight across the distance of the ice sheet, with risen tusks, jousting in the ice pools.

In all these stories, I felt the presence of ice itself. Frightening, moving unpredictably, spreading in brittle sheets across the ocean – reaching out with living intent for the small pocket of warmth that is brought with each person who ventures to the Arctic. It is as though the ice searches for the glimmer of fire that burns in the hearths, and the pulse of warm blood that flows through our veins.

8

'Over there,' Connor Herlihy said, 'you see the blink?'

He was standing at the bow of the ship, his boot wedged into the hawse hole, so he might lean on one leg. In his hand he held a smoked bloater, and was eating the flesh of the fish straight from the skin.

'Blink?' I asked.

He held his hand level, towards the distant horizon. 'Some of the lads say they see the blink already. It's the light shining off the ice sheet. A glow's what it is, you might say.' He grinned and turned his level hand into a questioning gesture. 'Meself, I'm not so sure, not till I'm standing on it. But you have good eyes, sir?'

'Yes, good eyes.'

'So, will that be an ice blink or not?'

I stared towards the horizon, where the sea was black and solid. A perceptible glow was there, low in the sky, in a wide band. But it was difficult to tell what it might be.

'There is something there – a lightness.'

'Aye,' he replied, taking another bite of the fish. 'You'll be a sailor, sir, for sure you will. You have good eyes.'

He threw the remainder of the bloater over the side and wiped his hands across the front of his jacket.

'Look at the water,' he said. 'The snow's not melting in the sea. Them grains is the ice crystals that are quite happy to raft.'

'Yes, I see. It's thicker.'

'Aye.'

A small flock of birds flew below us, their wings beating in great haste in groups of threes and fives, hurrying northwards to an empty horizon.

'Razorbills,' I said.

'Ah, is that right? Do you know all the names?'

'Most of them. The razorbill is easy to identify – the beak is distinctive, and if they have a good hunt, they will hang the fish from the sides of the beak – like gentlemen with beards.'

'I was told you're looking for a dead bird.'

'An extinct bird.'

'If it's extinct, then it can't be found, sir.'

'It seems so.'

'I like that,' he said, pointing to the woollen smock I was wearing.

'Thank you, it's a gansey I had knitted in Sheringham, in Norfolk. All the fishermen from that port wear them. It has a pattern here, see, of hailstones and lightning in the weave.'

'I see 'em,' he replied. 'I have this,' he added, showing me a tattoo on his forearm of a Celtic cross. 'Same thing.'

'How so?'

'Same purpose. So they knows our bodies if we drown,' he said, laughing.

After he'd gone, I studied the horizon closely, suspecting any gradual shifts in the quality of light to be an indication of ice. Instead of wonder, I felt that we were approaching a frontier to endlessness. A border where the world was rubbed away, and in its place was nothing but a wide, blank fear.

I was still there when Edward Bletchley sought me out.

'Ah, Eliot,' he said. 'Sorry about yesterday. I was confused and had only just awoken.' He was nervous. 'My cousin is a fragile person, you must understand. She is still quite ill and must not become excited.'

'She asked me to sketch her likeness,' I explained.

'Yes, yes,' he said, impatiently, 'but she is ...' He trailed off. 'Do you think her an odd person?'

'In what way?'

'I was considering it this morning. She is very beautiful, that is certain. But quite odd, don't you think?'

'I think she is very sensitive.'

'She feels she has a connection with you, Eliot. Quite strange: you hardly know each other.'

I felt cautious. 'I am flattered that she feels that way, but you are quite right. I hardly know her.'

'Of course, I know her better than anyone. When we were children our families kept us apart. I was' – he adopted a proud whisper – '*considered a bad influence.*' He tapped his temple, as if asking me to keep it a secret. 'You know what we used to do? I bet you don't – we used to take to our beds, at prearranged times, and we would communicate with each other.' He laughed, manically. 'I know, it sounds crazy, but our minds would talk. Yes, she is skilled.' He sighed, examining his fingers, looking blithe and relieved.

'Yet she is beautiful,' he repeated, almost talking to himself now. 'Quite a rare beauty.'

From the top of the mainmast, a shout was heard: 'The ice, captain!'

Bletchley sprang up, excited as a young foal. 'Tremendous! Did you hear that! We've spotted the ice!' He was almost too giddy to contain himself, and for a second I thought he might tip himself over the side. He straightened his jacket, as if expecting a visit from an aunt and, as if not knowing what else to do, actually polished his shoes against the backs of his trousers. He looked out to sea, rubbing his hands.

'But where the *devil* is it?' he asked, loudly, to no one in particular. Finally, he looked back at me, seeing that I was amused and a little bewildered by him.

'Forget what I was just saying, before,' he said, grandly. 'I was a little carried away.'

French and Captain Sykes were on deck, studying the changes in weather. A bucket had been lowered over the side, containing a thermometer, and when they brought it back on deck Sykes beckoned me over to have a look.

'You will smell the ice, soon,' French said, standing above me.

'If only these damned clouds would leave us, then we could take our sighting,' Sykes muttered, staring up at the masts. 'Run the log-line,' he ordered.

Wishing to see the ice for himself, Sykes began the long climb to the top of the mainmast, moving rigidly and purposefully, one hand above the other, his little booted feet stepping stiffly in the rope holds. He resembled a beetle climbing broad-backed up the wavering length of a stem, with little speed or pleasure. He soon disappeared into the maze of the rigging, the blocks and pulleys, knots, cleats and carcasses of meat that hung around him.

He was there for a long time, standing inside the barrel on top of the mainmast, turning his telescope this way and that. It must have been cold up there, for he kept stamping his feet like a woodcock. When he descended, he did it rather more swiftly, with that light-footed walk of his inching along the yardarms, inspecting the knots and fixings of the main sail. Finally he returned to the deck, jumping off the rail and landing with surprising grace. He walked swiftly to me, with a wink in his eye.

'Do you have the inclination for a climb, Mr Saxby?' he asked, not at all out of breath. He pointed at the lookout above. 'If you would like to see the ice, then you must climb for it.' He stepped closer, lowering his voice, conspiratorially. 'I trust you with your footing rather more than I do Mr Bletchley, so you might notice I'm not asking him. I don't particularly want my passengers falling onto my deck.'

'I have no wish to fall on your deck, either, sir.'

'Good, so you will climb, then,' he asserted.

'I will?'

'Of course, man.'

'Is it safe?' I asked, incredulous.

'*It* is safe. It is only men who are not safe. If you're a fool, you will drop.'

By the persistence of his expression I realised this was no casual invitation, but the setting of some form of test.

'Well then, yes, of course, captain,' I replied, firmly. 'I would like to see what you have hidden in that barrel of yours up there.'

He laughed, satisfied. 'Good man. The crew will teach you the ropes. Take my coat and hat.'

With little ceremony he placed his hat on my head and handed me the coat, pointing me towards two of the crew who were already waiting, with what I perceived to be an executioner's welcome.

'So, the captain's putting you up the mast?' one of them said. He was smoking a clay pipe, but the pipe had no stem, so the bowl was almost touching his lips. 'How are you with heights?'

I wasn't sure how to answer – I felt enrolled into a decision I had had little part in making. I noticed the captain had wandered off, amused. 'If you think you might faint, do this,' the man continued, demonstrating how to thrust an arm through the web of rigging and quickly make two twists of the rope either side of the elbow. 'I'll see you do it, and come up.'

'Thank you,' I answered. 'But how will I know if I'm going to faint?'

He frowned, sucking on his pipe.

'Tell me,' I asked him, 'your pipe has no stem – do you burn your tongue?'

'Not much, sir,' he grinned, 'but it scalds the cheek a little.'

'Do you not have another?'

He shrugged, unconcerned. I believe I noticed a blackening at the end of his nose, where the skin was sooty.

Above me, the masthead looked unbearably high. The barrel swayed perilously up there. But the first part of the climb was straightforward – up tapered rigging to the point where it intersected with the first yardarm. A slated platform with a simple balustrade was there; all very achievable, I thought. But when I stepped onto the rail and held the ropes, I was shocked to see that the rigging was also a sliding plane leading directly into the sea. Beneath my feet was nothing but a foaming current of waves as they ran by the ship.

With little alternative, I began to climb, remembering how the small-footed captain had done it. But where I'd expected the rope to have a rough grip, I discovered the tarring was actually worn smooth and difficult to hold. It was wet, too, and in places I had the sensation of my boots slipping on the glassy windings of the manila.

'How do you feel?' someone said, below.

'The rope is slippery.'

The man laughed. 'We'll have you up there in a frost rime!'

I reached the first junction, where the rigging joined into a tightly wound ladder fixed to the slats of the platform. I held the mast firmly, looking at the scars left by the carpenter's adze, and more cracks in the wood than I wanted to see.

Above me, the next section of rope ladder was far steeper, running up vertically beside the mast. Quickly I climbed behind the panel of the mainsail. It was pushed out, filled with air beyond my reach, but from its edges I heard the soft flapping of canvas as the breeze slipped around its corners. It seemed a living thing, with a wide skin across which the air rippled and channelled in a thousand conflicting tensions, creating a soft whir of sound. There was something of the pregnant form about it, a broad smooth belly behind which life was pulsing and a heart was beating. A draught sucked at my jacket, easing me gently this way and that as the wind moved the sail – a motion I had not anticipated. It toyed with me, aiding in one instant and knocking me the next, as a cat might play with a mouse. The sail filled then subsided, the buntlines pattering on the canvas like rain.

Despite the chilliness of the air I smelt the warming scent of canvas and was reminded instantly of boat sheds in East Anglia. Long dark sheds, each with a church-like serenity, with sails rolled and bound in rope, like bodies in shrouds. Beyond them, a glimpse of open estuary through a doorway passing by in brilliant sunlight. Each of those sails would be laid out on a trestle table, and tied with the same complicated knots that I noticed as I climbed further.

Above me the captain's barrel was perched on its stick, as awkward as an oak apple, bound with rope and weather-stained. I noticed a new breeze around me, carving into sections as it divided between the sails, and I listened to the ropes thrumming with air. Each one vanished in a tightly curving plunge towards its fixing on the deck. An invitation to fall. I was afraid to touch anything, lest it spin away or unwind or hurl me into the sea – the ropes capable of un-knotting in a thousand unexpected ways. At this height, the fixed rigging had not been attended to so frequently, and the footholds sagged when my foot touched them, bringing other lines towards me and giving the impression that this part of the mast was as soft as a warm candle. All was malleable where it should be rigid. I closed my eyes. Sounds I had heard on deck – the eerie shrill wind or the low moaning I'd heard from my cabin at night, the soothing sighs of ropes and canvas, the release and hold of iron fixings, or the creak of the mast, stretching like the tree it once was – these sounds surrounded me, explaining their origin.

The wind plucked at my clothes from several directions while, all around me, the empty chasm of air was over-whelming. It was the first moment that I truly looked out, away from the paraphernalia of ropes and clew lines, of bunts and footholds and bolsters, to a vast and empty ocean that stretched unbroken for as far as could be seen.

The mast swayed gradually to and fro, swinging its point from one side to another so that at one moment I saw the slated angles of the deck gliding beneath me, at another the cruel iron surface of the water. I concentrated on the small details and fixings that were the only things that held me: the nail heads hammered into the wood, the bends of the rope as they threaded through a simple iron ring, the carpenter's chisel marks.

The last few feet were a climb of several metal rungs ham-mered directly into the wood. Upon the deck, the mast was as broad as a man's shoulders, but here, it was a slender tree, a post that could whip and quiver in the wind. I could easily reach an arm round it. I grabbed the cold iron rungs grimly, feeling I had truly left the ship behind, that I was now hang-ing above it on a single point of wood.

Once inside the barrel, I braced myself while my toes gripped its thin rim, below which was a dizzying view of the deck. I saw the crewman peering up at me, his body foreshortened, a smile on his face. With immense satisfaction I let the floor fall back into position and I cowered, shaking and taking breath. As I peered from the top of the barrel the air was vast and thin; with its keen freshness, it wasn't the same air that passed over the deck. A steady wind poured towards me, undivided by the rigging or sails – a wind that had never before met an obstacle of any kind. There was a new scent to it, of coldness, perhaps a hint of the icy world we were drawing near to. These tall trees stood in an Arctic wind, overhanging the ocean with open arms.

The captain's telescope was slotted into a canvas tube, and above the rim of the barrel was a circular metal rail, upon which he rested it to gain a steady view. In this way, I scanned the horizon, but could see only distant miles of dreary and poorly defined ocean. I persisted, pulling and turning the telescope across its various sections, until I saw a startling sight: dark jagged waves, peaking and jostling in a crowded cataract. It was inexplicable, as if the sea at that point were racing in a torrent. Then I saw it, beyond the waves, a sudden unexpected whiteness as hard and flat as quartz. It was the ice sheet, that stretched for a thousand miles beyond, but which looked from this angle as thin as paper. Against its blunt edge, the waves slammed ceaselessly and with great fury. The worlds of ocean and ice were meeting in a frontier of rage, as if the Earth had torn in two along this line. This was a place, if there ever was a place, where you could disappear.

9

I jolted awake, convinced the ship was sinking. Men were running across the deck just as, below me, giant weights seemed to be moving around within the hull. We will be drowned, I thought, imagining reefs had torn a hole into the ship. I pictured a dark rush of icy water as thick and curled as ropes pouring in, the iron-black Arctic sea filling the hold, rising quietly and unstoppably until it welled through the hatches.

My mind in disarray, I pulled the curtain from the porthole and was halted by an astonishing sight: a few feet away was the edge of the ice sheet, almost touching the ship. I stared in disbelief. How could that violent border I'd seen the day before be in such quiet proximity now?

From on deck, where the men had arranged stores and sledges and were busily hanging fenders from the rail, the view across the ice was incredible. A low sun shone over the sheet, reflecting from the ice with doubled strength. The ship's woodwork took on a luminescence I had never seen before: in such white brightness the deck appeared freshly dried and salted, whereas the masts appeared waxed and glassy, with a reddish tinge. The metal hoops and fixings attached to them looked unusually hard and cold. The crew, also, were lit by a new intensity – the blue of their work clothes was suddenly the deep fathomless hue of the Arctic sea, and their hands looked pale and clean as they worked at their tasks. They seemed unreal, a painting in too-vivid colours, and almost as quiet and still, apart from the smoke from their clay pipes, which rose in soft floury curls.

'When did this happen?' I asked Simao, who was pouring out morning coffee from a large iron kettle.

'About four,' he replied. 'The captain tell the men to fix the ropes to the ice.' He pointed to the long hawsers fore and aft that had been tied to the floe, about forty feet in.

'It's quite unreal,' I said, seeing my breath plume in front of me. 'And it is very cold!'

'Mr Talbot is looking for you. He is busy to organise the hunting party, he would like to know if you attend.'

'Hunting for what?'

'Seal,' he replied, pointing vaguely at the edge of the floe with the spout of the kettle. In that direction, I saw nothing but miles of hard flat ice. It was difficult not to view it as a great danger, to think that the ship was in a catastrophic situation. The ice sheet looked highly untrustworthy. Small pools and grey rivulets lay in patches across its surface, giving it a porous, misleading firmness, and large cracks snaked in from the sea, some as long as several hundred feet. Parts of the front edge had risen, sharp and cruel as ploughshares.

'Is this . . . ordinary?' I asked. 'For the ship to be so close?' In the gap between the ship and the floe, the seawater glinted with the impenetrability of metal as it vanished below the ice.

Simao looked back, friendly. In this light his face was older than I knew it to be, with many lines either side of his eyes. His hair was slicked back with oil, and it glowed as dark and bright as a wet otter. 'Is very ordinary, sir,' he replied.

*

Soon enough, Edward Bletchley appeared on deck, wearing a fox-fur hat that covered his ears and tied beneath his chin, carrying his guns towards one of the sledges. The hat was an elaborate construction, and actually had a fox's tail hanging down the back of Bletchley's neck, resting on his shoulders. Talbot was with him, insisting the guns must be handed to the men so they could stow them securely. Talbot looked harried by Bletchley's impatience. I went to the stern, seeking privacy, knowing that otherwise I would be cajoled into a hunting party I had little enthusiasm for joining. The presence of the ice worried me deeply; I felt the need to resolve an issue I hadn't quite understood. Here was the endlessness Clara had talked of, right at our front door, larger, more featureless, more cruelly void of life than I had ever imagined. The sunlight poured across it with a burning ferocity, a glare that was punishing and inviting in equal measure. It was pure, distilled, without colour, unlike the soft glow of the English sun. Surely this was a light that could shine right through you, illuminating every part of your soul and leaving you with nothing to conceal.

I was thinking this way when Clara approached me, as if my worry had sought her company. Our recent conversation, about the ice sheet and its gateway to a vanishing, was almost a third person between us, and needed to be acknowledged. But she was more curious about its presence than anxious, squinting into the light and appearing quite composed.

'Well, Clara, here is your ice.'

She accepted my comment with a curling smile. 'Do not worry, Mr Saxby. I shall still be here when you return.'

'Please Clara, do not joke.'

'I have never been so serious.'

'I haven't decided whether I shall be joining them, yet,' I said, a little feebly. Again, she had disorientated me in a matter of seconds. 'The thought of a hunt fills me with worry. Nor do I know how to get out of it, should I be asked.'

'Face your fears with an unflinching eye,' she said. 'You told me that.'

I looked at her, confused. 'I did?'

'Yes,' she stated. 'I am sure you did.'

I watched her as she began to massage her temples and forehead, as if trying to relieve a pain.

'Well, if it helps you with your decision,' she said, 'you would be doing me a great favour by going.'

'Why is that?'

'Someone needs to keep an eye on Edward,' she answered, nodding towards her cousin. 'He is not what he seems.'

As if alerted to her comment, Bletchley looked up and stared in our direction. He appeared momentarily alarmed that we were talking alone. He frowned, then raised his hand in greeting, before turning back to harass Talbot with his requests once more.

'He seems quite capable,' I suggested.

Clara looked at me as if I had entirely missed her point. 'Don't be fooled by the impression he gives. He really is a most unusual person. He can be quite ... extraordinary. I need you to keep an eye on him.'

'Very well. For you, then,' I said.

'You make me shy when you look at me in that manner,' she replied.

'In what manner?'

'Intently.'

Was I? I had no idea. I felt out of my depth. My feelings for her had sprung once more, fully formed, as if I had been a jack-in-the-box, coiled with pressure for all those years, restrained by a lid and a simple clasp that the slightest nudge would unlock, and now I was sprung, gaudy and exposed and unable to retreat. I apologised, claiming it was the brightness of the sun that had made me so fascinated. 'Things appear new-made in this light,' I said. I believe I only partially managed to explain myself.

Taking my leave, I went to join the group of men, noticing Bletchley in their midst, now clapping his arms with excitement, as a wood pigeon claps its wings in spring.

Dressed in a thick borrowed coat and snow boots, wondering how I had agreed to this, I walked across the ice sheet, following the men and sledges. Talbot led the way, marching around the ponds and cracks with instinctive directness, never pausing, his figure bulky and hugely solid in his hunting gear. Men such as him make company with the wild. Only when he slowed could I discern the limp he had on board the ship, the result of frostbitten toes. The men followed him without question, silent in their labour, dragging the two sledges and making a twin track in the grainy surface as a path. They wore cork-soled boots and thick coats, some that were sealskin, two layers of mitts about sixteen inches in length, the inner of yarn and the outer of oiled leather. In appearance the men now resembled seals walking on hind legs. I stuck to the path they made as if my life depended upon it, which may well have been the case. Several times we passed crevass in the ice, some of which descended in sharp blue edges to a glimmer of trapped dark water beneath.

A couple of miles behind us, the tops of the *Amethyst's* masts were three twigs stuck in the ice. But the air was so crystal clear that the distance didn't seem to exist. I felt as though I could reach out and touch the wood. French had prepared me for this phenomenon. As I had waited to step onto the ice sheet that morning, he had explained the optical unreliability of the Arctic: 'There is nothing in the air,' he

113

said, 'except a lens that might bring an object several miles away to be the distance of this.' He had held his hand before us. His fingers were slender, with long nails. 'Men have marched towards an encampment, hollering their greeting, only to find it is an abandoned biscuit tin. Or they have drawn the outline of an unknown rocky promontory onto their charts, only to see that it was just a seal, sunbathing on the ice. The Arctic will catch you out, too, believe me.'

As we walked I wondered about Talbot, how he must feel back on the ice that once so nearly killed him. During that fateful night he must have sheltered in some bare hollow while the blizzard raged overhead. A starless night while his companions died, one by one, around him. Would they have held each other in desperation, or suffered privately, in silence, as their toes and fingers became painful, became numb, became solid, piece by piece, giving up on life? What had kept Talbot alive? What, in fact, determines a man's survival, when he really should have died? Talbot was inscrutable. Maybe that was the answer. He didn't think about it. He just acted, as an animal acts. Perhaps instinct will save, where thought will kill.

Abruptly, Talbot brought us to a standstill with an outreached hand, his frostbitten fingers spread out level with the ice. The men crouched, silenced, and gathered into a group. By the time I had caught up, he had already assigned various duties in simple whispered commands.

'... Mr Bletchley, you absolutely must refrain from talking,' he was saying, with barely disguised impatience. Bletchley nodded, chided, and Talbot proceeded to divide the men into two parties with a swift motion of his hands, directing them either side of a long ridge of broken ice that rose ahead of us.

'Is them saddlebacks or bladdernose?' one of the men asked.

'Bladdernose,' Talbot replied, uninterested.

Bletchley felt it necessary to explain to me: 'That's the sailor's name for the *hooded* seal,' he said, in a stage whisper.

'*Shh*, man,' Talbot commanded.

The sledges were unpacked, and a series of stout sticks, handspikes and clubs were laid out on the ice, most of which had iron or stone weights strapped to their ends. Several of them were hakapiks, used by the Esquimaux, a rigid implement consisting of a strong shaft with a hammer and spike fixed at one end. It was a popular tool among the men. I noticed Connor Herlihy wielding one, his eyes glinting with a form of murderous excitement, before he tucked a long-bladed flensing knife into the waistband of his coat. In this manner they armed themselves like a gang of brigands, selecting what felt best in their hands, holding hammers and sticks and feeling the edges of their knifes with the flat of their thumb. Only Bletchley carried a gun, with a second one slung across his back. He waited, patiently, his pale eyes made even paler by the glaring light, grasping the barrel with tightly clenched fingers.

Talbot singled me out. 'You want to hunt?'

'I shall watch.'

He shrugged. 'If you wish to observe, go this way. You will be downwind.' He indicated a route through the ice blocks, directly ahead. 'Once the shouting starts, it matters little if the seals spot you.'

With that he left, leading one of the groups, while Bletchley joined the others. They were a curious sight, working their way along and behind the ridge, crouching low as if in a parlour game, and in a minute or so they had slipped from view and I realised I was now totally alone. Stopping on the ice was all it took for a complete and oppressive silence to overwhelm. No wind, no birds, no air that moved; my ears felt hungry for other sounds. By a peculiarity of my position

I couldn't even see the ship. I marvelled at how suddenly and effortlessly all signs of man could vanish.

Perturbed by this, I crawled through the sharp blocks of the ridge until I found a vantage point. Ahead of me was a bare field of the ice sheet, blotted with broken water in several ponds. About twenty seals were scattered across the area, lying on their side, one or two with a head raised in the sunlight. They were a strange and wonderful sight: log shaped, limbless, lying without pattern as if they had been carelessly dropped. Most were a dark tea brown, with pale grey underbellies, and among them I saw several young, whose newborn fur was a gleaming ivory white.

Small noises rose among them, of subdued moans and the occasional cough. A mother began to hump her way across the ice, her belly shaking with a watery quiver as she moved. She approached a pup and their faces touched. Even at distance I saw her long bristles bending as she nuzzled the cub on both sides of its head, bringing it against her raised belly where it started to nudge her vigorously.

I was transfixed by the intimacy of the view, these animals making their home at the top of the world. But at that moment, a line of four or five men appeared, darkly silhouetted, from behind the tapering edge of the ridges on the other side. They ran towards the seals, waving their arms, and after a suspended moment I heard their shouts, a wild *hey-hey-ing* and *yar-ing*. Instantly, the colony reacted, waking and turning and raising their heads towards the noises but unaware of the second group of men charging in ambush from the other side. I watched in disbelief as both killing parties swiftly overran the colony, clubbing and kicking at the seals in the attempt to drive them from the open pools.

I ran also, climbing and sliding through the loose surfaces of the ridge, banging my knees and falling against the rough blocks of ice while, ahead, I watched in horror as sticks and clubs were brought down on the seals' heads. The seal I had listened to as it had coughed was now growling ferociously, raised up in defence, almost standing on its flippers as one of the men approached and struck it, deftly, with a heavy club. Its whole body shuddered as it fell. And amid all the movement and violence I saw Bletchley, kneeling in a practised shooting posture, bracing his brand-new gun and aiming it at a seal a few feet away from him, while two men stood either side of it to prevent its escape. I saw the flash of powder gust from the end of the weapon as it kicked back, almost at once I heard the crack of its report, and I noticed the seal had been shot in its side, where the bullet vanished without a wound.

By this time I was at the edge of the colony, passing an outlying animal that had been left because it was far away from any open water. As I stumbled past, it looked up at me, large eyed, without fear. I stopped, abruptly, held by such a steady liquid gaze. The eyes were as dark as onyx, but soft, too, as soft as amber. Their perfect roundness gave them a trusting, amused expression, and a compassion that was hard to face. They were full of such a human understanding that I knew that this brief, impossible connection between the seal and myself would be a sight that would haunt me. I was unable to pull my gaze from it – those eyes held me: they compelled me to ask myself, as one looks into deep wells, what depth can produce such stillness. This was an animal that was as near to a human consciousness as I had ever seen. It is no wonder that sailors are in fear of these creatures, not for worry of being attacked, but for their nearly human aspect. This was horrible, I realised, finally breaking away from its gaze, this was something I wanted to stop, and yet I had no power to intervene. Bletchley's gun fired again at his target, and this time I saw Talbot, briskly marching towards the chosen seal, repeatedly saying 'no, no, no.' He placed a finger on the stricken animal's head, between the eyes. 'Here!' he instructed. Bletchley nodded, quick as a schoolboy, and began to reload his gun while Talbot stood and waited, filled with a palpable disapproval.

Around me, the moaning of injured animals seemed unrelated to the tranquillity of just a few minutes before. I sat down, as if injured myself, in the middle of the area that had been their colony. Many of the seals were now lifeless and surrounded by a new colour, the brilliant flash of red blood, a redness that was more vivid than any I have ever seen. At the corners of my vision I was aware of the movement of clubs and hakapiks being brought down in swift motions, as if the air itself had turned sharp and murderous. Close by, one of the white cub seals was bleating loudly, before it was given an abrupt *coup de grâce* with a spiked boathook.

Among the carnage I gradually became aware of Bletchley, still in his crouched shooting posture, but now with his gun lowered. His fox-fur hat had fallen on the ice next to him, and he was rubbing his eyes with the back of his sleeve. The two men who had been guarding his seal were trying to coax it towards him, while fending off the repeated lunges it made at them. The seal was still very much alive, although a thin stream of blood was escaping several holes in its side. Bletchley appeared to be shaking his head. With his blood-stained hakapik in one hand, Talbot lifted Bletchley to his feet and pushed him to the animal.

'Here's your shot, man!' Talbot said, excitedly. 'Where I showed you. Right here!'

Talbot pressed the end of the gun against the seal's forehead, and the animal acquiesced, as if the feel of the hot end of the weapon was something it was grasping to understand.

'That's good,' Talbot said to the seal. And to Bletchley: 'You must shoot now.'

Bletchley continued to shake his head. 'Not – not while it watches me,' he managed to say, while still gripping the trigger with a clawed finger.

Talbot stared at Bletchley with a shrewd and cruel expression. 'What's got into you, man?'

Bletchley began to plead. 'Just ... go away,' he begged. 'Let it go.'

The men standing either side of the injured seal looked at Talbot for guidance. He gave a simple nod of his head towards them, then crouched down to Bletchley's level. 'Not got the heart for it, eh?' he taunted. 'You've come a long way with those pretty rifles of yours.'

Bletchley shook his head, beginning to cry. '*It is looking into me!*' he shouted, staring at the seal.

He pushed the rifle away from him, disgusted by it but unable to drop it, and I believe he was trying to shake it free of his hold when suddenly it went off, shooting the seal between the eyes. The animal dropped dead to the ground and slid towards Bletchley, almost pushing him over. He screamed with fear. Talbot stood, considering the pathetic man beneath him, then looked at the others.

'Skin her,' he ordered his men, as he turned away without a second thought.

Bletchley lay down on the ice, breathing heavily, his head turned away from the seal. His eyes were screwed tightly shut.

The sailors quickly abandoned him as they turned to the tasks of bending over or squatting on the ice, running their knives expertly through the sealskins, making a simple rotary incision around the tail flippers, then a long, cruelly parting slit down the belly. They worked the flensing knives in,

119

beneath the skin, bringing the pelt away and transforming the animals into vivid red carcasses. The eyes that had just seconds before looked so compassionately were now set within a bloody and socketed skull, lifeless and grotesque. Some of the seals were still moving with heavy thumps of their tails, trying to escape as their skins were worked loose. I watched one of the sailors holding a fist full of loose hide in his bloodied hand, while the animal he was skinning tried to roll itself away from him in a slick of its crimson blood, its flippers paddling uselessly at the air. This was a vision of hell, I thought.

Hanging lifeless from one of the men, a newborn pup was dragged across the ice before me.

'Wait,' I heard Talbot say, as he walked briskly towards it. He crouched, close enough for me to smell his jacket, while he examined the pup for signs of life. He touched its eye with his finger to know that it was dead and beyond reaction.

'Go ahead,' he instructed. 'Do you find it a hard sight?' he asked me, still with a remnant of his bullying tone.

'Yes,' I replied, surprised at the steadiness of my voice. 'It is a massacre.'

He regarded me with an appraising angle of his head, then surprisingly he nodded. 'Absolutely,' he agreed. He glanced at Bletchley, who was still lying face down on the ice.

'I knew it,' Talbot uttered.

'I'll go and help him up,' I said.

'No,' Talbot replied, sternly. 'Out here you help yourself up.'

He looked at the scenes of butchery around him with, I thought, satisfaction. 'Sykes will have his devilled kidneys tomorrow,' he added, grunting with pleasure.

A man called from the side of one of the pools: 'He's still under!'

Talbot went to him, and I decided to follow, towards a neat hole in the ice, the width of a common well, with a gently curved edge where it looked to have been nibbled.

'How long's it been?' he asked the man.

'Minute or two.'

'He might have another hole.'

'Not seen none.'

'Me neither.'

The hole in the ice descended to a perfect disc of black water. It was an eerie sight, a tunnel into the ocean, a deep airless world of mystery, beneath our feet.

A single bubble rose wobbling to the surface, bursting against it, spoiling the reflection of the sky.

'Told you,' the man said.

Another bubble rose, the men waited, then impossibly the flat level of the water began to lift, creating a dome which formed, greased and slippery, into the precise watery outline of a seal's head.

'Now!' Talbot instructed. Instantly the man brought down a hammer on the exposed skull. The seal slid below the water, stunned, and Talbot fell flat next to the edge of the hole, plunging the curved spike of his hakapik below the surface trying to get a purchase on the body. He thrust his weapon in again, his arm going in almost to the shoulder, but found nothing.

'Damn him! He's sunk!'

They watched the water for a while, as it rippled expectantly beneath them, but nothing disturbed it again.

10

Sykes tucked into his devilled kidneys with indecent gusto, smacking his lips deliberately after each mouthful.

'Finest breakfast upon God's earth,' he exclaimed, wiping his moustache with a satisfied flourish. 'Especially from the seal pup.'

I sat at the breakfast table, shocked by the display. Occasionally Sykes would shake smoked paprika across the kidneys, or sprinkle dried chillies from a small cruet with a silver spoon. A habit picked up in the West Indies in his youth, he claimed. It was an elaborate and precise routine, savoured and repeated each morning after the seal hunts. Each morning, I was invited to join him, and each morning I declined.

Edward Bletchley would refuse to sit at the same table, preferring to either stand by the stove or go out on deck.

'A peculiar fellow,' Sykes said at one occasion, once Bletchley had gone. 'Oppressed by many dark clouds, I believe.'

Over the next few days the *Amethyst* worked its way along the edges of the sea ice, landing wherever seals were spotted. The sledges would be dragged off into the distance, then return several hours later loaded with skins or, occasionally, empty. I didn't go on any more hunts. Bletchley refused to be consulted on the matter, either raising a hand to stop the offer coming his way, or simply turning his back with a deeply concerned expression. During those days he claimed many things: severe pains in the head, an itching across his skin, a malaise due to the fall in temperature, anything that required him to sit by the stove with a blanket across his knees, or spend entire mornings in his cabin until it was too late for him to join the expeditions.

His humiliation during the seal hunt was never directly mentioned, but he was treated differently by the crew. He was allowed space on deck. The men made themselves busy as he approached, turning the sealskins fur side down on the wood and rubbing them with salt, or junking blubber into strips and laying it into barrels where it would turn to oil in a few weeks.

Bletchley would look at their industry with open disgust, as if they were demons stoking fires. Only once did I overhear him speaking to the men. Impatiently, he said, 'Don't you miss coiling those damned ropes, now?' Surprised to be addressed, the sailor hurriedly agreed before continuing with his work.

'I do not like,' he told me, as he stared into the fire grate one morning, 'that the seal I . . . shot is on board this ship. I know it is down there.' He tapped his foot on the floor. 'In the cargo. And I very much wish it wasn't.'

I noticed his eyelids were sore with tiredness, and he had shaved badly. He sat still, not wishing to add anything, but repeatedly cleared his throat with a little swallowing sound. I held back from admitting that I, too, had become haunted by the seal hunt. That each night I relived the moment when the seal had slipped beneath the ice hole, the water masking the scene of its drowning.

123

In the evenings Clara sat with Bletchley, as she had done before, often with her eyes shut in trance-like meditation. I would sit across the room, reading my books or occasionally playing draughts with Mr French, but at every opportunity studying Clara and her cousin, too. Their relationship was deteriorating, with edges of tension and dependency I could not gauge and periodic spats of annoyance that were perplexing. Like a couple of magnets, they intermittently repelled each other with sudden force.

When I had the opportunity, and to escape the rendering of skins and blubber on board, I would take a walk on the ice near the ship. The very edge of the floe was a perilous border, against which the open sea slapped relentlessly, with deep cracks and misleading shapes able to slide a man in. Knocks and surges could be heard, travelling through the ice, vibrating the surface with a constant tremor – the sea had eaten away many caves and fissures. In some places the ice had a molten aspect, as pure as an ingot of glass, filled with a luminous blue depth and shot through with bubbles, entombed and motionless. Radiating deep into the darkness, hair-like filigree in webbed patterns indicated weaknesses and planes of growth. Further down, there was the shadow of the ocean, a cloak spread underneath. The captain had told me that the water was ten thousand five hundred and sixty feet deep at this point.

More commonly, the ice was grey or cloudy, a brittle and dusted white, through which nothing could be seen and no estimation of its depth guessed at. I had been informed that sea ice can be boiled and drunk, although it retains its saline flavour, whereas older ice might be washed in, and truly ancient blue ice – the ice of the bergs – can be drunk.

It was an unknown environment with its own rules. When the sun shone across the floe, the air became dazzling and bleached and curiously warm. There must have been unusual density in the air, because the horizon – which could only have been entirely flat – sometimes appeared to lift and buckle into unusual lumps and hills. Either that, or the distance would tremble with an eerie fluidity, as if the sea was attempting to break through. Most unnerving of all were the cracks that zigzagged in from the sea, sometimes for several hundred yards, like the jaws of open mantraps, revealing glimpses of terrible black water that shivered with current. If we had moored for several hours these cracks might appear, then close, yet it was a process which was never seen, as if the ice sheet opened its jaws when you looked away. It was most unsettling. A kind of frozen breath rose from these vents, wet and salty and chilled, as the waves moved beneath. Occasionally the ice would groan and shake, or sound as if it were being hammered from below, or a low thunder would roll briefly across the surface, then all would be quiet again.

We were forced by the arrangement of the floe to enter channels of open water, seeking routes through the ice. Often they were not much wider than the ship was broad. Fenders were hung from the waists, in protection, and sometimes the men had to haul the *Amethyst* upon its hawsers, while others boomed the sides from the edges of ice. Within these bites of the floe, bergs of ice sometimes moved at astonishing speed, as if pulled by wires beneath them, creating their own currents and disturbances in the water, although the rest of the surface was entirely unruffled. On one such instance, during an otherwise perfectly fine morning, I happened to be standing near French at the helm, when he suddenly shouted '*Clear men! Take hold!*' In the second after his command, with nothing but apparently still water ahead of us, I saw a seething of the surface, as if a vast invisible hand were sweeping low across it, followed almost simultaneously by a tremendous dark squall that punched the ship harder than any wave I had felt. I stumbled forward, as the shrouds and stays strained above me, the masts seemed to bend, and men cried out in sheer alarm. I thought we had hit the ice, or worse, but also knew that this was a dark and violent phenomenon of the weather that no one, save French perhaps, had had the presence of mind to recognise. A singing rang up the taut lines of the stays, as if travelling up thin nerves. The *Amethyst* shuddered back on its stern as French shouted, '*Aback! the rudder!*' and the men sprang to action, vaulting past me and letting fly several ropes from the clews. As I regained my footing, the ship nestled back against the ice, moaning and cracking but, mercifully, I knew the squall had vanished.

Bletchley appeared on deck, spooked by the sudden movement, as startled as a bird that's hit a window. He sought me immediately.

'What on God's earth was that!' he said, nervously scanning the ice, while the anemometer began to slow its frantic spinning. The scene was tranquil, once more, the gleaming ice restored and benign in the morning sun.

'I have no idea,' I replied. 'But it has gone.'

On several days, when the sun shone brilliantly like this upon the ice, the air was filled with a soft and marvellous spectral glimmer. The light glistened in a mysterious vapour as countless unbranched crystals floated in a haze above the ice, fallen from a cloudless sky. It was so tranquil that a wave of the hand would part and swirl the glitter, as if the elusive quality of its shine could be gathered, carefully, and held. It was eerie and enchanting, and created in me an impression that none of this was truly happening. Clara would accompany me in a silent trance as if sleepwalking. She would wear a dark satin day dress, with shawl and cloak, and kidskin gloves that did not look warm enough. When she spoke, it was in a soft voice, hushed by the enormity of the ice around us.

'I owe you an apology,' she said. 'When we first met on deck I think I was rude and untrusting towards you. Please disregard it – I am not used to meeting people, especially men, and I find it difficult to be in another's company. You have been patient with me.' She paused. 'I am ... a demanding person, I fear – I blow hot or cold – at least that's what I've been told. They like to tell you these things, don't they? Are you always so patient?'

'You are being harsh on yourself.'

She sounded nervous, as if picking her words carefully, afraid of a false step. 'My childhood has made me strange,' she explained. 'We're made by our childhoods, don't you think? Made and bent by them – like seedlings growing from the soil in search of this – the sky – but instead only finding our parents already there – large trees casting us in shade. We either grow towards the light they have found, or ... '

' ... or we wilt?'

'Yes. A mother should love you unconditionally, don't you think? But mine showed me no affection and would have little to do with me, and I think my father in turn held me responsible for the difficulty that I must have brought to his house. I do not blame him. Men change when they inherit wealth. My father was said to have changed. He inherited a large house and its accompanying duties,' she explained. 'He managed so many people, but was unable to deal with me. I don't think he has ever loved me – I have merely been ... a problem.'

'You don't have to tell me these things, if you do not wish.'

'But I feel relaxed with you, Eliot. It helps me to speak out,' she replied, with a forced brightness. 'And Edward is asleep,

127

so I am able to talk to you freely, without feeling that he is watching me.'

'You feel that?'

'He is a possessive man. He wants me all to himself. I think you understand.'

I nodded, worried, not for the first time, that I was missing entire elements of their relationship.

'I have always been surrounded by possessive men!' she quipped, without conviction. 'From what I have been told, my father was once a charming man, but that is unrecognisable to me. He is morose and distant, not really equipped to be a father at all when I think about it, and has recently been ill with a blood disease. I think he brought it upon himself. You have poisonous thoughts, it follows that poison must remain in your system. My mother – I'm certain she never wished to be a mother – was unable to comprehend the life of a child growing between herself and her husband. What is that bird that hatches her young in a stranger's nest?'

'The cuckoo.'

'Yes, the cuckoo. I was a cuckoo to them – I may as well have been.'

'Except, Clara, the cuckoo chick is looked after well by its false parents.'

She turned to look at me, a sideways smile on her face. 'You see, you *are* a kind man – you're trying to make me feel loved.'

'I'm sure you were, in a thousand ways.'

'Yes, yes, but only in terms of comfort, schooling, these pretty clothes I am wearing.'

'Edward told me a little of this.'

'Did he? Yes, sweet Edward – he was a ray of sunlight when we were children.'

'He said you were kept apart.'

'That too,' she said with an affectionate smile. 'He has always had a wild streak. They thought our behaviour was inappropriate. But Edward said we were free spirits – birds of a feather.'

'You flock together. And were you?'

'We developed a special connection. Isn't it true that the best things are always what's bad for you? Like sherbet.'

'Yes. And butterscotch and peppermint creams.'

She laughed. 'My personal weakness is for cherry tartlets! You also have a wicked streak, I see.' She halted, staring towards the shimmering, endless horizon of ice. 'Mother-hood made my mother humourless,' she said. 'She would leave the room as soon as I entered, or she would do this . . .' Clara raised a hand ' . . . if I asked an unwanted question, or just stare through the space where I was playing, so that she could look through the windows at the flowerbeds outside. I recall these moments with no lessening of their impact and hurt.'

I listened, watching Clara stepping tenderly on the sea ice, through the shifting patterns of sparkling air that glowed around her, remembering the autumn I had spent at her parents' estate. I had been a young man, eager to impress and willing to work in the most precise and methodical manner that was possible. But I had found the father to be an unusu-ally oppressive character. He rarely sat down, and would hover above my desk in the conservatory with a frowning air of displeasure. He had brooding, thickened eyebrows and flexed his fingers continually, either holding his hands behind his back or occasionally drumming the worktable or shelf, on which many neglected plants were struggling to exist in earthenware pots. The conservatory had smelt of soil and damp geraniums. He had treated me with little respect, as if

129

the fragility and unkempt nature of his sprawling egg collection were somehow my fault.

'You might see, Mr Saxby, that among these boxes are some of the rarest and most fragile beauties of the natural world. The goldcrest egg there, which is easily the most delicate of my collection, you might notice is smaller than the last fingernail on my left hand. If you crack that I shall dock you a guinea, you hear? And I will have you roaming the hedgerows when they nest until you find me another. The guardianship of precious items is a duty I take seriously.'

Had he been referring to the incarceration of his daughter? I could not be sure. Each morning he would stand before me, his arms crossed, daring me to make reference to her. I would sit, determined not to take my eyes from the eggs in the trays, while his daughter was led across the lawn outside, aware how badly my fingers were trembling. Did he know that by then I was trying to befriend her? Certainly, he had his suspicions. I was being watched, as a hawk watches the fledglings in its territory.

'My parents have ruined my life before it has even started,' Clara said. 'I can't bear the thought of returning to them.'

'Clara – you must forget your past, it is too heavy a burden to carry around with you,' I said. 'Think of this – of the world in such a strange and unexpected light as this morning. Think of all the possibilities you now have.'

'I am able to deal with the world when it is so brightly lit as this morning,' she replied. 'But at the end of each day I am faced with a long night, and I am afraid of it.' I held her hand. 'My feet are cold, Eliot. We should return to the ship. I don't want Edward to wake and see me out here.'

I nodded, unable to let her go.

'Why do you look at me so strangely?' she asked. 'It was the first thing I noticed about you. It's as if you know me.'

Soon, the weather deteriorated, and we were unable to remain by the ice for much longer. I was glad to leave. The sea became the colour of lead shot, unreflective and choppy, and squalls of rain and snow blew bitterly through the rigging. The spray froze quickly on the woodwork, turning the deck into a hazardous sheet of ice. Seals, we were informed, had the advantage over the hunter in such weather. The *Amethyst* stretched at her reins, much like an impatient horse, as the floe creaked alongside in a murderous fashion.

As I went towards my cabin, I noticed a small soft ball of fur blowing across the deck. I stopped it with the side of my boot, thinking it might be a mouse, but quickly I saw it was a very tiny bird. I crouched. A wheatear, no larger than the palm of my hand.

'Simao,' I called. 'A bird has landed – bring me some grains.' I had cupped my hands on the deck, and the wheatear had nestled quickly into the space I had made, instinctively seeking shelter. It leant against the warmth of my skin, but trembled most horribly. A film of skin descended several times across its eye, and its beak parted, almost in a silent call.

'Quick, Simao,' I called. He ran to me, bringing jars of seeds and meal with him. He crouched by me, and swiftly made a small pile of food on the deck. But the wheatear was in no state to eat. It shivered uncontrollably, falling into the palm of my hand with no more weight than that of a leaf.

'It has died,' I whispered.

Upset, I went below and sat in my cabin, wondering how it could be possible that such a small and fragile bird could live out here, upon the ice. It had blown out of a dense grey fog of freezing air, with no protection, no hope of survival. I sat at my desk, trying to study my books, attempting to calm my mind, but I kept thinking of the bird, how it had died, and then I started to think about Clara and the things she had told me of her childhood. Why hadn't I confessed, when I had had the chance, that she was known to me?

I remembered the day I'd first met her father. I had been walking on Blakeney Point, in north Norfolk, among the dunes and shingle, studying the nesting sites of sandwich and little terns. It was in May. I was fascinated by migration, even then, and I wished to chart the landings of the flocks coinciding with the arrival of the coastal herring and with the flowering of sea kale, toadflax and thrift.

I was observing the nesting site from within a shallow dune, when a tall man strode past, in full hunting attire, not six feet from where I lay. He failed to see me, but continued directly into the colony. The birds flew up as he approached, and he waved a walking stick angrily at them. Although I was frustrated that my studies would be cut short, I became fascinated when I saw him crouching on the shingle and placing something carefully into his bag. By the time I reached him, he was already straightening and beginning to walk off.

'I say! What are you up to?' I had asked.

The man had turned at me with an irate look. 'How dare you address me like that!' he replied. 'Why, I could ask the very same of you. In fact, I shall. What are *you* up to?'

That was how I met Celeste's father. In fear. He had the ability to destroy your nerves with a simple glance and, at that first encounter, I had faltered trying to explain why I had been hiding in the dunes.

'Migration, eh?' he had said, with a little less hostility. 'So you know about birds, I take it?'

'Yes, sir.'

He pointed along the shore with his stick. 'That?'

'A dunlin.'

'That?'

'A female oystercatcher.'

'And by the pool?'

'Redshank. He has been stamping his feet and flapping for nearly an hour – in courtship. I believe he must have lost his first brood and is trying again.'

'Very good!'

'Am I being tested?' I asked. For the first time he smiled, but it wasn't a pleasant expression. It was more like the smile a snake is said to give, when swallowing prey.

'What can you tell me of these?' he said, producing a couple of eggs he had folded into a band of cotton.

'Well, the more elongated one is a sandwich tern's. The other is a turnstone's. Its markings often have a smudged appearance, such as this one. If you would like my opinion I would say it is not a particularly good example—'

'Yes, yes,' he said impatiently. 'I will employ you. I have a fine egg collection which is in need of restoration and of cataloguing. I shall pay you well and feed you for the duration of the time you spend at the house. Are you interested?'

He asked without any possibility of being turned down. He was forceful and persuasive.

'We'll walk back to the staithe together and discuss the particulars.'

'Sir,' I said. 'What is in your bag?'

Celeste's father, Judge Cottesloe, gave an ugly smile, while he considered. 'You may look,' he answered. In a matter of seconds he had reached into his felt bag and pulled out a live Arctic tern, which I estimated to be a juvenile from the previous year. The bird splayed its slender wings in terror as

Celeste's father held it, expertly but a little too tightly, as if he was wringing water from a flannel. 'A sea swallow. I snared it in the colony.' The bird trembled under the pressure of his hand.

'For what purpose, sir?'

'A present.'

With that, he pushed the tern roughly into his bag, and it was then that I should have known: known that this man was a cruel man, known that I should never go to work for him. For as he forced the bird into the bottom of the bag his hand lingered for a second too long, and it was in that second that I heard a soft damp click. A noise that might easily have been missed. But I knew what it was. It was the bone in the tern's wing being snapped.

After we had left the ice floe, Sykes invited me to the chart room to explain the approach we would make to the island of Eldey, the last known breeding site of the great auks.

'There is no point in being at the ice in this weather,' he told me, unrolling the necessary charts. 'The hunting is poor and the conditions are unpredictable for the ship. It is near impossible to keep a bearing on it, and it behaves most aggressively. A storm at the ice edge is a most hazardous situation – you would not wish to experience it. In fact, you might hear the breakers, right now, Mr Saxby, a few miles away?' He gestured for me to listen and, distantly, I heard a low moaning roar, the sound of which had not previously been pointed out to me. It was a terrible and frightening noise. Sykes smiled, satisfied at my reaction. 'Yes, she's a hungry beast.' He placed four glass weights on the corners of the uppermost chart. 'Besides, I believe your fellow passenger, Mr Bletchley, has had enough of the hunt?'

'Yes, most definitely,' I answered.

134

'He is a fine one,' Sykes said, rubbing his chin. 'He prances like a gelding pony in those flashy trousers, showing us his guns and the like, then he has to be brought back to my ship howling like a baby. Most curious. I believe you witnessed the scene?'

'I did.'

'A child can hold a rifle, but it takes a man to fire it. Tell me, do I need to keep an eye on Mr B, or not?'

'I think Bletchley has conflicting emotions we know little about. I thought he was supremely confident when I first met him, but I was mistaken.'

'Yes, yes, I've seen his type many times before. A man like that, out here, it's a disaster. But I have more worries about him upon the ship than on the ice. This business in the evenings, with him and Miss Gould sitting as if they are possessed – well, I don't know. He'll have the crew spooked. Mr French has an interesting theory on the matter. Has he told you?'

'No.'

'He believes they might be communing with the spirit world,' Sykes said, conspiratorially.

'That's absurd.'

'My thought entirely. But that Bletchley is a piece of work. I won't have my passengers going mad on me, upon my ship. Do you think that is possible?'

'I would say you have little choice, Captain Sykes. If he wishes to become mad, we shall just have to look after him. At the moment I think he is merely agitated.'

'Agitated, you say.' Sykes considered the problem. 'I'll have French keep an eye on him. I believe they could be soulmates.'

'Why do you say that?'

'Oh, no reason. But Mr French has his own currents of disaster running through his veins. Have you seen how he stares at the candle flames? I do not like it one bit. When he does that I feel like slapping the man.'

'Perhaps you should,' I said, amused.

'It is no laughing matter, sir,' Sykes replied. 'I have a ship to run, not an asylum.'

Sykes waved his hand expansively over the intricate markings of the chart. 'So. This is the island you speak of.' He pricked the map with a finger. 'Not much to look at. A few hundred feet long. There are many underwater features and reefs in that area, and a racing current that is something of a trickster. It's a fine one to read. I was once caught in it and handled the ship in a most unprofessional manner. I shall leave the *Amethyst* with Mr Talbot, because he has a walrus's nose when it comes to water. I believe he smells changes as they rise from the depths. Mr French will command one of the whaleboats, and I shall skipper the other. Best you sit in my boat. In that manner we can gain access to many of the rocks without danger.' He pointed to an area of cross-hatching on one side of the island. 'Notice these markings?'

'A landing place?'

'Precisely. We shall be expecting a neap tide, so the reef should be accessible and reliable.' He cocked his head at the chart, as if a fresh perspective might reveal more. 'This island is a well-known feature on the approach to Iceland, Mr Saxby. It has a very distinctive profile, as flat as a table on top, but with sheer cliffs perhaps two hundred feet high. It is this shape.' He made an impression with his hands. 'Among English sailors it is called the flour-sack. You will see why.'

He began to roll the chart up. Apparently our meeting was at an end. 'Will we find your birds?' he asked.

'I doubt it.'

'Me also. But we shall try. And in any case we will have some sport, Mr Saxby. I'm looking forward to it.'

'As am I. I want to thank you, once again, for making all this possible.'

'Well, I have been chartered to steer this ship to these bird ledges of yours, let us not forget that. There's no charity out here. Did you enjoy the ice?'

'I thought it was the most extraordinary sight a man could wish to see. Do you ever get used to it?'

'I look at it merely as a farmer regards his field. Work to be done and machinery to maintain. Workers, too, to keep content. But I'm glad you were inspired – the first sight of the ice sheet can haunt a man for many years. I watched you with Miss Gould as you conducted your promenades upon the floe. You two seemed to be getting on very well indeed.'

I regarded the captain suspiciously, trying to ascertain his point.

'What is your opinion of her and Mr Bletchley?' he asked. 'What say you – are we dealing with an elopement here?'

'Captain Sykes!' I said, appalled by his indiscretion. 'You must withdraw that at once – such gossiping is beneath you.'

He sounded curiously happy to have riled me. 'It is a captain's role to be a gossip, sir.' He turned his back to me, busily putting the rolled chart into a pigeonhole. 'An attractive woman, wouldn't you say?' He glanced slyly at me. 'Ah, yes, I see you agree.'

'Yes, Captain Sykes.' His prying tone annoyed me intensely. 'I *have* noticed that Miss Gould is an attractive woman. I have also noticed she is delicate and should not be discussed in this manner.'

Sykes turned back, satisfied with his childish goading. 'Well, as I say, we'll have us some sport. I have enjoyed our chat. That is all, Mr Saxby.'

*

137

A couple of days later we were passing the barren treeless coast of Iceland's Reykjanes peninsula. It was a world away from the great sheets of ice we had been among. The weather was dreary, with a persistent Scotch mist drifting in bands and coating every inch of the ship with a cold wet shine. Little auks – or *rotges* as the sailors called them – constantly circled the ship in a small flock, their fast wings and aimless motion making me feel quite dizzy as I watched them. I wore a rain cap and greatcoat, and had tied the hat's brim to one of my coat buttons with a cord, as I had seen several of the men do. Peering with difficulty at the rocky peninsula, a mile or two off, I realised that what I was seeing was no ordinary land. This was a lava coast, where volcanic earth had risen and cooled in successive layers of black and grey, in heaps such as a child might make, in disorder and without scheme, some parts pushed roughly into the sea, other stretches in cliffs and crumbled ridges. The land was desolate, without houses or lights or signs that it had ever been set upon.

Talbot was at the helm that morning, stoic and wet through, one of his frostbitten hands resting on the face of a binnacle.

'Your island,' he said, simply, gesturing with a nod towards a point somewhere off the front port bow.

I could make out nothing but the grey on grey of bad weather on a dismal sea. A low brooding sky seamed to leach, at distance, into the ocean, both without colour.

'How can you see it?' I asked, more to myself than to him. He seldom answered a question.

Even the tops of the masts could not be seen. The crosstrees and captain's barrel had a feathery aspect as the mist drifted past. Yet strangely, corridors of clear view were emerging. At certain angles, whole mile lengths of sea were suddenly visible, the small black waves in sharp focus, and it was through one of these gaps in the vapours that I saw, or imagined, my first glimpse of Eldey. After all those years of dreaming the sight. This was it, the last rock on the earth where the great auks had stood. I felt a thrill shooting up my spine. Yet it had appeared as a distant window appears, a paler squared-off shape in the sky, which vanished as soon as I looked directly at it.

I remembered being in the upstairs corridor at Celeste's house. Waiting, in the chill damp air on a threadbare carpet, for sounds of her on the other side of her bedroom door. An awareness, as I bent my ear to the lock, that she was just a few inches away from me. She had spoken. A sudden, urgent whisper: 'Save me from this place.'

11

'Careful now,' Sykes advised. 'Sharp eyes, men.'

The mist was impenetrable, glowing with a pale light that played tricks on the senses. Sounds could be heard, not far away, of surges of water being interrupted by rock. Of flow and backwash.

'Mr French!' Sykes called.

'Aye,' French replied, some way off in the fog.

'Best ring a bell once a minute,' Sykes ordered. 'Or we'll lose each other.'

'Yes, sir.'

Sykes handed me a small bell. 'Do the same, would you, Mr Saxby.'

'*Christ and the Saints*!' Martin Herlihy yelled.

Appearing like some falling spear of masonry, a large bird – its wings folded – had dropped through the fog and pierced the water by our boat. It vanished, almost without a splash.

'Steady, I say,' Sykes said, calmly. 'What was that?'

I tried to see beneath the water, but even while I looked a second bird fell, plunging through the fog, wings closed, diving into the water.

'Gannets, captain,' I said.

More followed, perhaps half a dozen, falling like icicles

from a church roof and vanishing into the ocean. The two Herlihy brothers became unnerved, crouching on their seats and close to letting go of the oars. One of the birds, quite near the boat, could be seen paddling thickly underwater, its neck straining this way and that, a thin chain of bubbles escaping from the nostrils on its beak, before bringing itself back to the surface with a laboured drag of wings.

'Smack it!' Connor urged, trying to smite it with his oar. 'Devil!' Freeing itself from the sea it spied us, warily, before climbing into the air with a lizard's crawl, streams spilling from its wings as it flew away.

'Don't forget to ring that bell,' Sykes uttered, unimpressed, turning his collar up. I rang it, and a second later heard French's boat in answer. As if summoned, two puffins flew out from the mist, fast as hornets and low to the water, their wings beating so rapidly they were blurred. At the last moment they managed to avoid the prow of the boat, both turning at a precise angle to speed alongside and disappear. They were so fast I almost disbelieved they had been there, yet after they had gone, an image of an eye remained, large and comical and set amid the coloured flags of its beak, frozen in the air a few feet from where I sat. Soon, as we rowed, more birds appeared, guillemots and razorbills, rafting in groups, bobbing apprehensively as we approached, and it was seeing these birds that made us realise we had all been hearing a noise beyond that of the sea. It was a sound of hundreds or possibly thousands of similar seabirds, high above us.

'Here she is, men,' Sykes said.

Below us, we saw the first glimpses of boulders emerging on a seabed. The water lifted us with a new swell. Almost instantaneously a vast wall of rock loomed about sixty yards ahead of the boat, towering vertically and streaked with white as if lime wash had been thrown down it and smeared with a sea-blackened stain along its base. Dotted on its ledges were lines of birds – every inch of level ground turned into a roost or a nest. We must have been a curious sight, emerging from the mist below them, but they viewed us with indifference. I recognised the white breasts of razorbills, heads raised up to the sky, and the brightly banded beaks of puffins.

Eldey had emerged like a phantom, a rock obelisk rising sheer from the ocean. Making the same discovery as ourselves, French's boat began to work its way, as we did, in an anticlockwise direction to the cliff. Glimpses of the top of the island could be seen now and again, two hundred feet in the air, where the rock broke to an almost perfect level. Birds were launching off this ledge, gliding in a looping flight before plunging into the water.

'Well done, men,' Sykes said.

'There's a swell,' Martin replied.

'Not too close, now. She has a cross-tide,' Sykes commanded. 'And we don't know what's below.'

Passing so close to the rock was an oppressive and unnerving experience. New surges of water grew, lifting smoothly and regularly against the bare cliff, a glassy lip that trembled before falling away as if a plug had been pulled. Each time it happened, a raft of seaweed rose with it, a full beard which gave the rock a pliable, velvety quality to its foundations. It smelt as damp and earthy as a cellar, but with the sharp ammonium stink of rotten eggs.

'Are they puffins?' the captain asked.

'Yes.'

The captain smiled at them. 'They are sweet animals. It was once thought they were fish – did you know that?'

I shook my head. 'No, I have not heard that before.'

'It's true,' he replied. 'Fish.'

As we turned the end of the island, meeting a stiffer current, French's boat drew alongside.

'We'll be speared by these blasted birds!' he exclaimed, agitated. 'I swear one was aiming for the boat, can you believe it!'

'Have your gaff hook raised to fend them off,' Sykes instructed, more than a little amused, 'and we'll see if you can skewer one.'

'You'll look fine with one down your neck,' he replied.

Sykes shrugged, indicating the collar he had turned up. But he decided we should do the same, passing the hook from beneath his legs to me. I lifted it upright, pointing it into the mist. 'Move it a little,' he said. 'Anything of note?' he then asked his first mate.

'A wretched stink, sir.'

'Yes, my nose is not immune.'

'On the other side,' French continued, 'the isle has a low broken reef. It might be possible to land there.'

'The chart has outlying rocks to the south-west, a mile distant,' Sykes said. 'You'll hear them in this swell. Mr French, you look such a fine admiral of your craft – I would appreciate it most gratefully if you would inspect those, before returning to us at the reef. We will circle Eldey and find the best place to land.'

French gave a grudging nod, making it clear he thought the whole venture was a fool's errand, and commanded his boat off into the mist.

While this exchange had occurred, I had been searching the rock face desperately for any sign of the auks that had once lived here. But the lower ledges, the only ones accessible to a flightless bird, were bare, or had signs that the razorbills and kittiwakes had nested instead.

143

On the south side, low shelving rocks formed the only possible point for a landing. Above them, the cliffs were just as sheer as before, overhanging us with a presence that was unnatural and foreboding. Half the sky was rock; it felt as if the world had tipped upon its side. And the mist only made this worse. In places it was so dense it created an optical trickery, whereby new impossible cliff faces might be reflected, drifting above us where we knew they could not be.

Suddenly we heard a sharp fizzing sound as a shoal of fish broke the surface in front of the boat. An instant later, a rising tunnel of water arrowed towards us and a dolphin emerged just a few feet beyond the oars, breaching entirely from the sea with a smooth glistening arch of its back. It hung suspended in the air long enough for its tail to twist, like a weathervane swinging, before it dived back into the water. The dorsal fin of a second dolphin appeared in almost the exact spot where the first had jumped, this one scything the water in a sharp turn as the shoal of fish were harried against the surface. The fizzing returned, like a wave breaking on shingle, as the two dolphins hunted as a team, running through the shoal, dividing it in two. We watched, in awe, as each dolphin sped beneath, the bulk of their bodies enough to lift us as they passed. They used our boat as part of their strategy, utilising its shape and presence to corral the fish, both of them angling their heads to regard us. Joyously they leapt in front of the boat and cut like knives through the water, while the vibrations of their enigmatic clicking resonated through the boards.

We sat, rocking in our seats, enjoying the marvels of the spectacle. A fish jumped clear into the thwarts, landing on the wood with panic, thrashing and flicking its flanks until one of the men threw it back in. More fish leapt against the side of the boat and dropped back in a daze.

144

When the hunt calmed down, the dolphins raised their heads from the water, as if receiving applause. They nodded and lifted their beaks, clucking and singing with curiosity. Then, almost as quickly as they had appeared, the dolphins submerged and vanished.

After a complete circumnavigation of the isle, spying the rock ledges for any evidence of great auks, we landed at the low reef. The rocks were smeared with white guano, pellets, feathers and fish scales. It stank horribly. Several pools had collected, and they reeked with a fetid ammonia smell; in one I saw a drowned kittiwake which had been there a long time. One of the sailors referred to it as a *haglet*. The cliffs overhung us with a sense of precariousness that affected us all. I felt overwhelmed with bleakness, that this rock smelt of nothing but waste and death. Foolishly, some part of me, some residual ill-judged belief, had made me think that we might have found a great auk. It had felt possible, although I had never voiced this possibility. But to stand on the island, I felt chastened. I had dragged a whole ship to this spot. For nothing. It was a place of great absence. This damp forgotten rock in the middle of the sea was the last spot in the world, and yet man had still not let them be. And at that moment I felt ashamed to be part of the species that had done this. The previous year, three Icelandic fishermen had stood here and strangled the last two great auks. They had smashed the one egg that had been laid. And although the winter waves had swept any remnant of this species from the rock, the spectre of the violence that had finished them remained. This was the site of an atrocity.

The Herlihy brothers had climbed out of Sykes' boat and were standing with the look of the recently shipwrecked, not quite knowing what duties they now had to perform. I had no answers. Why had I directed a ship and its crew across the

145

Atlantic to land at this inhospitable place, only to be greeted by the undeniable proof of man's murderousness? This was folly indeed! Sykes, spotting my uncertainty and wanting to salvage something from a purposeless visit, pointed to a breach in the cliffs.

'Well, Mr Saxby, my only idea is that you, Martin and Connor might climb that gully over there – if you wished, that is – to see the top of the isle. There may be sights of interest to a naturalist?' I was thankful for his sympathy. A man used to salvaging situations, he seemed, at heart, equally disappointed. 'I shall be perfectly content,' he said, 'to sit here on this wretched boulder.'

'Thank you, captain. I appreciate your suggestion.'

The Herlihy brothers climbed swiftly, and several times we gathered to help each other onto the ledges, while below us I heard the distorted sound of the sea rising in false currents. I dared not look down. The rock felt harsh, with a mineral scent of saltpetre, and the streaks of guano resembled dry waterfalls spilling from ledge to ledge. In the cracks of the rock, what had appeared to be vegetation turned out to be bones and pellets that had formed mats.

Our relief on reaching the top was fleeting, for we quickly emerged onto a stage of dizzying and confusing sound that was diabolic in its feel. In front of us, largely free of the mist, was a perfectly flat field of bare rock, covered by a seething colony of ten or twenty thousand fully grown gannets, their white bodies forming what appeared to be an impossible covering of snow. They made a dreadful and insane noise, of barking and grumbling, formed from a restless sea of throats, most noticeable nearest to us, inflaming with vibration as we stood to watch. The egg yolk coloration of their napes, by the thousand, gave the colony a sunset shine, as if it had managed to emit its own light.

'I can't move,' Martin said, his boots placed awkwardly between the ragged territories of three nests.

'Me neither,' his brother replied, braving his fear. 'What's your orders, sir?'

The closest birds eyed us warily, falling from their nests and aiming at our legs as we passed. Their beaks opened wide and their throats were vivid with a bright pink anger. Their eyes were startlingly clear and empty.

'They's gutless, Marti,' Connor decided, setting off at a healthy stride to kick out a path. The air seemed to rise around us, full of black-tipped scythes, as birds took to the wing.

'*Hah! Hah!*' Martin shouted. 'Off you go, bastards!' The brothers began to enjoy the sport, giving heavy kicks to the gannets and swiftly pocketing eggs in canvas bags. I followed the path they created, as if we brought with us a rising wind, scattering the birds and causing a panic that spread far beyond.

'Watch the gulls,' I warned, noticing several glaucous gulls sitting among the gannets. They were large and ghostly white in plumage, and were considerably more vicious than the gannets. They would wade towards us, hissing, their wings unhinged and their necks low and strained. The colony was overwhelming. There was such noise, such a squalor of smell and scrabbling and unpredictable pecking, that our nerves were very quickly shot through.

'I'll not stand much more o' this, sir!' Connor whined.

'Me neither!' I shouted, stopping abruptly, all three of us standing as one does in a crowd, shoulder to shoulder. The gannets closed around us, a flowing mass acting as water does, filling gaps and rising unstoppably. I felt engulfed by a sense of drowning, that somehow an acre of the ocean had risen to the top of this rock and we would soon be overrun. I stood, in awe of nature's sheer abundance. Its noise. Its restless and unquenched activity.

'Would either of you have any complaint if we climbed down again, as quickly as we might?' I said.

The brothers laughed, relieved.

'We have us some eggs, anyhows,' Martin said, immediately turning back.

'Look at yous, Marti,' his brother jeered. 'Quick as a new bride on her weddin' day!'

'That I don't mind. You'll just be sitting down an' makin' friends with these winged bitches, eh?'

Connor prodded me with a finger. 'Was a cry-baby, that one was.'

'I heard that, Connor,' his brother said, laughing. He kicked a gannet as hard as he could. 'Whoa, that feels good!' he shouted.

The sound of his voice suddenly lingered, unnaturally, as silence swept through the colony. It had arrived like a wave, rushing across the tops of the gannets. For a second not one of them made a noise. The birds looked up, as startled as we were, daunted by the stillness. It was as if the world had ended, a pause in which I felt I had a true and complete understanding of the infinite. A second later, with the resumption of the gannets' endless moaning, the world began again, and this time the combined sound of the birds had the unmistakable tone of grief.

By the time we had climbed down, French's party had joined us. He had found the outlying rocks, but no traces of any birds.

'Same here,' Sykes confirmed, looking disheartened.

Some of the men had collected feathers and other debris and had placed them on a large boulder for me to inspect. It was evident, from a brief examination, that there was nothing more than guillemot and razorbill feathers, alongside various fish bones.

'There is nothing here,' I said.

Sykes gave me a sympathetic look. 'We tried, Mr Saxby. Do not be discouraged.'

'Thank you.' I looked at the others. 'Sorry,' I said.

As we pulled away from the island, I gazed at the mottled seabed as it vanished below us, thinking once more how the dolphins had appeared out of that mysterious shadow, rising, smooth and flint-coloured until they had breached the surface.

I turned to the captain: 'Do you think we might see that patch of water again, where the dolphins appeared?'

'What on earth for?'

I insisted. 'Where was it?'

He gave me a shrewd look, narrowing his eyes, before shrugging. 'It makes little odds. We can go that way.'

He directed both boats to row in that direction, while he continued to regard me with a curious scrutiny.

'This search of yours is affecting you,' he said, rather more to the men than to me.

'Perhaps so.'

We rowed on, surrounded by the mist. There was a sound of dripping coming from the tips of the oars. The sea was calm, almost with a lake's character. We could just as easily have been on a punt during a duck shoot on the Norfolk Broads. To close my eyes was all it took, to conjure the ghostly calls of the coot, the quiet dip of the paddle, the distant splash of a pike, and I remembered how I used to find birds almost by instinct, uncannily understanding them, where they would shelter, where they would feel most secure. Among the damp, exposed roots that grew from the banks. Under the willows in early summer. In the dark gaps between the lily pads. In the shallows of the lake. Birds know their own fragility, and are born hiding.

'It was about here,' Sykes said, the hint of a challenge in his tone. 'Lie on your oars, men.'

The men stopped rowing, and began to look beneath them, into the blackened water, as if expecting the dolphins to emerge once more.

I smiled and, unable to control myself, started to laugh. I held my hand to my mouth, incredulous.

'For God's sake man, what's entered you!' Sykes said.

I shook my head. 'Those dolphins,' I explained. 'They were such a marvellous sight. We were all transfixed by them, weren't we? *Look!*' I pointed thirty feet away to a bare platform of the rock where, calm sentinels, the distinct silhouettes of a group of great auks stood, half shrouded in mist, as if they were merely a sketch on paper.

12

There are many days when I have sat here and wished to God that I had never seen those birds. I have wished that the mist had remained thick, rather than parting briefly. Just a little further out to sea, or at a different minute, and we would never have found them. Yet through my persistence, my sheer obsession with finding what was lost, it seemed as if I had conjured them from beyond the impossible divide that separates the living from the extinct. It was all down to me, and to no one else.

Sykes was transformed by the discovery. He directed both boats to return to the place where we had previously landed, and he personally leant over the side to grab the rocks to guide the boat in. When he looked at me, it was with an expression of simple congratulation.

'Well done, Eliot,' he said. 'You are a marvellous naturalist. You have a nose for it!'

All at once the mood of the excursion had changed. The men in both boats were unduly happy. I remember French, when he brought his boat alongside, actually stood up and leapt to shore. He leapt, as he had done when I had first met him, jumping the hatch as if he was playing games with his shadow, or trying to escape it. But this time, I felt it was a leap of excitement. I felt vindicated, not just for the day, but for the whole journey. Against all the odds, a group of these birds had survived! Seventy feet or so away through the mist, were the last half-dozen great auks in the world. They had appeared so mysteriously, their bodies made almost glass-like by the mist. Yet they were real! On that single bare rock stood the future of a species. The thought was dizzying.

This discovery would be the making of my career. It was the reversal of an extinction that had readily been believed. And as I crossed the slippery surface of the reef, underneath the towering cliff of the island, I thought of Clara, back on the ship; how this simple discovery might transform her life, too. Fill it with a joyousness and hope and belief that had been missing.

To reach them we had to round a sheer boulder while clinging to a ledge above a small deep inlet. Essentially, this was the reason our search on the island had not found them, before. On the other side, all seven of our party – the four sailors, Sykes, French and myself – collected on an edge of the reef. About twenty feet away, still standing on their low plat-form of rock, the great auks eyed us curiously. They mirrored our number exactly – seven. They were larger than any of the other birds we had seen. Dark, goose shaped, with stout necks and prominent hook-nosed beaks, as if a child had designed them with little regard for grace and elegance. They sat low to the rock, on stubby legs with wide paddled feet, the skin there bluer than the rest of their plumage.

'These are your birds?' French whispered.

'Yes. Absolutely no mistake.'

'Then this is a miracle,' Sykes said.

A low murmuring sound emerged intermittently from the group, alongside a deep growl, far deeper than I have heard from any bird. It had the resounding thump of a bittern's call, even several dozen yards away, but was as rough as a bull's cough. It was an astonishing sound. I felt it reverberate in the pit of my stomach. Standing on the reef, I noticed we were among the detritus of a nesting area. Rafts of dried weed and fish bones adorned the rocks, alongside the glistening marks of guano and the soft sheen of fish scales. An hour earlier, I would have been overjoyed to find even these – a feather beneath my feet that I bent down to pick up – the feather of a great auk! This would have been prize enough, yet the riches of seeing seven adult birds, living, continuing, was an honour I found difficult to accept.

Captain Sykes instructed his men to sit. 'We must not scare them from the rock,' he urged. 'Mr Saxby, have you listened to the rasping sound they make?'

'It is quite incredible,' I replied.

'I have heard it said the great emperor penguins of the southern sea make a similar sound. But I have never heard anything like this.'

'Rather like the bittern,' I suggested, 'the bull-of-the-bog.'

He was almost childishly happy. French had said the captain was an enthusiast for nature. I was glad to have brought him here.

'Go,' Sykes said, gesturing eagerly with his hand, 'you must sit among them, to make your studies. We shall wait for as long as you wish.'

'It's strange, but I feel nervous,' I replied. I had waited for this day for so long. 'I don't want to scare them.'

'Look how their heads are sinking on their necks,' he pointed out. 'They are as docile as a Christmas goose! I suspect they have their bellies full of fish, and are intending to sleep it off.'

For the rest of my life I will remember the surge of feeling

I had approaching their platform, almost in a trance, acutely aware that this moment, this experience, should not be occurring at all. These birds had vanished from the world, and yet here I was privileged beyond my comprehension.

The great auks stirred as I stepped onto their rock. Each one watched me, closely, but none of them made any sign of alarm. Unlike the gannets earlier in the day, these birds were peaceful and apparently without fear. The sound of their chatter and growls was remarkable, as it reverberated through their chests and rasped through their beaks. But it also felt unnerving, to be among them, because their size was so similar to that of young children, perhaps three years old; it was as if I was treading through a nursery. I felt naturally protective.

Their eyes were tiny pebbles of glistening black, with a smoky hue I'd never seen before, set in a flat-sided head covered with rows of miniature oiled feathers. When one turned to face me, a subtle iridescence curled across its crown, like the reflected gleam from a polished helmet. Their wings were long and paddle shaped, noticeably missing any form of flight feathers, with front edges that were as bare and hard as wooden rails.

I sat down among them, perceiving a strong smell of fish and a musky odour of wet plumage as I began to draw them in my notebook. My fingers trembled as I tried to hold the charcoal. I still have this sketch. It is a sketch, I now consider, of innocence itself. They were perfect sitters. Quite still and tranquil, sometimes adjusting their fleshy webbed feet but otherwise showing little interest in me or each other. Occasionally one would raise a neck to its full height and gaze into the fog.

I drew them carefully, first as a group, and then individual studies. There seemed little difference between the sexes, or none that was strikingly apparent, but there were subtle alterations in their markings, a wider flash of white behind one's eye, a more prominent beak on another, that suggested a mixed group. In my *Compendium* the auk had been drawn as a noble and fierce dweller on inaccessible rocks, rather than the placid and communal birds I witnessed. I drew details – the sharp deep outline of the nostrils on either side of the beak, shaped like apple pips, the solid scaly leg as woven as a riding crop, and the curve of the wing which, even folded, had at its tip an oar's blade.

Every so often I looked back at the party of men sitting on the reef, at the base of the cliff. The sailors appeared aimless, but French and Sykes were in animated discussion. Sykes still had the eager expression he'd had since the birds' discovery. He was explaining something very thoroughly to his first mate who, even at that distance, looked uncomfortable sitting on the rock. French liked to stand. Like all tall men, he preferred to be elevated.

I turned back to the birds. 'Each one of you is a miracle,' I whispered.

When I felt I had drawn enough, and recorded as many aspects of their grouping and postures as I could, I walked back to join the others.

'I told you,' Sykes said, smiling, 'these birds are notoriously sleepy and quite trusting.'

'It appears so,' I replied. 'And considerably smelly.'

'This whole rock has a tremendous stink,' he said. 'Our clothes will not be rid of it for days. May I see your observations?'

I passed him the book. He looked carefully at the sketches, nodding and complimenting the accuracy. 'Most impressive. I shall probably begin an embroidery based on these, if I may?'

'I will make some further measurements,' I said.

Returning to the rock, I placed a yardstick next to one of the birds. It eyed me curiously, but allowed me to take detailed recordings of its beak and feet, its neck and wing. I felt a tingle the length of my spine when I touched the bird for the first time. How cold and slick it felt, how the front blade of its wing had a prickly, almost plucked aspect to it, and how the feathers on its neck were as smooth and polished as glass. I was absorbed in my observations, and needed to concentrate, and made gentle movements that would not disturb them.

After several minutes, I crawled back to the men and announced I was finished. I was enthralled by the experience. The absolute rarity of these birds made my observations unique. I was sure my notes would become a celebrated document. This would be a defining moment in my career and my life.

When I buckled my satchel, I noticed Captain Sykes watching me attentively. 'A most satisfactory visit,' he said. 'Your observations looked methodical and accurate, but most complicated. Do you think you have made enough of a record?'

'I think so,' I replied. 'Although I suspect it would take years to truly learn these creatures.' I gave him a grateful smile, wishing to show how satisfied I was.

'Good. We shall wait for you to move to one side, and then we will capture them.'

I started at his words, not understanding him.

'*Capture?* What do you mean?'

'It is best that we are very careful not to leave any marks on the bodies. We will drown them.'

I waited for this to be some form of untimely joke. I had seen it before, at the dinner table, moments when he tried to provoke others by a turn of phrase or outlandish comment, for no other reason than his own amusement. But the captain met my gaze head on, unflinching, and I knew very quickly that it was far from a joke. This was a very serious matter indeed.

'Captain Sykes, did I hear you correctly? You wish to kill these birds?'

He was unapologetic. 'Yes, Mr Saxby.'

The others in the party had grown quiet and still, noticing that their captain's tone had raised to that of a straightforward challenge.

'But you cannot kill them,' I said.

Sykes scoffed, with ugly intent. 'Of course I can. I am trying not to be blunt with you, Mr Saxby, but you must understand the nature of the situation. Open your eyes – on this rock is our fortune.'

'For us? What fortune?'

'Not just for me, you understand, nor the owners of the *Amethyst*. But all the hands on board are on a share of profits.'

'Is this a joke of yours?'

'Absolutely not.'

'You intend to—'

'Correct, Mr Saxby, I do.'

'I would never have anything to do with what you might be suggesting.'

He dismissed me with an offhand gesture. 'Your choice. It makes no odds to me.'

'Do you quite appreciate the discovery we have made here?' I continued. 'On this bare rock are the last birds of this species anywhere in the world. There are no others. We . . .' I looked around at all the group, searching for support, '– man – has killed all the others.'

'So you have said, on many occasions. It is that fact that I fully understand. If there were thousands of these birds, then they would be worthless, fit for a greasy meal or the stuffing of pillows. But you have explained the situation clearly. Each of these birds is a fortune, collectors or museums will fight for them, and if we bag the entire lot, then we can virtually name our price. Do you understand simple economics, Saxby? The last few of a commodity are precious. But the last *one* of a commodity is incalculable.'

'Economics! How dare you, Sykes!'

'Careful in your tone with me.'

'I will speak as I wish, damn you!'

'I am still your captain.'

'Not on this rock you aren't!'

Sykes took his time to reply, attempting to defuse the situation. 'Mr Saxby, I think you have a skewed impression of our trip.'

'What you are saying is disgusting. Men – can't you see what is happening here? These are the *last* of this species. If you kill these birds, it will be a moment that can never be reversed. Do you know what you're talking about, Sykes? Is that what you want? You are talking about conducting *an extinction*.'

Sykes tried to laugh it off, but this time I thought he sounded a little less sure of himself. 'What I am talking about is making money. I am talking about a comfortable retirement. I am in the business of looking after myself – just as the eider feathers her nest with her own down. You have seen the state of the *Amethyst*. She is worm-bored and iron-sick. Why, I could list the repairs required all day, and still I would not be finished. With the sale of these skins the damages of many years can be repaired, the debtors paid off, and I shall have a comfortable old age.'

'With Mrs Sykes and the roses around the door?' I said, reminding him of the displeasure he'd once expressed to me at the thought of retirement. It was privy information I was wrong to disclose. He glared, insulted that I should attempt to judge him publicly. I noticed the darkness of the ring that encircled each of his corneas, as if the colour of his eyes had a stagnant, dead fringing.

'You are wrong to ask the men what they think, Mr Saxby. I am their captain and they will do as they are told. You are also wrong to cast an opinion on my own private affairs. You know very little about me, but I shall tell you this: I have skippered these frigid waters of the North Atlantic and the Arctic oceans for thirty years. Indeed, you are not much older than that, I believe, so consider for a moment that when you were crawling as a baby, I was here, at the top of the world, looking across a dismal sea. I have lost friends and cargoes and I have faced winds and ruinous waves and errant bergs and I have hated every blasted year of it. You see? I am an old man and I will shortly be dying, no doubt, and here, on this rock, I have alighted upon a fortune. My business is not sentiment and it's not love. My business is money, and it's the business of all who are on my ship, too. I will remind you what we are looking at. They are *birds*, nothing more. I see little difference between these fowl and the Sunday roast which is served on my plate.'

'You are entirely missing the point, Captain Sykes. Knowing the difference between these birds and your Sunday roast is exactly what it means to be a man.'

Sykes stood up from the rock, exasperated. 'You've made your position clear. I think we have talked enough.' He looked to the men, all of whom readied themselves for his command. But Sykes evidently felt he had not won the argument yet. 'Say we left these creatures,' he began, trying a new tack, 'do you think they will live? If it's not us then it will be someone else. These animals will die, you can be sure of that.

I can sail my ship away but a different ship will be here, the masts will come over the horizon, perhaps this season, maybe next. A different captain will stand upon this very rock and I tell you he will be rubbing his hands and his conscience will be clear. It is the way of the Arctic: if there's profit, it will be taken, whatever the cost.'

We stood facing each other. I was aware that I was standing in his path, between him and the birds.

'I cannot stop you, Sykes. You have your mind set and you have men here to do your dirty work for you. But you *can* stop yourself. You may be right to think others will come here, but your argument is still that of a coward. You are hiding behind the prospect of other gutless men to excuse your own lack of fibre. It does not make you right. You are proposing the murder of these last few birds for what? For a few tins of varnish for one ship on one part of the world's sea. Your ship will rot one day, whether you repair it or not, and you and I shall be gone, too. But we have a chance here, to trade in a currency that you don't seem to understand – a currency of legacy. What is the purpose of being a man, other than to make sure that we can be guardians of what we have been given and pass it on to future generations? You have a chance here, today, to make sure this ledge of rock is not remembered as a place of permanent absence.'

Sykes adjusted his feet and gave me a wry smile. 'Pretty words for a young man. But ignorant, too. You seem keen to urge me to be true to myself. Well, I am a ship's captain. I look after myself and my men. You, sir, are a collector. You are paid by the very same museums that have demanded this wretched bird for their display cabinets. In my world this bird is a lousy meal of greasy meat. It is your world that has placed a price upon its head. I suggest you take note of that, and your responsibility within it. I shall act as a captain and you, Mr Saxby, should act as a collector.'

I looked at the other men, at French, who eyed me with a curious glance, and at the sailors who sat, oppressed and uncomfortable with the discussion. And I saw a great deal about human authority. All of us, equal in body, but completely under the rule of the captain. Only French would be able to defend me, but he remained silent.

Captain Sykes knew I could do nothing more. He straightened his jacket and addressed the sailors, directly.

'Men, go to the birds. You will do as Mr Saxby did. You observed how he walked softly on his heels and without sudden movement. Place your jackets round them and bring them to the inlet. We will drown them there.'

The sailors, all four of them, stood and obediently removed their jackets.

'Tread like this,' the captain said, demonstrating the lightness of step that I had noticed on board the *Amethyst*.

The men walked in a line down to the rock where the great auks stood, the place where I had sat, euphoric, making my sketches. As before, the birds showed no awareness of approaching danger, even while the men crouched down with their jackets held open. Again, I was reminded how similar in size the bodies of these birds were to those of young children, how the outstretched jackets resembled a gesture of fatherly protection, of offered warmth. Yet as the men moved, at a signal whispered by one of them, and four of the birds were gathered, I saw a struggle of wings within the jackets that revealed the true dimension of what was happening.

'*Please*, captain!' I implored.

The men quickly returned with the four birds. Sykes pointed at the inlet of water.

'For God's sake, do not do this!' I exclaimed, but knew it

was futile. The birds were already as good as dead. Sykes raised his hand at me, instructing me to be quiet, as the men took the auks to the edge.

One of the men waded into the inlet and was passed a bird. Without hesitation he pushed it underwater. I saw the muscles on his arms knotting with the struggle against the buoyancy of the animal, and then, after perhaps half a minute, a renewed struggle that boiled against the surface as the bird began to kick and fight below. The man shut his eyes as the water splashed his face, while the other men stood watching, holding the next three birds, until the inlet calmed from beneath, the water rising in soft folds then smoothing until it was still.

He brought the bird out, its neck hanging lifeless across his forearm, and laid it on the rock as he might a towel. I felt a sudden hotness within me, an urgency to act, yet helplessness, too. *I cannot stop the drowning*, I thought. *It will occur and I can do nothing. The water will take them. I am too late.* I felt a sense of peril reaching out for me, too, something I could not quite perceive, but rising as unstoppable as water, wishing to claim me.

A second man started to pass his bird down, but the first sailor wanted none of it.

'No. You do it,' he stated.

An anguished look passed between them, and I realised the second man to go into the water was Martin Herlihy. I watched him with acute awareness. We had climbed to the top of the island together, that morning. Alongside his brother, we had relied upon each other among the gannets. Allies of sorts: it gave me hope. And I remembered another aspect to Martin's character – how he had reacted when French had killed the greenfinch. His expression of doubt, then, and an expression here, too, of an intense and heartfelt worry. This might be the moment the day would be redeemed – if the sailors refused to act, surely Sykes would be forced to give up. I stood, and walked towards the inlet, offering my support and sensing a growing chance of salvation.

'Martin?' I said.

But Martin Herlihy was deliberately refusing to look me in the eye. He stepped into the water and thrust the bird below the surface, doing as the first man had done, until the auk was drowned.

All four birds were slaughtered in this manner and laid out carefully on the wet rocks.

'Well done, men. I'll see you get a good drink tonight,' Sykes said. 'Just the other three and we'll be done.'

The men raised no objection. Wet and sullen, they began to move back towards the rock. Feeling a surge of anger rise in me, at my powerlessness, at my part in this ugly display of human weakness, I ran past them, shouting and waving my arms like a madman at the birds.

In an instant the auks sprang alert, scrabbling across the rock and diving into the sea, launching themselves and paddling swiftly from their platform, just their necks raised above the water. I turned, triumphant, searching out the captain's expression, only to see him glowering at me, dark eyed, with a murderousness that quite terrified me.

'Bring him here!' he ordered.

'I am not part of this!' I shouted.

I felt my arms being held as the sailors brought me back up the rock.

Sykes visibly controlled himself, thrusting his hands in his pockets as if to prevent himself from striking me. 'Sit here, Mr Saxby. That's right, next to me. That was a silly and pointless thing to do. If you do it again I will have you sent back to the boat and you will be restrained.'

I sat on the rock. 'Not *quite* extinct,' I said, satisfied.

Captain Sykes raised his eyebrows at me and actually smiled. He sat by me and stared out to sea. Beyond the rocks, the mist was drifting thickly above the water. I thought, a couple of times, that I could see the dark silhouettes of the three birds, swimming this way and that, but the mist was dense and misleading. Many objects appeared to exist out there, where we knew it was just empty.

'We shall wait,' Sykes said, gravely.

We sat like that for about ten minutes, not speaking, but staring out at the greyness of the light and mist and water.

Eventually, a small shape began to condense and, pulling through the fog with an oaring motion of its wings, one of the great auks returned.

'Oh no,' I whispered, 'do not come back.'

It climbed out heavily, dragging its long wings and waddling up the wet rocks to the place where it had stood, before. It shook itself down, and nestled its beak into the soft plump shape of its throat. A few minutes later a second one appeared and, finally, the last. Each climbed out in the same manner to perch on the rock.

'Now,' Sykes commanded, quietly. In his tone there was no concealment of the warning he was giving me.

The men had lost their patience and their heart. They quickly gathered the birds, making no mistakes, and took them to the inlet, all three of them wading in at the same time.

'Captain Sykes, this time I shall watch,' I said. He regarded me, puzzled, but recognised too that I must witness what was going to happen. The moment of extinction.

'Very well,' he said. 'I understand.'

We stood at the water's edge while the birds were held under the surface. I watched their dark fluid shapes, kicking and struggling as the last bubbles of air escaped their beaks, and I watched as the water once more became completely still.

'It is done,' Sykes said.

For the first time, French spoke. 'Should we skin them?' he said. It was difficult to read anything into his expression. As always, his face seemed caught between conflicting attitudes.

'No,' Sykes replied.

'Very well. Shall I have the men carry them to the boats?'

'Not yet.' Captain Sykes was in no hurry. He stood presiding over the dead bodies of the birds, laid out at his feet, as if conducting a valuation. They occupied such a small space, their necks arranged in parallel, the entire species reduced to a row of wet feathers and lifeless bodies. It really was done. They had become extinct.

'Good,' Sykes said, solemnly. 'Men, we will sit on this rock and watch the sea.'

French shifted his stance, uncomfortably. 'For what purpose, sir?'

'We must make sure there are no others.'

I turned away, repulsed. The meticulous nature of his slaughter appalled me. 'When will you be happy?' I asked.

He didn't answer. Having no choice, I sat with the others, gazing into the mist, listening to the laps of water rising and slipping from the rocks and aware, pointedly aware, of the great absence that faced us. A sea that appeared not only empty of great auks, but empty of all life. The murderousness of the last hour felt as though it stretched across the ocean, without boundary. Man, his greed, seeing no obstacle, neither outside nor inside himself.

We waited for a long time. Once, Captain Sykes asked the men to sing, and they responded with a low-voiced work song about turning the capstan. Sykes appeared to enjoy the sound, tapping his foot and nodding his head, seeking a diversion. Not one of us looked at the row of birds by the side of the inlet.

At last, with nothing emerging from the grey sea or the mist that swirled above it, the captain ordered the men to take the birds back to the boats and return to the ship. He referred to the auks as 'our cargo'.

I looked at him, prompted by his callous choice of word. 'I wish to stay, for a while,' I said.

'Whatever for?' he replied.

'We will never again be able to observe these birds. I feel I should record as much as this rock can inform me – about their diet and behaviour.'

He regarded me, quizzically. 'As you wish,' he said, briskly. 'Mr French, stay with Mr Saxby for his observations. Make sure nothing untoward happens. We will return to the *Amethyst*. I shall leave two men for you in the second boat.

'Martin,' the captain ordered, 'make me a dog-vane of those feathers, will you.'

'Aye, sir,' Martin replied. He went to one of the birds and carefully plucked some of the finer feathers from beneath the neck. He bound them carefully on a length of twine and fashioned a small loop at the top, suitable to hang from a finger. When he handed it to the captain, Sykes held it up, satisfied, letting the air stir it.

'See, gentlemen, the wind comes from England today,' he said, proudly.

I waited until he had left, standing among the remnants of the nesting site. A feather by my feet, a pattern of their guano and the meals they might have eaten there. An almost painful absence. I was aware of the presence of Mr French, standing a few feet away. Upright and motionless, silent too, looking out at the sea.

I challenged him. 'What have we done here, Mr French?'

He looked back at me, grey-eyed. 'I had no idea the captain would do this.'

'Really?'

'Yes.'

'But you did *nothing* to argue against him.'

He had his argument planned. 'There was no point.'

That rigid inflexibility. I became emotional. '*This* is the point! These *bare rocks* are the point, Mr French.'

'I could do nothing, and neither could you,' he said, simply stating the fact.

I stepped away from him in disgust. Mr French, full of such unyielding posture, embodied everything I most detested. Man and his murderousness, and, hand in hand with his murderousness, his ultimate lack of conscience.

The inlet where the birds had been drowned had become quiet, the water was clear and pure. Seaweed and anemones shone in bright colours of blood and rust below the surface. There was no trace of the murder that had been done there. The water had closed and returned to all it was before.

I collected as much as I could. Scraps of feather, remnants of fish and shell that might one day tell the diet and habits of these birds. It was a desultory experience.

'I have enough,' I told French.

'Your cap,' he replied, pointing to the rock at the edge of the sea. It must have fallen when the men had brought me back to face Sykes.

I went to retrieve it, thinking of the moment I had scared the birds into the water. How euphoric I had felt. How senseless it had turned out to be. As I bent down to pick up my cap, something moved in a crevice a few feet beyond.

Almost instantaneously I saw the unmistakable head and beak of a single great auk, turned awkwardly at me, eyeing my movement with deep suspicion. Partly hidden, stuck at the tapering point of a crack through the rock, but a sight that was as miraculous as any that I have seen in my life. A great auk, watching, parting its beak, alive, beyond the certifiable fact of the extinction I had just witnessed. I stared at it, incredulous at this species' ability to flout the murder that has relentlessly flowed towards it.

Very quickly I had to make a decision. French was behind me, anxious to leave, and I had no reason to stay. I went to him brushing off my cap, and together we lined up to climb around the large boulder that led to the dock.

It was only on the other side, with the view of the tethered boat forty feet away, that I turned to French and held his arm.

'Mr French. There is an eighth.'

I watched him closely while he understood the implications.

'Show me,' he said.

I led him back to the rock where, as before, the great auk looked up at us from its position deep in the crevice.

'Is it injured?' he asked.

'Possibly.'

He stretched down and, with surprising gentleness, stroked it on the back of its neck. He looked up at me with a questioning expression.

'I don't understand. Why would you lead me to this bird, knowing what we have done here?' he asked.

I smiled, still jubilant with the discovery, but with growing doubt, also. 'I'm not sure, Mr French. But I do know this bird is not safe here. Sykes is right in one thing – other profiteers will come to this rock and kill them, I am certain of it.'

He nodded. It was an unavoidable truth.

We continued to look at it, knowing it was the last great auk in the world.

French sat down on the rock and held his ankles.

'What do we do now, Mr Saxby?'

I had already decided. 'We shall take this bird and conceal it on board. It will be butchered if we leave it here. And when we perceive the chance, I suggest we release it onto the most isolated rock, reef or skerry the Arctic can offer us. This bird, Mr French, will die a free bird.'

He seemed acquiescent.

'Mr French, you will have to help me with this.'

'Yes. I will,' he replied. 'I will help you.'

13

The birds are dead. I told her that. I felt the rage that had overwhelmed me on Eldey beginning to re-form. The captain is a mercenary, a simple and ignorant man. Despicable was the word I called him. A man of greed and no conscience. I told Clara these things as, in a rush, I conveyed all that had happened. How the mists had covered the cliffs, about the sight of the dolphins as they hunted, and how the day had started as one full of wonder and natural awe. I told her of the gannets spearing the water around the boat, like pieces of falling masonry, and how the same birds – by the countless thousand – had appeared brutal and ungainly on land. I described the miraculous vision of the auks in the mist. And the sense of miracle, how it had continued as we had approached them.

To all this she listened calmly, sitting on the edge of her bunk, her cabin the only true sanctuary the ship had to offer me. She moved just once, to stand and close the door with a soft click.

'Go on,' she said.

'We murdered the birds. The men were ordered to drown them in an inlet of the sea, and I watched them perform it. The captain has made these birds extinct.'

'But why?'

'For profit.'

'*Profit?*'

'Sykes will be able to sell his skins to museums and collectors for any price he fancies.' I looked out of the porthole, at the gunpowder-grey expanse of the ocean, which had an aspect of total lifelessness. An Arctic Ocean where every creature that lived there, whether as solitary as the whale or the bear, or in the colonies that clung to its barren coasts and isolated rocks, all the seals, geese, birds, walrus and deer, each one of them fit for murder, their bodies turned into barrels of oil and sacks of feather, their bones fashioned into corsetry, their tusks carved into ornaments and false teeth. Slaughter was everywhere.

'I had no power to stop them,' I said. 'I didn't know what to expect on this voyage, but it wasn't to find that man's most obvious mark on the world is of his violence. Life has no value here. Only the dead have value.'

I pictured the eighth bird, the one that Mr French and I had brought back to the ship, concealed in a slack cask. Saved, but now imprisoned. My joy in finding it had quickly been sobered – the species would still become extinct.

I knew I would need her help. I told her how by chance, on fetching my cap, I had discovered the last one of the great auks, that it was alive and, with French's assistance, I had secretly brought it back to the ship.

'Where is it hidden?'

'Below deck, at the bow ...'

Clara raised a finger to her lips, urging me to keep my voice down. 'Edward,' she whispered: 'he likes to listen through the wall, I am sure of it.'

I nodded, cautiously. 'There is a small locker containing the anchor chain and miscellaneous stores. French described it as a type of lazarette. It really is a particularly grim and dark place, but perfect as a place of concealment.'

'But do you *trust* that man?'

I felt at a disadvantage. 'I think ... Clara, I had very little choice in the matter.' She looked unsure. 'If the bird had stayed on the rock,' I said, urged to explain, 'it would have been killed by any other trader, collector or profiteer that sought it out, probably in a matter of weeks when the weather improved. I asked French because I couldn't save it by myself.'

To all intents a practical answer, not a preferable one. I remembered how gently French had touched the great auk, stroking its back as it had sheltered in the crevice, and how, when I had asked him plainly for his help, he had replied with a simplicity that was to the point and without edge. If I had doubted his motivations, or suspected him of duplicity, then his actions alone had reassured me. It takes a good deal to go against the law of a ship. I wanted to tell Clara how carefully French had concealed the bird in the slack cask, binding its beak to avoid its making a sound on the row back. How he had personally escorted the luggage, distracting the men and officers enough, and with calm authority, so that he could bring the bird below decks. 'I have placed it in the anchor locker,' he had told me, when we had met, soon after. 'It is a quiet store and the bird will not be disturbed as there is virtually no need for anyone to maintain that space.' He had been quietly satisfied with his achievement, even clicking his heels as if to indicate a job well done. 'At some time in the future we might be able to find a better location,' he added. I had watched him, grateful as he walked off, his hands held behind his back, a finger twitching in his grasp.

'Clara, Mr French has taken a huge risk in secreting the bird on board. For that alone I think we can trust him.'

She was apologetic. 'Please forgive me. I am not quick to trust men. That is something you may not appreciate yet about me.' She scrutinised me with an amused look. 'So this bird, it's there now?'

'Yes.'

'Right under Sykes' nose. Well, you really are quite a devious man!'

'Well, yes I suppose I am.'

'Devious, but splendid too. Will it be safe?'

'French seems to think so. There's a tradition of hiding things in that locker space, apparently. We bound the bird's wings, until it is used to its new surroundings. Our job is simple – we have to keep it fed and watered. When we find an isolated part of the coast, we can set it free.'

'That is your plan?'

'Absolutely.'

She considered it. 'Yes. I like it. And I shall be a part of it. I can promise to you – you and I shall set it free.'

We sailed west-south-west towards the southern tip of Greenland, resolutely; each time I passed the twin binnacles at the helm I saw the needle quivering at this same mark. The ship moved with a swift motion, helped by a steady wind that filled the sails for hours at a time. Going before the wind, it is called, with the ship's bow towards its destination, many sails billowing and useful, and all hands untroubled with the progress and trim. Yet for me, the atmosphere on board the *Amethyst* had changed.

As I stood beneath the masts, I felt the presence of the hams and meat hung above me, wrapped in muslin burial shrouds, as if the very ship was flagged in death. Bodies of seals and auks in the hold; the proximity of man's butchery. Bletchley had never truly recovered from the hunting excursion on the ice. He still talked about the seal that he had shot being on board, haunting him with its presence. He told me it had looked at him at the point of its death and stared right through him into his soul. When he said this – while he cracked walnuts in front of the wood-burner – I tried to make light of it. I answered the seal was not a sentient animal, that nature had given its eyes a largeness that meant the seal was often mistakenly seen as having compassionate and intelligent thought. He listened, his head angled birdlike, with a quizzical expression as if to say he was having none of it. Secretly I was greatly troubled. How could I forget the seal that had likewise looked at me at the edge of the colony? How the look in its eye had literally stopped me in my tracks. Hadn't I, too, felt my soul weighed by an animal that seemed more human than was possible?

Captain Sykes was indecently happy for the next few days. Whether it was the progress of his ship, heading towards Greenland, or the thought of his unexpected windfall in the cargo beneath his feet, he would trot across the deck with the light-footed gait of a man half his age.

'Mr Saxby!' he called one morning, loud enough for the entire ship to hear. 'Join me in my cabin, if you wouldn't mind.'

We had been on deck, and as he'd said this, he'd ushered me, without option, towards the aft companionway that led almost directly to his cabin door. I followed him, obedient, promising to myself I would not lose my temper.

Inside his cabin, Captain Sykes sat on a small padded armchair and instructed me to sit on the settee, as I had before. In front of me, on a low wooden table, Simao had already set up a coffee pot for two people, alongside a freshly baked cake. Sykes must have planned this moment. He gestured to the pot, which was covered in an embroidered cosy.

'Shall I?' he said, offering to pour. 'You are the kind of fellow that takes two lumps of sugar.' I let him do as he wished. He poured the thick black liquid into the coffee cups and added two lumps of sugar from a tray, using a surprisingly dainty pair of silver tongs.

'Would you like another game of draughts?' he asked, hopefully.

'Bullet against bone?' I replied. 'How ironic. Do you wish to test me again, or just want to beat me?'

He regarded me sagely, stroking and flattening his moustache either side of his nose, as if already considering a move of his players.

'I went to sea when I was twelve, Mr Saxby, working the slave route from West Africa to the Caribbean. My duties were largely below decks, spreading sawdust on vomit and blood and sweeping it up to the best of my abilities. We had the negroes on bunks, in the dark, and while we worked they would spit or they would shout in strange languages. Do you have any idea how much the negro can spew in the duration of a voyage? I will let you imagine how unpleasant it was down there. Please, take some of this parlour cake with your coffee. It is exceptional. On the return leg we brought spice and produce to Liverpool. There was nutmeg and cinnamon and pepper and fresh pineapples. We would sit on deck, eating mangoes and papaya, and had very little to do. I spent many hours drawing and that is where I began to practise my art of needlework.'

Sykes stopped for a dramatic pause, eating a slice of the cake with an elaborate savouring of it.

'As I said, delicious. I learnt very early on,' he continued, 'that the sea trades life and death with equal measure. We

175

stacked pineapples on the bunks where a few days before I had pulled dead men from their chains. Why, this very ship, Mr Saxby, was originally launched as a trader of slaves. You may not have appreciated that. I suggest, during your wanderings to the lower deck, that you examine the bulkheads, for there you will see the wood is riddled with fixings where the slave chains were attached. Quite hazardous, even now. If the negro could write, he would have scratched his initial there, too. The point being, ships have long lives that equal the journeying of any one of us. They might start sailing in warm waters, then are laid up in ordinary for many years on a Welsh beach or in an Essex creek, before some new vision is applied, they become refitted and re-conceived, new thwarts are cut in, bows strengthened, new masts erected or taken away, royals and upper topgallants added and cabin quarters refitted to accept the likes of paying passengers, such as yourself, Mr Saxby. The velvet settee and the mahogany table is for your benefit, sir, a sailor will sit on a bucket and he'll be glad of it. Through it all, these ships have lives very similar to our own – they adapt and survive and continue their purpose, and very little stops them, short of reefs and bergs and insurmountable seas.'

'Why are you bothering to tell me this, Captain Sykes? I am hardly in the mood to listen to you.'

'Because I wish to clear the air between us, Mr Saxby. On the island of Eldey we had a difference of opinion. You conceded to my authority, as you had no choice, but we are both men and I wish to put you straight. You may see the death of the birds as a loss to the world, but I see it as one day in the life of the sea. There are days of profit among days of privation. That is all there is to say on the matter. You will accept that as you will accept the order of this ship, to which, for the time being, you belong.'

176

'I believe you know my position very well,' I said. 'I have not changed my opinion at all.'

He gave me an appraising look. 'I am prepared to offer you a share in our profits.'

I refused to answer him. He faltered. The mention of money was vulgar, and only strengthened my moral position.

'As you wish,' he said, with indifference. He ate some more of the cake, making small appreciative noises as he did so. 'You will do one thing, though,' he said. 'While you are on board this ship you will not stand up to me in front of the men.'

'I understand. I shall not do it.'

'It has been brought to my attention that several of the men are not content with the events on that rock of yours. I simply cannot have dissent among the crew.'

I was surprised. Nothing that I had witnessed had suggested this to me. 'What have you heard?' I asked.

'Fo'c'sle rumours, that is all. But a captain should not hear even that.'

'Who has told you?'

'Mr French,' he replied, simply. 'I rely upon my officers, Mr French in particular, to inform me of all that is going on on board ship. Are you aware of Mr French's role?'

'Yes, I think so,' I said, cautious.

'He is a fool, of course,' Sykes said, lightly, his eyes squinting into narrow slits. 'He failed the navy in peculiar circumstances, that is for sure, but I am duty bound to give him a home here.'

'Why is that?'

'He is family.'

'Family?'

'A distant cousin. My wife believes there is a family resemblance in the way he carries himself, but I fail to see it.'

'I had no idea you were related.'

'It is little known. But you appreciate my point, Mr Saxby. Mr French is my eyes and ears.'

'An aide-de-camp.'

'You could say that.'

'You have nothing to fear from me,' I said, thinking rapidly how this news had altered the situation. French and Sykes, despite their regular spats, were to be considered in a different light. I could not estimate the unknown loyalties they might have.

Sykes pointed to an instrument that was bolted to the ceiling, above his bed. 'That,' he explained, 'is known as a tell-tale compass. I watch it from my pillow. You see, a captain is always at the helm, even when he's not.'

'Mr French was once in the navy?' I asked, trying to sound casual.

'He had an unfortunate – how shall I word it – entanglement,' Sykes said, amusing himself. 'To happier matters,' he continued, brightly. 'I have started a new image in needlework.' He indicated a small desk below the aft window, upon which was a wooden frame and the clear outline, even at this early stage, of a great auk, sitting on a rock.

'You really are a truly heartless man,' I said, half joking, but only half. He decided to laugh, loudly.

'Absolutely!' he replied. 'I am a rare specimen.' He laughed again, and his laugh developed into a hacking cough. His face went red and he held a handkerchief close to his mouth, attempting to muffle it. I had noticed this before, a cough coming through the cabin walls at night, or from on the quarterdeck when he was commanding the course. Once, on the ice floe, a chair had to be brought down to him when his fit would not abate. I had put it down to the rapid changes in temperature, but here I was not so sure. The captain was ill.

Seeing my doubt, Sykes waved his hand at me, as if swatting a fly. 'A trifle,' he said, as he regained control. 'Mrs Sykes claims she can hear my cough even while I am up here in the Arctic sea. It consoles her, she says, to know I am alive.'

'How comforting for her,' I said, sarcastically.

'And what of your upbringing, Mr Saxby? I suppose you went to a fine school?'

'I was privately tutored,' I said. 'My father was a physician, in Suffolk.'

'A boring county, I have heard.'

'A peaceful one.'

'With many illnesses?'

'As many as other counties, I am sure.' I had a fleeting memory of the times I had accompanied my father, visiting the sick. I was eight or nine. How he would enter the labourers' cottages, taking off his hat, and leave me outside to sit in the lane or wander the fields. Drinks would be brought out, but people treated me – even as a child – as someone they did not want near their house. My presence was part of the illness that had settled among them. My father would emerge, straight-backed and gentle, after twenty minutes or so. We would walk in silence to the closest church where he would sketch the architecture, especially the porches. It calmed him, he used to tell me, although I was never sure what it was that he needed calming from. We would make models of these churches, in the evenings, from balsa wood, sitting at a table in the parlour. And while he drew the church architecture, I would scour the graveyard and hedges for bird nests. I had built up a sizeable knowledge and collection of eggs by the time I was fifteen. It was the year my father had died, quickly and without fuss, from an illness he had not diagnosed.

'You are a curious man,' Sykes said, catching me somewhat unawares.

'Why do you say that?' I replied.

'It is my job to know the nature of the passengers I have on board.'

I regarded him, indignantly. 'What makes you so sure of your judgements?' I asked.

He laughed. 'We shall yet be friends, Mr Saxby,' he said. 'Let us shake hands,' he added, rising, offering me his outstretched hand. I shook it, perfunctorily, thinking how rare it is to shake the hand of a man who has conducted an extinction.

The fine weather didn't last long. As we neared Greenland the clouds lowered, brooding, onto a sea that rose in long high swells. Each wave stretched for several hundred yards either side of the ship, as if the surface of the ocean were rolling on iron bars, and French directed a course to meet them straight on, making the bow rise and lower with unpleasant motion. The ship sank heavily into each crest, and the water rose as high as the scuppers. The *Amethyst* headed as it had before, west-south-west, but now the weather was ominous and bleak in that direction, with a horizon that had almost entirely vanished.

On the pretext of examining my luggage, French led me, with a dark-lantern in his hand, to the place where he had concealed the bird on the lower deck. Although the arrangement of the ships was different, I recognised it as the same spot where Captain Bray had stored his frozen polar bear. 'It is in here,' French whispered, giving me the key to a padlock of a small door right under the bow of the ship. 'In the navy, it was not unheard of for a woman of dubious character to be concealed in this spot.'

'Then it is known as a place where people might search?'

'It is safe,' he replied. 'There is already a woman on board this vessel,' he quipped. 'She is pleasing to the eye – so I doubt whether the men would think to search for another.'

'I think that's inappropriate for you to say.'

'Really? Just a comment upon a lady's beauty, in case you hadn't noticed. Perhaps you are immune to such things.'

'Were you in the navy?' I asked.

He visibly stiffened. 'Briefly.'

Inside the locker, he hung the dark-lantern from a roof beam, showing me how I could close the slide to conceal the light. Below it, piled in a heap almost as high as my waist, were the giant links of one of the anchor chains. The light swayed above them, playing with their shapes and shadows, giving them a living, seething, snakelike texture. It was an eerie place. The locker smelt of iron and wet salt, and had the trapped frigid air of an ice-house.

'This is a horrid place,' I said.

'Exactly,' he replied, grinning wolfishly. 'A fine home for prostitutes.'

At that moment the ship must have sunk deeply into a wave. Being so close to the bow, it was as if the floor had risen to hit us. I stumbled against Mr French, who out of experience had braced himself against the door-jamb. I heard the wave sweep above me on the other side of the hull and realised that for a second or two we must have been below water level. The sounds of rushing water fell away as I regained my position, haunted by the feeling of a darkness that had swept through the room, unseen.

'Thank you,' I said. I smelt the scent of his cologne on my lapel.

The great auk was at the back of the space, behind packing crates and surrounded by the heavy outline of the anchor chain. It was a miserable sight. I thought, despite myself, of the dioramas that would be constructed at the world's great museums after they had purchased one of Sykes' skins. How the auks would be mounted on plaster, a few twigs or weeds arranged around their feet, a background painted in colours of the northern Atlantic: slate grey and moss green. The auks would be made to look magnificent, proud and wild and free, so unlike the auk that looked up at me in this horrid locker room. It felt like the darkest space in the world, a space that only men can truly make, filled with cruel machinery and the stench of bitumen and oil. Yet it held the most precious and unique of all of God's creatures. In this foul room, under the greasy light of the dark-lantern, I saw the brilliant flickering glow that only the last can emit.

14

Clara and I met on deck following dinner, waiting for the eight o'clock change between the second dog and first watches. As the crew were handing over in a boisterous manner, we quickly descended the companionway to the lower deck. Beyond the cable-tier we saw barrels and sacking, ropes and tins, metal boxes and wooden crates, all bending with the shadows that moved vaguely across their edges. It was certainly no place for a woman.

'Tread carefully,' I whispered. I held Clara's hand, leading her forward between the crates of the cargo, and her hand felt cool and strong in my own. It is good, I thought, good that she feels determined and calm.

'The bird is in here,' I said as we reached the locker door: 'be aware of the beam when we enter, it is low.'

Inside the locker room, I was relieved to see her undaunted by the smells of oil and iron or the sight of the links of the anchor chain, heaped across the floor.

'Here?' she said.

'Yes, quite the dungeon, isn't it?' I said, trying to be light, pushing against the anchor chain with the toe of my boot. It didn't shift. 'Forgive me bringing you to such a place.

The bird is behind those crates at the side.' I pulled the wooden chest that French and I had positioned, fully expecting the bird to have vanished. But as soon as I had moved the box, there was movement among the shadows, and the pale breast of the auk shuffled as it attempted to remain hidden.

'I can't see it,' she said. We listened as the rough feet of the bird scratched the floor of the locker then, beneath me, the anthracite gleam of the auk's extraordinary beak emerged, like the handle of a dark knife being held towards us. Larger than I had remembered, it was heavily grooved and as ridged as a tribal spear. The beak remained still, impossibly weightless above the floor, then it tilted to one side and the glint of an eye defined itself from the shadows, watching us, unblinking.

'*Shh*,' Clara soothed, 'are you afraid, little one?' The auk reacted to her voice, stumbling to the side and briefly losing its footing.

'It's restrained,' I explained. 'We tied cords around the wings and feet to keep it silent. There is another strap there, to close the beak.'

'Is it necessary?'

'It makes a most incredible growl. A resoundingly deep noise.' Above us, almost in warning, we heard a sudden laugh coming from the fo'c'sle, several feet away through the deck. Footsteps too, although the roof must have been particularly thick and solid. I touched the beam directly above my head, almost the trunk of a tree in width.

'You poor thing,' Clara whispered to the bird, her voice sounding soft and out of place in such a dungeon. 'But you are special – you are a very special creature indeed.'

I brought the dark-lantern down and placed it on the floor, giving, for the first time, a clear view of the great auk, leaning suspiciously away from Clara's hand. It spied the light from the lantern and seemed both curious and afraid, attempting to face it, then backing away. Again it stumbled, hampered by the bindings, and I watched as Clara instinctively reached to loosen the leather strap that was fixed around its beak. I decided not to say anything. She was confident in a way I hadn't anticipated. The bird allowed it, apparently soothed by the swift but careful way that Clara freed the knot, as if she was undressing a wound.

'There,' she whispered, satisfied, as she removed the strap. The auk shook its head, quickly, the plumage ruffling and flattening in a girdling motion as if it had been blown; then its beak opened, unhinging and closing several times with a small, dry click. She reached further, touching the bird on its back, stroking it along the neck and down towards its wings. I watched as the bird settled, lowering onto its feet and eyeing her, steadily.

'You have a gift,' I said.

'Yes, it has been said before.' She addressed the bird again: 'We are going to look after you, my love. Don't worry, you'll be free again, soon.'

It was unexpectedly poignant. Faced with the reality of the bird's incarceration, the grimness of the locker room – its menacing anchor chain, its smells of oil and turpentine – Clara had responded with a simple clarity of affection and care that gave me enormous hope.

Before I could prevent myself, I had reached out to touch her hair. My hand was already halfway there, poised, a few inches above her head. Staring at my fingers, in disbelief and elation, I watched as they traced the outline of the hair I so wanted to caress, to stroke, to call my own. This woman, once lost to me, now again so close, so very close. Beneath me, her shoulders tensed.

'What are you doing?' she asked.

Caught, I stumbled for an explanation, rapidly withdrawing my hand. 'I thought I heard someone approaching. But I must be mistaken.'

She turned to face me. 'Who would be down here, at this time?'

'Yes, quite.'

'Do they inspect this place?'

'No,' I said. 'We're safe here. Mr French was quite certain of it.'

'If we were discovered in here together, we would be the subject of a scandal,' she said. 'This ship is a gossiper's paradise – I am taking a risk being with you.'

'Yes. I know.'

'Scandal seems to seek me out.'

The auk appeared peaceful. 'You have done a wonderful thing here, Eliot,' she told me. 'Is this really the last one on the planet?'

'Without doubt.'

'Do you think it knows?'

I wondered. Had it seen the rest of its group slain? Can a bird have a notion of its own survival, its own unique self? I doubted it, and hoped that it couldn't be the case.

'I think not,' I replied. 'I have started to study it,' I added, squatting to Clara's level. 'Before it is released, I intend to be quite comprehensive. My notes will perhaps be invaluable one day. Notice how strong it is in the wing, yet they are totally unfit for flight. They are merely paddles. When we were on the rock, I watched them swimming in the sea. They were fast and very buoyant – yet on the land were as clumsy as old geese. It was easy – well – for the men to gather them in their coats. And that beak – it is really the largest I have ever seen on any seabird. When they were standing together they made a communal growling. It was a startling sound. Do you think it seems well?'

She considered the bird closely. 'I think so. It is hard to see. What are these?'

'Further bindings. Mr French advised it, to hold the wings. He was afraid it might escape.'

'From here?'

'He said it was a tenacious creature and he didn't want to see it running about on deck.'

I placed on the floor a dish containing strips of cod from my breakfast. The bird eyed the dish and its food suspiciously. 'We must give it time,' I suggested, easing back. When the bird moved, an oily shine, almost iridescent, flashed across the back of its neck. Its beak was truly huge and wondrous, the ridges carved into it as if sculpted by a chisel. It gave the auk an ancient expression.

'He has a general's face,' Clara said.

'Yes, like Caesar.'

Clara picked up a strip of the cod and held it towards the bird. The auk leant back, warily, then in a quick movement it opened its beak and took the fish with its head angled sharply to the side. She laughed happily, shrugging her shoulders like a child and looking at me with complete satisfaction.

'Astonishing!' I said. 'Clara you are a *magician*!'

'Thank you,' she replied, squeezing my hand. Expecting her to let go, I was surprised when she continued to hold me.

'And you must thank Mr French for making this possible.'

'I have learnt something,' I replied. 'Mr French is a cousin, or distant cousin, to our own captain.'

'Oh,' she replied, letting my hand go. 'That may change things.'

'Hopefully not, but we must be careful.' Even mentioning

the man seemed to bring the scent of his cologne into the room.

'How did you learn this?'

'From Sykes himself. He told me in his cabin. He claims they have a special obligation to each other.'

'What kind of *obligation*?'

'Well, perhaps that is something we have yet to learn.'

Clara was thoughtful. 'I have something to admit, too,' she said. 'I have told Edward everything.'

'About the bird?'

'Yes.'

'Why? Is that wise?'

She looked a little insulted, so I quickly attempted an explanation: 'I say that only because he is behaving in a strange manner.'

'I think knowing about this bird, and its survival, it might give him a cause,' she said, 'for hope.'

'But what if, during a strange mood, he were to tell the captain?'

Clara was amused. 'Edward and the captain are not friends. Edward believes the captain is determined to make a fool of him. Haven't you noticed?'

'I'm afraid I haven't.'

She reached up and brushed my cheek with a finger. 'No, there are many things you fail to notice, aren't there?'

That night, as I lay in my bunk, my mind raced with thoughts of Clara, of her touch, the coolness of her fingers, her expression. But also I thought about the girl I had known as Celeste, who had similarly possessed my spirit. It was inescapable. I would never be free of her. I never wanted to be free of her. But just what had she meant by touching me? Had I imagined it? In the middle of the night all things are possible.

I tried to calm myself by concentrating on the great auk, hidden in its grim locker between the giant links of the chain and the containers of oils. I thought of its eye, dark and wild, among the shadows, and the bindings around its wings and legs. Survival, but at the cost of freedom. Perhaps on these terms it was no survival at all.

At about three in the morning, still not asleep, I heard a commotion coming from on deck. Several voices were raised and a laugh rang out, rough and clear. I lifted the felt curtain from my porthole and looked across the dark ocean. The clouds were brooding, overlapping in blooms of density like writing ink spilt in water. Then I saw below them, in the distance, as black as driftwood, the unmistakable outline of cliffs. Jagged and hideously cruel, they had the appearance of rotten teeth jutting from the sea.

I watched, transfixed by such a bleak and lonely view, and decided to go on deck. I only reached the saloon. Because as soon as I had opened the latch to my cabin, I was halted by the sight of Edward Bletchley, sitting in his customary arm-chair next to the wood-burner. His legs were straight out in front of him, as stiff as a corpse, and his head was slumped forwards so that his chin rested almost on his chest. He appeared dead, or dead asleep, but as I walked up to him he opened his eyes and fixed me with a strange, bleary gaze.

'Aha,' he said, vaguely, before shutting his eyes again.

I stood, unsure what to do. The fire had been damped to its slowest burn, to last the night, so only the faintest glow shone through the glass. The only other illumination was from the oil lamp that hung in the rear of the saloon. It spread a grey-ish half-light, similar to the Arctic dusk, throughout the room, and cast a stony pallor on Bletchley's face. He resembled a cemetery sculpture guarding his chosen grave.

'You cannot sleep,' Bletchley said, his eyes opening once

more. In his expression I saw a drifting consciousness which roamed, before settling with renewed focus upon me.

'You too?' I replied.

He bent his legs slowly. 'I can, but choose not to.'

I stepped up to the wood-burner and rubbed my hands above its hotplate. A constant dry warmth rose there, but it was hardly enough to warm the room.

'We are passing Greenland,' I said.

Bletchley didn't reply. Again I saw a glaze of something dark and clouded drift across his eyes. He frowned, as if trying to understand what I had just told him.

'I am not surprised you are unable to sleep,' he said, quickly. 'You are full of many secrets.'

I thought I would sit by him, thinking he was unpredictable and to do so might prevent him raising his voice. The saloon at night was an intensely quiet place, the cabin doors were of thin wood and I had no knowledge of who might be listening.

'I am?' I replied.

He raised a finger and pretended to admonish me, as if I was a child. 'Oh come, come, Eliot, we should not play games.'

I smiled at him, steadily, certain that he was drunk.

'My cousin is an attractive woman,' he said.

'What of it?'

'Most attractive. I know you have a similar – how should I put it – *appreciation* of her.'

'You are talking about Clara.'

'Cla-ra. Yes. The fashion for such ringlets is beguiling, I feel they resemble a spaniel's ears, but really, she is beautiful.' He focused on a point in the air between us and, strangely, lifted a hand as if to move it away. There was nothing there. His fingers made a little brushing motion. 'She

190

is precious to me, you understand that, Eliot? I told you of our special connection, didn't I? How we used to lie in our beds and communicate with each other?' He placed the palm of his hand upon his throat, then, quite deliberately and slowly, he stroked it down his chest and onto his thigh, purposefully sensuous. I was appalled. 'She is like a piece of sunshine that we have brought with us,' he said. 'There is very little sunshine in the Arctic seas, have you noticed? But we have it, on board. We have the sunshine with us, among the shadows.'

I stood, determined to leave him at once. Whether he was drunk or not, his incoherence was alarming. He raised his hand again, trying to prevent me leaving. 'Do you think,' he whispered, with stage theatricality, 'that you will get away with it?'

Looking down, I saw him as prone and vulnerable in his chair, almost childlike, his stockinged feet pointing in at each other. A slump to his right shoulder made him look injured. He was pathetic.

'Yes,' I said, finding an unexpected certainty in my voice. 'I think I will get away with it.'

Bletchley laughed, loudly. 'A drink then, Eliot, to the sea-witch you have brought on board. A drink to the last great auk.' He lifted a large silver hip flask and offered it to me.

'Please keep your voice down.'

'A drink!'

'I would rather not,' I said.

'Nonsense,' he replied. '*Non*-sense.' He unscrewed the cap and poured a healthy measure into a small glass he had on the table.

'Greenland, you say?'

'Yes.'

'You are agitated, Eliot. I can tell it, in here.' He tapped his forehead. 'Your mind is burning from the inside. Have this, it will mollify you.'

He gave me the glass. I smelt it, but didn't recognise the origin of the spirit. It had an unusual greenish colour.

'I do not think so,' I repeated.

'Please have a drink with me. Or else I will do something.'

'You are sounding foolish.'

'I will shout.'

'I have had enough of this. Go to your cabin right now and lie on your bed. You are delirious.'

Edward Bletchley took a deep breath and opened his mouth. I really feared that he was on the verge of doing just what he had threatened – that he would shout, God knows what.

I downed the measure of spirit. 'Satisfied?' I said. The drink was sweet and woody, similar to anisette and not at all unpleasant, but I still could not place it.

'Another, and you will sleep like a baby,' he said, kindly.

I drank a second measure, fuller this time, by way of taking my leave of him. 'The drink is poisoning your mind, Edward. You will become ill and useless,' I said.

'But at least, not sober. At least that, my friend.'

'Go to your room,' I said, turning towards my own cabin.

As I lay on my bunk I heard Bletchley stumbling towards his cabin. A candlestick fell loudly on the dining table. He probably would not remember our encounter by the morning, but it still unsettled me greatly. I stared up at the ceiling, perceiving a strange thickness to the air, an underwater quality that made the knots and joints of the wood swim and reassemble and fade. I thought of the coast of Greenland, several miles across the ocean, and its dark-toothed cliffs felt like the jaws of a mantrap that was widening around the ship.

Soon, I felt a pressing weight almost pushing me into my

bunk, a darkness growing, sweeping into the room as I had felt in the great auk's locker when the wave passed outside, and I was ushered into a terribly deep sleep as if a burial cloak had been laid across me.

I woke almost immediately, sensing calamity. There is no one, I thought, to witness our sinking! There is no one to survive this! There is no hope. It was a feeling so strong, so overwhelming, that I gripped the smooth rail at the edge of the bunk. In the dim light I looked at each of my fingers, an inch or two away from my face, faithfully holding the wood; the clenched grip of a drowned man.

In the same instant I realised there was something far closer and more present to alarm me. Within my cabin, I became aware of a solid shape in the shadows near the foot of the bunk.

I was suddenly, intensely awake. There were only two sources of illumination coming into the cabin. One, a glimmer of pale grey light where the thick felt curtains didn't quite meet the frame, and a second glow coming under the doorway, where the night-lantern left on in the saloon shone on the varnished planks. It was in this light that I could see a pair of boots in my cabin. Man's boots.

I sat up. 'Is someone there?' I asked, reaching for my oil lamp and tray of matches. My fingers were shaking as I struck the first match, and in the brief initial flare of the flame I saw a startling vision: a man, hooded in sealskins and fur, looking directly at me from the foot of the bunk. Smoke curled up where the match hadn't caught, and the vision disappeared, like a theatrical trick.

Struck more slowly, a second match caught, and I managed to light the wick of the lamp. The glow sprang across the room and illuminated the man. I saw his pupils contracting. I had never seen this man before.

'Who are you?' I said, afraid.

The man was large, broad-shouldered and heavily bearded. A hood of fur-lined sealskin was pulled low across his forehead. His nose looked cracked and raw and the skin on his cheeks had a frozen, worn roughness to it. A thick and unkempt moustache overhung his mouth entirely, joining a grey and black beard, but it was the eyes that impressed me most. They were startling, jet black, and piercing.

'Who *are you?*' I repeated.

The man leant forward, bracing his arms on his knees. He seemed curious.

'Do you speak English?' I asked.

I heard the hems in his coat cracking. His clothes were ragged. The sealskin overcoat was frayed and scratched and stained with dried blood and oil. Rough repairs and patches had been sewn into it with strong stitching of a twine cut from skin. The trousers, too, had several layers, of hides wrapped and bound or stitched into each other. I waited, appalled and confused. 'I understand,' I said, at length. 'I understand that I'm dreaming this.'

The Arctic is the place for dreams, the man replied in a sombre, deep voice. I almost cried out in terror.

It was silent again. 'Do you have a name?' I asked.

I tried to think rationally. 'Why are you here?'

He squinted, his eyes almost disappearing in the creases and shadows of his face.

'What *was* your name?' I asked.

His voice was quieter now, as if he was moving away. *They called me Huntsman.*

15

That was my first vision. The following morning I woke agitated from my dream, for I could not think of it as being anything other than a fantasy. It had been an outrageous and disturbing vision. A man, a stranger, had sat at the foot of my bed, watching me while I slept, and the details of him – the smell of his rough seal coat, the cracking sound it had made as he moved – felt more real than I could account for. Even at breakfast, I still felt his presence, and with it an awareness that the ship had a troubling new dimension to its empty cargo spaces and bare decks. Among the shadows that filled the hull, or against the grains of wood and coils of rope, at any time I might see him again.

Simao served me, polite and attentive as always, but I could tell he was aware of my anxious state. Bletchley, too, who emerged from his cabin with his customary loud yank of the latch, but then stood so awkwardly, staring at the fire, then at the back-rest of his chair, and finally at the companionway door, that I knew he must be remembering parts of the conversation he and I had shared the night before. *Do you think you will get away with it?* he had said, enigmatically. It still hung in the air as an unanswered question between us. *I can tell it, in here,* he had added, tapping his forehead as if he were privy to my inner thoughts. *Your mind is burning from the inside.* The man was in a very dangerous state, that much I knew. And it seemed the only possible conclusion that it had been his drink, with the strange but not unpleasant odour, that had conjured up the vision.

Bletchley was uninterested in having food. In fact, I had rarely seen him eat during the previous few days. Unshaven, roughly dressed, with one wing of his collar sticking upright, he stamped his boots into place over his stockings, issued a rough 'good morning' to clear his throat, and went up on deck. I was glad not to have to deal with him.

'You are not well,' Simao asked, with the tone of a statement.

'I had a troubling night,' I answered.

'The sea runs many ways in this area,' he said, weaving his fingers together as explanation. 'The ship ...' He began to rock his hands.

'Maybe that's it,' I said, happy with his normality, his constancy. Beyond him, I saw the companionway door swinging eerily on its hinges. I was again haunted by a presence of something I could not explain.

'We are in sight of Greenland,' Clara said to me as she stepped from her cabin arranging a bonnet on her head. It had an aigrette of grebe feathers, pinned to one side. I watched her fingers tying a small bow in the silk ribbon, fixing it under her chin. On her skin I noticed a dot of reflected shine from the apricot silk, as one does the glow of a buttercup held in the same place, and I realised that Clara's health had continued to improve.

'I saw it, during the night,' I replied.

'I will be on deck, if you would like to join me when you are finished,' she said, kindly.

'I will.'

I sat through my breakfast alone, listening to the sounds of crewmen winding the bilge pump, a duty they performed at eight bells each morning. Simao brought me oatmeal, tripe in egg batter, bread and preserves, but all I had was coffee, which Simao refilled three times and eventually he left the pot by my side. I tried a glass of ship's water, but it tasted of rhubarb and rust. 'The water is foul,' I said.

'We will get fresh in Greenland,' Simao answered, apologetically. Then he removed the uneaten food without comment.

On deck I watched the coast passing several miles away to the north. It was barren, utterly treeless, and coloured with dark browns and greens as if it had risen, stained and weeded, from the ocean bed. It lay with this stranded aspect, so gullied and interrupted with islands and inlets that its true coast was impossible to perceive. Only in the distance, where the hills rose into bleak and cruel mountains covered in ice and mist, could I imagine a land that stretched without barrier almost to the top of the world.

I joined Clara as she watched the many islands and fjords that allowed glimpses into a sheltered coastline. She informed me that a man had been put on ice watch, at the bow. I could tell she was perturbed. She laughed quickly. 'Eliot,' she said, 'striking an iceberg would be doing us a service. This land is such a desolate sight, I wish I had never seen it. Isn't that how you feel, also? But still, it's right to face things with an unflinching eye. I would rather face it than turn my back upon it.'

'Clara, I need to tell you something. Last night, I had the vision of a ghost in my cabin.'

Her expression dropped sharply. 'What do you mean? Did you know him?'

'No. He was a stranger.'

'What kind of stranger?'

'A hunter,' I said, sounding and feeling foolish. 'An Arctic hunter. It was merely a dream, Clara, there is no other explanation, but it was so *vivid*, so unnatural. He was as real as you are, right now. He was in my cabin, dressed in animal skins, watching me as I slept. It was his presence that awoke me.'

'But you said you were dreaming?'

'I was. It must have been a dream.'

'Did he speak?'

'I think so, although it is difficult to remember. I believe he told me his name. Huntsman.'

She listened attentively.

'It followed,' I continued, 'a most distressing discussion with your cousin.' I explained how I had discovered him, in a half-conscious state, sitting in his chair by the wood-burner – so stiff and still that I had initially considered placing a mirror in front of his mouth to see if he was breathing. Then I explained the volatility of his mood and, in short, how peculiar and aggressive he had been. I stopped short of relaying what he had said about her. How he had run his hand down his body in a crude and vulgar way.

'Edward can occasionally enter a very strange disposition,' she explained. 'But he tends to forget what he has said. From his attitude this morning I should think he is unlikely to remind you of your talk. Even so, we should be careful not to spend too much time together.'

'Why?'

She laughed, quickly. 'Because he is so *jealous*.' She brushed her hand against mine. 'He has been warning me against you. He says that you are hiding something.'

'How ridiculous – Clara, don't listen to him – he is ill.'

'He has a playful mind, that is all.'

'But he knows about the bird,' I tried, chasing a doubt I couldn't explain. 'It may have been a rash decision to have told him.'

With some dismay, I saw that she agreed. 'Yes,' she said, 'probably it was my mistake. But last night I thought about the bird and it seemed so perilous. It is so dear and so vulnerable surrounded by all this. We will need allies – we will need Edward, I'm sure of it.'

Whether prompted by this, or by a feeling of being watched, I remember turning then and noticing Quinlan French, pacing the quarterdeck with the captain. He was a good half-foot taller than the older man, but was stooping to make this less apparent. At one point I saw him brush something from the captain's shoulder, and they both laughed.

We saw a whale later that day. My first glimpse of it was a shot of steam which appeared impossibly from the surface of the ocean, about a mile distant. It was followed by the sound of men's boots as they dashed to the side, full of excitement, as they leant out across the bow rail, pointing, one or two lifting their caps in mock greeting. The steam lingered, cone shaped, as if a cannon had fired from that part of the water. A couple of seconds later, as the mysterious plume dispersed, we heard a great rasp of breath across the deck, accompanied by a cheer from the men. I remember looking above me, for it had seemed that some parts of the sound of that breath echoed from the sails.

'It has a calf, sir,' someone shouted from the front, in a thick Irish accent.

I went to join them at the bow, and noticed fairly rapidly that the helmsman was bringing the ship towards the area where the whale was surfacing. Breaks of white water could be seen where the blows of breath erupted. I was very excited. This was not only the first whale of the voyage, but the first whale I had ever seen.

I was quickly informed that, by the peculiarity of the spout being a V shape, this was most definitely a right whale, and if I were to look closely I would distinguish the separate profiles of a mother and her calf rising alongside each other.

I was thrilled that the ship was bringing us closer to this spectacle, presumably for the benefit of the passengers, so I went to fetch Clara. 'Why are we steering towards the whale?' I asked one of the men in passing.

'That'll be Mr French, sir. He likes his sport with them.' From the look on the faces of the men I saw the sport was well anticipated.

'I can't wait,' I said.

'Oh, it'll be fine, sir. That it will.'

The men were so full of a joy that was rare to see that I felt happy with them. For the first time since being on Eldey, I sensed they welcomed my presence among them.

I brought Clara on deck so we could admire the sight. The long smooth back of the mother could be seen, rising elegantly in a curve that barely interrupted the water before descending. A couple of seconds later, a smaller back rose alongside, in perfect imitation. A breath blew up to mix with the larger one that still hung in the air. They swam in this perfect rhythm, a graceful running stitch through the miles of the sea, their backs arching as smooth as horse saddles. Occasionally the edge of a fluke would lift from the water, point hesitantly as if in a partial wave, before slapping the surface and pushing the whale lower.

The direction of the *Amethyst* was clearly at an intersection to the line the whales were making. We were closing the distance rapidly, and it was a beautiful motion, bringing us towards these magnificent creatures who were oblivious of our presence. Petrels and ivory gulls dived repeatedly into their wakes. As I watched, with Clara at my side, I felt a certain timelessness, that these journeying whales were on some invisible route through the oceans that they must have followed for many thousands of years. We were privileged to witness it.

As if the presence of the ship were a great magnet, repelling the bodies of the whales, their course started to bend away from us. First, the mother began to turn, creating a small distance from her calf which, by instinct, the calf closed. An adjustment was made to our own route, and the *Amethyst* steered until ship and whales colluded in a curving line in the sea that might be the beginning of a spiral.

'The helmsman must be careful,' Clara whispered to me, 'or we will strike them.'

'Yes,' I replied. 'I believe Mr French is giving quite close instruction.'

Below our bow we followed the choppy trail of white foam the whales left in their wake. Their backs rose, as before, but not as smoothly. The tail flukes lifted erratically, being brought down in a vigorous fashion, slapping the water with the sound of laundry being smacked dry on a washboard. The mother could now be seen almost in her entirety, both above and below the water, occasionally turning on her side, possibly so that she could watch us.

'Do you think they are becoming distressed?' I asked Clara.

When I turned to face her, as she had not replied, I found she was looking beyond me, to the men.

'What is the matter?' I asked.

'Those,' she said, pointing along the rail. I looked, immediately appalled to see guns being handed out by Mr French.

201

'No,' I said, quietly, realising how naive I had been, watching the ship being brought closer to these creatures and yet not expecting it would end like this.

'I cannot watch this, Eliot,' Clara said, urgently.

'Mr French!' I shouted. 'What is going on?'

'A little sport, that is all,' he replied, directing his men to the task at hand. 'Do not worry, the bullet is a mere pinprick to them.'

A rifle was fired. I saw the ball enter the water, below the hump of the whale's rising back. It had absolutely no effect; as if the bullet had vanished into glass. Other shots were fired in succession, as Clara flinched next to me. The men fired freely and as fast as they could reload, clouding us with a hot stink of gunpowder as bullet after bullet went into the backs of the whales. Someone yelled with disappointment, 'They can't feel 'em, sir!' and I saw French nodding, his gaze intent and bloodthirsty on the sport that was now taking place virtually below us. The whales thrashed clumsily, the mother's tail crashed down upon the back of her calf, and in the melee I saw French's long arm raised above his head directing quick adjustments to the course being steered by the helmsman.

The ship veered across the path of the whales and the bow was brought straight and as heavy as a lock gate right against the animals.

'*Stop them! Oh stop them!*' Clara begged me as, below us, with a deep sickening crunch the ship struck one of the whales.

'Yes, yes,' I promised, trying to push the men away as they came down the rail. Right beneath where I stood, a long and impossible flank of pure black skin was rolling to one side, as dark as polished basalt. The animal was stunned, but still pulsing frantically, as if a thrust of its tail might yet lever the ship from its path.

I noticed French, forcing his way towards us. 'The *calf*, you fools!' he shouted. 'Aim for the calf, you bastards! Stop the calf and we have the mother.'

The men raced past, leaning over the rail and shooting wildly beneath the ship or hurling loose weights and spars of wood down at the animals. Despite the scramble there was much laughter and calling out. I was knocked to one side and instantly I felt Clara grasp my hand and pull at my elbow. I turned to see her face, close and wet with tears, as she buried herself in the front of my jacket. I held her, as any man would have done, feeling her sobbing against my chest and, amid the smoke and the rough smell of the men and the blasts of the guns, I smelt the scent of her hair – the scent of hops and attar of roses I had smelt before – and felt the tight-fingered grip of her hands reaching round my middle, beneath my jacket.

'Oh Clara,' I whispered. 'Let me save you.'

She raised her head and looked into my eyes, a few inches away from me. What I saw there was an instant acknowledgement, an understanding that yes, that was what she wanted. I was sure of it.

I led her towards the saloon, bearing her weight. The saloon would be a sanctuary not touched by the callousness and violence of men. That is what I hoped and what I promised her. Simao joined us, holding Clara's other arm and sensing that she might be about to faint. A few hundred yards behind us in the ocean, the two whales had come to a halt. A small tail, belonging to the calf, was raised at an unnatural angle, pointing to the sky like a broken weathervane. The mother thrashed alongside it. A couple of shots rang out; each time a gun went off I felt Clara's body tense, and for the first time I saw the captain, not looking at the whales but ordering the ship's course to be corrected.

203

'Don't waste your shots,' he ordered.

At the companionway door, with Clara virtually limp between Simao and myself, I turned, feeling the sensation of someone watching me. A few yards away, French was facing us. He stood, rifle in hand: the rigid stance of a hunter excited with the heat of his blood. But what shocked me was the look in his eyes. With an unguarded expression he glared at me as I led Clara away. It was a look of accusation.

16

Rowing across the bay, I noticed clouds of grey effluent suspended beneath us. The water had been dark and crystal clear, but suddenly it had turned murky, and in the gloom I watched nameless sections of carcasses, fluke tips and dorsal fins, jawbones and ragged white-fleshed cartilage, all swaying eerily above the seabed.

Across the shore this same carnage continued in a filthy tideline. The boulders were slick with grease and had torn strips of dried flesh on them. There was a large congregation of birds: gulls and skuas squabbling and rising, watched judiciously by ravens as black as anthracite. Stinkpot petrels too, sitting happily, at home among offensive odours that only their foul bodies could equal. They scavenged the shore, pulling at the debris and hovering and crying in a frenzy of feeding and appetite.

The whaling station stretched along the bay for several hundred yards. Huts had been built of ship's planking, caulked and tarred and smeared with rendered oils to make them weatherproof. In front of them and alongside, large winches stood among the stones and cables snaked across the shore, some of them reaching straight out into the bay.

Perhaps twenty Danish men lived there, rendering and

junking the whales, seals and walruses that were brought throughout the Arctic summer until the weather closed in. They were as dirty as Bray's crew on the *Jester*, dressed in flushing jackets on their backs and shoulders, and some with cow-tail wigs upon their heads. I was told they were made from the roughest wool sheared from the sheep's hind legs, and must have been remarkably itchy upon the scalp. They wore long fishermen's boots at least a yard in length, that were as wide as tree trunks, giving their legs a curiously elephantine look.

I was shown around by an enthusiastic boy called Johannes, who spoke some English and made up for the rest of it with intricate hand gestures, explaining the processes of sizing and slicing and boiling the blubber before it was barrelled and stored. He had the blondest hair I have ever seen, almost pure white, somehow untouched by the grime and dust that covered virtually every other surface.

'We boil,' he said, proudly, at the entrance to the try-works shed. Inside, four men worked in a pall of greyish-black smoke, as if they were stoking hell itself, loading cauldrons with the rendered strips of flensing. The smoke was oily and had a distinctly fishy aroma, and parts of it carried a fine ash that could be tasted on the tongue. I held my sleeve to my nose against the smell. 'You breathe in the mouth, it is better,' Johannes advised, leading me away. 'My pallet,' he said, pointing into a shed with a curtained door but no window. He made a hand gesture of *to the right and high* as if explaining exactly where in the shed his bed was. 'And there is the place we eat,' he said, showing me a section of the shore where long trestle tables had been set up.

Overhead, the barbarous skuas intimidated the other birds into dropping their catches. The men had learnt to ignore the birds and the hellish shrieking they made. Occasionally, as a man walked across the shingle, he might try to kick a path between the scavengers, but work was obviously hard and harassing the birds was a job not worth undertaking.

'We see whale, come come,' Johannes said, eagerly. As I was led I noticed French, a list of stores in his hand, regarding me. He was apparently amused at the tour I was being given, as if I was a visiting dignitary. He smiled, but not for the first time I considered it an expression that he found uncomfortable, as if his face could not quite sustain it. As he looked down at his list of trading goods, the remnant of the smile was closer to a sneer. I recalled the moment when I had fallen against his shoulder, in the anchor locker. The scent of his cologne. The hard fleshless aspect of his chest.

Johannes pointed out the bundles of rolled-up sealskins, barrels of salted meat, eider down, feathers, seal oil and white whale oil, with an attitude of great satisfaction. But he knew the most impressive sight was further along the shore. He led me to a section of beach that had become a whale graveyard. Three whales, or parts of three whales, had been tethered to the rocks with long cables, from where they stretched half submerged into the water like staved-in boats. They had been stripped of their blubber, leaving a visceral mess of oyster grey and vivid red matter partially spilt, partially held in place by the structures of bone and cartilage that remained intact.

'The whale, you see,' Johannes explained, 'is finished.'

I nodded in grim understanding. As the water lapped around the bodies they rose, eerie and wallowing, and the water that surrounded them was a fetid cloud of foam and grease. The smell was appalling, quite honestly the worst smell I have ever experienced, and it was only being this close to the dead whales that I realised the origin of the curious odour everywhere in the bay. Even the birds were reluctant to gather in this spot, although this had obviously not always been the case, as the bodies had been badly pecked and shredded by tools that were not entirely man made.

'The stench is horrid,' I told Johannes.

He held his nose, grinning. 'I have lost my nose.'

I laughed, hoping it might prompt us to leave the carcasses, but Johannes was keen for me to study the whales' anatomy that was revealed here in all its complications. I began to appreciate the sheer size of these creatures, how heavy they must have been, and how strongly muscled and smooth the contours of their bodies still were. They did indeed seem animals of mystery, even in this form. Those bodies had made great journeys, they had known deep oceans and bleak coastlines, star-filled Arctic nights when the aurora borealis had spanned the sky, forming a glittering path they could follow. They had dived beneath the waves and had heard the bellows and moans of other whales, several hundred miles away. They had followed migratory routes passed down from generation to generation. And to finish in this state, chained, then peeled as one might an orange, discarded on this abhorrent shoreline. I realised they had never truly revealed their secrets. Somehow, miraculously, a shred of their dignity remained.

'Let us go,' I asked Johannes, quietly.

French had made the men assemble some of the ship's stores around him so that he could detail their contents for the station's commander, an elderly man with an odd-shaped leather hat pulled low across his forehead. As the list was read out, the commander kept removing his cap so he could rub his head with his sleeve.

French read in a monotone, obviously unhappy to perform a shopkeeper's duty. '... lances, towline, toggle irons, gun irons, boat masts and booms ...'

'We have no need of the masts.'

'... cask flagging, cask sawdust, a turning lathe ...'

'... that is good.'

'... percussion caps, two quarts of flints, fish line, jack-knives, sheath knives. You had those last year. I should strike them off. Let's see, various manilas, hemp twine, wax, window frames and glass, hacksaws, wire of varying thickness, screws, nails, putty, linseed and turpentine oil, sandpaper, rifles and ammunition, sets of loading tools, cookery ware, pipes, tobacco and playing cards.' French raised his hand, preventing the commander from interrupting: 'Also flour, beef, pork, rice, meal, coffee, tea, vinegar, butter, soap, dried apples, sugar, corned beef, pears, potatoes, onions, mustard, spices, beans, peas, raisins, codfish, molasses and pickles.'

The commander had begun to laugh.

French straightened. 'What is so amusing?' he asked.

'You, sir,' the commander replied. 'You do this every year.'

'Do what?'

'You bore me with your list. Can you not see I have eyes?'

'It is my duty,' French replied, vexed.

'Ja, ja, your job.'

'Any Esquimaux?' French asked, impatient to change the subject.

The commander pointed to a position a few hundred yards away up the slope of a valley, where several huts could be seen, their roofs made of turf.

'They trade?'

'Furs.'

'Good, we have beads and needles and hooks and the like. We'll visit when we fill with water from the stream. I wish to have a bathe. How's the water?'

'Straight from heaven.'

*

During the afternoon I wandered up the valley, following a brook that bubbled joyously through the rocks. I picked several Arctic buttercups, their yellow petals fresh drips of egg yolk against the darker greens of the sedge and mosses. I identified pink lousewort, dwarf willowherb and Arctic cinquefoil. But there were many grasses and flowers of a kind I had never seen before, nor could identify in my botanical guide. These were not the soft-petalled flowers of East Anglia, but small robust blooms of mauve, white and yellow, as if they had been dipped in ship's varnish. The air was cool and fresh and a pale sun shone into the bay across the water. I felt a relief to be alone, away from the ship. But the natural subtlety of these flowers made me homesick, for a softness and peace that I associated only with England – and East Anglia in particular. The lavender light of late summer, whose echo I had occasionally seen along the western Arctic horizon, and the dry flaxen colour of the harvest crops. The estuaries in Suffolk and Norfolk, reflecting a morning sky as pure blue as a goshawk's egg. The hang of the willows over silent river pools. I missed them deeply. No other place than East Anglia – where the land is held in a cradle of tides swinging back and forth – can give such a feeling of balance, such equilibrium.

Occasionally a breeze descended from the crags, making me turn away from its chill. It was an Arctic breath, sterile and still frozen, without life or scent, reminding me that beyond the valley was a thousand miles of ice desert. It was as if Greenland had been rubbed away in its centre. It made me reluctant to venture far from the whaling station and the view of the *Amethyst* in the bay beyond. They say that men swimming from a ship in the middle of the ocean will not leave the side, because the thought of the depths beneath and the miles around are too much to comprehend. And I felt a little of this too, that however revolting the whaling station was, it was my only connection to the world that I came from. I recognised it, understood it, and it was where I belonged.

With my collar turned up against the cold air, I bent down to pick a variety of the flowers and folded them into the leaves of my notebook. I would give them to Clara when I returned to the ship. I would give them to her and I would tell her that she was as rare and as beautiful as anything I'd ever known. That she was as miraculous as these drops of colour that had grown from the Arctic waste. They would look pretty, set in her hair or hanging as a posy from her wrist. Beauty needs to gather in such a place as the Arctic. Among the sedge, I reached to pull some of the stems, and I smelt the damp scent of mud. Mud, and sodden vegetation – the hint of an English woodland. Not just a general smell, but one woodland in particular, I realised with a shudder, where the ground had turned marshy, where rhododendrons grew so densely they blocked out the light and, among them, the silent dark waters of a lake covered in lily pads.

I left the flowers where I'd picked them.

Down the slope, where the stream crossed the shore, I noticed French, standing naked, pouring a bucket of water over his head. His pale skin made him look like a candle set among the dark stones. I watched him slick his hair back with a comb, before he walked to the pile of clothes he had left on a boulder. For a while he stared, naked, towards the ship across the water.

There were half a dozen houses in the Esquimaux settlement beyond the brook, built with low rock walls and buried, it appeared, in the turf and grasses of their roofs. Thin grey lines of smoke rose from the buildings, and the ground surrounding them was worn away to bare earth. Several of the

Esquimaux could be seen, tending to racks along the side of the largest house. From this distance they looked small and wide in body, moving deliberately and without hurry. Children played outside the dark doorway of one of the houses, throwing stones against a small cairn, and I heard the faint sound of the pebbles landing. The sound of each pebble vanished quickly in such a large landscape.

As I began to walk back to the whaling station, I noticed one of the Esquimaux children, standing in thick sealskin trousers and no jacket, waving at me. I waved back and held my arm in the air for a long time. I saw him point to the sky, then down at the ground. I copied his gesture. As he began to do it again, we did the gesture together – up at the sky, then down at the ground.

That evening we ate around a large fire that had been set on the shore, while the crew of the *Amethyst* and the Danish whalers mallymarked with dances and songs. They forgot they could not talk a common language, or had drunk enough Akavit not to notice. French had returned to the ship after his bathing, not wanting to mix further with the men. Unsurprisingly, we were offered whale meat. On a butcher's table, a piece of flesh had been laid out, as long as a cow's leg and consisting of the most remarkably dark and smooth meat I had ever seen. There was absolutely no gristle or fat to it, and hardly any grain. In the twilight it was as black and impenetrable as obsidian, yet to the touch it was as soft as butter, leaving an impression of my finger long after I had removed it. One of the Danish men cut it with a cruelly long carving knife into steaks, as wide and as thick as a man's hand, which he then slapped onto a hot greased skillet. Each steak sizzled quickly, curling up in lifelike contraction, before the cook flipped them to seal on the other side. I watched,

212

fascinated by the darkness of the steak, and struck by a meat that still recoiled from man's touch.

I glanced at the row of men on the other side of the fire, who were watching the preparation of the meal. I had become used to the thickly bearded faces of the sailors and the roughness of their skin and clothing, but at that instant – lit by the devilish flicker of wild flames – these men looked ancient and harsh. They lived their lives on the frontiers of land and sea, and they resembled the rocks themselves, the craggy coastlines and isolated skerries that only they inhabited.

Johannes, with his smooth skin and fine hair, was looked upon by the whalers as something of a curiosity – a boy they could relentlessly mock and tease. Several times he was asked to do pointless errands, fetching articles from the sheds that were not required, being then told to put them back, and I saw him refusing to drink from one of the cups that was offered. These whalers had searched for amusement among their own, and Johannes seemed quite used to this role. He even sang, in a light voice that was not tuneful, but a little feminine, and I noticed several of my own crew beginning to laugh along at him. It had an edge of cruelty I didn't enjoy, and stopped only when some of the Irish sailors broke into one of their shanties, about the Blood Red Roses.

When the shanty was nearly finished I leant forward and asked Captain Sykes the meaning of the words.

'It is a favourite in these parts,' he said, 'and a good tune to raise the topgallants. The "blood red roses" does have a meaning. It is the moment when a whale is slain, and its final blow from the spout is filled with blood' – he made a graceful gesture with his hands – 'resembling a bouquet of roses.' He laughed at the macabre nature of his image. 'But not a bouquet that one would present to a sweetheart!'

He held his look, waiting for me to smile, then repeated his gesture of the bloody flowers once more.

'It's a gruesome song,' I said.

'Very much. But not the worst I know.'

The whale steaks were passed around on tin plates, accompanied by slices of rough baked dough and a few spoonfuls of a pickled green vegetable. I tried this first, by dipping my finger, expecting it to be cabbage or samphire. But instead it had the most bitter and acrid taste, and within the little leaves were many wooded stems that clearly shouldn't be eaten. Sykes noticed my tasting of the herbs and whispered, 'From the shore, my friend. A foul concoction favoured by the Esquimaux. Some place it on the meat, as one might mustard, but I prefer to flick it into the fire.'

'Yes. I think I might join you.'

'Ear wax,' he added, with great pleasure.

I tried the whale meat. It cut effortlessly, but inside it was bloody, and as soft as pâté. It resembled beef steak, tasted of beef, and it was possible to convince oneself that it was, in fact, supplied by a regular butcher, except that occasionally there was a strong aftertaste of fish, similar to the dark meat of mackerel or buckling. In this respect, it tasted like beef that must be rancid, a most unpleasant sensation, and I doubted that I would be able to finish even a mouthful. Around me, the sailors and whalers were eating hungrily, without concern, and I wondered why I, among them, was the only one to show such reservation. I thought of the mother and calf whales that the *Amethyst* had steered towards. How they had been harassed and shot at and eventually rammed by the ship's bow. How the calf had obviously been terribly wounded by such a senseless collision. I remembered how its tail flukes had pointed lifelessly at the sky, far behind the ship, as I had led Clara away from the commotion. And yet here I was, just a few days later, the memory fresh in my mind but now a chunk of whale meat in my mouth.

I put my plate down and looked to the ship, silhouetted on the black bay in front of a sky that never truly turned dark. Several petrels flew past it, skimming the water as if they were skating on its surface. A couple of lanterns had been hung from the masts, and I could distinguish further illuminations coming from Simao's galley and the cabin quarters. I imagined Clara eating her supper, with French at the other end of the table, freshly bathed and with his hair oiled. Bletchley would be by the fire, not wanting to talk. Simao would be serving the meal, attentive and precise in his gestures. Clara would be tasting the food, pushing parts of it away with the flat of her knife, as I had seen her do before. French would have his eye drawn towards the candles, as always, with moth-like fascination, or would be dabbing the side of his mouth with the napkin, as if blotting an ink stain. Dabs of cologne on his neck. I had an overwhelming sensation of anxiety. That I was missing something. That events beyond my control were already presenting themselves, but unseen.

I thought of the great auk in its chamber and imagined how it must have been when the *Amethyst* had dropped its anchor this morning. All those iron links suddenly springing to life like the dreadful animated skeleton of a giant serpent, dragging in a deafening rush through the chain pipe, heavy and lethal, clouding the air with iron dust. Clara and French would have checked the bird by now, and I had an equally worrying impression of them, in that miserably confined locker, sharing such a small space. French had an awkward presence about him which became magnified in small spaces. A presence that demanded attention and could make your skin feel sensitive. He made you itch. With Clara, he liked to stand too close to her, as if he was deliberately inhaling a sweeter air. Or poisoning it.

'Tell me, captain,' I asked. 'I was intrigued by what you told me of Mr French. He served in the navy, you say?'

'Indeed. A master's mate. Until he was thrown out.'

I was intrigued. 'Was it inappropriate behaviour?'

'Now, now, Saxby, I do not possess a wagging tongue,' he replied, regarding me with amusement. 'But I can tell you this – I do not know whether Quinlan French's blood is unusually hot, or whether it is ice cold. Do you have a theory on this? No, I see you are afraid to speak your mind. Well, perhaps we should cut him to see.' With that, Sykes deliberately turned away, as if to physically close the exchange.

As nightfall descended, as much as it was possible in those latitudes, I watched the distant clouds to the west as they deepened into cobalt blues and lichen grey. Veins of light tunnelled through them, illuminating them with a fire unlike that of any sky I had seen in England. Held between forelands that were as dark as a blacksmith's pliers, parts of this strange light were reflected briefly on the sea, as if a shine was emanating from beneath.

Captain Sykes had begun to tell the whaling commander about the great auks, his voice lost in the simple pleasure of a boast as he related the events on Eldey as an adventure, an outrageous gamble. He had secured a fortune from nothing, he was claiming.

'You must have them skinned,' the commander said, speaking in good English. 'Then soak them in alum and salt.'

'I have them cooled and in good condition. They are too valuable to cut.'

'The Esquimaux will do it. They are better knife-smiths than you have in England.'

Sykes considered it. 'Well, we shall see. Personally, I don't trust an Esquimaux with a knife. I have seven birds. Their sale will allow a new refit for the ship. Next year, I shall be dressed as a sea lord, Jesper, just you wait. I'll have none of your whale muck on my boots, thank you.'

'I cannot wait, captain,' the commander replied, taking his strange leather cap off and running a hand through goatish hair. He looked at me with a curious glance as if I had been the subject of a previous conversation, before replacing his hat.

Sykes reached into a canvas bag he had set in the rocks by his side, and passed the commander his nearly completed needlework image of the auk. In the firelight I saw the familiar profile of the bird, standing heroically on its bare rock, an unfinished sea behind it.

'An ugly creature with a big nose,' Sykes said. 'Very much like Mrs Sykes. I shall hang it by her dressing table and be secretly amused.' Sykes laughed loudly at his joke, until he began to cough, and could not stop. It was the commander of the whaling station who, at that moment, voiced something that had not been mentioned before.

'You are ill, Kelvin,' he said. He spoke it as a statement from a man whose duty it was to notice illness before it became a problem.

'*Pah!*' Sykes responded, brushing the issue aside with a wave of his handkerchief. 'No, no. Not ill at all.'

'I hear it in your chest.'

'Merely the rattle of old bones, Jesper. I am cursed by all this journeying into the dampest and foggiest part of the world.'

'I think you have had enough of the *Amethyst*. Am I right?'

Sykes treated the question seriously. 'One should never be outlived by one's ship.'

*

217

We rowed back to the *Amethyst* in near darkness, across water that was as smooth and black as Indian ink. I thought of the grim clouds of whale flesh billowing beneath us, now invisible. Those parts of fins and flukes that I had seen wavering in the tide earlier in the day were still there, and the fact that I could no longer see them made their presence all the more terrible. The night is a great obscurer. Looking back to shore, I saw the fire burning claret red among the rocks, and some lanterns shone brightly from inside the sheds. They were not short of lamp oil, that was certain. Behind them, the valley slope and crags had vanished into a solid blank depth without definition. The Esquimaux settlement had sunk into this impenetrable blackness without any illumination, in the same manner that the sound of the pebbles landing on the cairn had vanished in such vastness. I thought of the child I had waved to, asleep in some dark corner of the stone house, with an unwashed face and a smoking fire near him. And moving across the shore towards where the whales had been tethered, I thought I could see the pale outline of Johannes, his hair as ashen as a wandering ghost.

Back on board I knocked lightly on Clara's cabin door, even though it was past midnight. For reassurance, I needed to see her; my sense of foreboding was difficult to overcome.

She opened the latch almost immediately. 'I'm glad you are back,' she said.

'And I am glad you didn't venture onto the shore,' I replied. 'It was a vile and horrific place. I fear I might stink of it ...' I stepped into the cabin. 'What is wrong?' I asked, urgently.

'Eliot,' she said, quickly and short of breath. 'It has been such a long day, you must never leave this ship again – I have been counting minutes until you came back – but a clock moves so slowly, doesn't it? When you look.'

'What has happened?'

'I thought I heard the oars in the dark, an hour ago. But it was nothing – there's nothing out there but emptiness.'

I held her hands to soothe her, she was so nervous with energy – I could feel it in her wrists and in the way her fingers would not keep still.

'Tell me,' I asked. She lowered her eyes, taking breath.

'The bird is ill,' she said. 'I think it is dying.'

17

Perhaps it should have died, that night. Perhaps, with the bird's death, other things more precious might have been saved. Things that were slipping away from me, although I failed to see them at the time. It is difficult to look back, with the knowledge of what happened, and place your finger upon the moment when an outcome might have been averted. A journey is made of right and wrong decisions, always, and I think we acted then as we should have done. We tried to save it, we tried our best.

As soon as it was light, French, Clara and I went secretly to the anchor locker to decide the bird's future.

'The bird may have been ill even from the start,' I suggested, wanting to initiate a frank and straightforward discussion. 'Remember how it was discovered, cowering in the crack between the rocks?' French looked back, dubious. I felt uncomfortable with his presence – he was too angular a fit for such a room. Too tall and too brisk for shadows and corners and low beams. I continued: 'There has been a distinct deterioration in the last two days.'

Clara was about to speak, but stopped herself to listen to footsteps pacing the deck just inches above. When she spoke, it was in a hushed voice. 'I know very little about birds, but it seems listless and unresponsive to anything we've tried. It seems as if preparing for death.'

Behind the packing crates the auk lay slumped, like a parlour goose, its neck turned to one side as if half-wrung.

'Can we do anything to make it more comfortable, at least?' I asked. 'It was a proud and inquisitive bird. Is it eating?'

Clara shook her head. 'It has not eaten for two days.'

'Then we must release it,' I said.

French placed his hands on the beam by his head and contemplated them. 'It's too weak,' he said, carefully. 'Release it now ... and we'd watch it drown. You don't wish to see that, do you?'

'None of us want it to die in captivity, Mr French,' I replied. 'That is what we promised when we found it.'

'Oh I remember the promise and all that,' he said. 'But the circumstances have changed.'

'Our principles do not need to change.'

He narrowed his eyes and began to gaze at a fingernail. With a sigh he said: 'I don't know the point of principles, when we have a dying bird on our hands.' He pushed the toe of his boot towards the auk as if trying to stir it into action, but stopped short of actually touching it.

I was instantly reminded, purely by his attitude, of the moment when he had killed the greenfinch. How he had reached into Martin Herlihy's hands and taken the bird and wrung its neck. The force of the memory struck me. How had I been so foolish to trust this man?

'So what do you suggest?' I asked, a little aggressively.

French regarded me, watchful but patient, in no hurry to reply, the attitude one sees in a hunter who is happily concealed.

'Might it be melancholy?' Clara asked, sounding brighter. I appreciated her efforts to keep the situation positive. 'It's a

221

wretched place in here, next to that chain and oils. Perhaps it has given up hope?'

French sighed with impatience. 'A bird has no concept of hope, Clara, it does not understand such a thing,' he said.

'But what makes you so sure?' Clara replied, with some steel. 'They say swans die quite regularly soon after their mate has gone. I have heard of that often. In Norfolk they say kill the cob swan and you kill the lake too – the whole place loses hope. That must be from the swan having a broken heart.'

French shrugged to show he had no wish to be drawn into such talk. 'I know little about swans or the things that might kill them. Eliot is our expert in this matter.'

'Do you mean with swans, or with affairs of the heart?' Clara asked, recklessly responding to French's provocation. Unexpectedly, I felt my cheeks reddening. I looked down at the links of the great chain by my feet, feeling surrounded by their entrapment. I became aware of French watching me with an expression that – at the edge of my vision – was now curious. After a few awkward seconds he brushed the dust from his hands and straightened his waistcoat.

'If you will forgive me,' he said, in the voice of an officer, 'it is a great risk for me to be down here, and I have many duties to attend to.'

Clara nodded, grateful. 'Quinlan,' she said, 'I will continue to nurse the bird until the end.'

He smiled, an oddly shaped smile that was close to a grimace, before bowing his head in a formal manner and smartly leaving the room.

It was as if a hotness vanished with him. He carved a particular presence, demanding attention, reluctant to relax, wherever he was. I looked at Clara, glad to be alone with her, but needing her as an ally.

'On first name terms?' I asked.

'Was I?'

'Yes.'

'Perhaps it makes sense, to be friends with someone you are unsure about.'

'He is unknowable,' I sighed.

'He behaves strangely in front of you.'

'He does?'

'Yes. And you are right. We should be watchful of him.'

Perhaps it was an unusual motion of the ship that prompted it, but all at once I had a startling image of lily pads floating on a dark lake fringed with trees. They were rising and settling among themselves, although in the water beyond them nothing moved any more. I shivered, needing to escape.

'What's wrong?' she asked.

'You're very perceptive,' I replied. 'Someone crossed my grave.'

She closed her eyes. I saw the shape of her pupils through the lids, as if she was still watching me. She sighed, opening her eyes and crouching to be with the bird again. As she stroked its neck I watched as the auk relaxed, opening its beak in quiet appreciation.

'I won't let you die,' she promised.

The first icebergs we saw were blocks that drifted towards the ship, some large enough for several men to stand upon, but most much smaller. They floated on the black water of the fjords with an unnatural calm and unknowable purpose, the ice shining with a brilliant white gleam, and glowing pale blue beneath the surface. They had a beautiful and lonely character, drifting one by one out to sea, already weathered into strange but recognisable forms: necks and bodies, occasionally an outstretched limb that would wave, eerily, in a frozen greeting.

At the bow a large wooden arrow was pinned to a

weathershield that could be swung from side to side to let the helmsman know of obstacles. But mostly the man on ice watch leant against the boarding with his hands in his pockets, and the smaller blocks of ice were allowed to knock into the prow below, sending them spinning and revolving along the side of the ship.

I went to stand alongside him. Just a few feet below us the bird was still wedged with its head in the corner of the locker, the way animals tend to huddle when they sense death is near. Perhaps death materialises in the air, first, before making its approach, and to face a corner is to turn a back upon it? It felt appropriate to stand at the bow, in a form of vigil, a few feet above the great auk, and wait for what might happen. I filled my pipe and offered my tobacco pouch to the sailor on watch, before asking his name.

'Ralph, sir,' he replied.

'You are from Ireland, also?'

'Sligo.'

'From a farm?'

'Na. Me brothers are turf men. But it's bad country, sir, it's real bad country.'

'The blight?'

'Aye. It's bad.'

'I have heard.'

He sucked on his pipe, hard, wincing in the sunlight.

The ship was rounding a rocky promontory, following a wide sea channel between the coast and islands. Lit by a low sun, the coast of Greenland was intensely rich in its colours of loose brown earth and low-cropped meadow. Treeless, and virtually without sign of man, it was like a country which had been born overnight.

'What is that?' I asked, pointing to a distant area of the channel that appeared clogged with broken ice.

'Ice field. It come from the glacier.'

'Will we steer through it?'

'Aye,' he replied, patting his arrow in explanation. Above me I felt the sails loosing their hold of the wind as the helmsman prepared to tack. 'There's bay ice, sludge ice, field ice, all sorts of ice. This gut of sea is shorter by fifty miles.'

'Is it harmless?' I asked.

'All things are harmless till they ain't,' he replied.

The ice field resembled shattered glass flung across a darkened mirror. It was a peculiar and unnerving sight. And fairly soon we were among it, first individual blocks, then into more concentrated drifts. Blocks as small as a man's fist bobbed furiously as the ship struck them, as buoyant as cork. Occasionally, much taller bergs passed, some as high as the lower rigging of the ship, sharp edged and cruelly solid in appearance, and it was these that Ralph alerted the helmsman to.

'The captain told me at length about the ice beams he has had fitted, beneath us,' I said.

'As long as he don't want to test them, we'll be right.'

'Is he known to be a cautious man?' I asked.

Ralph shrugged. 'Can't say, sir. But if you was in trouble, the only one I'd risk my life on would be Mr Talbot.'

The glacier emerged beyond a promontory, its front edge a jagged collection of filthy white cliffs, perhaps two hundred feet high, with deep cracks and fissures stretching from the sea at its base to the very top. It filled the space between the mountains like a great tongue stretching tens of miles inland, roughened and misty across its surface, and ancient and brittle where it met the sea.

As we passed, keeping our distance by about a mile or so, I marvelled at how strange it was. A thousand frozen rivers, congealed and piled, serpent-like, a back and spine that

225

twisted and nestled into its own valley. It seemed capable of rushing towards us, a giant scythe that would sweep us away. Sounds of cracking resounded across the bay, as loud as cannon shots, every couple of minutes, making me feel that it was intensely, unnervingly alive. The air began to cool as the ship sailed closer. It was the very breath of the glacier, I realised, cooling the area as if we were entering a vast stone cellar.

I watched in disbelief as one of the cliff edges slipped, a solid curtain of ice, sliding in a vertical plane straight into the sea. The section vanished, in perfect silence, among the litter of ice in front of the glacier, before rising again like a launched ship, while a great rolling crack of thunder swept across the bay.

Gradually, as if time itself beat twice as slow in this frozen place, a bulge of water began to swell, stretch and roll across the channel, raising the floating blocks of ice as if the sea was merely a piece of silk being lifted by a breath from beneath. The wave rolled slowly towards us and, perhaps a minute after the ice cliff had fallen, the entire ship rose as it passed underneath. I felt as if something beyond my experience and scale had drifted through each and every one of us, as the shadow of a solar eclipse is said to cross the land, a glimpse of the mystery that lies at the heart of our world but beyond our view, revealing itself and disappearing, the ship, crew, even the dying auk beneath us. We all felt and were touched by its passing.

The following morning, having cleared the ice field, the *Amethyst* was in open water. A hunting party had assembled on deck after one of the spotters had seen a colony of walrus. I decided to accompany them, not wanting to miss the opportunity of seeing such exotic creatures. Even Bletchley, after being sullen and withdrawn for nearly a week, was standing among the men, donning his hunting attire and fox-fur hat with the tail hanging down the back of his neck. His face looked scrubbed clean and raw.

'Walrus,' he said to me, as if it was a magic word. As if out to prove his determination, he marched to the side of the ship and took a wild shot at a group of black guillemots that were rafting alongside. He missed. Instantly, the group dived, and we watched their white-tipped wings and red feet kicking underwater, a chain of pearls escaping each of their beaks.

'They have nowhere to go so must come up,' Bletchley said, eagerly reloading his rifle, the boast of the hunter he had once been. But when they surfaced, he didn't take a second shot.

We rowed in both whaleboats in a wide arc that took us downwind of the walrus colony.

As the water shallowed, one of the men passed me a bucket with a glass pane fixed into the bottom. 'You might want a look,' he said, pointing over the side.

I leant over and pressed the bucket into the water and gained a vivid view of the seabed, perhaps twenty feet below. Strange creatures covered the stones, moss-fringed molluscs at least eight inches long, next to soft corals in bright yellows and reds and an abundance of hydroids, sponges and starfish, the spokes of their limbs nearly as large as a pram's wheel.

'It's so colourful,' I said, enthusiastically, privileged to have this view of quite unexpected beauty. 'The starfish are giants.'

I continued to gaze as the occasional cuttlefish swam underneath with a languorous fanning of its rippling tail fin, aware that I must be the first person to have seen this particular sea garden.

The smell and sound of the walruses began to reach us. Strange bellowing and grunts and snorts, much deeper than the familiar barking of the seals; and their scent was more pungent. As we approached, the animals lifted themselves, humping their way across the stones like sacks of flour coming to life. There were several hundred, dun-coloured and massive, lying in a disordered collection across the gravel bank. Tusks rose in the air, and the sounds of groaning and bellowing increased at our arrival, as if those tusks were the raised bows of an orchestra playing an infernal overture.

The mist we had seen at sea rose from the backs of the walruses, added to by their breath which stank of a deep musky animal odour, like that smelt in a cattle shed but here with a horrid addition of fish and weed and the excrement that smeared the stones.

We pulled the boats onto the shore and waded through the shallows, skirting the animals at a safe distance with several of the men raising their pikes and gaffs in case of attack.

'See those,' Connor Herlihy said, pointing out several carcasses, 'they've been killed by a bear. A polar bear. It's attacked the colony and killed two of the youngs.'

I examined the bones. Connor was almost certainly right. The carcasses had been picked clean and neatly pulled apart in several places. It was the site of a feast: something large had eaten these animals without hurry, unconcerned about the colony so near by.

Bletchley came to my side. 'Is it a bear's kill?' he asked.

'So I have been told.'

He looked along the shore, then out to sea, imagining the route of the attack. 'It ate the pup in full view of the others,' he said, fascinated. His tone intrigued me. From the look upon his face, it was clear he was searching for some revelatory fact among the bones.

'It seems, Edward, that the Arctic is always this way,' I said. 'Despite all this emptiness and space, there is no room for ceremony or discretion. Animals are killed and disposed of wherever they are.'

'First the bear, then the birds,' he replied. 'They have pecked the carcass clean.'

The party of men stood in a loose group, close by, casually selecting animals from those at hand and deciding on their merits. A tureen of soup was passed around, of meat and potatoes and hard peas with toasted sippet, and several men sat among the stones to have their fill, before lighting their pipes. Talbot, in their centre, was retelling a story – among men and their weapons, ahead of a hunt, it was the only time I ever saw him animated. At all other times he was barely able to say a civil word.

'You had better stand back,' he instructed Bletchley and myself in a loud commanding voice. The men put their bowls down and stood alongside him, as he pointed out various positions.

As the men crouched, preparing for the hunt, the walruses turned away. The men advanced, using gaffs to hook an animal and try to drag it from the others. The walruses were a sea of overcoats, like a crowd of large men pushing each other. The chosen one turned several times, lunging angrily at the men with its flared tusks. A great sound resounded from its throat, a gutteral cough and bellow that mixed with the clamour that was rising among the colony as the panic spread.

The colony acting as one was an impressive spectacle. Several large individuals had herded the cubs into a protected corral, while the rest of the walruses massed and rose in height, creating a formidable and impenetrable wall of bodies. But the men worked relentlessly with hooks and lances, trying to gain purchase on their animal. Several times the hooks merely bounced off the thick whorls of blubber, and it was only when two of the gaffs were secured through the tail flippers that this animal decided to turn and fight.

It twisted, a limbless bull, and swung its head at the men, its tusks stabbing and plunging in open air. Behind it, the colony continued to roll back, until the animal was isolated. The men jabbed it from all sides with the points of their lances. It bucked at them, raising and rolling and throwing itself with incredible vigour and weight. Several times the lances were slapped out of the men's grip. But other lances found their mark, and were driven into the walrus with little discrimination, as if they were attempting to puncture it. The animal roared horribly, the insides of its mouth a wet livid pink.

One by one the men ran at the walrus to club it across the head with hakapiks or rocks. It reacted with surprise, turning towards the spot where the man had attacked, but already someone was coming at it from a different angle. Agility and speed gave the men an advantage, as they effectively hunted in a pack. Still, the animal's sheer weight made it a contest that could not be called. The thickness of the skin, blubber and skull was immense.

The assault went on for the best part of ten minutes, then without any overt sign of wounding, the walrus lowered its head to the stones in apparent submission. It looked strangely peaceful, as if withdrawing from the violence or falling into a deep sleep. Once or twice it moaned, lifting its head, but gradually its motions lessened.

'That'll be it, lads,' Talbot said. 'Well done. He was a big 'un.'

The men looked on with a little wonderment at the prey they had slain. They were sweaty and ragged and this had been a tough life to extinguish. Yet the animal was clearly still alive. The seal has no heart, the captain had said to Bletchley during that first meal of the voyage, and perhaps the same was true of the walrus. Despite the invasions of the lances, despite the clubbing from the hakapiks and hammers, that great heart had still not been found.

'The axe,' Talbot said.

Now, I thought, they are going to hack the head off this dying animal right in front of my eyes. They will swing an axe as if they are felling a tree trunk, and I will be able to do nothing but wait until the job is completed. I sat on the stones, on the putrid shore, while the axe was raised for the beheading. I wanted no memory of this. But even with my eyes firmly shut I felt each awful blow as the axe was sunk into the flesh, searching for the neck bone. It took the best part of several minutes, the axe being passed from one man to another, for them to share the burden.

When I opened my eyes, the shoreline was slick with the most vivid red blood imaginable, poured thickly over the stones as one might do a sauce or preserve. The men were drenched in this same butchery from their hands to their shoulders. On first impression, it looked as though they had reached into the very body of the walrus in the search for the twist of the bone that would bring it apart, the lock that would unhinge this great animal.

All that was left of the walrus was a folded stump of oak, still bleeding. Headless, but with a force of pressure inside that brought blood to the severed end of the animal with constant welling. I have never seen a creature bleed so much – or be so full of blood – in all my life. And I doubt I ever shall, again, God willing.

And all of this for the two tusks that I could see being held by a couple of the men as they eased the great head, as large as a cannon ball, into a canvas sack. The tusks were very valuable, I had been told, as they could be sold at a high price to dentists in Liverpool for the manufacture of false teeth.

It was only then, with the violence of the hunt receding, that we noticed Edward Bletchley, sitting in the blood, his palms pressed into the stones and tears streaming down his face. He was moaning in apparent grief and, when all the men had stopped to look at him, he raised his hands up, covered in blood, for them to see.

Talbot stood squarely in front of him, a scolding father above an infuriating child.

'Lift this man from the slick and get him to the boat,' he said.

Back on the *Amethyst*, Bletchley was taken to his cabin and laid down on his bunk. I tended to him, helped by Simao and a couple of the men. We removed his bloodstained clothes and helped him into his nightshirt. I noticed how pale and thin his legs were, and how surprisingly weak his chest looked. Tremors ran through his forearms and flicked at his fingers. During the return journey he had not spoken, and didn't speak then, in his cabin. But as I was about to leave, he grabbed hold of my wrist. I bent my ear to his mouth.

'My flask!' he whispered, in a hot breath. I gestured for the others to leave. Alone with him, I quickly found his personal hip flask and filled a glass with the odd green liquor. He drank it feverishly, then turned away from me to face the wall of his cabin. He fell into an immediate sleep.

I felt deeply shaken, and kept looking at Bletchley's flask and its promise of instant relief. I tried to recall its strange taste and the drowsy sensation of swallowing it. Some remained in the glass, left in his haste to consume it. I took a breath, filled the glass to the top, and drank it in one go.

Clara was waiting for me outside his door, upset. 'You must tell me what happened,' she insisted. I took hold of her hand

and led her directly to my cabin, where I shut the door behind us.

'I think he will sleep now,' I said, gesturing for her to sit by me on the bunk. The taste of the drink burnt in my throat. My head felt strange. I told her what had occurred that morning. How Bletchley had been exposed to a sight of slaughter that was too much for him to accept. I described how he had sat, childlike, in the blood of the dead walrus and how he had taken on the responsibility for what had happened. I hoped he was peaceful now. I didn't describe the delirium tremens that had run through his arms.

Clara sat, deep in thought. Her ringlets hung to the side of her face, so gentle, so feminine, so at odds with all that I had witnessed a few hours earlier.

'I will go now, Eliot.'

I nodded. Already my vision was beginning to spin.

I'll never let you go, I replied. I'm sure I said it, as I lay down on my bunk and turned to face the wall, unable to fight the wave of tiredness. A sense of dread overwhelmed me.

Huntsman appeared, agitated, pacing the cabin back and forth, so tall that he had to angle his neck to one side. I smelt the stink of his clothes and listened to the brush of the rough sealskin along the edge of my bunk. Wringing his hands angrily, he kept stopping, trying to listen, occasionally lifting a finger as if he had heard something and needed to alert me. I lay on the bed, moaning. He refused to look me in the eye, but began to pace once more, touching the walls of the cabin and attempting to peep through the cracks in the wood. His manner was utterly caged, utterly feral; he seemed determined to peer through every wooden plank of the ship if he had to.

I cried out, shielding my eyes and pushing past him to reach the door. I crossed the saloon and went straight to Clara's cabin.

'*Clara!*' I whispered. 'Open the door.'

Almost immediately she was there, as if she'd been waiting for me.

'I'm so afraid,' I said, reaching out to hold her. She put her arms around me and guided my head onto her shoulder.

'*Shh*,' she whispered, consoling. 'I know, Eliot. I know.'

'I'm so weary, with all the hunting and slaughter.'

'We try, Eliot, it is all we can do. We try and we believe. I feel it working, don't you? If we believe in each other we can overcome everything.' She put a finger to my lips. '*Amor vincit omnia*,' she whispered: 'love conquers all. See, you must calm.' After a prolonged moment she placed her hand on my chest, near my heart.

'Do you feel that?' she asked.

'Yes.'

She nodded, her lips becoming taut and thin as she smiled. 'And I feel connected to the bird we have saved, Eliot. If we are strong, it will recover. Do you feel that now?'

'I think so.'

'It is,' she underlined. 'We are able to save it.' She nestled against me and brushed a cool cheek against mine.

'Believe,' she whispered.

18

The town was draughty and damp, with bitter curls of wood-smoke blowing around the house corners and water running from the eaves and down the walls. A persistent and heavy drizzle fell, filling the few streets with the sound of dripping. I walked with Clara, holding a waxed umbrella above us and supporting her arm as she stepped in and out of the wheel ruts.

'At least we're off the ship,' I said.

She gave me a thin smile.

Godthåb was the country's largest settlement, but it was a bleak and lonely place. Several houses had been painted a rust red, with white window frames. Built in the Danish manner, they had heavy timber doorways on stone foundations. These buildings were gentle and civilised, reminiscent of fairy tales and warm Scandinavian evenings, a glimpse of the familiar and welcoming. It was in the largest – which acted as a covered market – that French had arranged his trading goods in front of several interested merchants. I had his sales list on a sheet of paper.

'Listen to this, Clara, it's as if we've brought enough to furnish an entire town: oilskins, sou'westers, undershirts, overshirts, duck coats, blankets, tin pots, tin pans, mittens, stockings, razors and mosquito netting. Then there's thread, coverlet cloth, combs, towels, some handkerchiefs – that's kind, given the colds that must be rife in this place – thimbles, sets of dominoes, beads, calico, needles, glover's needles for the long Arctic winter nights, knives and forks, scissors, chopping trays and chopping knives, axes, snow knives, shingling hatchets, saws, bastard files, gimlets, awls and fish hooks.' I folded the paper away. 'Exhausting.'

'Tell me, Eliot, have you revised your opinion of that man?'

'French?' I considered how I felt about him. 'I believe he has his own interests at heart. But what is actually in his heart is a mystery. Why do you ask?'

She shrugged. 'He can be charming when he wishes to be.'

'Charming? Not a word I would associate with him.'

'Being pleasant seems to take a toll on his energy. Certainly he finds smiling a tiring business – it doesn't surprise me the crew are not keen on him.'

'Has he told you this?'

'A little.'

'When?'

'The evening when you dined with the whalers. He showed me a more considerate side to his character.'

I remembered how he had bathed in the stream that day, pouring bucket after bucket of water over his body. That, and his impatience to return to the ship.

'But where was your cousin that night?' I asked.

'Oh, wandering the ship.'

'So you ate alone with Mr French?'

'It was peculiar at first. He couldn't look me in the eye. I wished you had been there – but he relaxed. He told me about his days in the navy, but that he wished to get away from the sea.'

'He was thrown out of the navy. Did he tell you that?'

She was thoughtful. 'He pushes people too far. And he likes to play games. I think he is beginning to play a game with us.'

I was alarmed. 'What form of game?'

'Does it not seem to you that in the last few days he has been watching us rather too closely?'

I was sure that Clara was not commenting on any specific incident, but was reacting on intuition. Yet her instincts were often correct. I remembered the way she had touched my cheek, telling me how much I tended not to notice what was occurring.

'Why should he do that?'

'That man is conflicted,' she said.

'He has much at stake in concealing the bird. If the captain discovers, he could be discharged. Perhaps he is thinking about his future.' I was stumbling to defend him, and not sure why. 'Clara, I am sure he is still a man of his word.'

'Have you noticed how he stares into the flame of a candle?'

I pondered her observation carefully. 'Yes, Clara, I have noticed it.'

'Do you not think it odd?'

'The captain referred to it once. He said French would ruin his eyes.'

'But he persists, Eliot. It is unusual.'

Clara, wearing a dress of watered silk trimmed with bands of plum velvet and black lace flounces, was attracting much attention. Her height, the elaborate plaiting of her hair and the waxed umbrella made her an exotic sight among the deep ruts and gravel drains.

'You are being looked at,' I commented, wishing to lighten the conversation.

'Yes, I noticed. Do you think it is my bonnet?'

'Quite definitely,' I joked, regarding her bonnet with its

apricot silk ribbons and the ornamental grebe's feathers. She was a bird of paradise in this place. 'They prefer a skullcap of seal fur here.'

As we left the centre of the town we entered a poor area of rough stone houses, partly dug into the ground, with turf roofs and chimneys where the smoke escaped liberally through the gaps in the rocks.

'We should turn back,' I suggested.

Clara was reluctant. She wandered a few steps further, towards an open moor stretching for miles.

'There's nothing here,' I said.

'Let's go on.'

'What do you want to find?'

'Warmth.'

We continued, between the rough dwellings, even though we'd been told that we would not be welcome in this quarter, as the town was suffering greatly from diseases brought by Europeans. Illnesses that might last a week or two in England the Esquimaux had no immunity from. In the open door-ways, several women had come to look, mostly dressed in sealskin. They were small people, with long flat black hair centrally parted or wound into a knot on top of their heads. One or two wore a cloth head cap, or a brightly beaded bodice, but on the whole they were clad in a uniformity of tanned hide, making their legs padded and baggy, even with hide lacing wound around them. Their boots were gaudily painted.

Children began to follow us, making a sweet chatter, and we found ourselves being invited into one of the houses by a young woman.

'It appears we are being asked in,' I said to Clara.

We stooped to enter a long dark corridor of bare earth and smooth rock, and then a kitchen where the air was grey with smoke. It felt damp and warm. The walls were entirely soot covered, with a range of utensils and cooking implements hanging on pegs and wires. Alongside them, various types of hunting and fishing equipment were strung up to dry. On a large cooking range, built of stone, sat a blackened pot filled with a thick stew. Several seabirds – I noticed a diver, a pink-footed goose, a pintail and eider, alongside a knot and wheatear and smaller birds – hung on meat hooks fixed to a beam.

We were guided to a second room, which was long and low, with a sloping floor almost like the pitch of a ship's deck in a storm. At the far end was an old man, sitting in a hand-made chair and coughing regularly. He didn't seem to notice our arrival. Woven stools were brought to us, and from neighbouring houses food was quickly mustered: white biscuits, wooden cups of fresh milk, a berry liqueur and several eggs that were small and elongated in shape. 'I will try the biscuit,' Clara told me, smiling. 'It's the thing I most recognise.'

'You are thoroughly lacking in courage,' I replied, holding a hard-boiled egg up in front of her. As I began to peel it, one of the elder women indicated for me to wait. She went to the kitchen and when she returned she held her palm out flat for me, revealing a pile of coarse salt. She gestured for me to dip the egg into it.

'Gosh,' I said, 'slightly more than I bargained for!' I dipped the peeled egg into her hand and ate it quickly, in two mouthfuls. It was surprisingly sweet, with a chalky yolk that tasted a little of fish. Or perhaps it had been her palm that smelt of fish. 'Thank you,' I told the woman, as she wiped her hand on her leggings. There were many other stains there, in the same place.

Clara relaxed, playing with a boy and girl who had come

in to watch. She asked for string and made a simple cat's cradle with it, inviting the children to participate. The children laughed continually, and it was a scene I had great pleasure in watching.

The women smiled and chatted among themselves and wanted to touch Clara's hair. They tried to emulate the plaiting across the top of her head, and bunch the sides into ringlets – but their hair was relentlessly straight and jet black, and their show was only for amusement and affection.

Was this really the same woman with whom I had formed a strange and anonymous relationship on the other side of a plain bedroom door in a manor house in Norfolk? It was incredible that now we should be together, at the far end of the earth. I had noticed, wandering with Clara through Godthåb, that her shoulder brushed mine, and when she wished to point something out she would touch my forearm and hold it with a lingering gesture.

'Why are you watching me?' she asked, coyly, still playing with the children.

'Seeing you in this room. In this room you seem ... precious.' She smiled at my choice of word. 'As precious as our bird in the anchor locker. Surrounded by all this,' I said, pointing to the dirt and smoke of the room. 'You seem rare.'

'Thank you, Eliot. You make me feel special.'

'You are. I've always known that.'

'But you've known me only a few weeks,' she said, smiling.

'Yes. Of course,' I said, glad when one of the men of the house decided to show me his hunting hooks. They were fine and carved from bone, despite Sykes' claims that the Esquimaux preferred British steel. I thought of French, down in the trading post, listing his cargo of hooks and rifles, wires and cables, while I held this exquisitely carved pale fishing hook: a secret I had been let into.

'Do any of these people speak English?' Clara asked.

'I am sure they don't.'

'Then we can talk. What shall we do about my cousin?' she asked.

'How was he this morning?'

'Reluctant to speak. He is approaching a crisis. I have seen it in him before.'

'Is there any way I might help?'

'Perhaps, if he lets you.'

There was an element in their relationship that was still deeply troubling. 'He seems to have a hold upon you,' I said.

She gave me a quick, dark look, before resuming her play with the children.

'I do not know what you mean,' she said.

I felt urged to explain myself, but also out of my depth. 'When I saw your arrival on the ship, I felt as though you knew nothing about where you were. Did Edward force you into embarking upon this voyage?'

Clara appeared momentarily thrown. 'What do I remember of the weeks before this ship? Very little, I can tell you. I recall Edward standing up to my father in a courtyard, how he shouted at my father that I should be allowed to find my own way in life. That is imprinted on my memory, and I am indebted to him for it. But what else? Interminable coaching journeys across the country, the most horrid lodgings where we were the subject of lewd insinuations. I remember being ushered in and out of rooms, not knowing where I was and not caring either, and I remember the doses of medicine that Edward gave me. Yes, more than anything I recall that leather case of his, and the vials of liquid.'

'Tell me what the medicine is.'

'Is it important to know?'

'Not all medicine is meant to make you well.'

She considered how to respond. 'You asked if I felt pressured – well, I did, I felt pressure surrounding me, but the medicine relieved that. But to answer your question, I no longer require it.'

'Yet when you sit with him in the evenings, Clara, it's almost as if you are in a trance.'

'Is that what Edward's told you – that I am in a trance?'

'I'm not sure. He said things about you two, as children. What you did when you were apart.'

Clara laughed. 'He loves to tell that story! I suppose he told you we communicated with our thoughts while we lay in separate beds? He is quite a fantasist, my dear. An endearing fantasist quite capable of elaborate conclusions.'

'So, it's not true?'

'Edward believes I have a gift. That I am able to channel between this...' she waved her hand around her, 'and the spirit world.' She smiled, wishing to leave the subject. 'He thinks the medicine encourages it. But I am not convinced. A childish game, really, but he is most involved.'

Was this an admission? A further deception? I wasn't sure, but felt reluctant to be guided away so easily. 'I have also noticed,' I persisted, 'that the health of Edward and your own well-being are intrinsically connected. He has an influence over you that causes me concern. You were very fragile when you first boarded the ship, and I wouldn't wish for you to become ill again.'

'Again?' she answered with practical finality. 'There are days when I am able to cope, and days when I cannot, that is all.'

I sighed. 'I think it might be time to leave.' I gestured to the Esquimaux, then thanked them for their hospitality, and gave my metal-nibbed pen to the man who had showed me the hooks. He marvelled at it, looking along it as you might sight down a rifle.

As we went out, I wondered whether I should have told Clara about a conversation I'd had that morning, as we had moored at the harbour. French had come up to me and asked, without preamble, if Edward Bletchley was a user of drugs.

Quite taken aback, I had asked him what made him suspect such a thing, and why he should mention it at this specific moment.

'Because of the way he hugs that damned doctor's bag of his,' French had replied, mirthlessly. 'You must have noticed it too.'

'Of course I have.'

'Well, what do you think?' He was in a great hurry to know. I shrugged, feeling cornered by his urgency. 'And what's in that hip flask of his?' he asked.

To get French away from me, I decided to offer him some information, and mentioned the occasion when I had tasted the drink. I told him of the drink's colour, and that it was not unpleasant but as a taste it was unknown to me.

He knitted his brows, listening attentively. 'Very interesting,' he said.

'But we all have our comforts,' I continued, thinking I had already said too much, 'as you have with your fondness for your pocket watch. I believe Edward needs all the comfort he can get, the poor fellow.'

French pulled out his watch, examining it on its chain, as was his habit, but this time as if proving a point. He slipped it back into his waistcoat and made sure he had my attention before he spoke:

'Opium.'

19

The ship made cracking noises as it cooled. My cabin became cold. When I placed a hand upon the wall it felt chilled and damp, like the walls of a Norfolk house in winter, where the heat does not reach. I took my hand away quickly, as if it had been seared. Our direction was relentlessly north, crossing once more into the Arctic Circle, but this time Sykes made no mention of it. There was no pantomime of kissing hands at the dining table. For several days a cold mist enveloped the ship. The decks, masts and fixed rigging became coated with a thin layer of ice and the wood turned cloudy as if it had been sugar glazed. The *Amethyst* was transforming, as a chrysalis encases the caterpillar, into a different material. On one occasion I ran my hand against the mast and a sailor grabbed my sleeve, in caution.

'Don't touch the iron, sir,' he said. 'The skin might freeze and tear.'

Illnesses were said to arrive in weather such as this, and sometimes the mist encroached so thickly it seemed possible to slice the air and gather it, with darknesses looming in the near distance suggesting rocks, or other ships. It was our shadow, leaching into the fog, but the walls of ghost ships veering towards us made me so unsettled that several times I truly believed I could smell the dampness of their wood and sails.

There was much studying of the water. Shoals of seal, loons and ducks, floating seaweed – all were signs of the proximity of land; several times we heard breakers surging on rocks, and the men would stop to listen, gauging their closeness. I clenched my hands in my pockets, braced for the crunch of wood against a reef. Every few minutes a sounding of depth would be taken, and the leadsman would call back to the helm, *brown sand, fifty-five, mud, fifty* or *gravel, eighty*. It was hardly consoling. We appeared to be blind men feeling the seabed with a finger. Occasionally the same sailor would call, *off soundings, at one-hun'erd twenty fathoms*, the simple announcement that the world had fallen away from our deepest touch.

There were glaciers near by, many of them, of great size. The number of sails had been reduced, enabling the ship to be hauled to the wind in a moment, and two men were on ice watch now. Men with good eyes and a reluctance to talk, who knew when layers of the fog were in fact the walls of icebergs. They would swing the wooden pointer and yell a hearty warning several times each hour, although it was rare that we ever saw any of the obstacles they steered us round. Only once during those days did I see an iceberg. I had been pacing the deck, nervously trying to light my pipe with a frustratingly damp match, when I felt the presence of something close by. A sensation of sudden alertness swept through me. It was as if the air had developed sharpened edges. Looking beyond the ship's rail I saw, veiled in fog, an unmistakably cracked and grainy texture passing, a solid wall that had either been seen too late, or not seen at all. The ice was ancient and stained and looked as if it had drifted the world for centuries, spreading its sickly copper-green pallor to the surrounding air. I stared in disbelief, expecting to hear the disastrous sound of the hull splitting, but nothing happened. The fog concealed the berg, wrapping it once more, the ship carried on, and the men at the helm laughed loudly.

As I headed for my cabin, I was halted by the sight of footprints upon the boards of the deck. Not footprints made from dirt or grime, but made of water. I crouched low to examine them. A line of footprints made by bare feet, walking towards the cabins. Small feet, that could only have belonged to a woman. Yet the temperature was below freezing, and there was no other sign of dampness on the boards that had not already turned to a thin glazing of ice. I stared at the prints and placed a finger upon one of them, wondering whether it was the cold I felt, or wetness, and as I wondered, I watched the line of footprints vanishing, or drying, so that after a minute or two, there was nothing at all.

Clara and I took turns nursing the auk. She would show great patience, offering the bird morsels of food, or would stroke the back of its head where the feathers were flat and sleek and so small they could hardly be ruffled. 'Tell me abut your life,' she would ask it. 'Tell me about the storms you have faced, standing on your rock – or swimming on the ocean – tell me about swimming, dear one, with those strong feet of yours. Those storms were so large but you were undaunted, remember? This is not a place for you to die in, is it? Not here.' She even sang to it, soft nursery rhymes, as if the bird was a child in her charge.

When I was able, I took measurements. I sketched the patterning of its plumage, the scales on its legs, the join where the beak entered the head and the soft concavity around its eye. I was preparing for its death, when its sound and smell and the way it moved would be lost for ever. These notes would be valuable. Either it slept, with a second milky eyelid half-descended across its eye, or it sat in the shadows, observing me with a pupil that was as small and black as a polished bead. Surrounding the eye was a pure white marking as wide as a goose's egg, and often it seemed this marking was a larger more curious eye, regarding me, clown-like and sad. I could hardly bear it. For this bird, the ship was a coffin.

It had no fight left, no struggle, and I felt ashamed that the last great auk should die a captive bird. Its kind had existed throughout millennia, long before man had ever set eyes on them, a lifeline filled with ocean currents and the secrets of migration and breeding. All those thousands of years, only to be eradicated in a couple of decades of senseless greed, and finally coming to an end in this room, next to a chain and witnessed by a man who had failed.

'What is happening outside?' Clara asked me one morning. 'I can hear the men shouting.'

'We are travelling through an ice field,' I told her. 'The Jakobshavn icefjord. The men are giving warnings of bergs and packed ice.'

'How do they see them, in this fog?'

'That, I'm afraid, is a mystery. Clara, you must take some time away from this cell.'

'I think it will die today,' she said.

I nodded. Surely the bird could not last much longer. Clara was sitting on the floor, with it resting across her lap, as long as a dog. It breathed haltingly, with a rasping sound. Occasionally it gave a cough. 'I am concerned, Clara, about what this might mean for your health. I do not want to see you becoming ill. If the auk dies, it is not because we haven't tried.'

'You have a caring soul, don't you, Eliot?'

'Yes. I care very deeply. But not just for the bird.'

247

She knitted her brows, as if in pain. 'I had a vision last night, Eliot. It was Huntsman.'

'*Huntsman?*'

'Yes.'

'In the sealskins – a bearded man – the stained sealskins?' I asked.

'He sat in my cabin, watching me.'

'This is horrible!'

'Eliot, it was just as you said. A vision, that is all.'

'But how is it possible? This ship is haunted!'

'I don't know how it is possible.' She seemed suddenly tired. 'All I can say is that I saw him.'

'But what did he do? Did he speak to you?'

She shook her head. 'I can't—'

'You can't what?'

'I can't tell you.'

'You must! What happened?"

'He said nothing.' She held her head in her hands as if dealing with a great pressure. 'He sharpened a knife.'

I took a step away from her, holding the roof beam for support. This was terrible, I thought, *terrible*! I felt quarried by a sense of dangers all around me. Dangers in the shadows of the room, dangers below and upon deck, in the hearts and minds of men, and dangers in aspects of this voyage that were beyond my comprehension.

Clara placed the bird on a nest of sacking she'd prepared, laying its neck out like a short length of rope. Her dress had a deflated appearance, as if she had crumpled, without struggle, next to her patient. I looked at them both tenderly, realising she understood the plight of the bird better than I could ever do. She had, after all, dealt with her own incarceration when she was younger. It had made her ill. And illness seeks its own reflection.

I spoke quietly. 'You used to dream about a poacher.'

She looked up at me, startled. 'What did you say?'

'A poacher. A wild man – or spirit – who lived in the woods near your home. You used to dream about him.'

She stared at me, alarmed and unblinking, as if I had broken her trust.

'I have deceived you, Clara, please find it in your heart to understand me. As soon as I saw you on board this ship, I knew who you were.' I held out my hand to prevent her from speaking, I was so afraid I wouldn't continue.

'Ten years ago, when I was twenty-two and you were just sixteen, I was hired by your father to curate and restore his egg collection.' Below me she sat perfectly still, breathing shallowly, but I knew I had to say it all, now. I had no choice. I had never had any choice. Even as I spoke, even while she bit her bottom lip, confused and preoccupied, relief was spreading through me. Dismantling a barrier is a job that becomes easier.

'I worked for several weeks of the autumn at your parents' estate in Norfolk, sitting in that draughty conservatory over-looking the lawn. Clara, I can tell you remember. It was I who came to visit you in the corridor outside your room. It was I who used to talk to you through your bedroom door. You used to tell me of your visions and dreams back then. You told me you dreamt of a poacher, living in the woods. Only, you were not called Clara then. You must have had reason to change your name. You were called Celeste.'

'*Celeste?*' Her whisper was barely audible.

'Forgive me,' I said. 'When I saw you on deck that night I recognised you – I should have told you. But I have been so confused, and you appeared so frail, I was afraid to alarm you. I feel wretched now. The last thing I wanted was to deceive you – you are the only worthwhile thing on this ship.'

She stood and, without once looking me in the eye, put her arms around me.

'Please,' she whispered, 'say nothing else.' Her breath was in my ear. She angled her cheek upon my shoulder. Her body felt limp and suppliant, but her hands clenched themselves tightly behind my back. She began to sob, her face tucked into the lapel of my jacket, urging me forward into a tighter embrace.

'I know you remember me. I know it,' I said.

I wandered the deck, reeling and elated after my confession. My feet barely seemed to touch the boards. Yet I have often wondered about this moment, wishing that I had paid more attention to Clara's reaction. Did I miss something? Did she reveal something in that shadowy locker room that would have explained all that subsequently happened? I don't know. Sometimes, when I recollect being with her among those shadows, I feel she was deliberately concealing herself.

The ship had been brought to a halt by the thickness of fog and the proximity of icebergs. All was silent, except for the solitary barking of a seal, somewhere across the water. But even though I had been just a short time beneath decks, I could see the sun was now trying to clear a path through the mist, as if wanting to shine on me alone, and the happiness I felt. It burnt with a cold haze, pouring its pale light across the deck, as through a high window in a cathedral. The air had begun to sparkle with the dust of minute crystals, a phenomenon I had first witnessed on the ice floe. A simple wave of the hand would part and swirl the glitter, as if the air contained a thousand pinpricks of sunshine.

I noticed an unusual and bewildering vision: a burning disc of sunlight emerging in the fog. It grew in intensity, thirty or forty feet out to sea, surrounded by rings of rainbow coloration running in a haze. As I watched it I began to discern in the centre of the circle, burning, as it were, the hovering spectral appearance of a man. A man, where a man could not possibly be, suspended above the water. I stared, dry-mouthed, as this spirit-figure floated and shimmered. Around his outline, a coruscating wheel of Arctic light and glitter seemed to radiate, pinning him to the centre and lifting him in ghostly levitation.

It was only when I took a step back that I realised the man was, in fact, myself. My outline, captured by the sun, projected within a tumbling vortex of light radiating from the air crystals. When I raised an arm in greeting, the figure responded, exactly, but it was unlike any other shadow I have ever seen. It was like meeting another living part of myself.

By evening, the mist had cleared. Across the bay several hundred icebergs floated, their shapes doubled by the perfect mirroring of the calm water. As the light changed, the ice began to glow, a pale steel blue and then an ivory white that lingered, until the entire bay had a magical, transparent quality. I listened to the seal, once more barking, but I could not see it. Distances became deceptive. Some icebergs seemed to hover above the horizon, overlapping others like pieces of coloured glass in a magic lantern. Greys and blues shifted in bands across the sky. I had never seen such beauty as this, such elemental grandeur, such peace. Mesmerised, I watched as icebergs appeared to melt into clouds, their solidness temporary and untrustworthy. Yet others hardened, turning into cliffs of pale rock, revealing new facets and dimensions: eroded hearts, the fragments that they would become one day, the stone kernels that must lie in the centre of each one.

Eventually, it was difficult to see any of the icebergs at all. The ship's deck became grey, then lighter, then finally dark and featureless. The sea turned glassy. Instinctively I knew something magical was about to occur. I remained on deck, even though the night was bitterly cold and I could feel the ache of the low temperature spreading into my fingers and toes. For a long time there was nothing at all, then swiftly it was everywhere, a strange and luminous green glow that stretched in a braided pleat of ribbons across the sky. A revolving phantom, spreading wings, pulsing with life. The aurora hung above the ship and flowed towards the horizon. It glowed dull green on the wet wood of the mast and the pale rolls of the furled sails; even on the dark wooden stem of my tobacco pipe. The sea had flattened, as if the lights pressed a quietness beneath them. Even the seal had stopped barking. I felt that the lights were spilling upon us all in simple grace. That we were all touched by this dance of mysterious energy that flowed across the sky and through us too.

I was moved to tears, thinking of all the sights I had seen: the slaughtering of the seals, the whale and calf, the gull with its wing shot clean off, the flensed whales at the Danish whaling station, the flukes and body parts that drifted in the murky water beneath our rowing boats, the colony of walruses, steaming with breath and fear, and the kill there which had been long and terrible. Through it all, a vividness of blood which almost hurts the eyes. The piercing red of a yew berry. All that slaughter and aggression. Mankind's failure to be anything other than a beast of greed and profit. All that, and then to see the majestic aurora above us – gentle proof that the Arctic was beyond any one of us. It draped across us like a blessing. And that is what I felt. I felt blessed.

Clara came to my side. I saw the play of green lights on her cheeks. Her eyes were wide and as dark as oil. I knew she was in a mood I couldn't grasp. Something had happened.

'My dear Clara,' I whispered, 'tell me.'

She shook her head, unable to speak. Instead she took my hand and led me across the deck, under the lanterns that had been hung in the rigging, their pale wicks in odd competition with the spectral greenness beyond, past the hatches of the deck that once more appeared like open jaws. She led me down the companionway to the lower deck, where we passed under the greasy light of the storm lantern, feeling the dusty air of the stacked cargoes, the smells of all the skins we had collected, their musk adding a soft reminiscence of death to the air, past the hooks and chains where once – many years earlier – rows of African slaves had been manacled, on their way to the West Indies, their bodies tormented with grief and illness. All of this pressed in on me with immediacy, as if past and present had truly overlapped, until we reached the anchor locker where I knew the auk had finally died, even as Clara was opening the small padlock on the door.

She led me into the room where the air felt thick with shadows, and here the bird sat cornered. The difference in its posture filled me with confusion. Then awe. Pushed up beneath its breast, the unique pattern and brittle symmetry were unmistakable. The bird had laid an egg.

20

I cannot remember how long we stayed down there, with Clara crouched by the bird, whispering and stroking its back. The egg was easily the size of a man's fist, tapered at one end and decorated with a lattice of brown and grey lines against a cream white background.

Pointed like a razorbill's, but more elongated, closer to a guillemot's, the markings had the yellowish brown hue of many terns' eggs, but a lighter background. The veining was as distinctive as serpentine. Of all species it resembled most closely the egg of a Brünnich's guillemot – a specimen of which I had only ever seen once.

'This is the rarest egg in the world, Clara.' A tingling sensation ran the length of my spine. *The last of its kind*, I thought. Irreplaceable. Beyond value. I felt like a man who unexpectedly discovers a large rare jewel, or nugget of gold. He is struck by its beauty and its rarity, its natural quiet splendour. And its ability to change his world – the stroke of luck every one of us needs at least once in a life. This egg would grace any display case. Private collectors would fight for it. The gentlemen who had paid for my passage, idly betting that this species might still exist, would now pay treble or more to own this object. They would happily contact the museums, eagerly anticipating a bidding war. Men admire eggs. Perhaps it is their fragility, or their rarity, or simply the fact that within an open palm it is possible to hold the entire encapsulated life of a bird. Perhaps it is all these things, but men covet rare eggs, they collect them, and they will spend a great deal to make sure they have what others may not.

The bird sat upon its prize with a splayed belly. Occasionally it would lower its head and nudge the egg sideways with its beak, as if in disbelief. When Clara offered some food, the auk ate quickly.

'Now you are hungry!' she said, laughing. 'Well, you must eat as much as you wish, because you have been truly splendid, and we have been so worried about you. Eat, and rest, and we shall continue to look after you.'

It eventually became so cold in the anchor locker that Clara and I were forced to return to the saloon. We stood by the stove, trying to warm ourselves. Bletchley was in his customary armchair, next to the fire, fast asleep. I noticed the scratched shape of the star, on his right boot, to remind him which side port and starboard were. It had been inscribed by a different man than the one I recognised, now.

'He is peaceful tonight,' Clara said, regarding him with the same caring attitude as she had in the anchor locker. 'He was quite excited earlier, when he saw the northern streamers. They were a little too much for him to take.'

I nodded, afraid we might wake him. Briefly, a tremor flickered across his face and I wondered – not for the first time – whether he was merely pretending to sleep. Soundlessly, I took Clara's hand, and led her to my cabin. Inside, we sat together on the bunk, sharing whatever warmth we had, and it seemed the most natural thing to do. There was an air of celebration.

'Do you mind being in here?' I asked. She shook her head shyly. 'Thank you,' I said. 'It's quiet tonight.'

'Yes.'

'I like the silence.'

'Me too.' She seemed thoughtful. 'I was used to it as a girl. But they say silence is the bedfellow of madness. It can make you hear things.'

'Such as what?'

'Things you didn't want to hear.'

I nodded, blowing into her cupped hands to warm them. Her skin smelt of the bird's feathers.

We sat listening to the sighing of the ship at night, as it moved against the anchor. There were occasional footsteps on deck above us, the gentle knock as ice touched the hull, the ticking of the ship's clock from the back of the saloon. Every so often, a distant bird, screeching, a lone skua searching the bay. We could hear Sykes, asleep in his cabin, coughing every ten minutes or so and, directly through the wall, an ominous silence from French's cabin. Often, I had heard him long into the night, writing, the scratch of a harsh nib on the paper. But at that moment, all was quiet. He might have been fast asleep, or he might be staring at the flame of the candle that he liked to have burning upon his desk. This image of him, intently awake, unnerved me. I remembered how he had glared at me as I led Clara away from the whales being targeted. Equally it was possible to imagine he was angled, tall and insect-like, against the wall, trying to listen through the wood.

'We must be quiet,' I whispered.

She took off her shawl and folded it carefully, stroking the fabric until it was smooth. She placed it on my desk and, in an unexpected and swift movement, climbed beneath my blankets. I sat perfectly still, perched at the end of the bunk, unsure what to do. She lay very quietly. I thought she might be falling asleep, and that it would be thrilling to watch her do so. Then, quite suddenly, with her eyes firmly shut, she broke into the most wonderful smile. She pulled the bed-clothes to one side, inviting me in.

I remember that night more vividly than any other night of my life. Quickly, I lay down beside her. My familiar bed was filled with strangeness, the feel of Clara's satin dress, her sleeves trimmed with lace and ribbon bows, her feet in woollen stockings, her toes wriggling happily to keep warm. Her fingers, too, seeking to interlock with mine, as if in extremity she was a different person, active and playful. I lay rigid and bewildered alongside her, trying not to touch her, but the bed was so narrow it was unavoidable. She turned upon her side to face me. We were inches apart.

'You are trembling,' she whispered.

I nodded, unable to speak. I was thirty-two years old, but without any sensual knowledge or experience of women. I felt completely at a loss.

'You may hold me,' she said, quietly. The cabin was unlit, and her eyes were two perfect holes in front of me, without expression. I smelt her breath mingling with the perfume of her hair. This was everything I had dreamt of, to have Celeste this close, to call her mine. I placed a nervous hand upon her waist.

'This is perfect, Eliot,' she said. 'You make me feel like a child again. Edward and I used to get into bed together and hold each other. We would pretend we were married – sometimes we would put the blankets over our heads and imagine we would never be found.'

My hand felt awkward and heavy upon her side. I tried to brace it with my elbow, not wanting to remove it, but afraid of keeping it there, also.

'Have I said something wrong?' she asked. 'Is it because I mentioned Edward?'

'No,' I replied, 'of course not.'

'I don't want to upset you. We don't have to talk, not if you don't wish to.'

'But I want to know everything about you.'

'Just hold me,' she said.

'Like this?'

'Do you ever wonder whether moments such as these are really happening?' she asked. 'It feels as though I'm dreaming this.' She stared quietly at me. 'Pinch me,' she said.

'Pinch you?'

'So I know this is real.'

I hesitated. My hand felt hot on her waist.

'On my leg,' she urged.

'Why?'

'To know this is not a dream.'

I moved my hand, full of doubt, to the soft length of her dress and the leg beneath. I pinched her.

'Harder,' she whispered.

'No.'

She looked entirely lost. I pinched her again, more firmly. She winced, taking a sharp breath. Then her mouth relaxed and she smiled, gratefully.

'We're not dreaming.' She paused, watching me. 'Thank you for all that you told me, earlier.'

'I should have told you before.'

'But let us not talk about the past. Not now.'

I nodded, obedient to her lead. But I felt nervous, unable to move, afraid I might be indecisive, afraid I might start to shake.

'Eliot, you must breathe deeply,' she whispered. 'That's right. Now, let the breath out, it will calm you.'

I took a second slow intake, before releasing it. And as I did so I felt her bend towards me.

'Shall I tell you where to touch me?' she said.

'Yes.'

'Here.' She took my hand and guided it among the pleats of her dress. I felt the soft flat texture of the silk, in complicated arrangements of hems and folds, then the touch of her skin beneath – and a single quiver jumping from the tips of my fingers to her body.

'I will show you what to do,' she said. I believe she said it, because I felt I was drifting towards her, crashing with softness against her and feeling her roll into me. I noticed her hair laid across the pillow, like a dark stain spreading through water. I stopped, afraid, momentarily haunted.

'Don't lose heart,' she whispered. Emboldened, I felt a strength in my arms and across my shoulders, a completeness of spirit and courage that ran down my spine.

'This?' I said.

But she seemed already beyond me, drifting, as if slipping underwater, her body rippling with a current that lifted and moved her, surfacing, sinking, resurfacing once more.

I thought of the aurora streamers. Perhaps they were still lying across the ship like a blessing; how blessed I had felt to see them, and how blessed I felt now, to lie next to her. When I touched her wrist, it was as if a residual charge of static, heaven sent, remained on her skin, rising in each one of the tiny hairs on her forearms.

'The Northern Lights have transformed us,' I said.

'Yes,' she replied. 'I will tell you a story. When I was a child I had a book – a hand-tinted book with water-coloured illustrations, where a ship was besieged in the ice. It was such a beautiful book. The ship – I forget its name –

was surrounded by bears, and then the Northern Lights lit up the sky and all the bears sat to wonder at it, and the men saw a path across the ice to safety. When I used to turn the page and see those lights, my whole body felt joyous and lifted. They do say books can transport you – I've never forgotten that feeling.'

'I like that: how the lights shone a path to show them the way out. I had the notion, all day, that we were on the verge of seeing something wonderful. And then that egg. It felt like a premonition.'

'The Arctic is a place for visions,' she said.

I was immediately struck by her choice of phrase. It was the one Huntsman had used, when he had appeared in my cabin. 'Why do you say that?' I asked.

'What did I say?'

'That the Arctic is a place for visions.'

'Did I?' she said, falling asleep.

'*Celeste?*' I whispered.

She smiled, vaguely. 'My name's *Clara*,' she replied. 'I feel unreal – I feel as though I have been lulled into a dream … You're not real, either, are you, Eliot?'

Her hair still lay across my pillow. The neck of her dress had an inlaid pattern of rose petals embroidered among the fringing. The tops of each stitch had the same smoothness, and I was struck by how soft and feminine she was. The ship was a world of men. It was made from cables and hawsers, canvas and barrels. And its currency was muscle. The men wore dark and heavy woollens, with mittens against cold and boots against grease. Their faces were dirty and aged. Clara was made of a different substance altogether.

We curled together into the space, the blankets rising so that a draught kept my back almost permanently cold. She filled my bed with her smell, of perfume, of a malty warmth that I had often smelt on board but never quite realised where it came from, of her breath.

'Thank you,' she whispered, her voice thick with sleep.

I stroked her hair tenderly, knowing that this moment, which felt so simple and pure, was one of the best of my life. As she sank further into sleep, drifting away from me as I watched her, I felt urged to chase her, a remaining question that was in need of answer.

'For what?' I whispered.

It took her a few seconds to reply: 'For saving me.'

In the middle of the night I woke, startled. Clara had gone. I sat up in bed, trying to read the unfathomable darkness at the far end of the cabin. It was solid and menacing. Carefully I pulled the felt curtain to the side, expecting to see Huntsman, and was relieved to see nothing but the bare planking above the washstand, the knots in the wood that were so similar, at times, to eyes.

Through the window I saw the bay filled with icebergs, their bases darkly shadowed, and the tallest of them topped with brilliant orange light from a rising sun.

21

Sitting in the rowing boat, I felt watched by the men at the oars. Privacy is a luxury not afforded on a ship, and I was uncertain whether I was already the subject of rumour or not. Cabin doors opening in the middle of the night, the tread of a woman's feet, in stockings, crossing the saloon. The soft click of a latch.

The men were taciturn, pulling rhythmically at the oars, grimacing with the effort, and in their grimace there seemed to be an edge of amusement, directed at me. I tried to ignore them, as a gentleman should do, trying instead to concentrate on the glorious forms of ice we were passing. It certainly was a beautiful morning. The ice glowed bright blue and was carved smooth by the sea, dripping in the crisp light, each drip catching a single jewel from the sun. The air was brittle and cold, as if it too might have an element of ice in it, and like a lens that was sharply cut, it brought everything into vivid focus and intensity. I should have been captivated, but all I could think about was her. The night she had spent with me. Then her disappearance. I had not seen her at all since I woke.

Even French made time to admire the ice, although his orders were given in his usual dismissive tone. Pull here, avoid that, and so on. One berg passed so close it had to be boomed off by the men. The tip of the gaff hook glanced off its side as if it were glass. On the other boat, Sykes sat hunched in his thickest pea coat, a handkerchief held close to his mouth, and his collar turned up as was his habit in small craft. 'This is the last stop we shall make,' he had informed us, after breakfast. 'If you wish to go ashore, you are welcome, although this trading place is poor and insubstantial. When we landed here last summer, the Esquimaux were preparing a dish of Greenland shark – the so-called *blind shark* – the flesh of which they had buried for a year. For the shark is poisonous and putrefaction is preferable. It was a repellent smell, which has never quite left my nostrils.' He took no pleasure in his joke. 'Its liver alone weighs a ton. But if you wish to visit, do.'

Bletchley, looking tired and restless, had listened to the captain, then shrugged his shoulders and moved to his seat by the fire, already wrapping his blanket around him.

'We'll leave you in charge of the ship, Mr Bletchley,' the captain muttered, a hint of his old amusement returning.

Waiting on deck, hoping that Clara might emerge from her cabin, I went to the helm and observed the dipping-needle compass by its side. Its magnetic steel pointer was mounted in such a way as to tilt vertically the higher up the world we travelled. I had heard that compasses behaved erratically in the Arctic, that they wanted to point inward, towards the structure of the ship, or became so burdened by the need to point down into the earth that they were no longer free to turn. Sure enough, when I looked closely at the dipping-compass, its needle pointed straight through the deck. Up here, it points to hell, I had heard the men say.

As the boats were being loaded I took French to one side, pretending to ask his opinion of what clothes I should wear. After giving general advice and noticing I had taken him away from the men, he looked askance at me and said: 'I assume you have something more pertinent to say than to get a mother's advice for your warmth and comfort?'

'The bird,' I said.

'Dead?' he replied, quite without emotion.

I laughed, somewhat abruptly. 'In fact, no. I have some surprising news for you. It has laid an egg.'

He stared at me, incredulous. Once more I was struck by the mixture of expressions that seemed to flit, ever-restless, on his face. One moment impatient, then curious, as if these feelings rose to the surface beyond his control.

'I take it this is an amusing joke you have devised, to pass the time?'

'You will see for yourself.'

'I shall.'

'It is feeding again. You might try it with some strips of fish.'

'If I have the time.'

Why was this man so constantly infuriating? 'You seem uninterested, Mr French,' I asked, with a politeness I certainly didn't feel.

'I slept badly last night,' he said, an edge to his voice suggesting I ought to take note. The image I'd had of him, pressing his ear against his cabin wall, perhaps had a degree of accuracy.

We had moored at various Esquimaux settlements along the coast, where French would trade the Sheffield steel plates, hooks and needles for freshly prepared animal hides. At this one, it appeared as though we were keenly expected. Laid out in one of the sheds were many bundles of sealskin, bound in hide strips, as well as reindeer skins and musk oxen, whose hides hung off each side of the trestle table, touching the floor, and were so deep with dark black hair that I could easily bury my hand and wrist in it. There were also various artefacts carved out of walrus bone – brooches, pipes and letter openers. A couple of wolf skins were held up to us, grey as smoke and darkened along the spine, and a small pelt that was of pure white which was said to be from an arctic fox.

'No bear?' French asked, disappointed.

In broken English the local man described a late blizzard when three bears had come to the village. He went to the side of the shack and pretended to peer round the corner, acting afraid.

'You must shoot them, man,' French said, with great dismissiveness. 'My captain wants bearskins, you understand? He'll pay for the white bear.'

'Yes, yes,' the man replied. 'Shoot bear. *Skyde isbjørn.*'

'Any bear?' Sykes called, standing on a rock near the shore.

'No, sir,' French said. 'Ask this fellow why, if you can be bothered.'

'Do we have a coward?' Sykes said.

'Yes,' French replied, before turning back to the man. 'A coward, my captain says.'

'Yes, yes,' the man agreed. 'We shoot *isbjørn.*'

I wasn't keen on this general mockery. It contradicted the easily seen evidence that this was, in fact, a great haul. Sykes came to the shed, refusing to look at the Esquimaux, but addressing French directly. 'We'll have the men start ferrying, and we'll fill up with water from the stream over there. I've drunk from this place before. It's certainly good water, crisp and straight from the ice.' He looked at me as if I was a separate problem for his consideration. 'How are the preparations of the skins?' he asked French.

'Very fine.'

'Who does them?'

French shrugged. 'One of the old hags, I believe.'

'Any nicks?' the captain asked.

'They are very fine, as I said.'

'Have the men bring over the birds we have. I have decided they must be skinned here.'

'Right, well, in that case I shall return to the ship. This fellow stinks.'

'What are you in such a hurry for?' Sykes asked.

'You are well aware of my thoughts on the Esquimaux. Riddled with lice, and that's just the start.'

The captain looked at me, smiling softly. 'No bears!' he scoffed. 'We shall be here a while, if you wish to entertain yourself.' He looked out across the bay. 'Interesting,' he said. 'The petrels are flying. We'll have bad weather ahead.' With that he turned, a captain without a ship, but pacing a deck nonetheless.

I had come ashore not to partake in the trading, but to be as far away from it as possible. From the deck that morning I had spied the great slab of bare rock that rose behind the settlement and known that it promised all the solitude and escape I needed. I hadn't seen Clara. Not at breakfast, nor as the men finished at the bilge pump, bent the sails and made the whaleboats ready for the trip to shore. I had waited until the last minute, hoping the commotion on deck would bring her from her cabin. But to no avail. Holding her during the night, calling her Celeste, then her disappearing before dawn, it made me quietly anxious. As I climbed behind the settlement, up a small path that led steeply to the crag, I wondered why I had insisted on calling her Celeste. I felt I had let a djinn from the bottle. For ten years my feelings for Celeste had been secret. A secret obsession. To call her by her true name was a shattering of the spell. And dreams are best not spoken of.

As I climbed, I distracted myself with the spectacular view. First, the settlement receded into its sheltering cove, the turf roofs virtually disappearing among the rocks and grasses, as if they and the few people who lived there were negligible. Then the bay widened in size, filled for as far as I could observe with icebergs, a great fleet at anchor, their sides as white as sails set for ocean journeys. In their middle, the dark wooden shape of the *Amethyst* appeared spidery and fragile, a nest of twigs among the swans.

The sounds of dogs yapping behind the settlement came and went. I watched the whaleboats busily ferrying water and supplies back and forth between ship and shore, soundless at this distance. I thought of my own cabin, how cosy and welcoming it had felt last night, so homely, a bed shared by a man and a woman, a bed I had never known before. Yet here, surrounded by the jagged ice, that same intimacy felt seconds away from disaster. Was she still in her cabin? What was she thinking? She had once asked me never to leave the ship again, yet I had. I felt fearful. She had asked me to pinch her. And I had obliged, willingly, not understanding why, enthralled and out of my depth.

The air grew cold and very fresh, with a gritty breeze coming off the land. Perhaps it was this wind that set sail to the bergs, pushing them out to sea. I felt strong and invigorated by the climb, and was glad I'd aimed for the summit, for when I reached it I was greeted by one of the most astounding sights of my life.

Stretching from where I stood was a glacier that curved in a vast snake of movement and ancient cracks, rising for several hundreds of feet and pierced by a chain of black mountains several miles away, shrouded in mist.

I climbed down towards it across rocks glazed with a fine and perfectly transparent coating of ice. It was difficult progress and I was afraid of slipping, but gradually the slope eased and I stepped onto the glacier. I was scared that my legs might sink into it, as if stepping upon a cloud, but the ice was as hard as granite; harder, in fact, than I could have imagined. The surface was weathered and jagged, stained dirty white and pitted with erosions. In some places a hard crystalline grit had blown and refrozen, with the texture of ground glass.

I have wondered at times why I chose to walk upon it, but I knew even at the time that it was irresistible. It was as solid as rock but made of water, frozen and ancient yet moving with the curved spine of something animal. How tremendous! Beyond its fragmented edge, the glacier became smooth. For several hundred yards I walked towards the line of black mountains – or nunataks as they are known – that snagged the fabric of this great sheet.

When I turned away from the wind, the only sounds were a distant rushing of water, impossible to place, and the small trickling of a stream that must have been very near or indeed below my feet. It is difficult now to understand how I failed to notice the wisps of cloud that had drifted above, gathering in strands. But suddenly a freezing mist settled around me, and as I tried to run back a fog descended, swamping me, arriving as if from nowhere.

The light diminished to a grey twilight and after a few rapid steps I realised I was utterly disorientated. I sat, deciding to wait. With dismay I felt the fog grow thicker and colder. I buttoned my jacket and turned up the collar, sickened by my recklessness and naivety, that I had so foolishly walked into a landscape I knew so little about. I thought about shouting, but knew I could not be heard and something, even then, prevented me from calling out for help. There was a dimension to the fog's blankness that I felt wary of. Shadows and solid outlines appeared and vanished, as theatre wings might slide back and forth across a partially lit stage. I remembered when I had been on deck as the ship had been guided through a similar fog, with the men on watch looking for bergs and reefs, and that only I had seen the sheer cliff of ice that passed alongside the boat, before it vanished. The Arctic, I thought, it is a place for visions. So vast and empty, with air so crystal pure that distances appear foreshortened as though all exists in one perfect view. You might reach out your fingers and touch all that you see, yet a few steps away is always this: a blindness. It's a wilderness that can encircle you, remove your perception, and dull your mind. I thought of the filigree of cracks that veined the sea ice like frozen cobwebs, then the breath of the whales, rising like the puff of smoke in a conjuror's trick; of how the carcasses of meat hung in the rigging had frozen and clouded with ice, and the first sight of the auks appearing through the mist. There were many shrouds and partial obscurations. The seal in its breathing hole had slipped under water, never to return. It had sunk into a deep whose shadow beneath the ice was as black and impenetrable as oil. It was an animal that had drowned, but it had died like a human. A face slipping into the eternal. Water consumes. It takes away. And it lingers long in the memory.

I remembered her whispering *thank you* to me, during the night. *Thank you, for saving me.* I had held her, tightly, afraid that she might slip away from me again. I had held her wrists, not able to let her go.

Please, she had murmured, *not so tight. You are hurting me.*

In the fog, a distinct new sound emerged: a scraping noise, intermittent. I tensed, knowing the sound was that of an animal, a large animal. The fear left me dry-mouthed. I crouched, silently, staring into the cloud, trying to discern any

269

silhouette that might appear. The scraping continued for a few seconds, then stopped. I tried to hold my breath, sure now that it was a bear, a great white bear.

An outline began to emerge. I thought of Captain Bray's warning of how, after shaking hands with the polar bear, the scent of the mother would be on me, unable to be washed off, rendering me visible to a vengeful offspring. I took an involuntary step back, trying desperately to conceal myself as the ghostly shape moved, in the forlorn hope it might not come my way. I smelt the scent of musk and, at the same time, the animal stopped to face me. The fog thickened briefly, then without warning it parted. I saw, standing, not the outline of a bear, but a man, dressed in a thick coat, looking straight at me. I gasped, thinking it must be Huntsman, fearing what this meant, as the man walked rapidly towards me. The briskness of his stride was familiar. So was the way that he spoke, in a matter-of-fact and concise manner.

'You are lost, Mr Saxby,' Talbot said.

My relief was overwhelming. 'Oh, thank God it's you,' I replied.

Surprisingly, he smiled, quite warmly. He stood close and, in no immediate hurry, offered me some pipe tobacco. 'Thank you,' I said, 'the fog came swiftly.'

We smoked our pipes together, regarding the cloud that surrounded us. 'This is a strange place,' he said. 'They say hell is flames, but I disagree. It is this – it is frozen.' He squinted at me, knowingly, and again gave me that unexpectedly warm smile. He slapped me hard on the back. 'What possessed you to venture onto the glacier?'

What indeed, I thought. Curiosity? Surely, but it was more than that. I had been drawn to it. Drawn by a force that was stronger than my will to resist.

'I think you understand,' I said.

He regarded me, narrowing his eyes, a look I had seen when he weighed up one of his team, deciding on an order to be given. 'No. I don't understand,' he replied. 'Come on, man, let's get you out of here.'

'I thought you were a bear,' I told him. He laughed, telling me it had been said before. 'Your jacket,' I added, following a few steps behind him, 'your jacket stinks like a bear.'

'It does?' he replied, amused, smelling his own lapel. 'I think you are right, Mr Saxby.'

'When you were coming through the fog, I listened to the scraping sound you made – I thought you were some terrible animal, wounded and hungry, scenting me out. I realise now, it is merely the way you limp, Mr Talbot – perhaps as a result of frostbite?'

He stopped, fixing me with a questioning glance. He looked at his boots for explanation. 'I have no *limp*, Mr Saxby. I was merely leaving scuff marks, so we might find our way off this infernal slab of ice.' He kicked his boot against the surface. 'See? Scuff, scuff.'

The men had made a fire on the shore and were cooking reindeer steaks upon a griddle, much as the Danish whalers had cooked the whale meat earlier in the voyage. As I walked between the houses a dog ran past, wagging its tail with excited greeting. Then a child approached and – for no apparent reason – passed into my hand a pebble she had found on the shore. The stone was warm, from her touch, and it felt smooth and soothing as I closed my palm around it. With this simple gift, I welcomed all that I saw: the fringe of humanity that clung to this wilderness. I was hungry for the cooked reindeer, I wanted the company of the men, I wanted to be in a place that I recognised and understood.

'Mr Saxby,' Talbot said, breaking the silence he had

adopted on approaching the settlement. 'I might have been a bear, you understand that?'

'Yes,' I replied, grateful, and humbled.

Along the shore, the seven bodies of the great auks had been skinned and laid out across a flat rock. An elderly Esquimaux woman was rinsing the last of them in the bloodied water that lapped against the shingle. I looked at the pelts, reminded of their first drowning in the gulley on Eldey. The poor animals had been drowned a second time. The woman's hands looked leather-thick and greasy with the business of skinning. As she walked away, she spat on the stones, shook her head and uttered something. It sounded like *Djævelen fugle*, which I have since learnt is Danish. It means *birds of the devil*.

22

It was late in the evening and I was sitting on my bunk, looking across the saloon at Clara's cabin. Her door was very firmly shut. I sat there for several minutes, staring at the details of the wood, the small brass handle that folded flat to the panel, within its own housing, the glimmer of light that I thought I perceived coming from underneath. Perhaps she had her lamp lit, or possibly it was merely a reflection from the edge of the metal tread. I couldn't decide. Above the dining table a yellow pallor shone into the room, from a sky that had never entirely gone dark. It gave the saloon a sickly air, like corridors of convalescents; a light announcing that true light is elsewhere, where the world is vital, but here it is ill and in retreat and heavy with time.

I hadn't seen Clara all evening. I hadn't seen her, in fact, since arriving back on the *Amethyst*. Not while the men unloaded the boats or while the captain, in a boisterous mood, had handed round extra rum for the crew.

'To our futures, men,' he had said, grandly, 'for tomorrow we shall be hoisting the Blue Peter and leaving this grave-yard of bergs for our return journey.' He had said it, I felt, for the benefit of his passengers, and was unconcerned that none of them was listening. Bletchley leant against the rail, wrapped in his faithful blanket, polishing the tops of his shoes against the backs of his trousers, frowning at the drink that was passed to him. I had sat near the mainmast, still chastened by my experience on the glacier – the knowledge that I had had to be rescued was quickly known by the men.

Sykes, never one to miss an opportunity, toasted me. 'To Mr Saxby!' he had offered, a touch cruelly, 'who apparently wished to make his mark as an Arctic explorer, this very afternoon.'

I didn't respond, apart from the most wan of smiles. It didn't dissuade him. At supper, he had continued his tease: 'We watched you disappear among the rocks and knew very keenly the perils on the other side. What was in your mind, Mr Saxby? Please do tell us.'

I was unhappy with Sykes' little theatre, which he presided over at the head of the table, his glass still raised and his head cocked to one side, waiting for my reply. It had a brutish edge.

'Well, as you say, Captain Sykes, I was merely taking a walk. I was wishing to cross through the heart of Greenland and wait for you to pick me up on the other side.'

'A stroll of five hundred miles, sir!' he said.

'Correct.'

'And no provisions to speak of?'

'Only my boots, with which I intended to make a stew.'

'You are a lucky man,' Sykes said, keen to win the exchange. 'Mr Talbot informed me that you were quite disorientated. The Arctic does not welcome casual strolls. Still, you have learnt your lesson. We sail tomorrow. Once we clear these bergs we shall steer for the open sea and make as swift progress as possible. There is no more trading to be had, our hold is full of skins and we have civilised many of these poor settlements with fine British manufacturing products.'

'In Godthåb,' I said, 'the Esquimaux preferred bone hooks, rather than our steel ones.'

'They do that,' Sykes replied, dismissively, 'in front of the Europeans. They will have cupboards full of our plate and needles, you can be sure of that.'

During the exchange I had been acutely aware of Clara's cabin door being resolutely shut. Her setting at the table had been cleared away, mid-meal, by Simao. No one had commented.

By the time the others had retired, I was desperate to see her. But sitting at the end of my bunk, facing her cabin, gave me no answers. *Don't be foolish*, I whispered to myself. *You do this each time. You build up your thoughts. You let them rule you.* But I could not resist. I walked lightly across the saloon and pressed my ear to her door.

I listened there, just as I used to do at her father's manor in Norfolk. The similarity of my gesture was so precise, the memory so intense, that for a second I imagined I heard the distant call of the coot upon the lake in the woods. I thought I heard the sighing of the trees outside, their boughs cracking gently in the breeze, or the sounds of the old house settling in the cooled air of late autumn. Oh, how terrible to be imprisoned by such thoughts! I touched Clara's door, but instantly felt that other door, the heavily painted one of her bedroom at the top of the house, with the promise of her within the room, trapped in there like a bird in a cage.

Abruptly, the door opened. Clara stood, facing me, showing no surprise.

'I thought it might be you,' she said, quietly.

I didn't know what to say. 'I have been worried about you.'

275

'You worry too much,' she replied.

'You didn't eat this evening.'

'No.'

It was the first time I'd seen her since the events of the previous night. Why had she left? Why had she hidden all day? What was I meant to think? All these questions were unanswered and I was afraid to blurt them out. She was calm and wise. I felt unsteady and unprepared.

'Come in,' she said.

'Should I?'

'You should.'

I stepped into her cabin, thinking how little I knew about women, how easy it was to make a mistake, to push them away, to frighten them.

'I don't wish to frighten you, ever,' I said.

She turned quickly towards me. 'Why do you say such a thing?'

'I want you to know that I have been thinking about you all day,' I replied. 'I nearly became lost, this afternoon, on a glacier.'

She softened. 'I heard.'

'You did?'

'Edward told me. What happened?'

'Upon the glacier?' The recollection seemed surer and more certain than the feelings I had at that moment. 'I ventured onto it and was caught in a cloud. A fog that had rolled down its surface. It was quite sudden.'

'Why were you there?'

I sighed. 'I was greatly relieved to see Mr Talbot, although I thought at the time he might be a wild animal.'

'Why are you trying to make it a joke, Eliot?'

'Because I feel stupid,' I said apologetically. She gestured for me to sit at the foot of her bunk, then raised the wick on her lamp to brighten the cabin. 'The captain enjoyed my misfortune,' I said.

'Yes,' she replied. 'He is the worst kind of man – he hides behind his humour but he is a bully. And a bore.'

'When did you hear?'

'During your supper. It's hard to avoid the talk that occurs just outside your cabin – these walls seem to be made of paper.'

I noticed she had tacked silks and other fabrics to her cabin walls. 'Did you do these?' I asked.

She gave a proud nod. 'I had to do something. I have a vase here, but no flowers to put in it. I miss flowers very much.'

'I picked some for you, when I went to the whaling station.' She sat, propped up against her pillow, the length of the bed between us. 'But I'm afraid I dropped them.'

She gave me a lingering look, as if weighing which way to guide our talk. Is this how Bletchley felt, in her presence, hanging upon every word?

'How is the bird?' I asked.

'She is very well,' she replied, brighter to be on the familiar ground where we had always been allies. 'I fed her several times and cleaned the area where she appeared to have made the nest.'

'That's good. Did you show the egg to Mr French?'

'Yes.'

'And what did he make of it – or was he in one of those curious moods where he doesn't seem to make any effort?'

'You really are not keen on the man.'

'No. Should I be?'

Clara didn't answer. 'He picked it up.'

'The egg? But did the bird let him?'

'The bird had very little say in the matter.'

'But what was he intending?'

Clara shrugged. 'I asked him not to. But he was keen to make a joke. He said an egg of that size would make for a fine breakfast, although it would threaten to overflow the frying pan. He has been trying to make me laugh all afternoon.'

'Why?' I asked, dumbly. The thought of French acting in such a cavalier manner, flirtatious too, made me uneasy. I had an image of him in the anchor locker, grinning wolfishly, caring only for himself and what he could carve from second to second. 'He might have dropped the egg,' I said, annoyed.

'Sometimes,' she continued, 'I believe he thinks all this is just a game for him.'

'All what?' I asked.

She raised her eyebrows. 'All that is happening on this ship.'

I wondered what she meant. Not just the auk, but other things too; I was afraid she might have told him about all that had occurred between us the previous night. 'French has a peculiar way of amusing himself,' I ventured, 'but he has at least honoured the concealment of the bird. At least we can say that of him.'

'He was asking many questions about you, today.'

'Why?'

'Perhaps it is as you say, he was amusing himself.'

'What form of questions?'

'About where you are from, and the nature of your employment. He seemed to think I knew much about you. But it isn't really the case, is it, Eliot? I know very little about you, if anything.'

I was growing wary, hearing a new directness to her tone.

'Where did you grow up?' she asked.

'In Suffolk.'

'Where?'

'Near Woodbridge.'

'Woodbridge? Yet you told me you have been to Aldeburgh on only one occasion.'

'Perhaps I have been more.' She let my lie pass. 'I cannot remember . . .'

'I need to trust you – to believe everything about you. My life has taken place entirely under the shadows of unreliable men. I go from one shadow to the next – I've forgotten the feel of the sun on my face.'

'You *can* trust me.'

'Do you have siblings?'

'No.'

'Are you married?'

'*Clara!* What do you mean by this?'

She grasped a hand in the air, as if trying to hold something. 'Please answer.'

'No. No, I am not married.'

'You see, you told me you have been thinking of me all day. Well, I have thought of you all day, too. It happens once you have spent time in a man's arms. And I have been quite upset.'

'But why?' I asked, knowing I was dreadfully losing my way with her.

'When did we meet?' she said, flatly.

'You know this. We met on board, several weeks ago.'

'But you say we have met before. Isn't that what you told me? I wish to know about it – when did we meet for the first time?'

I felt enlightened, arrived at the kernel of her doubt. Had she engineered this moment in order to admit who she was? It made me calm to tell her. 'At your parents' house, near Somerleyton in Norfolk. It was in 1835, in the autumn. Your father had engaged me to restore his collection of birds' eggs. I worked for several weeks in the conservatory at the side of the house. You remember – at the bench below those dead geraniums.'

'Several weeks.'

'Yes. It was quite an exacting job – and your father was very particular.'

'Did we speak to each other?'

What was she trying to establish? I felt dispirited, and wanted to stop this exchange, to gain some breath. 'Do we have to talk like this?' I asked.

'Did we?'

'No. Not at first. I wasn't even aware of you in the house. Your father, you understand, he never made any reference to you. Not once. But I used to see you being led across the lawn.'

'But you were in the conservatory?'

'I took it upon myself to find you. I discovered your bedroom at the top of the house. I used to listen at your door, and ... eventually we spoke to each other.'

'How often?'

'But you remember! Do you have to tease me? Daily, from either side of your bedroom door.'

'But on no other occasion?'

'I do not want to continue with this talk, Clara. You are distressing me.'

'At what other occasion did we talk to each other?'

'On the day when you escaped. When I stole the key from your father's study and I unlocked your door.'

She sat back, apparently exhausted. But I was afraid that if I touched her, she might cry out. When she spoke, it was with a tenderness.

'What happened?' she asked.

There are times when I remember this, and I am sure I was crying. But other times, I imagine I replied with a steady voice. 'You ran past me,' I said. 'You escaped the house and . . . and we found you.'

'Where was I? Please tell me where I was.'

I was worried I wouldn't be able to say the words. 'You were in the woods. I found you in the woods. I have tried not to think about that day.'

'And my name?'

'*Celeste*.'

She took a deep breath. I felt destroyed, and weak. So weak. I closed my eyes. I felt her touch my cheek and, a moment later, the softest of kisses on my brow.

'Eliot?' she whispered. 'Thank you for telling me. I can see it was a very hard thing for you to say. But this is very hard for me, too. Because you are confused, my dear friend, you are so confused.' She looked with great sadness. 'My name is Clara,' she whispered, urgently. 'It is *Clara*. I do not know anything about a girl called Celeste. You have described a sad story, but I know nothing about what you have told me, nor of what this other girl may have done to you.'

My cabin was dark and silent and intense. I remembered how I had first lain upon my bunk while the ship was still docked at Liverpool, how the floating sensation of the ship had felt, disconcerting and eerie, and how I had never quite become used to it. It lifted you in fragments, questioning your reality, changing the weight of your footsteps and the lean of your spine. On the sea, or merely on board the ship, I had felt different, not entirely there.

I could not sleep. I tried not to think about Clara and the things that she had said. Something was missing. I tried to imagine all that I had left behind. The willows that hang over

281

a silent river as it pools and bends through an East Anglian meadow, the sound of a bee going from flower head to flower head and passing close to the ear – a delicate greeting between man and insect, or the sound of skylarks, so high they cannot be seen but their sound descends like sunshine on the meadows. The glow of mustard fields. A hand pressed against old bricks warmed by a stove, or touching the smooth facets of knapped flint, whose surfaces are always cool, whatever the season. The tall ragged crops before harvest, the angle of late summer sunlight, almost waxy in its lustre as it shines on the dry barns. Comfort and security in every texture. I thought of the sea, the North Sea off Suffolk and Norfolk, breaking in long languorous waves against a shingle shore – oh how I missed it. Or the mouths of the estuaries, where the brackish river meets the salt water in curling spines of current, braided in ribbons as it flows out to sea. Smooth-trunked beech trees, water pooled in their hollows. Bracket fungus on a fallen log. The chirping of sparrows. Peaceful churchyards, the gravestones powdery and leaning, names eroding, the iron gates that swing with heavy grace, their handles polished by decades of use. Horses dragging carts laden with hay, a scent of their horse musk and the sweetness of the hay as they pass. Brick and flint outbuildings that are dark and calm, filled with dust and tools that are seldom used, their walls held together by the single span of a cobweb.

All that I loved. All that I missed. I thought of these things, trying to dispel the Arctic sea that I felt pressing against the ship. It was the jagged ice, out there, dog-toothed, and an icy sky too, pure and empty. We were merely floating and at any point we might tip and spin and fall into its nothingness. I grabbed my bed frame and tried to concentrate on the sounds that would remind me of where I was. My breath, the tick of my fob watch: a child's trick, to count the small things, when he first realises life has an ending that is unavoidable. I could hear French in his cabin, still awake, writing at his desk. The scratch of his writing nib, punctuated only by the silence of the frequent dips into an inkhorn, suggested that he was marshalling a cockroach back and forth across the page. So strong was this image that I could not dispel it. I pictured him hunched over his desk, watching the insect moving, touching it with his finger until it did as he wished.

Eventually there was nothing I could do but go into the saloon and gently knock at his cabin. The noise of the writing stopped at once. I heard him push his chair back and, just before he opened the door, I heard a lock being slid.

'I cannot sleep,' I told him.

He looked beyond me – involved and confused by the work he had been doing – into the darkened saloon, with its single night lantern hanging above the table.

'What time is it?' he asked.

'Late.'

'Or early?' he quipped. 'Depends. Come in.'

I felt so lost, in such need of company, that I was greatly relieved by his offer. I entered his cabin and sat on his bunk, while he turned his chair from the writing desk and sat to face me. There was little legroom between us.

'I heard you writing,' I began, although behind him his escritoire was now noticeably clear. 'I hope I am not disturbing you.'

He shrugged. The only object upon his desk was a candle, set in the middle, burning brightly.

'What are you writing?' I asked.

'A letter. Why can't you sleep?'

'I feel a long way from home.'

My frankness caught his attention. 'Yes. Well, we are. We couldn't be much further.'

'Does it not play on your mind?'

'A little,' he said. 'But I don't really have a home: not on shore. My home has always been ships.'

'Why did you leave the navy?' I asked.

French laughed, putting a hand to his mouth. A dark, venal expression passed across his face. 'I had, let us call it, an entanglement.'

'With another ship?'

'The *object* ... was not another ship.'

'Oh, I see,' I said. 'I'm sorry I asked you that. It was quite rude of me.'

'Well, it is the middle of the night. It is the best time to be rude, wouldn't you say?'

'I suppose so.' The candle burning behind him made it difficult to see his expression. 'You place your candle very close to you, Mr French. Does the light not pain you?'

He smiled and as he half turned towards the candle I saw its light flash across his profile, making him as untrustworthy and false as a theatrical performer.

'You might wonder why I adore the flame of the candle so much, Saxby,' he said. 'I shall tell you. It is an exercise of mine. I stare into the flame for as long as I might take it, in the wish that the fire will fill me. Do you follow? So that it might purge me from within.'

He leant across his desk and opened a small cupboard that my cabin did not have. Inside it, he had several bottles. He poured a mixture of liquids into two glasses, stirred them with a finger, and handed me one.

'To the night,' he toasted, licking his finger.

'Thank you,' I said, accepting the drink. When I tasted it, I was once more unsure of what I was drinking. It had a dark

284

conker colour, and a blend of syrupy and woody tastes that made it impossible to identify.

'What is this?' I asked.

'Arctic liquors,' he replied, smiling slyly. I saw the points of teeth between his lips.

'To the night, then,' I replied, downing the drink and knowing, instantly, that I shouldn't have taken it. *Mr French does not drink*: that was what the captain had said, a day into the voyage, and I knew that French had no intention of touching the Arctic liquor he had poured for himself. He had licked his finger, but the glass remained untouched, in his hand.

'I will go,' I said, standing.

'I hope you sleep, Mr Saxby,' he said.

At the door I turned back: 'Only the innocent sleep.'

I returned to my cabin knowing that I had been drugged. The pressure that bore upon my head was similar to when I had drunk from Bletchley's flask. I lay on my bunk, fighting sleep, wondering what connections I might have overlooked between my fellow passengers, fighting against the thickened cloak that descended on my thoughts, realising I was going to have a vision. I felt afraid.

'Who's there!' I called. It was the middle of the night, and my cabin was almost completely dark. I had awoken with a jolt and had pulled myself upright to stare at the shadowy wall at the foot of my bed. The shape of a man, I was certain of it, was sitting there. The thing remained, as still as a jacket that I might have hung, except I knew there was no hook or nail in that place.

I struck a match. But in the flare of light I felt the blood drain from my face, for it was not Huntsman that I saw, but a woman, a young woman, her face pale and drawn and her hair soaking wet, with river weed clinging to her clothes and her eyes shutting, shutting, as water poured from her mouth. I gasped, dropping the match as it burnt my fingers. The cabin became intensely dark. I breathed harshly, staring at the wall. Whether she was still there or not, I could no longer tell. I laid my head on the pillow and turned away, knowing with sudden clarity that it was a vision that I'd had many times before, and I brought the blanket up to my face and then over my head.

23

Celeste had told me where the key to her bedroom door was kept. 'In my father's library,' she had whispered. 'He works at a bureau by the window. You must look inside the central drawer. The key has a pale blue ribbon tied through it.'

She had given me these instructions as I leant my head against the cold paint of her door, the empty corridor stretching either side of me like a small pathway. I should have been downstairs. I had no business at the top of the house. The attic floor of a Norfolk manor in the late throes of autumn is particularly quiet, I had thought. Through the window at the end of the corridor I could see the fields, bare after harvest; the soil and grasses had a withered look, as if waiting for the frosts that would soon come. Solitary rooks flew across the landscape, landing heavily in the tops of the oaks, where they would lurch angrily from branch to branch, noisy and restless. A few remaining leaves clung to the ash and sycamores, but mostly the leaves were blown and heaped in wet piles along the hedges and across the lawn.

The house had smelt damp, as if the plaster had soaked up this autumnal breath, loosening the wallpaper and bending the floorboards. It had become a creaky and depressing place.

'He walks after lunch, you must have noticed it. He has strict routines. First he follows the hedge and disappears behind the trees and his route returns across the pasture and meadow. It always takes him three-quarters of an hour.' This is what she told me. 'It will be your chance to go into his study.'

While she spoke I remained silent, unable to reply, knowing my time in the house was virtually over and knowing I had become unhealthily drawn to this bedroom door. I was unable to sleep well at night, I thought of Celeste constantly, I planned my day around the rare glimpses I would have of her being walked across the lawn, where the small pattern of her daily exercise had begun to leave a worn mark in the grass. I found myself whispering her name at my workbench. I had finished my restoration of the egg collection, and had been busy for several days trying to create more work for myself, relabelling, reclassifying, and I had even broken an egg, purely with the intention of having to restore it, gluing it, sanding it, filling the cracks with gesso and painting across the hair-like joins with a miniature brush.

'Will you do it, today?' she had urged. 'I would love to see your face. I think about you often. The time passes so slowly in here.'

I had returned to the conservatory, descending in stock-inged feet the second staircase and taking a route through the kitchen passage to avoid the main areas of the house. I had greased the hinges of the doors with linseed oil, and trod only at the edges of the steps where they joined the wall. I had enjoyed the challenges of navigating around a house without being seen, creating a silent path, knowing where the boards were noisy, ducking beneath the window-panes, listening for the rapid walk of the housekeeper as she marched back and forth. There were spaces where I could sit for hours, if it was necessary, where I was never seen. A corner recess beyond a window where a dusty vase had been placed. A shadowy corridor where the air was several degrees cooler because the rooms were used only for storage.

That day, I had sat in the conservatory, beneath the dying geraniums, arranging and rearranging the alignment of several pencils on my desk, but imagining the moment I might enter the father's study, the moment I would find the key, the moment when I could open the door and meet Celeste. When I saw him walk briskly past the conservatory, dressed in his long boots and thick coat, I was already picturing where I would be in a few minutes' time, running towards his study without my boots on. My actions seemed unavoidable and planned. Even while I could still hear his footsteps crunching on the gravel of the drive, as he headed towards the lake, I had moved swiftly to the door.

I ran into the main drawing room, where a glorious fire was burning in the grate. A thread of steam still rose from the coffee cup he had sipped, after lunch, and his pipe lay forgotten, to one side of his armchair. I remember pausing, knowing that he might come back for this, but also feeling a momentum that was impossible to refuse. Did I wish to be caught? I wondered. His study was silent and lined with books, with family portraits hung on the walls, each one of them a severe reproach for the action that I was bent on undertaking. Generations of Cottesloes, a similar vein of meanness running through their expressions, condemning me as I ran beneath them. His chair, his desk, his private papers. As I touched the brass handle of the central drawer it felt as though I had been stung by a nettle, it was so wrong. When I pulled it open I saw a pouch of gold coins, letters tied in a soft bow of silk, and, just as she had described it, the small key with the pale blue ribbon.

From several windows – as I climbed the back stairs towards the attic rooms – I saw the dark tall figure of her father, paused on the river meadow beyond the drive, checking his pockets, looking back at the house. I stopped to watch him, attempting to influence his decision with the power of my thought. He leant forward on his stick, poised, keen as a hunter, and I saw his attention caught by the same rooks I had studied earlier. They were thrashing about in the tree above him, dark as devils.

'Go on, damn you, go on,' I had whispered, the feel of the key in my hand almost singeing my finger. I had imagined Celeste, standing by her own window, looking at her father with a similarly tense attitude, urging him on.

'I have it! I have it, Celeste,' I said, breathlessly, a little louder than I should have done, when I reached her door.

'Wait!' she replied, from within. Was the key already in the lock? I cannot remember. I recall how it had felt, once the key was in, the tension of the bolt being held by my fingers. Just an extra half-twist and the door would open.

'Now, Eliot, do it now,' she whispered. Her voice was tight, excited, strained by the months of her captivity, my own obsession with it, and my transgression, all now converging at the point of the key in the lock. And as soon as the bolt clicked, the handle had turned, the door had sprung open, recklessly, with no regard for the noise it made, and Celeste was suddenly exactly where the door had been, tall and urgent and searching for me and pushing forward so that I was forced back on my heels. Her eyes settled briefly upon mine, but with an expression that was as quick and as nervous as a trapped bird. She was wild and unknowable as she leant against me. I braced her, her soft warm weight, her hair pressing against my face so that I had to close my eyes. I felt the silk gown that she was wearing as it turned and slipped and vanished through my fingers and when I looked it was as if she had never been there. I saw a glimpse of her room through the open doorway, shadowed by blinds and drapes, with clothes strewn across the floor, and a sensation of urgent movement made me look back: I saw Celeste, barefoot, at the end of the corridor, running headlong down the stairs.

I had pursued her, as fast as I could, as she fled noisily through the building. At a landing on the main staircase we both passed the housekeeper, who pressed herself into the corner with a startled expression of horror. My flight through the house said it all. I was a doomed man, even at that moment, or at the next, when, as Celeste threw open the main doors, she virtually knocked over her father as he climbed the stone steps, returning for his pipe.

Celeste did not stop, she fled like a sheet caught in a wind, streaming across the wet lawn. It was I who was halted, fixed by the sheer presence of her father who had been flung against the stone balustrade. He glowered at me, hatefully off balance, insect-like, his eyes burning with accusation and contempt.

'She . . . she escaped,' I blurted out.

He straightened his jacket and stood, erect and command-ing, his entire authority and condemnation brought together into a single word:

'How?'

I stood dumbly, fixed to the spot, out of breath. We were both aware of Celeste, who was vanishing into the trees at the end of the lawn. But despite the urgency, he was keen to indulge in this moment. He had me pinned, a man he could watch being destroyed in front of his very eyes, and he was going to enjoy it.

'I shall ask you again, Master Saxby. How?'

There was no possible explanation, other than to admit I had let her escape. Behind me, the housekeeper had joined us, adding weight to my guilt. I shook my head, unable to speak.

If a man is able to snarl, then I believe I saw it then. His expression clouded, as if a pain was forming within him, and I thought he might strike me with his stick. Possibly only the housekeeper's presence prevented it. 'So,' he said, savouring every second. Every part of every second. 'Can you run?'

'Yes, Your Honour.'

He looked down the length of his lawn, to the spot between the shrubs where his daughter had vanished.

'Then run. Bring her back.'

I spent most of the day in my cabin. By lunchtime we had cleared the icebergs around Jakobshavn, and had made a good mileage into the Davis Strait where, with stiffening winds and a mounting sea, the *Amethyst* started to labour as it sailed into turbulent weather. I decided to stay lying on my bunk, an injured space for an injured man. Why had French given me that drugged liquor last night? I was sure it had prompted that terrible hallucination. My mind was filled with thoughts of Clara. Parts of our conversation from the night before kept returning, unresolved and troubling. *You are confused, my dear friend, you are so confused*, she had said, *my name is Clara*. But she had been tender with me, at least I had that, yet also so forthright. She had looked me in the eye and said that I was mistaken. She was not Celeste.

Outside my porthole the sea had darkened to the colour of pewter. My head ached. White horses broke and rushed by, leaving an angry spindrift across the surface. When I closed my eyes it was as if trees were being felled around me, their branches and leaves whipping past each other in sprays of sound. The ship began to pitch – I opened my eyes, trying to fight the nausea that was growing, trying to steady a liquid world – and I realised the view from my porthole had briefly become a view of the sea itself, as it flooded and surged. Again and again the ship lurched forward and down then slowly, so slowly, rose once more. It felt as though we were permanently in the process of sinking, digging into each wave, not returning but sinking further.

The surface of my bedside desk trembled, and occasionally my cabin would shudder with the compression of the ship. The spars cracked aloft, whipping the stays and rigging taut, each crack more irreparable, more catastrophic than the last. I thought of the captain's fortification timbers holding us all together, the ice beams he had had fitted taking the slap and smash of the waves and dispersing them, evenly, throughout the structure of the vessel. But it felt as though each wave that struck must be loosening some joint or fitting. I imagined the *Amethyst* separating into hundreds of unconnected timbers and bindings, opening out like a fruit held in the palm of a bear.

A shutter of wood was lowered outside my window and fixed. And it was the application of these deadlights, with the storm still howling beyond them, that made me feel truly cocooned. I lay on my bunk, staring up at the dim ceiling, trapped.

There was a knock at my cabin door. Simao appeared, dressed in an oilskin, but his appearance as always was impeccably neat and ordered. He had the calmness that comes from being an islander. He was a most welcome sight.

'Sir,' he said, 'are you ill?'

'Ill? I don't know. Do I look ill?'

'A little.'

The pitching of the ship made the door-frame swing from side to side, nearly touching each of his shoulders.

'I feel sick,' I managed to say, turning away from him to stare at the ceiling once more.

'Everyone is sick,' he said, cheerily, placing a small drink on my table. 'Aguardiente,' he said. 'Portuguese brandy. I return in one hour,' he added. 'No dinner tonight, but some cold cuts are there. And candied fruits.' He pointed behind him. 'The galley is in deep flood.'

He made to leave, but I stopped him. 'What flood?' I asked.

He grinned back, miming a large wave sweeping the deck. 'Was very big,' he said.

When he had gone, I wondered helplessly about the great auk sitting on its egg in the anchor locker, right at the front of the ship where the storm must be most severe. It was impossible to contemplate going forward to see it. That space must be plunging under the waves at least twice a minute, more than likely flooded, too, by water pouring in through the chain pipe. I decided I must seek out French, who would hopefully put my mind at ease. Despite his aloofness and his unpredictable moods, he would be good in a situation such as this.

The cabin floor pitched and rolled as I went for my door, and I listened with despair as the ship strained in the storm. The saloon looked incongruously calm and serene but the lights above the table swinging almost flat to the ceiling were a mad sight. So, too, was the glimpse of French, bent almost double at the far end of the saloon, one arm grasping the side of the settee, and the other grappling Bletchley in a silent, furious wrestle. I stared, disbelieving and alarmed, as both men saw me at the same time. French had his arm round the other's neck, and was attempting to hold him down, but Bletchley, although smaller and less broad, was putting up a surprising and wiry resistance. I watched, grimly fascinated, at this insane *danse macabre* evolving before my eyes, as

294

Bletchley began to force the taller man away as if bending a sapling. I stepped back into my cabin and sealed the door behind me.

My relief to be running across that lawn had been considerable. I was glad to be leaving the scowling dark presence of Celeste's father and had thought, hopefully, that by catching his daughter I might, against the odds, enact some restoration of my position. Quickly I reached the shrubs and ran through them, roughly where Celeste had vanished, and entered a wooded area thick with damp bracken and briars. I became snagged almost immediately, and wondered how Celeste had managed to run through this, barefoot and scarcely clothed. It was only then that I realised I, too, was without my boots. The wood was shady and peaceful, with a pungent autumn smell of earth and fungus. Nothing stirred. Above me, the blasted rooks flapped from branch to branch, their splayed wings falling like axe heads. I searched for glimpses of Celeste's pale silk gown, half believing I could see the outline of her brown hair among the undergrowth. I thought I saw her standing, poised as deer can be in the distant shadows. Perhaps she was hiding? Crouching in the bracken, watching me. Perhaps it was a game she was playing? But I knew I had broken an order and discipline that I knew nothing about. I felt as if I had pulled apart the workings of a clock and would never be able to replace the cogs and springs in the correct position. I began to run again, forcing my way through the tangled briars that seemed like arms trying to impede me. On a muddy track I found a line of bare footprints. I could see where the heels had slipped and the toes had clenched in the attempt to grip. Several yards later they vanished, then appeared further along the track, a fleeting trail, but enough to follow.

Behind me, from the direction of the house, I heard men being called as her father mustered more hands to help with the search. A dog began to bark with excitement. From the opposite direction I became aware of distant snaps, the startled cry of a pheasant, scraps of sound that only I could hear. But did Celeste want to be found? Why had she run past me in the corridor, why had she tricked me into unlocking the door?

The ground became more sodden as the wood sloped into a natural hollow. Rhododendrons grew in thick stands, obscuring the view and creating impenetrable barriers. I pushed blindly through the leaves and saw the dark hearts of the trees, the gnarled and twisted trunks, as a marshy smell of decay and stale water began to grow around me.

'*Celeste!*' I shouted.

I had carried on further, impeded more and more as my feet sank in mud. An oily sheen covered the ground, and I saw the beginnings of reeds and marsh grasses through the dark shrubs. It stank, as if air had never properly circulated in this part of the wood, a breath that felt wrong and trapped. But I sensed I was close. As I pushed at last through a thick wall of leaves I emerged at the side of a round lake which was entirely fringed with rhododendrons. A coot floated in the centre of water, chipping with alarm. Birds flew up, startled, from the trees on the opposite bank, perhaps two hundred feet away. The water looked unbroken and ancient, encroached on all edges by thick rafts of lily pads. Then I noticed a faint rippling of the surface, spreading in a delicate shell pattern from one side of the lake. The coot bobbed calmly among these ripples, instinctively turning towards the direction they had come from, and that is where I saw Celeste, her body floating face down among the lily pads, her hair spread across the surface of the water like a stain.

I plunged into the lake and paddled and dragged and tore at the weeds but was held back – with dreamlike insistence – by the roots of the plants. Cloudy black water rose around me, as dark as ink, smelling of death, as I thrashed my way through. Celeste's silk gown floated before me, bubbled with air, her arms extended in a stretch I could not reach. I touched her fingers, reached for her wrist and pulled her to me, trying to lift her from the water, and plunged several times beneath the surface. Eventually I managed to clasp an arm around her waist and drag her towards the bank, her silk gown slipping through my hold for the second time that morning as, nearing the edge, I became aware that two other men had waded in. They pushed me away and took her from me. They lifted her from the water. I saw Celeste in fragments as I coughed and spluttered: her hair, hanging in front of her face, the weed and mud woven into it, an arm that appeared to hang lifeless, a glimpse of her mouth that looked alarmingly serene and at peace.

The sight of her, laid out cold on the bank, was the last reliable memory I have of that day. That, and the memory of the coot, floating in the centre of the lake: those images feel certain, everything else feels unclear. I didn't see Celeste again. Each time I try to remember, I am held back by a numbness. I didn't see her father, nor my place of work in the conservatory. I was ushered away, told never to enter the house again, or ever set foot in the grounds. The eggshell I had broken would remain on my workbench, forever unglued.

24

The storm was the beginning of the end, I can see that now. It shook the frame of the ship, as a dog might shake a length of old rope. But ships are designed and built to resist natural onslaughts, whereas people may or may not be. It was the passengers, in that storm, who became loosened from their fastenings. That is how I perceive it, now. I cannot recall how long it lasted. Perhaps it was for twenty-four hours, perhaps a good deal less – bad weather bends the notion of time – but I slept, and at some point I became aware that the howling of the wind had receded and been taken over by the hammering of men, fixing and repairing, a comforting replacement. I fell back to sleep, listening to the fall of hammers and the hauling of rope, imagining a ship re-forming. When I awoke, Clara was in my cabin, laying a damp flannel across my forehead.

'Hello,' she whispered, kindly. 'We have been worried for you.'

When I looked into her eyes, it wasn't Clara that I saw. I saw Celeste. Glad, and relieved that she was back, that she had come back for me, I smiled. Hers was the expression of peacefulness that I remembered and cherished, so distinctly, as she had been carried from the Norfolk lake. Celeste's body had hung across the back of one of the men who had waded in among the lily pads; her head had been turned towards me, and I had stood in the cold water, gazing at her in a stunned silence.

'You're wet,' I said, confused.

'I have been on deck.'

The deck, of course, I am on the ship, I had thought. I sat bolt upright. 'Is the ship not sinking? What about the bird – is the bird *drowned*?'

She put a finger to my lips, humoured by my confusion. 'I have brought you some sweetened milk syllabub, it will make you well.' Then she bent to my ear and whispered, 'The bird is fine. Do not worry about her. She has told me she intends to survive. And right now she is sitting on her egg as proud as a hen in a coop. Shall I describe her to you?'

'Please.'

'She sits on the egg so just a part of it might be seen, between her feet in the soft down of the underbelly. Sometimes she guides it onto one of her feet, to prevent it touching the floor. She still takes a step or two away from it, every hour or so – I think the egg amazes her, continually. She did this ...' Clara rested her head on her shoulder ... 'her beak lay across the egg and she growled, deeply, as if communicating.'

'Did it not flood down there? Simao told me the ship was flooded.'

'A wave overran the deck and washed through the galley, that is all. He lost several pots and goods, but it is all repaired.'

'It was a terrible storm.'

She smiled. 'Yes. Hailstones broke several of the windows. I expect you heard. The ship is covered with a frost-rime –

you cannot touch the rails for fear of cutting your fingers on the ice.'

'Clara,' I said. 'I saw French wrestling with your cousin.'

She listened, thoughtfully, and I imagined I saw a flicker of a smile at the side of her mouth. She took the flannel from my forehead and dipped it in an enamel pot filled with warm water.

'I know something of this,' she replied. 'Edward found it difficult to cope with the storm.'

'But they were *fighting*.'

'Perhaps, but not now. Have some drink.'

'It was a demonic sight ...'

'Edward is in my cabin – he has been for several hours – asleep on the floor.'

'What is he doing there? Is he injured? Why is he in *your* cabin?'

'No, he is not injured,' she answered. 'I am looking after him, in the same manner that I am damping your brow. You are both my patients, and I am your nurse. If you wish to know, I enjoy the role – it is something I always intended to be one day. When I was young, I would dress as a nurse and tend to birds that had been hurt, and I would try to heal them. It was said I had a gift for healing birds, as you have also told me. I would keep them in the drawer of an armoire, where I could stroke their feathers and band-age their wings.'

'What happened to them?'

'Sometimes they lived, but not always. I think I learnt that often a bird never gets over its fright. When they are injured, they are also very frightened, and it is the fright that kills them. They are nervous.'

I remembered again how I had first met her father, on that spring morning among the dunes of Blakeney Point in Norfolk.

How the man had been cruel and aggressive from the start, and how, in pushing the tern back into his collector's sack, he had deliberately snapped one of the bones in its wing. He had called it a *sea swallow*.

'And did your father bring these birds to you?' I said, spurred on with the memory of the outrage. 'Did he catch them and break their wings for you?'

Clara recoiled, shocked. 'Eliot, that is … is an ugly thing to say. Why would you say such a thing?'

My memory of that period of the voyage is unreliable. When I shut my eyes I see glimpses of Clara, continuing to nurse me, and with her help I began to regain my strength. I remember asking her to tie her hair back in a braid across the top of her head. She obliged, saying it gave her a youthful appearance. Quite so, I replied, but secretly I had viewed her with renewed elation and amazement, for it was the same hairstyle that Celeste had had. 'Another thing, dear Clara,' I had ventured, 'a couple of weeks ago you wore a pearlescent silk dress. It was very lovely. Would you mind wearing it again?' A simple request, one that in ordinary conversation would have been an innocent remark to make. But not for me. Pearl silk was the colour of the gown that Celeste had worn, as she had been led along the brick path by her mother.

Re-dressing Clara, re-creating Celeste, it had been a natural urge. And I was delighted as, each time Clara obliged, it felt as though she was allowing it one step at a time. Allowing herself to become Celeste once more.

As the ship was put back in order, I sensed a restoration of my own spirits too. Whatever malaise had struck me, I believed I was able to overcome it. The body can lead the mind out of its troubles. I would walk the deck at a brisk pace, try to eat as much food as Simao would supply, and at all costs I would avoid any preparation of drinks that Bletchley or French offered.

Preoccupied as I was, I failed to notice how the storm had affected Edward. Ever since it had ended, he had spent much of each day on deck, wearing a sealskin hat he must have procured from one of the Esquimaux settlements. He wore it pulled low across his forehead, as he would a bandage, and paced from side to side, examining the countenance of the sea and looking towards the distant coast of Greenland with one of the captain's telescopes. He was distracted and I generally avoided him, but there were occasions when his and my routes crossed, and it was at one of these times I decided to press him for answers.

'What is it you are studying, Edward?' I asked. 'You seem fascinated by the sea, yet all morning it has not changed one bit.'

He looked at me curiously from beneath the brow of his sealskin hat, as if the complexity of replying was beyond him.

'The sea?' I repeated.

'Yes, yes,' he answered, impatiently.

'Would you care for some tobacco?' I offered, hoping it might settle his nerves. He reached for his pipe and held out a hand, much as a child might do.

'That sailor standing by the blocks,' he muttered, 'he has no stem to his pipe. Have you noticed?'

'I have, Edward. In fact, I have asked him about it. He told me that he scorches his cheeks when he smokes.'

'They are strange men,' Bletchley snorted. 'Happiest near flames. They are devils.'

I chose not to comment, hoping he wouldn't become agitated.

'I have been meaning to ask you about Clara,' I said,

between the puffs of lighting my pipe. 'It has perplexed me since the start of our voyage. I have been wondering whether I recognise her.' I nursed the flame in my pipe, trying to calm the rapidity of my heartbeat. 'I was raised in Suffolk, you see.'

'What of it?' he asked.

'Well, I believe Clara is from Norfolk. I am familiar with several of the Norfolk families. Was her home near Somerleyton?'

'I was never allowed to go to her home,' Bletchley replied, remembering an old slight. He looked out to sea once more, as if I could not entirely hold his attention. 'Her father banned my visits.'

'Yes, her father,' I mused, seizing an opportunity. 'Am I correct in thinking he is a magistrate? He has a fine collection of birds' eggs.'

'The father is an ogre, that is the sum of what I know of the man. I am only in contact with Clara now because it's behind that man's back.'

I couldn't decide whether Bletchley was being open or dishonest in his responses. He appeared to be both, and I was in danger of making a fool of myself. I decided to take a bolder approach, thinking it might cause the breakthrough I required.

'It is strange, but I believe Clara has not always been her name.'

A flicker of vexation flashed across his face, but it was fleeting and may not have meant anything. He had the tendency to try out expressions, even when he was alone. Even while he slept by the stove, with his blanket wrapped around him, his face flinched with tremors and twitches.

'An intriguing theory,' he replied.

To stop at this point would have been maddening for me,

but I could tell Bletchley had little interest in continuing. 'Was she once known as Celeste?' I asked.

'*Celeste*, you say? A pretty name – she would be deserving of it. We have discussed her charms and attractions at an earlier occasion, have we not? But Mr Saxby, I do not quite understand you. You are suggesting she is two people?'

'One person, but with two names.'

'How queer. You have a curious mind. But in truth there isn't any one among us who is one person. We are all many personalities. Now if you will excuse me, I have much thinking to do.'

I reached out and held his elbow, frustrated by his evasions. He looked surprised, staring at my hand as if it was something he could not comprehend. 'You are holding me,' he said.

'Edward ...' I wondered how to continue. 'What is the nature of your friendship with Clara?'

He turned in my grasp, a little hostile. I thought of him wrestling with French, how he had forced a stronger man up by sheer tenacity. 'She is my cousin,' he said, properly. 'More than that I do not know it is any of your business.'

'She cares greatly for you.'

'Yes, she does. We have this –' he tapped his head. 'A connection.'

'My point is that she cares for you, and I do not wish your actions to hurt her.'

'My *actions*?'

Our exchange was rapidly slipping away from my control. Already, several of the men had noticed I was restraining Bletchley by the arm. I adopted a kindly tone towards him: 'This voyage appears to have changed you considerably.' I let go of his arm and he deflated somewhat, as if I had been bolstering him.

'Yes, that is true,' he conceded. I glimpsed a relief in him, that he was able to acknowledge it publicly. 'The journey has not been as I expected. I have told you, Eliot, about the expression the seal had, when I shot it? I can see that it troubles you for me to mention it again. But I am still haunted by it. And this ship is haunted by it, also.'

'The *ship*? In what way?' I asked.

He chuckled, as if it was clear to anyone who bothered to notice.

'You will have to explain,' I pressed.

'The Esquimaux are interesting people,' he began. 'It is their belief that all things have a soul. Not merely man, but also the animals and the world at large. In this manner, all things are connected by a continuation of life that we have little understanding of. If you wish to know what troubles me and forces me to wait by the stove night after night, it is because this journey has made a great imbalance. We have filled the hull of this ship with dead things. It is the weight of their souls that has caused us all to suffer.'

I listened with alarm at the elaboration of his thinking. Nights of vigil at that stove had enabled him to construct something quite wild.

'Some creatures have several souls,' he reflected, to himself.

'You were fully aware of the nature of this trip before you started,' I tried. 'Why, you even had guns made for you, with engraved stocks for the purpose of your hunting . . .'

He scoffed. 'Those guns!' he said, disgusted. He looked on the verge of tears, haunted by the man he had once been, a man he now wished to deny. He stared at me with an appeal in his expression I had never seen before. His mood was very volatile. 'Illness is a small death of the soul, and I have been ill, Eliot, as have you. I recognise things in your eyes, my friend. Deep secrets. I *see it*.'

305

'What do you see?' I asked, cornered.

'Damage.'

I wanted to escape him. I felt my blood pounding in my ears.

'My remedy has been extreme,' he continued. 'May I tell you?'

'You must.'

'I have been tying myself to my bunk,' he said, 'so that my soul might be freed from my body. It is a practice of lustration performed by the shamans of these communities we have visited. I can see you are horrified.'

'I am attempting to understand you, that is all.'

'My conclusion is that the ship and all of us upon it have committed a wrong. It is full of the dead and we have not been forgiven. This ship is carrying a migration of souls, but it is upon a route not of their wishing.' He looked at me as a teacher might, who has outlined a theory but is disappointed that the student cannot grasp it.

'It is why we were in that storm,' he explained.

'Edward, I have to stop you. It was a *storm*, a natural occurrence, that is all – it was nothing else.'

He continued to look at me with disappointment. 'It is why we were in that storm,' he repeated, as if to say it once more would validate his theory, 'and it is why the voyage shall end in disaster.'

This time, it was Bletchley who reached out to hold my elbow. 'But do not worry. I will correct the imbalance,' he said confidently. With an enigmatic wink he added:

'I shall see to it myself.'

Occasionally, the distant coast of Greenland would appear, little more than a charcoal smudge above the horizon, as if a wipe of a cloth could remove it from the world. We had left a curious litter on that land: a scattering of manufactured goods, Sheffield steel, needles, rifles, shells and primers, flints, hooks and line, forged tools and blades, cutlery and cloths. We had left the bones of the auks on the shore at Jakobshavn, for the gulls and ravens – Sykes had overlooked the fact that even their skeletons would have value to museums – and we had left the headless stump of the walrus on the shingle where it had been slain. Perhaps we had left illness, too. It is said that the Europeans are murdering the Esquimaux, simply by bringing influenza and smallpox. So that was the sum of our trade: a hull emptied of English steel, and replaced with the skins and feathers and bones of a wilderness. Bletchley was correct. It was a hold full of death.

It was the same story with all the ships that travelled north. They arrived empty, hungry to be fed, at an Arctic where they would feast and feast until they could take no more. The whales would be lashed to the ships and their blubber sliced, peeled in strips as wide as a mattress by flensing hooks and cables, before being boiled and rendered and poured into barrels. Jawbones would be opened and baleen extracted with axes, for corset stays and parasol ribs, and ambergris would be searched for in the rank miles of intestines, men reaching up to their shoulders into unimaginable filth, groping for secretions more valuable by weight than gold itself. Birds would be shot from the sky or plucked from cliff ledges, their eggs gathered or smashed and their pelts reduced to pillow down and writing quills. Seals would be clubbed with oars and hakapiks and hammers and spikes, their colonies would erupt with slicks of blood on the ice. Some of their hides would be unsheathed while the animal still thrashed with life and their pups looked on bewildered. This Arctic, so grey and white and endless, contained a welling of blood that was as bright as fire, and this frozen sea that was as vast and lonely and as wild as any place on earth, it had been set fire to. It was a burning sea.

The men who came here plundered indiscriminately: wherever they saw life there was profit or trade. Some animals were a greater challenge than others, but for every animal there existed a method, and all could eventually be killed. Knife, hammer, wooden stick or gun. It was a larder with apparently infinite resources, yet it was clear the Arctic was not infinitely replenished. The seals are harder to find now, the whales are scarcer. The nesting ledges are falling quiet.

We had stumbled across a rarity akin to a pot of gold at the tip of a rainbow: the last family of great auks. It had been a test, where the conscience and nature of man would be questioned. He had met it with a simple, practised answer: to slaughter, and slaughter, and slaughter again.

From this fire we had extracted a single flame of hope. A bird that, with the true tenacity of nature, had become a bird and its egg. A single thread of life on which might hang the future of an entire species.

The bird was now eating voraciously, either from Clara's hand or my own, taking the fish with a dry parted beak, much as a parrot carefully takes a nut, before throwing back its head to swallow it whole, with quite a flourish. The auk's eyes were glistening with a new-found lustre, and it growled and wheezed so comically and loudly that we had to tie the binding around its beak to keep it calling for us when we were elsewhere.

'She is quite a character,' I said to Clara. 'She fusses with that egg as if it's a hot potato.'

'And she mumbles considerably. Sometimes at night I think I hear her, grumbling and complaining. I lie there wishing she would be quiet – even though I know it's not possible to hear her from the cabins.'

The *Amethyst* was making good progress, flying before a zephyr wind, which meant time was running out.

'Clara,' I whispered, alone with her after breakfast one morning, 'it is only a few hundred miles of ocean between here and England. We might not even *see* land, let alone discover a sheltered cove or appropriate cliff or reef where we might release the bird.'

She stiffened in her posture. 'I wish those men would stop winding the bilge pump and let the ship sink!' she said, vexed. 'What shall we do?'

'We must bring the bird to England.'

'Oh no! That is impossible!'

'Speak quietly.'

'But England is part of the disease that has killed these birds.'

'I am aware of that.'

She looked cornered. 'Has French told you to say such a thing?'

'No. No – of course not. I haven't spoken to him about this.'

'You sound like him,' she replied, disappointed. 'Forgive me. What I mean to say is – there is nothing for this bird in England. Nothing but hunters and cruelty – you know that in your heart, don't you? It would either be killed and stuffed, or it would be paraded around like a circus animal.'

'But in England we *might* be able to find a safe haven for it.'

She looked steadily at me. I wasn't even convincing myself.

'Then we shall have to take a greater risk,' I conceded. 'We have no choice. We must tell the captain.'

She flinched, quite openly, as if she had been stung. I held her hand to console her.

'We tell the captain,' I continued, 'and we appeal to his greater nature. He is the only person who would be able to find a suitable place for the bird and its chick. He has his haul and fortune – what difference would it make to him?'

'But you tried to appeal to the captain's good nature before,' she said. 'Sykes is an open book. He is out to make a profit.'

I agreed, but it was an impossible situation. She had to understand that. 'Yes, dear Clara. I tried with Sykes. But it might be different if we *both* tried.'

The idea made her curious: 'Are men so easily unlocked?'

I shrugged, at last feeling I had made some ground in the conversation. She was willing to grasp at straws, as I was. 'I had a game of draughts with him once – the black pieces were flattened bullets, and the white ones were discs of seal bones. When we played, I had the feeling that all he cared about was the playing of games. He likes to joust and kid. Perhaps there is nothing more to the man.'

'Do you really believe that?'

'I do not know. But there is another thing. He is ill. You have seen him coughing into his handkerchief until he is red in the face. He *knows* he is ill. I witnessed a moment at the whaling station when he was unguarded, and I am beginning to think he might act more favourably towards us as a consequence.'

'But why?'

It was difficult to answer, other than admit it was purely a guess. 'Surely, if you feel your time might be running out, you might have empathy for the predicament of this animal?'

'You think a dying man suddenly becomes interested in the last of a species?'

I laughed. 'Something like that.'

She smiled, happily. 'What I love in you is that you are an idealist.'

'I wasn't sure I was one, until this voyage.'

'I think that you should hold me.'

'Here?'

'Of course. And you wish to save things,' she whispered.

'Yes. That is true.'

I put my arms around her. She was thin and fragile; the hard lines of her shoulder bones felt as curved and delicate as walking canes.

'Now,' she continued, 'squeeze me. Until my breath has gone.'

Alarmed, I broke free of her, but she clung to my arms with an insistent grip. 'Please,' she urged.

'But why?' I tried. She brought my arms around her waist and guided them across her back, waiting for me to oblige her.

I pulled my arms tight, interlocking them and gradually pressing her within my hold. I imagined all there was to her, her bones and flesh, her densities and the spaces of her body that were filled with air. I imagined them contracting, disappearing.

Clara gasped in pain; quickly, I let her go, shocked by a pressure I hadn't known I was exerting. She looked back at me, flushed and unembarrassed, with a triumphant smile that faded as quickly as it had formed.

'Tell me, who won at draughts?' she asked, unnaturally composed.

I stared back, bewildered. She raised her eyebrows.

'Oh, he did,' I said, 'quite easily.'

'Then he's always going to win, I suspect.'

'Did I hurt you?'

'My cousin told me of your conversation with him,' she

said. 'Did he tell you that he has been tying himself to his bunk, in the attempt to free his spirit?'

'Yes.'

'Tell me, Eliot – do you think him mad?'

How to answer? I wasn't sure. The journey had certainly affected him. 'I'm not convinced that I would recognise madness,' I replied.

'But you think he is an addict?'

'An addict?'

'Of opiates.' She looked at me without judgement. 'I can see you do.'

I told her what Bletchley had said, how he had insisted this voyage had become a migration of souls, but that it was a damned migration that had offended a natural balance. 'I must admit I didn't quite follow him. Has he said this to you? He is planning to correct the imbalance.'

'I am looking after him,' she said, formally.

'By tying him to a bunk?'

'If that is what he needs, I think I shouldn't refuse him,' she answered. 'He believes a demon wants to find mischief with him.'

Bletchley performed his correction one night, as we approached Cape Farewell and our last sight of Greenland, from the stern rail. Apparently the three men on watch – curious as to why he was cloaked and dragging a large package – had attempted to stop him, but he had shrugged them off with great strength. Thinking he might be about to leap into the sea, they had been relieved when all he had done was to throw the tightly wrapped bundle away from the ship. It had caught briefly in the moonlight and they had heard the splash. It must have been weighted down, for it quickly sank.

The men had stood away from him, naturally wary of a man they had never understood.

Apparently he had spoken in a clear, calm voice: 'One of you devils should inform the captain that I have saved the ship. Please tell him I have thrown his cargo of great auk skins into the ocean.'

25

Within minutes of Bletchley being brought down from deck, I had been summoned to the saloon. Pacing with frustration, Sykes was already mid-rant, flushed pink as a lobster and burning with frustration. He was overdressed in his sea coat, which appeared to have been hurriedly buttoned on top of his night attire, and his constant agitation made the saloon feel crowded. French and Talbot stood awkwardly on opposite sides of the room, as if between them they were pushing the captain from one to the other, as in some diabolical maritime game. Sitting stoically on a wooden chair, Bletchley was more serene than he had appeared for several weeks. But he was obviously guilty of something, and although he sat with his eyes half closed, placid and untroubled, I felt there was a coiled tension hinged within his body, making him at any moment liable to spring up.

'I should have you in irons!' Sykes shouted, marching back and forth in front of his passenger in the manner of a bullying schoolmaster. 'And to think that my officers – my own officers – warned me of your increasingly errant behaviour. All your peculiar night-time vigils by that stove and the like. But would I listen to them? I did not! I believed you to be an eccentric, but this is not the case is it, man? Is it? You are little more than a criminal – you have meddled with the business of the ship and as a consequence you have wilfully ruined our financial returns.'

Bletchley accepted his role without complaint, allowing the rant to fall on him with phlegmatic patience. He showed no sign that he was even listening to the captain's words, let alone preparing to defend himself.

'You are maddening!' Sykes said, in disgust.

Emerging from her cabin, Clara made a swift assessment of the judicial nature of the gathering.

'Captain Sykes!' she said. 'I have been hearing your accusations from within my cabin. It is intolerable. How dare you address a gentleman in this tone? What has happened to your manners? What, sir, has happened?' She deliberately stood directly in Sykes' path, preventing him from completing one of his crossings of the room. He looked startled by the obstacle put in his way, and I realised that, despite his parade of authority, despite this being his ship, a woman's presence instantly quelled him.

He regarded her gravely, picking his words. 'Perhaps your relative will explain,' he said, dismissively.

'Well, Edward?' Clara asked.

But Bletchley made no motion to speak. He closed his eyes, his silence not one of guilt, but of the morally wronged. He would take no part in this.

'He is determined not to speak,' the captain stated.

'What have you done to him?' Clara said, indignantly.

Sykes deferred to his first mate: 'Mr French, if you please.'

French looked up, a little surprised. Quickly clearing his throat, he adopted a serious demeanour sufficient to outline the crime. 'He has thrown the skins of the great auks into the ocean.'

No one spoke. The news silenced the room, the way

315

irreversible fact always does. I have often tried to recall the moment of this announcement, how Clara jolted with surprise, whereas Sykes stared dark-eyed at the floorboards. And French, a quickening tension in his expression, avoiding everyone's eye. I had imagined a blank depth of water that pressed around me, and had the urge to reach within it, into its featureless and lightless fathoms, chasing something that could not be found.

I knew Bletchley's warped logic. This was the corrective gesture he had promised. Of course it was. How could I not have seen?

Clara was the first to speak: 'Is it true, Edward?'

Bletchley snapped open his eyes, as if waking from a pleasant daydream. 'Oh, yes, quite true,' he answered, in a blissfully light manner.

'But are they *lost*?' she asked.

Captain Sykes sighed, looking deflated. 'He weighted the bundle, madam. It has sunk to the ocean bed.'

The finality of the act subdued the room. The last breeding colony, needlessly slaughtered, now entirely vanished. And alongside that, a further fact: history would have no record of this journey. The captain's logbook would be proficiently filled with hourly readings and separate columns for knots, fathoms, course, wind and leeway. Navigation and speed would be calculated and plotted with the utmost accuracy. But there would be no mention of the birds that were found and lost. No one would ever know there had once been a chance to save this species, but that chance had not been taken, because of greed, because of man's weakness. All of us, present, would be too ashamed of the story to tell it.

Whether or not Bletchley became, at that moment, aware of what he had done, he was suddenly keen to elaborate.

'I used a length of chain,' he explained, demonstrating with his hands how he had wrapped the package. He looked happy in the precise nature of the task: 'In order for it to sink.'

'But why, man?' Talbot asked, fed up beyond bearing with a man he'd never understood.

Bletchley regarded Talbot with curiosity, his mouth half opened ready to shed light. But Talbot's sheer presence, his broad bearded jaw and straightforward expression, the countenance of a man requiring blunt solutions to practical problems, seemed only to amuse Bletchley rather than require an answer.

'We might consider the ocean bed a more fitting grave for these birds than the public spectacle of them being mounted within display cases, where our guilt might be looked upon for hundreds of years to come.'

'*Avast!* I have had my fill of your prattle!' Sykes roared, his strength regained. 'You talk of these birds as if they have *souls*. They are *cargo*, and you have destroyed them. Perhaps Mr Saxby here will explain just how valuable each of those birds might have been.'

I crossed my arms, reluctant to take part. 'I do not wish to comment,' I said.

'But you shall, Saxby, because I am your captain and I have asked you.'

I felt a restless energy in the room, keen to find a new victim. 'All I have to say is that the collection of those birds was a doomed and cynical venture from the start.'

He dismissed me with an impatient wave of his hand. 'The cost, Mr Saxby?'

'The cost in pounds is probably several times the value of the rest of your cargo, if that is what you require from me.' Before he could answer, I made it clear I had more to say. 'But the cost to the animal kingdom was immeasurable, and it was not Edward, but you, who committed that crime.'

'Enough!' he spat back. 'I will not be judged on board my own ship!'

The captain's anger was fierce, but it bounced off me. I felt emboldened by the realisation that for once I was not afraid of him. 'It is not being judged on board this ship that should concern you. It is the rest of the world that shall judge you, sir. You may be captain on this plank of wood, but as soon as this vessel docks in Liverpool you will be seen merely as a profiteer. A man who recklessly murdered a species for the sake of a few pounds. That is your crime and it is for that you will be judged.'

Sykes turned on me, squaring up like a street brawler, even though I was a good few inches taller than him. 'You are young, and foolish,' he snarled. 'I am in the business of survival, Mr Saxby, of making a living and a profit. I am doing what every Englishman was born to do, and I am proud of it. My type is strong and it is in the majority. You, on the other hand, are in the business of trying to save the things that are already lost. For that, you are foolish. And you are mistaken, too, in considering that the world of this ship is inconsequential.' He held out his fist and opened it, revealing a wide, fleshy palm. 'Your life and all the lives on board this ship are in my hand, right now. We are surrounded by a cruel ocean and dangerous coasts. This ship, sir, *is* the world.'

He turned away from me, contemptuous and in command. Beyond him I noticed French regarding me curiously, as if I was a problem he could not solve. As usual, he showed no sign of standing up in my defence. Instead, it was Clara who came to my aid.

'The birds are gone, captain,' she said, her voice impeccably

318

reasonable. 'There is little point in venting your frustration now.'

Sykes looked at her, apparently considering a futile response, knowing he had no answer for her. Instead, as he assessed her proximity to me, I saw a glint of amusement flicker in his eye. He nodded, reluctantly, and addressed his officers:

'We shall not take passengers upon this ship in the future,' he said. 'They are supernumerary, they do not understand the sea, and when they speak, I do not understand what they say.'

Talbot actually smiled, as if he'd wished for this moment for a long time. I remembered how he had looked at me during the first meal on board the ship, chewing his beef with greasy, unpleasant lips.

Oddly, Bletchley thought this the best time to voice an opinion. 'Captain Sykes,' he said, speaking when he should have absolutely kept quiet, 'in actual fact I believe you should *thank* me for what I have done.'

'Are you quite insane?' Sykes replied.

'I have saved you,' Bletchley continued, blithely following the logic of his actions. 'It is the Esquimaux who believe that—'

'We have heard enough from you,' Sykes interrupted. 'You are nothing but a mountebank and you are preferable when you do not speak. French, the men will want to know the situation. Go for'ard and inform them, I will have no secrets on board. Have the yards set acockbill for an hour tomorrow.' He turned back to Bletchley with the attitude of a parent who can't get enough of admonishing a child. 'You shall be confined to the passenger quarters for the remainder of the voyage. Under hatches, you understand? You are a liability about the ship, you have proved this most convincingly, and

I can therefore not vouch for your safety among the crew – you must understand that they have lost quite a dividend, too, as a result of your foolish actions. They are hardworking men, sir, and they might express their anger in an ungentlemanly manner.' He clenched his fist and regarded his knuckles, whitening with pressure.

Sykes turned to his cabin and went inside, closing the door with a slam. In his absence the room felt misshapen, with a scolded air. We remained positioned around Bletchley, who looked content on his seat. French nervously examined his fob watch, his usual gesture, before walking briskly up the steps to the deck without a second look towards the rest of us. Talbot followed him, clearing his throat loudly and walking wearily to the companionway.

'I will look after Edward,' Clara said, when the officers had departed. 'Let us decide what to do with him in the morning.'

'Did you know he was going to do this?' I asked.

I placed a hand on her shoulder. She looked sadly at me, then sighed:

'How could I?'

In my cabin, I lay on the bunk and pressed a hand to my forehead. I was shocked by what Bletchley had done, and the brutishness that it had unleashed in the captain. I remembered the miracle of discovering those birds in the mist, the sheer joy at finding them alive, then the agony of having to watch as one by one they were drowned, an entire species meeting its extinction. To battle through all this with the captain, to witness him bragging of their worth with the Greenland whalers and listen to him negotiate with the Esquimaux to have them skinned. All this, for them to be thrown into the sea. So futile! I imagined them, descending through the complete night of the Atlantic Ocean. They were probably still sinking, even at that moment, tunnelling into uncharted depths, never to be seen again.

Over the next couple of days a troubled air persisted throughout the ship. The officers went about their tasks with perfunctory routine, ordering the sails to be trimmed and re-trimmed, the masts to be greased, the rigging tarred, and the deck to be sanded and scrubbed with stone bibles. A spinning wheel was brought up on deck, and the sound of the yarn being made was a constantly whirring accompaniment, much like the sound of a nightjar patrolling its woodland territory, coming and going, coming and going. Oakum was piled up, and in groups the men unwound ropes while further along the deck another group replaited them. Senseless work to occupy idle hands, with intermittent, perplexing orders being issued by the officers: *Mr Talbot, will you see that the men cover those ropes with new foxes*, or *stuff the sides and be ordered about it*, or *address the top nettings and fringes*. One of the men was hoisted up the mast on a boatswain's chair so that he could pour hot fat from the galley onto the wood.

The crew set about this work without complaint, but perhaps because of my sensitivity to the situation on board, I glimpsed a difference in their attitude, a flat disappointment. Bletchley did as he had been instructed, staying in his cabin. Meals were taken to him, and at night he no longer sat in his chair by the side of the stove. Of the captain, I saw very little. He spent his hours in his cabin and at noon he took sightings of the sun before retreating to the chart room. The possibility of seeking his help to save the last bird had become inconceivable.

The weather improved; it lost the bite of Arctic cold, and instead became wet and softer. I fancied I smelt the coast of

321

England, many times, while walking the deck at night. For the first time I began to anticipate our return, imagining my disembarkation at the quay in Liverpool, very much an enlightened man. Free, too. Free to plot a future – a hesitant farewell to Clara hand in hand with a desire to meet again. I imagined travelling to Norfolk, this autumn – when I would walk up the long drive to the manor near Somerleyton, crossing the once familiar damp lawn in front of the old house, and it would be she who would rush out to greet me, healing a wound that had remained open all these years. And as we embraced, the rooks would rise from their roosts in the trees as if a curse had been lifted.

Two nights after Bletchley had destroyed the birds, I was considering these things, smoking my pipe at the bow of the ship, when one of the crew came to my side asking for tobacco. It was Connor Herlihy, who often smoked at the same spot. He placed his foot through a hawse hole, as he'd done before, so he could lean on one leg.

'Thank you, sir,' he said, sucking on his pipe stem. He seemed intent on gazing at the horizon. 'A nasty business, to be sure, with the loss of them birds,' he said.

'Yes,' I replied.

'A great loss.'

He puffed at his pipe, in no hurry, then tapped his foot in the hawse hole. 'It's said, you enter the ship by them hawse holes, you come into the service at the lowest level.'

'I didn't know that,' I replied.

'Mm. It's true,' he said, thoughtfully. 'Anyhows, we'll be back soon. You'll be glad to be home?'

'Maybe.'

'You think you'll be a-sailing again?'

'Well, that also feels uncertain.'

'Like I says, you have the eyes for a sailor.' He viewed me

quizzically, sucking on his pipe. 'Very pale blue, sir. I think they would suit the Arctic.'

'Thank you.'

'I suppose those eyes of yours wouldn't be missing nothing, now,' he continued. I regarded him, a little wary of his direction. 'I have been wondering sir, might I ask yous a question?'

'Of course, Herlihy.'

'It's been botherin' me, an' that younger brother of mine,' he said. He sucked on his pipe and relit the tobacco, taking his time. I watched the light flickering on his strong face. 'I been wondering, sir, what happened to the eighth bird?'

I looked away, too startled to face him.

'Juss wonderin', sir,' he repeated.

'I don't follow you,' I managed.

He smiled, and the impertinent fellow actually gave me a wink. He waited, allowing me to leave, should I wish to. When he saw that I was going to remain, that I had to hear what he had to say, he seemed satisfied.

'It's just, when I was on that rock with them birds of yours, I saw it hidden in the crack.' He made a gesture of pointing at the planks near his feet, as if re-creating the vision of the auk concealed in the crevice. With apprehension, I realised he was also pointing straight down to where the anchor locker was, several feet below us.

'I do not know what you are talking about.'

He chuckled. 'Like I says before, a good sailor is devious.' He raised his eyebrows at me, and I saw the flicker of indecision in his expression. Surely he was uncertain how far he might question a gentleman? Yet there remained a stubbornness to the line of his mouth and the directness of his gaze that made me think he was past caring. He was difficult to gauge. Eventually, he took a step away from me, allowing me

323

to take my leave. Again, he saw that I was going to hear him out. He smiled knowingly.

'You have the bird on board?'

'I think it's impertinent of you to ask me this.'

'Aye, right you are, sir. And that would be the ordinary position, it would. But my tongue is quick on account of the things are bad at home. The crop has failed again. It has given me a desperation, to think of them digging in that wet earth and them fingers findin' nothing in there but the rot and the disease.'

'Be that as it may, if you continue, I shall have to report this conversation to the captain.'

'Yes, sir.'

'He wouldn't take kindly to the things you have said.'

'No, sir, he wouldn't.'

'Insinuation is what it is.'

'Aye.'

I prepared to leave, looking him in the eye and seeing nothing but a flat reflected gleam of the night's sky. His face was a patchwork of shadows and ambiguity.

'So you are wanting money from me,' I stated.

He sounded surprised. 'For what, sir?'

'For your silence. And for your brother's silence.'

He looked out to sea, knitting his brows, as if the answer was out there. He considered his options.

'Is that what you think?' he said.

'Yes. It's what I think.'

'No,' he sighed. 'I don't want your money. I just want to know about that eighth bird.'

It appeared a simple, honest appeal. I looked at him, at the strong square face that was both open and impenetrable.

'You're an unusual person,' I remarked.

'Aye, has been said before,' he replied, smiling.

'Do you remember when we climbed the cliffs and stood among the gannet colony?' I said. 'It was a mad place, wasn't it?'

'Yes, sir, I thought we'd be pecked ragged.'

'You amused me, that day, you and your brother. We were fairly scared, weren't we?'

He laughed. 'Well, in truth, me brother was more scared than me.'

I tapped my pipe out against the brass top of the capstan. 'It's hidden in the anchor locker,' I said.

He broke into a broad grin, revealing the strong even teeth of an honest working man. 'I said you could be a fine sailor. You *are* devious.'

'This time I'll take it as a compliment.'

'It's been there all this while?'

'It has.'

'Will you be selling it?'

'No, Connor. I want to set it free, where it will be safe.'

'It has value.'

'Yes, but not a value that can be measured in pounds. And I have some news for you. It has laid an egg.'

'An egg? Well I'll be blessed!' He stood, shaking his head.

'I am sorry about Ireland,' I said. 'I am sorry about the potato crop.'

'That's fairly odd, to hear an Englishman say that.'

'I don't really know what being an Englishman means,' I said. 'But Connor, what about your duty to the captain? To tell him what is on board?'

He pocketed his pipe and wiped his hands on his jacket, preparing to leave. 'What duty would that be, sir?' he said. 'We're just his Irish bastards.'

I had little choice, after this exchange, to relate it to French. The knowledge that two or more of the crew knew that there was a concealed bird on board forced my hand. Connor might be genuine, but others might not be. I didn't truly comprehend the workings and hierarchies of the ship, so I felt I needed advice in the matter.

I found him in his cabin, once more writing at his desk with the nib of his scratchy pen. Yet as before, when he welcomed me in, his desk had been conspicuously and hurriedly cleared, although the familiar candle burnt brightly, right in front of where he had been sitting.

'Quinlan, I am sorry it is late, but there has been a development of our situation. I have just come down from deck, where I was accosted by one of the crew. He knows all about the bird.'

I had expected a reaction from French, but he remained almost impossibly impassive. 'He knows it is in the anchor locker,' I continued.

He sat, quite comfortable in his chair, and began to rub the side of his finger where the writing ink had left a stain.

'The name?' he asked, at length.

'One of the Herlihy brothers. Connor.'

'Yes, yes. I could have guessed it would be that one.'

'Possibly there are others, too.'

French's self-interest was quick to show: 'Do they know my part in it?'

'He made no reference.'

'I see.'

'So what should we do?'

'Do?' he replied. 'I suppose we should do nothing. They know better than to challenge the authority of the ship, especially if they suspect an officer might be involved.' His manner became quickly overtaken by a barely controlled anger. 'I hate them, Saxby, are you aware of that? I hate the way those men sing their mindless shanties and smoke their foul pipes and the way they obey orders with a knowing look. I hate the smells of cooking that come from the fo'c'sle and the sound of the laughter. It must be fetid in there, and yet they love the stink and the grime. They are little more than pigs.'

Even by French's standards, he was in a volatile mood, partly surprised at his own outburst, partly relishing it. I realised the underlying current that welled in him, which occasionally broke the surface, was a thing he was greatly fascinated by.

'You were writing again. I am sorry to interrupt you,' I said.

'Oh, it is nothing,' he replied, his tone still torn between self-control and its release. 'It is wasted effort – she will never read it.'

Abruptly he turned away, as if dismayed. I saw he had been caught off guard, and was attempting to conceal a revelation. Sensing the nearness of an answer I understood to have been long bothering me, I asked him:

'She ... ?'

French stared at me with a look of excitement, attracted to the idea of telling me, of telling someone of the conflict that had been keeping him awake all these nights.

'I have been writing a long letter – but it is so difficult – it has taken me several drafts. I don't enjoy writing, not in the least. The words take me off on routes I didn't predict.'

'To a sweetheart?'

'I hope that will be the case.'

'I see. So it's a letter of persuasion.'

He nodded. 'But the words are hard to find.'

For the briefest moment I saw a glimpse of the man French held too much at bay. A youthful man, still believing in a world of hopes and desires.

'It is good to see you in this spirit,' I said. 'I have often wondered what really lies within you.' He looked back at me, a little quizzically. 'So,' I continued, not wanting to relinquish this new openness from him, 'have you known this lady for long?'

'A while.'

'In what capacity?'

He sounded amused. 'We have ... dined together, on several occasions.'

'You like her character?'

'Yes.'

'And is she pleasing on the eye?'

'She is—' He broke off, grinning unpleasantly. 'Eliot, what is the point of this silly game you are playing? Are you making fun of me?'

He looked confused, as if I was not following him at all. 'I am talking about *Clara*,' he said.

I felt a sudden hotness, possibly even a blush, which doubled in intensity under his scrutiny. '*Clara?*' I managed to say. 'But how is that possible?'

He spoke warily. 'Surely you knew my feelings?'

There are moments when merely the postures of two men, sitting a few feet apart in a small cabin, reveal more than anything they are prepared to say. A certain awareness; facts seen in complete clarity. And I felt it right then, facing this acquaintance who had quickly become a rival. French knew it too, I could see it.

'Oh,' he uttered, knowing for the first time the true extent of my own feelings towards Clara.

I nodded.

'I would like you to leave now,' he ordered.

I returned to my cabin, troubled, and lay upon my bunk just a few feet away from a man whose presence had a palpable

328

heat to it. I imagined him bringing his desk candle close to his face, regretting his *lapsus linguae*, his slip of the tongue, and staring at it until the flame purged his soul.

By breakfast, everything had changed. Clara was refusing to emerge from her cabin, the sound of her inconsolable tears quite evident to all on board. Two men from the crew had been brought to stand sentry in the saloon. They stood, awkward but dutiful, one outside the captain's quarters and one with his back to the stove, avoiding anyone's eye. And in the captain's cabin, Sykes was gazing at the great auk, which had been placed in the centre of his table. Proudly, he tried stroking its plumage, then prodded its breast with a curious finger. With his free hand he reached for its egg, lifting it carefully, examining it and gauging its weight as if it were an ingot of pure gold.

26

Even now, five years later, the image of Sykes with the bird in his cabin has the power to upset me. It was a sight that ran against the grain: life hanging by its most fragile thread from a hand that weighed its potential for profit. I felt defeated and ashamed. Ashamed for ever having tried to meddle with fate. Extinction, I realised, is a process that cannot be negotiated.

The reversal of fortune had made Sykes amiable and relaxed. He welcomed me heartily, like an old friend, inviting me to sit on his settee; once he was sure I would comply, he replaced his glasses on the end of his nose and continued his observations.

'It is quite a remarkable creature,' he said, with pleasure. 'Either you have tamed it, which I think is unlikely, or this bird really has no fear of mankind. Regard this, if you will.' The auk was standing squarely upon Sykes' table, without bindings around either its beak or wings. It was contented and almost sleepy. Sykes reached forward with an inquisitive finger and gently nudged the bird's neck. The auk stirred, watching the finger curiously. With a swift movement, Sykes flicked it hard upon the side of its beak. The bird flinched, snapping its neck back, and I heard the sound of its claws trying to grip the polished wood, but with startling ease it quickly resumed its previous pose. Sykes laughed, satisfied: 'See, it forgives me immediately! I believe it regards the slight against it as having emerged from my finger, not myself.'

I felt utter disbelief. Disbelief that I should ever have to see this. The bird had for so long been a secret, belonging to the shadows of the anchor locker. It belonged to Clara and myself. It was our bird and our secret alone. As usual, Sykes was allowing me no time to consider the new complexities of a rapidly changed situation. With the gesture of a prearranged signal, he rang a small handbell on his desk, and almost at once his cabin door opened. Quinlan French entered, somewhat hesitantly, but rigidly upright, glancing first at the bird that was standing on the table, and next at the captain, who was choosing which chair to sit in to admire his new prize. Eagerly, I sought French's expression, hoping for an ally, but he was reluctant to meet my eye. He looked awkward and shifting, undecided between standing or sitting, and it appeared as though he had not slept well.

'Now I see there are aspects to my needlework image that were incorrect,' the captain continued, deliberately cheerful. 'She is much plumper around here, and down this line towards the belly and legs. Something of a baggy-trousered look. And in the manner that she sits upon her haunches she is more womanly than I expected.'

I decided to speak. 'Is no one going to attend to Clara? It appears you are unable to hear the obvious distress that she is in.'

Sykes rocked his head from side to side, but chose to ignore me. Instead, he picked a fillet of dried fish and held it in front of the bird, excited by the possibility of making it perform. The auk saw the morsel immediately and raised its neck in the manner a goose has. I watched the miniature glossy feathers aligning down its throat and the adjustment of its body as it shuffled towards his hand.

'Aha!' Sykes cried, delighted. It was not an unusual sight for me. Countless times I had watched Clara offering it food.

'It is not a circus animal,' I said, disgusted by the captain and suspecting his every motive. 'If you will permit me, I have had enough of this show, and wish to leave.'

Captain Sykes leant back in his chair and regarded me, stroking his moustache in a deliberate gesture.

'I can see you are shocked,' he said.

'Yes. Very.'

'But I am intrigued,' he said. 'Just how long did you think you could maintain this charade? Did you really think that I could not know about a bird that was concealed on my ship?'

'How long have you known?' I asked.

He waved his hand at me, dismissively. 'It is not important.'

'I would like to know.'

Sykes smiled, weighing me up. 'Then I shall tell you. I have known from the start.' His eyes sparkled with the pleasure of informing me. 'I see this surprises you. But I think you have underestimated the workings of a merchant ship, Mr Saxby. It is more than a few planks bound together with line. It is a living thing, you see, and it is bound together with sinew, and all those on board have to assume a part of this connection. Why, it was I who gave Mr French the key to the anchor locker – I believe I even told him of the tradition in the navy that women of dubious character used to be concealed within that lazarette. I told you that, didn't I, Quinlan?' From the corner of my eye I saw French give a single nod of confirmation. 'That was a thing he did not know, despite his brief spell in the services.'

French was determined not to catch my eye. 'You are a despicable man,' I told him.

Sykes clapped his hands with pleasure. 'Well said! I like my passengers to have fire about them. You hear that? He called you *despicable*. You may add that to the list of accusations I have heard against you over the years. What were they now? Immoral, heartless, selfish ...'

Sensing he might hide behind the playfulness, French was keen to join in: 'It was also said that I was cunning, disloyal—'

The captain raised a finger. 'No, Quinlan, not that. I would say that being disloyal is not one of your faults. You are most loyal.'

I had had enough. I stood to leave.

'Where are you going?' Sykes asked.

'To attend to Miss Gould. It appears that there are three men in this room but only one gentleman.'

'Yes, yes, attend to Miss Gould's tears, of course you must, but we shall have a small discussion first. Please, let us sit down.' He waved to the couch with an expansive gesture.

'I would prefer not to,' I replied, clinging to all I had left – my dignity. 'I have had enough of your games.'

'As you wish,' Sykes replied, casually. 'Mr French, bring that lamp, would you?'

French quickly went to the captain's bedside table and brought the oil lamp. He set it in front of the captain. Sykes raised the flame, then picked up the auk's egg and held it to the light. He gazed intently, examining the egg through his glasses.

'Mr Saxby, what is your opinion? Is the egg viable?' From where I stood, the egg glowed a milky yellow, darkly speckled with the lines and flecks of its marking. Sykes glanced at me, raising his eyebrows, before setting the egg down once

333

more. It rocked on the flat tabletop. The auk noticed, and quickly scrambled to gather it.

'See!' Sykes cried. 'She sits like a statue, but when she moves, she waddles like a washerwoman!'

'Goodbye,' I said.

'Stop,' Sykes instructed. 'Please, sit.'

I refused, intent on leaving.

'So,' the captain continued. 'We appear to have one problem, which is a bird, and another problem, which is an egg. We have two problems.'

'Mr French knows how to wring a neck,' I said, pushing past French with the satisfaction of shoving him against the wall as I left.

I knew what I had to do. The thought had occurred to me with the clarity of a crystal of quartz. Hard, smooth-edged, filled with its own perfect right to exist. For a moment in the saloon, I actually thought of how the world might be, if it accorded to such beautiful and natural lines of geometry and precision. Rightfulness, existing with the power to cut through all that was wrong and bent within men's minds.

Across the room I faced the two sailors who had been put on sentry duty. They were not men I had spoken to, and they eyed me with suspicion, encouraged by the warning they had no doubt been given that I might be trouble. Trouble! What a thought. I stared at them with an unflinching resolve and saw that it was an attitude they hadn't anticipated. One, a tall man in a smock whom I had seen at the bow of the ship, patiently bent over the spinning wheel making yarn, lowered his chin and eyed me as you might give a shrewd glance at a particular problem – an incorrectness in a carpenter's join or a door that wasn't hung straight. He scratched his chin and relented, looking to his mate for advice. I scoffed at him and went directly to Bletchley's cabin, marching straight in without knocking.

Inside the room I was quickly unnerved by what I saw. The porthole was entirely closed off with material, making it a very shadowy place, and Bletchley was not on his bunk; he was instead on the floor, covered in several blankets so that even his head could not be seen. But there was no doubt he was in there, for he was moaning in a most disconcerting and injured way.

'Wake up, man,' I said, overcoming my trepidation. 'Edward, get off the floor.'

From among the blankets I heard a strange and muffled groan.

'Did you hear me?'

'I *am* awake!' he replied, irritated.

'Get up, then.'

'Why?'

'Can't you hear your cousin?' I said. Clara's cries were clear through the thin divide between their cabins. 'I'm talking to you – I said can you hear your cousin's distress?'

He whipped the blanket away from his head. 'Of course!' he snarled, as an angry child might do, backed into a corner.

Despite the situation, I laughed. He really was quite pathetic. Only then did I notice that his clothes lay in a tangled pile strewn about the floor, several garments ripped to shreds as if he had searched among their expensive linings.

'What's been going on here?' I asked.

He stared at me, wild eyed. His hair was tousled and unkempt and there was a sour unwashed odour coming from his clothes or body.

'I have to do something,' I said, pushing my boot through his clothes and shovelling them to one side. His cabin had the same layout as mine, which meant the locker underneath the bunk would be the only possible place where they could be. I crouched down and opened the hatch, reaching in among his stuff.

'Are they in here?' I asked, more of myself than Bletchley. He was quietened by my attitude, and watched me with a curious expression. I quickly found the case and dragged it onto the floor, springing the catches as if I had done it a thousand times. It was only with the lid open, and at the sight of the three gleaming and immaculate rifles, that I felt my determination crumble. Their hard steel, their engravings, their sheer workmanship and plain intent were unavoidable.

Bletchley shuffled on his hind quarters across the floor towards me, pushing his hair back from his face and eyeing the guns with excitement.

'Now, Eliot, that's my gun case, you know that – I mean, those are my guns, yes?'

He couldn't take his eyes from them, and neither could I. The barrels were long and made of a dark steel that had a wavering pattern within the roll of the metal, akin to agate. The stocks were of flat polished brass, and the butts of a beautiful walnut, deeply polished and smoothed until the grain shone. Each gun was nestled within a plum-coloured velvet indentation in the case. The engraved stocks had scenes of seals and walrus sitting atop the ice floe, with a proud hunter aiming a similar weapon in their direction.

'It is no wonder you couldn't cope,' I said, unexpectedly.

'Close the case,' he whispered. 'Go on, shut the lid on them, it's best.'

I picked up the closest gun and felt its weight. It tipped awkwardly in my hand, as heavy as a pickaxe. I pushed it towards him. 'You don't understand,' I said. 'You have to load it for me.'

He shrank back from it, and me, raising a hand to shield his face. 'No no no,' he said, 'I can't touch the thing. Put it back.'

I thrust it at him and let it drop onto his lap. 'Do it, Edward, or I shall strike you.'

He stared, incredulous. 'Would you?'

Someone gave a loud knock on the door. 'Is you all right in there, sir?' one of the sailors demanded.

Bletchley looked at the door with pure hate. 'Get lost, you devil!' he spat, then turned to me with a wolfish grin. 'Give me that,' he said, urgently, pointing at the case.

'What's wrong with the gun I gave you?'

'Pah!' he replied, the sound of an old boast in his voice. 'Only a fool would use that. The short-barrelled one, the snub one,' he said, clicking his fingers with impatience.

Seizing my chance amid his erratic mood swings, I quickly passed him the smallest of the guns. He took it gladly, a favourite pet, appreciating it once more, running his hand along the barrel and stock.

'I like this one,' he said, a little sadly. 'Give me the powder then, before I change my mind.'

I passed him the powder flask. Eagerly he took it and began to pour powder into the muzzle, his hands working quickly and expertly and following their own set of practised routines. He unclipped the ramrod and slotted it down the barrel, giving the powder a hearty push that made his eyes gleam with pleasure. Ignoring me completely, he reached over and picked his own bullet, a small spherical ball of lead that he sat in a precise square of fabric before easing into the end of the muzzle. It was a beautiful and satisfying fit. He pushed it in with the soft part of his thumb before again tamping with the rod.

'It's done?' I asked.

'You really know nothing about weaponry, do you?' he replied, chiding me with a tutting of his tongue. With care, he slid back the percussion mechanism until the spring creaked and the lock clicked into place with a precise snap. Delicately, he placed a small percussion cap upon the nipple of the gun, as if it were a miniature top hat upon a figurine's head.

'Ah,' he uttered. 'Now she's ready.'

He passed the rifle, reverently, then sat back amid his blankets, his eyes glinting. 'So, Saxby, who will you point that damned thing at?'

I didn't answer. Expecting to have met more resistance from him, I felt a renewed sense of doubt. A gun, primed for firing. I felt unable to concentrate, overwhelmed with a sense that my actions were not properly of my choosing any more, that I was on an uncertain path that was more dangerous and inevitable than I had anticipated.

'Thank you,' I said.

He gave me a single nod and pulled his blanket tight around him. 'The trigger is stiff. Pull it as if you are snapping a wishbone.'

I pushed open the cabin door with the barrel of the gun and stepped into the saloon, immediately turning the weapon towards the first of the two sailors.

'Ah Christ!' he said, raising his hands to his face and stumbling backwards towards the stove. 'Jesus, don't shoot that!'

The second man was not far off, but had pressed himself against the wall, near the companionway door, and seemed to be stuck there, pinned by a force that came from the weapon. He began to slide, his face pushed against the wood panelling, a fevered eye on me and a hand outstretched to the other man.

'Don't speak,' I commanded, my voice more level and assertive than I could have imagined myself capable of. The gun had that effect of power, as if it concentrated an energy and made a taut line between myself and what lay in front of me. A target, I thought, randomly. The room has become a series of targets.

And these men, who just a few minutes before had swaggered with a casual sense of their own brute strength, for them now to be watching me with utter fright and confusion was almost impossible to believe.

'Don't, sir, please don't,' one begged. His mate flashed him a look of contempt, but said nothing. He still had his hands raised in front of his face, and was peeping at me, furtive, between his fingers.

'Now, get out,' I said. 'Both of you.'

The men didn't need a second command. They went quickly for the door and scrambled up the stairs, shouldering each other out of the way as they went. I listened to the sound of their boots running across the main deck to the fo'c'sle. Men and force would be mustered. Someone would take charge – Talbot was at the helm – he would be called. He would know what to do.

I went at once to the captain's cabin and flung the door open. Along the barrel and lined up by its sights I saw Quinlan French, slouching at the end of the red chaise longue. As soon as he saw me, he curled into the corner, like a thin strip of paper being singed by a flame. His arms went up beseechingly and he started to writhe, as if already trying to catch the shot that might fly towards him. It was a revealing sight, to see such an eruption of fear and anguish in a man so commonly upright and determined. But I couldn't linger, for on my right I saw the captain moving rapidly and I swung the gun towards him, pinning him to the edge of the cabin as I had the sailor in the saloon. Sykes grabbed his desk and froze, eyeing me with a strange mix of excitement and fascination.

339

'Most surprising,' he said.

'I think it's best you don't talk,' I replied.

I pointed the gun towards French again, making sure he didn't move. He seemed quite incapable of doing anything other than squirming in a childlike manner, grasping at imaginary bullets. I kicked the cabin door shut with the heel of my boot.

'Sit next to the snake,' I said to the captain, aware that the men were too far apart for me to keep them both under control.

Sykes obliged, walking nimble-footed across his cabin to sit next to French. On the table I noticed the great auk, lifting its neck to view me with suspicion. I lowered the gun a touch, not wanting a flapping bird to add to the situation.

'May I speak now, Mr Saxby?' the captain asked, picking up on what he may have felt was a softening of my attitude.

'I haven't decided yet.'

'As you wish. I shall wait.'

Outside I heard a large commotion as men charged down the steps, yelling and shouting. It sounded as though it was the entire ship's crew, flooding the saloon with their noise as they sought me out. Quickly, I heard them close in on the captain's door. Faced with it, they fell silent. I had the impression of a wall of men a few feet behind me, irrepressible with energy and prevented from entering by the merest of obstacles. The door was not locked.

'Sir!' Talbot called. 'You want us in?'

Sykes took his time, regarding me and raising his eyebrows. 'The men want me to say something,' he said, calmly.

'Go on then.'

Again, he was in no hurry. 'Best not come in, lads,' he called. 'One of my passengers is currently pointing a gun at me.'

'We're ready, sir, all of us is,' came the answer.

'Don't be smart,' I said to the captain.

He sighed. He still regarded me with fascination, quite unlike French, whose face had gone bloodless.

'What is your plan?' Sykes asked.

The auk, standing on the table, opened its beak and made the deep-throated growl that was so familiar. I felt the sound reverberate in my stomach and tips of my fingers. Then it shook its head, ruffling the neck feathers and letting them settle before closing its beak with a hollow, dry sound like that of two coconut halves being brought together.

I raised the gun at the captain again. 'You will take the bird on deck and release it into the sea.'

He smiled, then nodded, as if complimenting me on my suggestion. 'Just drop it over the side?' he asked, miming the action with a theatrical gesture of his hand.

'Yes.'

'Would it not drown?'

'Its home is the ocean.'

He rubbed his chin, considering.

'Then what?'

'I shall lay down this rifle and take the consequence.'

His eyes brightened at the word. 'Yes, consequence. We should perhaps talk about that.'

'You do not scare me, Sykes. At this moment I care only about the survival of this bird. What might happen to me is of little concern.'

His reply came at once. 'I was thinking, not of you, Mr Saxby, but of a wider consequence. You may have overlooked it, with your rush of blood.'

'Enlighten me.'

'The egg.' He looked triumphant. 'Release the bird and the egg will die.'

French shifted in his position, letting his hands drop to

view me properly for the first time. A look of curiosity flickered in his eye. Someone banged on the captain's door, loudly, and Talbot followed it with a shout: 'What's your order, sir?'

'This isn't one of your damned board games, Sykes.'

He wasn't so sure. 'Between the bullet and the bone?' he mused. 'I rather felt it was. So what do we do?'

'You're forgetting an important thing.'

'Pray, tell?'

'I am still holding a rifle.'

'Oh yes, that.' He looked directly at the gun. 'One of Mr Bletchley's toys, I believe. The short one, for when the prey is close at hand. It really is a ludicrous design.' He let out a sigh and, light on his feet as always, stood up abruptly. I tensed, feeling the harsh curve of the trigger against the inside of my index finger. The captain was by far the most unruffled person in the room. I felt as though I was an axis of pressure that existed in a line between the captain and the men behind the door, waiting for their order, an axis of pressure centred on the point of my finger upon the trigger.

Sykes took a step towards me and looked me straight in the eye.

'I must bung that hole,' he said. He lifted his hand and inserted a finger into the end of the barrel.

I stared, white with fear, disbelieving, as he took the rifle from my hand.

Events happened rapidly and at an unnatural speed. I remember only small details. I remember the captain flicking the tiny top hat percussion cap from the firing mechanism, then the way he turned his back on me as he put the rifle against the wall. French, in the same instant, leaping from the settee and flinging the cabin door open. An awareness of men, rushing in, filling the space with shouts, and myself being hurled against the table as if a wave had swept into the room. A glimpse of the great auk as I was physically lifted – one arm tightly held around my neck – and carried out into the saloon.

Talbot grabbed me by the throat, seething with anger, seeking instruction. 'What shall we do, sir?' he shouted.

Captain Sykes came to his doorway, looking a little breathless.

'Remove Mr Bletchley's rifles and ammunition from his cabin.'

'Will do, sir, and what of this one?'

Sykes looked at me, but not with any sense of triumph or jubilation.

'Oh, leave him,' he ordered. 'He's harmless.'

Bletchley's cabin was quickly searched and his rifles removed. The men stayed in the saloon for a while, excited and prepared for further trouble, but gradually they realised that it was over and they should return to their duties. Within half an hour I was the only person left there. I sat, defeated and lonely, haunted by glimpses of things I had done, all I had nearly done, the feel of the gun that had been in my hands, the smell of its steel that still clung to my skin. That unnatural quiet that had returned, as if nothing had happened.

On instinct, I went to Clara's door and leant my head against it. I heard her move on the other side. I tried not to remember. My forehead, placed against the chilled wood – *Celeste, come to the door* – a cool head but a mind that must have been feverish with desire and imaginings. *Please, just a glimpse of you.* How I had pictured Celeste, trapped in there, wan and thoughtful, how I had wished to save her from a torment that I could neither appreciate nor understand. Those memories and the turbulence of the present seemed to merge. I struggled to understand the entire picture, the sum of all this yearning and obsession. But I felt clear-headed and sure of my actions. So when Clara opened the cabin door, and stood in front of me, I took her in my arms and kissed her, I kissed her, and would not let her go. I felt total peace. This was a world within a world, away from the greed and betrayals of the ship and the cruelties of an ocean which stretched immeasurably around us. Clara and I were in the centre, a spark and warmth surrounded by incalculable coldness, but that coldness could not reach us.

After some time we sat, perhaps a little shocked, but unashamed. The room felt honest and pure and I felt stronger than I had done for days. We sat on the bunk, with her cabin door still open, looking at a plain view of the saloon. I noticed the polish on the bare wood of the dining table, the glint of silver mounts on the lanterns that hung above it. I looked at the grains of wood that ran along the planks, imagining as a child would do the intricacies of worlds that exist alongside our own, all of them necessary and vital but none as essential as the one you truly felt was yours.

'I heard the commotion,' she said. 'I was afraid.'

'Me too.'

'What happened?'

'I tried to resolve things. I was a fool.'

'But are you all right?' She touched my brow, sadly. 'Is the bird still alive?'

'Yes.'

'But it's distressed? Tell me.'

'The bird is fine.'

'Was it Mr French?'

I felt so thoroughly exhausted. 'It was. He has been informing the captain from the start.'

She accepted the information without surprise. Without reaction. At length, she spoke again: 'He has presented me with a letter. It's a love letter. A billet-doux. We have fewer and fewer options,' she said.

'Do you wish me to confront French?' I asked, appalled at the thought that I might have to.

Clara spoke with a defiant calm that I hadn't expected: 'I think you should go back to your cabin, or on deck if you prefer. You've tried hard, and for so long. It's my turn now. I shall resolve this.'

It is difficult to recollect the exact sequence of events of that day. I think I remember being on deck, in a dreary wind of drizzle and greyness. I certainly remember the sight of the ocean, a bleak horizon on all sides, with clouds that seemed as wet and as thick as the water below them, the entire world made of a single element that bled its pigment between sky and sea. A simple longing to see land. I needed a reminder that there was a solid world at the edge of all this. Just the sight of it – the merest glimmer of lights around a familiar harbour – would be enough to believe in. To believe that there was warmth and comfort and an old age waiting for me in a thousand different possibilities that were not there, right then, on the bare ocean. The ship had seemed different, too, made of the repairs and fixes that kept it afloat, the grandeur I had once seen in it now a mere attempt to put off the inevitable progress of decay. I remember the crew attended their duties with practised, unhurried motions across the deck, and the way they avoided me. All that day, I had the sensation that beneath me, in the captain's cabin, a negotiation was under way – from which I was excluded. Overwhelmingly, I remember a distinct feeling. I felt lost.

Several hours later, Simao brought me a note to say the captain requested my attendance in the chart room. I stared at the paper, the captain's signature written in a flourish of dark ink, then looked at the steward for guidance.

'He is not angry,' Simao said.

'And the bird?'

He reassured me the auk was still alive.

'Did you know we had it on board?' I asked him.

'Yes, sir.'

'Well – thank you,' I said, grateful for his honesty.

The chart room was small, not much larger than its table. Not the ideal place to meet once again a man I had so recently levelled a rifle at, but Sykes, as always, was determined to assert his own mood. I found him in an unbelievably jovial frame of mind.

'Mr Saxby!' he exclaimed, quite unnecessarily. 'Just the man. I wonder if you could help me with this.'

In his hand he had a half-unrolled maritime chart. 'Please take the opposite corner to mine and place some weights upon it.'

He began to unravel the paper across the table; obediently I held it, to keep it flat. He was keen to make our meeting brief. It suited me also.

'You will see that this chart refers to the outer isles off the west coast of Scotland,' he said, running a dry hand across its surface and gazing with some excitement at the contours and depths. I listened, but only to learn his intention.

'We have St Kilda, the Hebrides, Skye, do you see their shapes and outlines? The Hebrides are rather like the vertebrae of a whale, poking out through the sea, do you not think? Imagine – the Vikings navigated through this labyrinth with just a few bare scratchings carved upon bone and the like. It is quite humbling, as is every day upon the sea – it is a constant reminder of the bravery and vision of the men who have gone before.'

346

'What is your purpose?' I asked.

'Aha, yes, thought you might ask. You will know of it presently,' he said, enjoying, as always, the sound of his own voice and his roundabout way of coming to the point. 'We have had a strange voyage, would you not say? I must admit, I had no reckoning of it when I first saw you on deck. I thought you to be a most meek and obedient fellow – a flash of humour here and there, of course, but nothing like you turned out to be. I have been most educated by you.'

'I think we can safely say that goes both ways.'

'Yes, yes, I know you are infinitely disappointed by me, but I have little regard for what you may or may not think. We had a pretty little scene this morning and I have no intention of getting into that kind of situation again. I have seen many men like you, Mr Saxby. They all slow down and fatten up in the end, it is the way of the world. Men are born with sparks in their eyes and fires in their veins. But fires become embers, and finally ashes – there is no other way.'

'Am I in this room for a lecture?'

He put his hands up, in mock surrender. 'No. Absolutely not.' Then he regarded me with a sly smirk. 'But we have learnt about each other, nonetheless. You have also surprised me with your intimacy with another of our passengers. That has had me quite amused.'

'I'm glad you have had your fun.'

'Let us not spar, Mr Saxby, do you not see I'm here to offer a solution?'

I waited.

'There is room for manoeuvre in the smallest of spaces, would you not agree? And also in the thorniest of situations and negotiations. It is my role as a captain to spot these changes in tack – and I must admit that this morning I was quite at a loss as to where I might steer my craft with you. Or, indeed, why I should even bother.'

'You are talking in riddles, sir, as usual.'

Sykes clapped his hands with delight. 'I have the tendency, for sure I have,' he said. 'I will come to the point. It has been suggested to me that various choices might be made at this juncture. Miss Gould really is quite a remarkable person, isn't she? Well – what am I saying – you know that full well, from what I gather. Yes, a most intelligent and clear-thinking individual – she is able to see through situations with the utmost clarity. In fact, she would make a fine ship's captain – her skills are wasted being a woman.'

I glared back at him, unimpressed.

'So, to the point,' he continued. 'Are you interested to hear? Yes, good.' He placed his finger on the chart, keen to make the meeting brief. 'Here are the isles of Lewis, Harris, North Uist, Benbecula, South Uist and Barra. Together they form the Hebrides. The chart is precise in the surveys of ports and anchorages, but less specific with general coastline. At the southern tip – here – is the hamlet of Castlebay. The word is written there, you see? In a couple of days you shall be put on shore at that spot, with your precious bird and its egg, and this ship shall continue to Liverpool, as before.'

He straightened, satisfied.

'How has this been arranged?' I asked.

Sykes regarded me, an avuncular look in his eyes.

'Please tell me,' I said.

'Accept good news, sir,' he said, assertively. 'Do not question it.'

Late at night the *Amethyst* passed the solitary outcrop of Rockall for the second and last time. It appeared, several miles distant, a black void against a dark sky, with only the scarring white of breakers surrounding its base to give it away. Upon first sight, it appeared as if there was a tear in the fabric of the world, through which an angry but silent torrent of water was pouring. Even as we neared and the glint of moonlight began to shine from several of its sheer facets, it was difficult not to view it as an empty and unholy object. I shall never see it again, I am sure, and neither do I wish to, it is such a bleak and distant sight, and the memory of it returns to me with sadness. I stood by the rail, noticing a solemnity cast across the deck, with several of the crew halting their tasks to watch its passing. In the near silence, I believed we could hear the waves as they shook the island, but the sound came and went with a phantom quality. It seemed that all the land of the world had shrunk into this single blunt finger that pierced through the ocean. I felt as if I was facing all I knew of land itself. Land was sheer and inhospitable and something that could not be clung to.

Clara refused to discuss the deal she'd made. It was late at night. She had opened her cabin door, but only after I had been knocking for several minutes. She didn't want to come out, nor to invite me in.

I decided to be straight: 'Did you pay him?'

She stared at me, tight lipped and fearful. 'I offered, but it was refused.' She looked pale and distracted. The talking of the day had drained her.

'I was summoned by Sykes this afternoon,' I said. 'How did you achieve it? What could you possibly have said to persuade him?'

'Him?'

'Sykes.'

She smiled, but it was strained. 'I didn't go to *Sykes*,' she said, 'I went to Quinlan French.'

I felt a stab of panic. 'French? That snake in the grass!'

She seemed to consider the problems of the day anew. 'A snake has a useful bite,' she said, dreamily. 'Even you must admit that.'

'So you got French to talk on our behalf?'

'Something like that. I'm tired, Eliot.'

'But what could French say to change Sykes' decision?'

'You told me once before – they have a special obligation to each other. Persuade one, and the other follows.'

'It cannot be that simple. If you have put yourself at risk I shall need to know. What are you concealing?'

'I answered French's letter. That is all. Please be glad.'

'Have you promised him something?'

She smiled. 'The promise is theirs – you are to be put ashore, with the bird and its egg. I have been made aware of the arrangements.'

'Clara ...' I urged, 'please don't face this alone. Tell me what you have done.'

'French seemed to think it was not the bird – but you – who was the problem,' she said, enigmatically. She shook her head. Her skin looked paper thin, blue beneath the eyes and her mouth looked as though a child had drawn it with a simple straight line.

'Oh Clara!'

She leant her forehead against the door-jamb. 'I am very tired, Eliot, and my head hurts with a terrible aching. It will all be fine.'

'Are you in trouble? Let me help you.'

'Sykes told me what you did this morning, with Edward's rifle.'

'It was a rash and stupid thing.'

'No, it took courage. But it is not you, Eliot. You must not be like the rest of them, do you understand?'

350

'Yes.'

'Men find it easy to kill. Yet the true mark of a man is not to kill, but to save.'

She looked to be in pain.

'Will you tell me the story once more, Eliot?'

'Which story?'

'About Celeste. I want to hear it again.'

'No.'

'Please,' she urged. 'I am going to shut this door and listen to your voice. It will help me. Please, let me do this.' She began to close the door – I resisted it with the pressure of a single finger. She looked at the finger, where it touched the wood.

I let go, and she closed the door with a soft click. I heard the lock being turned from within. Then her voice, close to the wood:

'You talked, like this, a young man and a girl, on either side of a locked door. It must have been brave of you, to go up there, to the top of the house, and whisper to her every day.'

I leant my forehead against the wood. 'It was.'

'Did you not think you would be caught?'

'I didn't care.'

'And when you let her escape – when she ran past you – what did you think?'

'I don't want to remember it.'

'You must, Eliot. Please, do it for me.'

'Let me in.'

'I cannot.'

'*Celeste*, let me in.'

'Tell me . . . how you felt when she ran past you.'

'I felt betrayed.'

'Yes, of course you did. But you followed her, into the wood? You didn't give up. You never give up, do you, Eliot? You followed her until you found her. Where was she?'

'I don't want to remember.'

'You must.'

'But I can't. I've forgotten . . . I've learnt to forget that day.'

'You found her. Where was she?'

'In the lake.'

'Yes. In the lake. Did you rush in to save her?'

'There was a coot, floating in the middle of the lake.'

'Do you see the coot, now?'

The coot, bobbing silently on the dark water, turning towards the ripples that radiated across the surface.

'Yes.'

'Tell me.'

'It floats on the water, in the middle of the lake. It looks so peaceful.'

'But it's not peaceful, is it, Eliot? It is a place of great hurt and pain. Let me know what you can see.'

Celeste's hair, spread out on the water, her back half submerged, her dress dragging her under.

'She's in the water,' I said.

Reaching for her, her arms extended towards me, but in a stretch that is not far enough.

'Celeste drowned, didn't she, Eliot? She drowned that day.'

27

'I wish you well,' Sykes told me. I really believe he meant it. We stood together on deck, watching the whaleboat being lowered over the side, in mutual resignation.

Below us, I remember how still the water was, surrounding the ship like quicksilver, then the soaring easy flights of the gulls and terns as they wheeled above the headland, lazy flight so early in the day. I remember how low and unassuming the shape of the Hebrides island of Barra was, dark and without definition, and the few scattered houses of Castlebay, around its sheltered cove. Wood and peat smoke collecting above the roofs, a light on in the windows here and there. I tried to fix that time in my mind as one remembers all turning points in a life. With clarity. With precision. You remember them in the same way a fork in a path is etched into a memory. The feel of a flint wall, the particular shape of an oak's trunk. Remember these moments, and you won't become lost.

'These are for you,' Sykes said, offering a handkerchief in which he'd placed one of the flattened bullets from his draughts set, and one of the discs of seal bone. Objects in opposition. I took them without comment.

'You have what many naturalists do not have,' he added.

'More than curiosity or observational rigour – which are easily come by – you have the desire to save. It makes you unusual.'

'Goodbye, Captain Sykes,' I replied, seeing the boat nearly ready. 'We shall not meet again.'

Sykes smiled at my turn of phrase, pursing his lips in a half-whistle. He nodded, amused. 'Who knows,' he said, deliberately teasing. 'Take good care of that little bird, now. Remember you told me the Scots clubbed the auk, for they thought it was a sea-witch.'

'Yes, I told you that.'

'Bear in mind, then.' He touched his nose, emphasising the secret. Below us, the auk and its egg had been lowered into the whaleboat in the slack cask.

'I was becoming quite fond of the bird,' Sykes said, 'it has a comical expression that makes it endearing.'

Before I could reply he had turned away from me, crossing the deck in the pursuit of some task. I thought about calling after him, needing to say the last word, but, really, the last word is never necessary.

Clara and I had agreed that she shouldn't come up on deck to see me leave, and that it was best to say goodbye in her cabin. I had sat in there while my luggage was removed from my room, trying to ignore a sense of dread and finality.

Clara had attempted to be in a bright mood. 'I think the egg will hatch in a matter of a day or two,' she said. 'I held the egg this morning and I thought there was movement inside, although perhaps I was just wishing it. It will be a miraculous moment – but you will have much to do and organise.'

I nodded. I was holding a cup of coffee, and very aware that as soon as I finished it, I would have to leave. The sounds of my case being taken up on deck could be heard. In just a few minutes it would be placed in the whaleboat and the men would be sitting, resting on their oars.

'You are quiet,' she said. I imagined the turbulence she must have been concealing, her emotions channelled into trying to be practical, being brave, being anything other than dealing with the here and now. She began to tie her hair, her fingers working quickly at a knot at the back of her head. I watched the silky winds of her hair being gathered and turned, a knot developing that was intricate and soft.

'Remember I told you, once, about the place I used to imagine, when I was a child – a place where all the lost things of the world might be found? It's up to you now, my heart, to find that place, and keep this bird and its chick there. You'll do that, won't you, Eliot?'

'Yes,' I promised.

She looked back, her eyes bright with bravery and doubt in equal measure. 'And as soon as I am able to, you know I shall come back here, don't you? I'll come back and see what a fine hiding place you have made in these coves and islands. See, you'll have to work hard, because you won't want to let me down, will you? I'll be back to see our bird and ... and the chick and I will come back to see you ...'

'I don't want to leave,' I said.

She nodded, and sat next to me. 'I know,' she sighed. She had let go of her hair – the knot sprang open, half finished. I watched the plait slowly unravelling.

'What will happen?'

She placed her hand on mine. 'The egg will hatch,' she replied.

'It's not what I meant.'

'I know what you meant. But I cannot answer that.'

*

355

I had climbed into the whaleboat, as if in a dream. The *Amethyst*'s planks had smelt tarry, and my last touch of them was something I felt on the tips of my fingers for a long time after. I sat in the tender, where the two Herlihy brothers were waiting to row me to shore. I remember the simple push that one of them gave the ship, to cast us off, and the sense that with it I was leaving the one thing that I truly shouldn't leave, nor should ever leave. And as the brothers rowed me to the quayside, I turned my back upon the ship, tried to listen instead to the soft rhythmic dip of the oars in the still water, the sound of the great auk murmuring from within its container, occasionally adjusting its footing in there. I tried to concentrate on the egg I was keeping warm in the fold of my lap and tried, but failed, to ignore the presence of Quinlan French, standing like a column of dark troubled air behind me, at the quarterdeck rail.

I arranged my lodging at the Castlebay Inn. They had an outbuilding where, above a store, there was a bare loft that could accommodate myself and my luggage. One window, at the end, offered a small view of the loch and the sea beyond. It was through that window that I watched the *Amethyst* preparing to sail. I followed the familiar routines of unfurling the mainsail. The men, from so far away, appeared like a row of knots in the fixed rigging. The window had four panes, and I sat perfectly still, watching the ship lean gradually away from the wind, begin to drift from the bottom right pane into the centre of the window, and then into the upper left pane, further sails becoming loosened, flapping then tightening, being brought under control, the ship growing ever smaller, eventually vanishing, removed from my sight beyond the curve of the world.

I lit a strong fire in the stove and arranged my books on the shelf. I hung my jacket on a peg near the fire, where it would naturally warm. I ate the two coconut biscuits Simao had given to me on leaving, with a jug of hot tea that the innkeeper, Mr MacNeil, had brought over. I sat long into the night, disturbed by aspects of my departure, a separation I felt increasing, second upon second, between myself and Clara. I was perfectly still, seated at my desk, but she was leaving.

In the early hours I fell asleep, not in my bed, but on the armchair next to the fire, with a blanket across my lap, in the same manner that Bletchley had spent most of the voyage. Long into the night I sat there, gazing across the room at the dark bird with the two patches of white plumage above its eyes. Comical indeed, as it regarded me as if I was a puzzling companion. Fellow traveller, both of us a long way from home. In the shadows, I had watched as it occasionally turned its head, the light glimmering a dull graphite shine on the side of its beak. The auk sat on or near its egg, adjusting its posture, sighing or grumbling deep in its throat, keeping vigil. In this room, two days after I had landed, the egg hatched.

We both heard the sounds of movement coming from within the shell. A scratch at first, which soon developed into a tap, a series of taps, then a rhythm that came and went in little bursts. The great auk regarded the event with curiosity, angling its head to watch the egg as if not quite comprehending why it should be emitting a noise. I sat still, not wishing to disturb it. After forty minutes or so, a hair-like crack began to appear, about as long as a small finger, followed by a dense ring of fractures that developed part way along the line, caused by the concentrated stabbing of a beak within. Concentric rings broke the shell further, the way ice will crack under pressure, and a glimpse was revealed, within two parting edges, of a diaphanous membrane which stretched with the single, insistent pulse of life that I had come to recognise for as long as I had known these remarkable birds. The shell took on a flexible, living quality, pushed from within and then rocking from side to side.

I was struck by the hypocrisy of my joy: this was without doubt the most valuable egg in the world, the shell that any collector or museum would gladly fight over, a shell that I had longed to see and hold for the entirety of my life, yet here I was gladly wishing it to be destroyed by the simple life that it held. Oh, if only Clara had been there, at that miraculous moment! Within an hour, watched by the bird and myself, half of the egg had unhinged, unveiling a wet and confusing interior of feathers. What I could see of the chick lay panting, taking breath and twitching with vital energy. Every few minutes it would resume, rocking and pushing and attempting to lever the shell away. It was a most humbling experience to witness. I had seen many chicks hatch before: swallows' eggs, as fine as the birds that lay them, wrens' eggs, too, so delicate it seems they are made of wasp paper, but this struggle, this elemental birth, through a shell that seemed as set as china, was one of the most moving things I have ever observed. Every second it took, every movement of the chick, the world didn't deserve to witness, and would never see again. I felt privileged, and in awe.

When I saw the beak emerge, fronted by the minute appendage of its shell cutter, I was overcome with tears. The head turned within the open egg and, even at that size, the distinct profile of the characteristic beak was clear. With a sudden tipping of the egg the chick tumbled out, damp with albumen, unsteady and spiky, its wings flared against the bare surface of the floorboards. It staggered and fell, its beak hitting the wood as if it was a weight that had not been anticipated. I immediately knew the chick had died, that the

358

struggle of its hatching was too much for it to have endured. For the agony of several minutes it did not move. It lay, wet as a fallen leaf, on the floor. Then with two eyes as black as ink, as precise and as piercing as any I have seen, I saw it perceive its mother, and the chick began its struggle towards her.

I kept all this secret, and until now I have never, in fact, told a soul. These birds were too rare for their existence to be known. I have learnt that man places a special price on the unique, and that it will blind his judgement until it is too late. My job in those first few weeks was purely to keep these birds alive, to record them in every detail I could, to make sketches and notes, observe their behaviour and, above all, to make them invisible. My arrival in Castlebay had created interest among those who lived there. I believe I was viewed as a spy acting for one of the estate landowners, and my enquiries about the area and outlying islands were greeted with some suspicion. To some extent this was useful. I kept my room locked and no one dared pry. I was able to study local maps and charts, explaining that I wished to observe the nesting sites and migration routes of indigenous birdlife, and know that this information was given willingly, because they feared I had a more onerous agenda. It was only after several weeks, with no calamity befalling their community, that I felt I was truly believed. A gentleman naturalist. It was a term that suited me well, and one I could hide behind.

During that first summer I purchased a ten-foot sailing skiff, which I spent several weeks restoring. I arranged for a new standing lugsail to be made and bought two nine-foot sculls. I caulked the keel, stem and sternposts with cotton-wick, which I forced in with a blunt chisel, and addressed the planking with a holding-on hammer, tightening up where I saw fit. I attached air-cases either side of the midship thwart and bought several fathoms of new rope and an anchor. I scraped the little craft down, before applying new coats of varnish inside and out, and finally I painted a black rail and a white underbody, the personal livery of the great auk. My secret homage. It was difficult but instructive work; using my hands upon the boat both restored and asserted a sense of purpose in me.

In several excursions into Castlebay harbour, I learnt the rudiments of handling the boat. In the flat water of July and August I explored the complicated chain of islands that extended, in a series of reefs, grazing islands, cliffs and barren shores, to the south and west of Barra, each day pushing my knowledge of this region further.

On fine breezy days I would leave early, hanging a dog-vane of auk feathers and cork from my hand to feel the direction of the wind. I would raise my simple lugsail and beat to windward into a sea that was as iron blue as the ocean fjords of Greenland. With the sun on my face and my back to the wind, I chopped at the waves, enjoying the spray that splashed me from the bow and the smell of the new canvas of the sail. My lungs felt full of this vital air and sense of achievement. Close to shore I raised the keel board to drift through kelp forests, their wide bronzed arms stroking underneath the boat like horses' tails, and I would pass mirror-calm bays, fringed with coral-white sand, where the wake of a sea otter would create a single, precise scar.

I learnt the names then explored the islands – Vatersay, Muldoanich and Sandray, Pabbay and Mingulay – noting the coves where I might be able to make a safe landing, and the stacks and bays and cliffs where one day the auks might be placed, safe from predation by land or by sea.

As my journeying increased, I began to overnight on some

of these islands, hauling my beloved skiff onto the sand and sleeping next to it by the side of a fire fringed with rocks. I would lie on my back, staring up at the deep azure heavens of the summer night sky, finding there the stiff cruciform silhouettes of shearwaters flying in from the sea in mysterious flocks, making the stars blink as they passed beneath. The eerie callings of the birds, the spitting of my fire and the sighing of the shoreline, the pops of bladderwrack and the settling of the boat next to me were the most peaceful sounds I have ever heard.

Some of the islands were inhabited, and here I would eat with the crofters, sitting in their kitchens while a stew of mutton was prepared, or bread baked in the stove, while through an open doorway I would gaze at the sparkling light of the sun on a lonely shoreline. The crofters told me much about the nature of these islands. How the months could be read with the flowering of the plants, how each wind brought new elements of optimism or strife, how the currents encircled the rocks and bay and promontories like the runes of an ancient language that, given time, could be read like any other.

I performed all these tasks and excursions with diligence and enthusiasm, believing fully that one day I might be joined by Clara. She had hinted as much during the last few days of the voyage. *Believe, Eliot,* she had told me, *remember to believe. It is what you are good at.* I would work hard, I promised her, to build a home for myself and find a haven for the birds, so that all we had strived for would not be in vain. There will be a day when we will be together once more, I had said, and we will know that we have made a difference in the progress of the world. That we might live a simple life next to the birds we had saved spurred me on in those first few weeks. This belief kept me alive in spirit and endeavour,

361

right to the moment when, three months after my arrival, I received a letter from Edward Bletchley.

He had a curious and unkempt writing style, as if his hand was trying to catch up with the race of his thoughts, but I could tell, even within the first few words, that this letter had been written in difficult circumstances and brought news that would be hard to bear. I sat, on the edge of my bunk, as sailing had taught me, in preparation for the unexpected.

I reacted to the news of Clara's death as if I had been struck. I stared at the words, disbelieving their shapes and message, wishing I could rapidly undo the news they formed.

Bletchley wrote with great consideration for my feelings. He acknowledged that Clara and I had shared a special bond that had developed during the voyage, and it was this which had without doubt restored her health, albeit briefly. He made reference to the fact that he had found the voyage – and hunting in particular – a very difficult experience to bear, and admitted that he had become disengaged from the day-to-day nature of social interaction. 'I had been withdrawn, for the entire second half of the trip, and I thank you for being able to be Clara's strength in this period. She benefited greatly from having you to rely upon.' He had written generously, anticipating my sadness and shock and apologising for all he might have done to exacerbate the situation on board. 'My soul was dark,' he wrote. 'I was hardly the pilot of its woeful direction.' His sentences were muddled at times, as if the entire experience of the ship and its journey existed as one present and immediate sensation for him. 'She was ill at the start, from a mental exhaustion which I believed was a result of the escape from her wretched father – and the impending day when she would have to face him again, but I have since concluded that my own presence may also have contributed to her oppression. I am truly sorry for it.' He wrote of his reliance upon her, and said that it must have taken a toll. And there followed a lengthy passage where he explained the sins we had all committed against the balance of the world, suggesting his recovery was far from complete.

Becoming more lucid, he wrote of the situation on board following the day I had been left on Barra. He described an uneasy truce, with the captain having retired to his cabin for much of the day, and Clara and Mr French in lengthy conversations long into the night. He described French as a leech, sucking the blood of life from whomever he latched onto, and wished that he had thrown him over the side, rather than the pelts of the great auks. *My mistake!* he had written, as an afterthought, in the margin. 'It seems that Mr French had developed an unhealthy obsession with my cousin,' he wrote, 'which could not be easily satisfied.' In an oddly formal comment he added: 'Rest assured, Clara did not once lose her natural and splendid dignity.' But it had been clear, he continued, to all on board, that French was exerting a most uncomfortable pressure upon her, a pressure of expectation, and a tragic air had descended upon the decks of the ship. Near the end of the voyage she had, in his words, 'been virtually unreachable'.

He informed me that Clara had stepped off the ship's rail within sight of the English coast. Several of the men had seen her fall, and she had done so without a cry. The boats had been lowered but her body had not been retrieved. Captain Sykes had performed a full ceremony on board, which all the crew had attended.

28

It is five years since I received that news. I did not believe it at first. How could I? How could it possibly be true?

As soon as I had read his words, I thought of the impenetrable wood in Norfolk, where I had fought my way through the rhododendrons, trying to find the girl I had let escape. I had remembered the way my feet sank in the mud, the way the branches and foliage seemed complicit in preventing me from reaching her. Then the startling sight of the almost perfectly round lake, fringed with dark trees and, in its centre, that solitary coot, turning quietly towards the ripples that had just reached it. I had remembered the feel of Celeste's body as I pulled her from the water, and the sight of her, at peace, as she was carried from the lake. How could it be possible, after I had saved her, that she would return to the water once more, this time for good?

I didn't accept the news of her death until an event that occurred several weeks later. I had been travelling to South Uist on a small sailing ferry, in search of boating supplies for the skiff I was restoring. It had been a blustery day, and I had seated myself in the lee of the wheelhouse, where I could read one of my books in peace from the wind. Occasionally I would look to the craggy inlets and promontories that passed by, always keen to spot otters playing on the shore. It was a joyful sight.

Out of habit, I had absorbed myself in my book, not wanting to draw attention to myself. But when the boat tacked into the sea loch, approaching South Uist, the water had become sheltered and I had put my book down.

At the stern rail, a woman turned to face me. It was Celeste. Taller than I remembered, dressed in the rough woven shawl that is common in this area, but with the same appeal in her eyes that has filled my dreams for so many years. She smiled at me, wishing me a good morning, and I must have stared back, in my confusion, my inability to comprehend what I was seeing. Perhaps I had paled, as if about to faint, because she quickly came to me and asked if I was feeling well.

'Celeste?' I managed. She looked back at me, wondering what I had said. When she spoke, it had been with the strong island accent of this part of Scotland.

'Why do you not ... don't you recognise me?' I asked, in a mixture of sadness and fear. She seemed undecided, puzzled and unsure whether I needed assistance. I noticed her hair was shorter than I remembered, and darker.

'Shall I fetch help for you?' she asked, quietly.

'Please, tell me you know me,' I replied forcefully and she took a step back. I saw that a couple of men had come to stand near by. One of them – looking quite fiercely down at me – put an arm around her to guide her away. I saw her speaking to him and, after some minutes, he returned to confront me.

'I don't know who ye are, man, but you scared me wife. I'll not have it,' he said.

I put my hands up, fearing he might strike me, but it appeared he was not interested in making any further scene.

'I am sorry,' I said. 'Very deeply sorry.'

He gave me a single nod and returned to his wife. We had nearly reached the harbour. She glanced at me just once more, when no one was looking, and alongside my recognition that she must be Celeste, I knew at that moment that I would see Celeste, that I would keep seeing Celeste, when I was least expecting it – in the fragment of a face in a passing carriage, in the back of a room sitting by the fire, on the shore just after sunset – for the rest of my life.

Since then, I have largely avoided being in the proximity of people. I cannot trust myself, I cannot trust my perceptions, and I cannot trust where those perceptions might lead me. No. I have chosen to devote my life not to the things I have lost, but to the one true thing that I have ever saved.

I have been living this way for five years. No one knows the true nature of my business or, if they do, or at least suspect, then none of them realises what I have done. It is my secret, alone. I am meticulous in my arrangements, for I live in a community which is small and therefore naturally suspicious. In these five years I have become a good boatman, I sail my skiff with a keen eye, noticing the cat's paw of the wind upon the water, or the curl of the tide as it pulls to ebb. I have learnt about nature, most profoundly learnt about nature. I have charted the migrations of birds and the arrivals of fish, and the cycles of breeding they announce. I watch the hares as they fight and pant. The swallows in their scattered flight, flying in ribbons beneath the boathouse doors, their wingtips an inch above the water, where they swoop up to their fragile mud nests under the joists. I have counted the shearwaters as they fly in at night, hundreds of silhouettes against the moon, before they drop screaming to the ground to search for their burrows. I have studied the weather, am able to interpret the sky and the clouds, and the colourings of the sea. The black shine of cold water, or the blooms of plankton that drift in mossy clouds each June, heralding the arrival of the basking sharks. I am able to mark the changes of the seasons by the transformations of the insects and by the simple budding of a flower. I have made a good and comfortable shelter where I can sometimes stay overnight. But what I do, year after year, is also dangerous. I could drown a thousand ways, each day, alone. Or fall from the cliffs, where the rocks are almost permanently wet from the sea mist. I might be a victim of a sudden squall or a gust of wind, and my vanishing would hardly be noticed. A cry and a splash in the water, and I would be gone. It is for this reason that I decided to write down the story. You see, I have had plenty of time to think, out here. And my hope is that in writing this I might spot the details I missed at the time, on that voyage, and recover what was lost. I might see where it all began to go wrong. Yes. Plenty of time to think.

Edward Bletchley pays for my lodging and the maintenance of the boat. He has written to me many times. Often he tells me not to be so frugal, insists that I must be incurring additional expenditures, but he is wrong. My life is Arcadian. I have all that I need. He is the only contact I have with the world beyond this island and, as such, I believe he is probably to be counted as my only friend. It is remarkable the companions we end up with, some of whom we never chose. From each letter I have learnt more about him. He has decided to live in Norfolk after all, and has let a portion of the estate he inherited go wild, encouraging waterfowl and migratory birds, well away from the blasts of hunting rifles. He describes it as the only safe landing spot in all of East Anglia. He tells me that his soul is clear and that he is to be considered a free spirit and an integrated part of the nature of all things. I truly believe he is an extraordinary man, compassionate and interested in his role in life, and that it was the Arctic that first opened his eyes. I recognise now that the voyage on the *Amethyst* changed my life, also, as voyages are meant to. It taught me that there are some things that can be saved, truly saved, in a life where I once thought it was not possible.

Celeste drowned, that day in my early twenties, when I recklessly stole the key and unlocked her bedroom door. I let her out. She escaped. She died. I know now that I had been obsessed with her, that I might have been too blinded by this obsession to realise the consequences of my actions. It was I who let her escape, and I who should take the blame.

Perhaps her life was always going to end that way. Given the severity of her father this really may have been so. But I was instrumental that day, and for that I am truly regretful.

It has been harder for me to accept that the sightings of Celeste – over the years – have been chimeras of my own mind, delusions arisen from my own feelings of guilt and longing. Only now do I understand that I have also seen her in the country lanes of Suffolk, standing on staithes and quaysides in Norfolk, in the windows of passing carriages in London, even on the ferryboat to South Uist, and I saw her on the deck of the *Amethyst*, in the eyes of a woman who was vulnerable and in need of solace. I have seen Celeste in all these women, and each time I have sought her out I have been absent from myself. Clara, I was mistaken to think you were her, but I wasn't wrong to love you, too.

I think of Quinlan French when I see a candle flame near to me. On several occasions I have tried to find what he saw, by staring at a lit candle until my eyes hurt with the intensity of light. But when I experimented in this way, it wasn't the dance of the flame that disturbed me – it was the ring of darkness that surrounded me at the edge of my vision, like an impenetrable wall of shadows as I stared at the light – a darkness that felt thicker and more oppressive than I thought could be. Perhaps this is what he saw, and wished to observe. I shall never know, because I never wish to meet that man again.

If Sykes lived beyond the onset of his illness, then he must be retired by now, and I think of him sometimes, stitching his elaborate embroidery in the cottage home he was so dismissive of. In my vision, I like to think of him as an embroidered character in one of his own creations: a small, portly man by a suffocating fire next to a wife he is trying to ignore. I imagine him sitting in a church pew on a Sunday morning, or pruning the roses around his front porch, and occasionally smiling privately at the anchor-shaped knocker on his front door. No one has ever known that this little and fairly old man once had the chance to save a portion of the world's animal kingdom, and that he failed to take it.

I am still haunted by what he did. One by one they had been taken to the inlet. And I must state a truth here: a drowning is never peaceful. But there on the rocks, faced with the aftertaste of an extinction, something transcendent had been illuminated: this scene, of man's destruction, of his heartlessness, would inevitably be repeated time and time again, across the decades and centuries with all the world's creatures. Man will murder whales and seals in their thousands, he will pluck the birds from their rocks and shoot them from the sky.

*

It is 1850, we are halfway through this century, and I have little notion as to whether my efforts have all been in vain. It is said the whales are becoming scarcer in the Greenland Sea. The seals are more infrequent among the ice floes. The walrus colonies are dwindling, their tusks and bristles raised impotently against gaff hooks and grappling irons. Even that most invisible of the polar beasts, the white bear, may one day entirely vanish.

Clara once told me to believe, and I try to stay true to this each hour and each day, even when I lose hope. I have chosen a solitary life in order to complete all I promised to her, but there is still a kernel of anger in me that wishes to tell the world what I have tried to save. I have been greatly affected by the death and slaughter I saw in the Arctic. It has stayed with me. I think of it constantly. I want to confront the men who have ruined our world. I want to go to the cities – where the Arctic's great animals have been reduced to collar stiffeners and parasol ribs, corset stays and combs, where their oil lights the lamps and greases the axles and gears and chains of a relentless industry – and list the crimes that have been committed in the Arctic in the name of profit. How a man like Captain Sykes, who I truly believe was not an evil-hearted individual, can nonetheless be warped by greed until he can make no moral judgement. Perhaps one day, man will save the Arctic in all its multitude of extraordinary life, but perhaps by then man will be too late, as he always seems to be. It is a fight that will need to be fought, and it is for this reason that I have written this account.

I often sit on Mingulay's headland, on granite that is warmed by the sun, surrounded by the blowing scents of the grasses and heather. Crickets chirp around me, bees, moths and butterflies fly delicately in the air. Flowers grow in even the smallest cracks and lichen clings to the bare rock in a coat of brilliant colour. Below me, a thousand acres of sea roll quietly towards me from the west. It is such a vast sight, such emptiness, that it fills me, overwhelms me, every time I sit here. There is nothing to interrupt the eye, apart from the gannets as they spear the water beneath the cliffs, or occasionally the tip of a basking shark's fin – a lonely, roaming point of life in all this view. Sometimes I feel as though I am floating, yet surrounded and connected to all that I adore. Everywhere is the reminder that nature is tenacious, it clings to the bare, it abhors a vacuum, and will fill a void. Nature replaces, continually.

It is strange to think that when it came down to it, the great auk's future was a simple throw of the dice. The odds were even, but nature won: the auk chick was a male offspring. Within two years another egg was laid. With plentiful feeding, a second batch succeeded that same year. I think of it being the largest of journeys that began with a single step.

On fine days I launch the skiff from the white sand of the coral bay and row around the brittle limbs of the promontories that reach out to sea. I scull towards the west of the island where the cliffs rise, ever steeper and more sheer, until they tower above me by several hundred feet. They are a formidable sight to pass beneath, black and stained and as ancient as any rock I have ever seen, splitting into stacks and coves and sea caves along their foundations. As I move alongside them, their brooding presence begins to affect the motion of the sea, as if they have their own gravity, lifting and pulling at the skiff even on the calmest of days, sucking the tiny boat into their shadow where the water swells up and surges. It is a humbling experience to pass below these wonderful cliffs, hearing the echoing shrieks of the nesting birds high on the ledges, feeling an intruder beneath a primeval landscape. After the third stack, which rises as sheer as a cathedral's spire, I turn the boat into the shadow of the cliff and let the current guide me in. I pass a narrow entrance, a collapsed cave, not much wider than the span of my oars, and bring the boat into a cleft in the rock, where I can tie the painter around a boulder. It is a damp, slippery hollow in almost total shadow, with drips and streams falling from the cliffs, and black rock overhung with vivid green ferns and trailing vines. But beyond this natural barrier, there is a small protected cove which opens onto the sea, and this is where I sit, among the group of great auks that have made this place their home.

They are my phoenix birds. I have saved them from a sea of flames.

Sometimes I close my eyes and listen as they murmur to themselves. I like the way they preen each other in a small social group, their necks rising and rubbing each other in new-formed greetings, several times an hour. They have a tendency to face out to sea, gazing at the waves and the horizon beyond. Weather does not concern them. Neither do the calls and shrieks of the other bird species from the cliffs above. They have taught me a great deal. Sometimes they allow me to approach. I may sit on the rocks near their feet and reach forward to stroke them. They are wild and they have no friendship with me, but I am accepted as I never believed I could be. I am considered a part of the family that lives in this hidden cove. When a chick is hatched, I am allowed to hold it, and in the slate-grey reflection of its eye I know that I am the total protector of this fragile strand of life, and beyond me there lies only one thing: extinction.

It is summer now. Each year, at this time, they follow some unknown signal and swim out to sea. They are gone for several months, and there is no one on earth who knows where they go. I imagine them in the rolling dark slopes of the North Atlantic, where they have been for thousands of years, their plumage the same colour as the blackened waves. I imagine them out there, beyond my protection, and know that I have played my part in saving them. I imagine them fishing with one another, paddling across the surface and diving into a shadow that is complete and enveloping. I shall never know, until I see them again, whether they will return.

Jeremy Page grew up in north Norfolk and has worked as a script editor for Film4 and the BBC, in addition to teaching on the Creative Writing MA at UEA. He lives in London with his wife and three children. He has published two previous novels: *Salt* and *The Wake*.

Pine River Library
395 Bayfield Center Dr.
P.O. Box 227
Bayfield, CO 81122
(970) 884-2222
www.prlibrary.org